PAST GHOSTS ECHOED

Jordan Buchanan

Contents

Acknowledgement

I wish to acknowledge that Sudbury, Ontario is on the traditional territory of the Atikameksheng Anishnawbek and Wahnapitaeping peoples with lands protected by the Robinson Huron Treaty 1850.

Dedication

2

This book is dedicated to my parents

Marilyn and David Buchanan and my wife Brenda

Foreward

The investigations and events in this book have been inspired by real cases. Names, locations, time periods and most of the details have been changed to fictionalize these incidents. Many of the cases come from mythical verbal accounts by police officers in Sudbury, Ontario. You may view them as police fables.

I have tried to be historically accurate in what I have written for these time periods with regard to police procedures and practises from that time. Any mistakes, errors or omissions are mine and mine alone.

I would like to thank all past and present police officers and civilian employees of Sudbury from Sudbury Regional Police Force (and included police forces from before Regional government especially Coniston Police and City of Sudbury Police), Greater Sudbury Police Service, Ontario Provincial Police and Royal Canadian Mounted Police. I would like to thank the Ontario Police College and the Canadian Police College Polygraph School for technical information and context. I would like to thank the City of Greater Sudbury Archives and the Sudbury Region Police Museum for providing information and context to these time periods.

Past and present police officers may see something of themselves and others in the characters in this book. No officers in this book are real people but each is an amalgamation of officers I have known in my career.

I wish to recommend reading and thank the authors of "Reading Rock Art: Interpreting the Indian Rock Paintings of the Canadian Shield" by Grace Rajnovich, 1994; "DNA and Social Networking: A Guide to Genealogy in the Twenty-First Century" by Debbie Kennett, 2011;

"Twelve O'Clock and All's Well" by E.G. Higgins, 1978; "Forensic Psychophysiology Using The Polygraph" by James Allen Matte, 1996; "Memory-Enhancing Techniques For Investigative Interviewing: The Cognitive Interview" by Ronald P. Fisher and R. Edward Geiselman, 1992; "A Guide To Crisis Intervention - Fourth Edition" by Kristi Channel, 2012; and, "Principals of Neural Science" by Eric R. Kandel, James H. Schwartz, Thomas M. Jesse, 1991.

Introduction

Purple lightning, high winds, driving heavy rain. I leaned forward trudging through deep brush to try to return to my canoe. Vicious pain as though my head exploded. Nothing. I awoke to bright sun, light warm breeze and birds singing. How did I get here?

Visions begin to rotate through my mind. I am on a horse. I am kneeling beside an old time car and there is a dead man beside me. I am in a hallway standing over a body with blood everywhere. I am at a wedding in a jail or police station. I am sitting in a dingy bar nursing a beer. I am speaking with a family about a loved one. I flash through all these scenes. As I shake my head, I feel the veil lift from my mind. I don't know if any of this is real.

I am in a hospital room. I can see, hear, feel. I am solid. Real. It has a smell of antiseptic clean. It is warmer than it should be. The air is not moving. I faintly hear voices without hearing the words. It is so bright.

"Come back. Stay relaxed but feel yourself slowly beginning to open your eyes", the doctor's voice says.

I am Enoch Brown. The doctor is sitting vigil in a chair. For the third time the room has changed for me.

"How do you feel?" the doctor queries.

"Rested. But I don't seem to know where I am or how long I have been here." I respond.

Yet all of this is a dream.

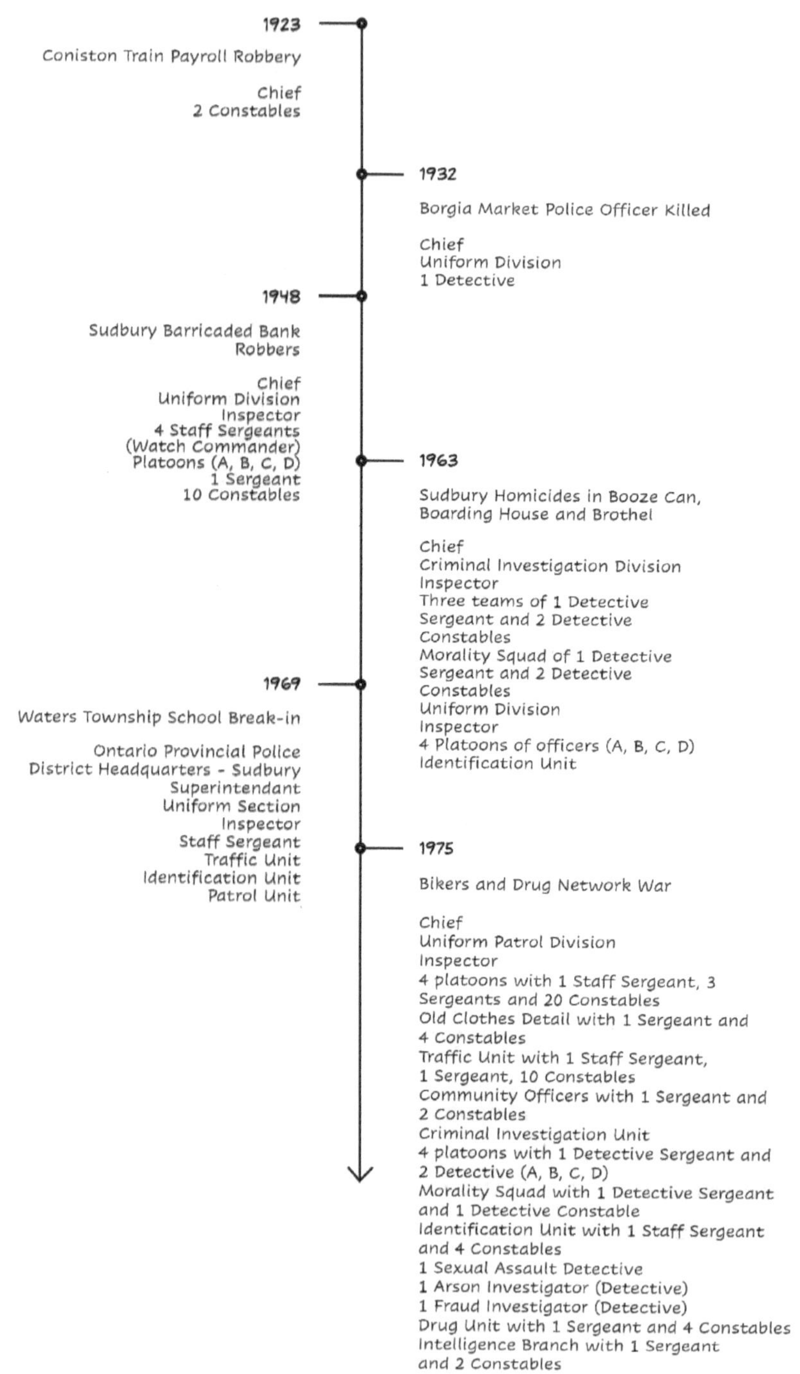

1923
Coniston Train Payroll Robbery

Chief
2 Constables

1932
Borgia Market Police Officer Killed

Chief
Uniform Division
1 Detective

1948
Sudbury Barricaded Bank Robbers

Chief
Uniform Division
Inspector
4 Staff Sergeants
(Watch Commander)
Platoons (A, B, C, D)
1 Sergeant
10 Constables

1963
Sudbury Homicides in Booze Can, Boarding House and Brothel

Chief
Criminal Investigation Division
Inspector
Three teams of 1 Detective Sergeant and 2 Detective Constables
Morality Squad of 1 Detective Sergeant and 2 Detective Constables
Uniform Division
Inspector
4 Platoons of officers (A, B, C, D)
Identification Unit

1969
Waters Township School Break-in

Ontario Provincial Police
District Headquarters - Sudbury
Superintendant
Uniform Section
Inspector
Staff Sergeant
Traffic Unit
Identification Unit
Patrol Unit

1975
Bikers and Drug Network War

Chief
Uniform Patrol Division
Inspector
4 platoons with 1 Staff Sergeant, 3 Sergeants and 20 Constables
Old Clothes Detail with 1 Sergeant and 4 Constables
Traffic Unit with 1 Staff Sergeant, 1 Sergeant, 10 Constables
Community Officers with 1 Sergeant and 2 Constables
Criminal Investigation Unit
4 platoons with 1 Detective Sergeant and 2 Detective (A, B, C, D)
Morality Squad with 1 Detective Sergeant and 1 Detective Constable
Identification Unit with 1 Staff Sergeant and 4 Constables
1 Sexual Assault Detective
1 Arson Investigator (Detective)
1 Fraud Investigator (Detective)
Drug Unit with 1 Sergeant and 4 Constables
Intelligence Branch with 1 Sergeant and 2 Constables

Chapter 1 - 2024

Detective Staff Sergeant Enoch Brown walked quickly through the hall in a hurry with sirens blaring in the distance. The sirens hold meaning to him in this moment. He has another report of a fire to an abandon building. That makes three fires this month. He remembered back to his time on the beat finding a homeless man burned to death in a garage fire. The fire today was also an old garage. It was not far from the deadly fire he investigated all those years ago. The man back then was beyond recognition as human. His figure was burned into Enoch's memory and intruded at the oddest times. He had roast beef for supper that night. He could still smell the crime scene. To this day he could not eat roast beef as the taste always brought the smell that took him back to that moment. It had been an accident as the homeless man was trying to stay warm and the fire got away from him while he slept. It was the most gruesome scene he had ever attended.

The smell of fresh coffee hastened him to his office. Something different and enjoyable to shake the thoughts and images he was seeing from his past. He slowed himself as he passed through the door looking around in the bullpen at all the desks seeing his detectives were seated and working.

"Another day," thought Enoch. "My last day before holidays."

The Criminal Investigation Division's (CID) Administrative Assistant, Franklin, held up his mail while he spoke on the phone to someone. He covered the phone with his hand.

Franklin loudly whispered, "There is a fire on Lorne Street they're now calling it arson. Uniform is loudly on their way as you can hear.

The Comm Centre is asking for a detective to attend. The Uniform Staff Sergeant has already approved Forensics who are on route."

"I heard. Who's calling it arson? Are we even on scene yet," Enoch asked.

"The Platoon Captain from Fire. Uniform is just arriving. More fire trucks are on their way as you can hear," replied Franklin.

"Well, send Detective Sergeant Phillips and Detective Jackson. Good experience for Jackson in his first month and Phillips has an arson investigators course from the Fire College in Gravenhurst. Have they called the Fire Marshall to attend?" queried Enoch.

"Yes sir, they were called first and had someone in North Bay who is on the way in about an hour or so. Here's you mail," replied Frankiln.

"Okay. Tell Jackson and Phillips to call the Comm Centre to get details, go to the scene and call me from there when they have more. Oh, and tell them to keep the Uniform Staff Sergeant up to date and Media Liaison. We'll need to get a media release out or something on social media," said Enoch.

Enoch took his mail and walked into his office. He put in a coffee pod. He saw his trip map pinned to his bulletin board. He took it off to study it. He gazed over the map imagining the canoe trip he was taking. It would be the first peace he had felt for a while. He had so much unfinished work his head was wrapped around. He looked forward to gaining some clarity away from his desk.

Jackson, the new detective stuck his head in the office doorway. "Need a coffee or anything while we're out Staff?" asked Jackson.

"No," replied Enoch. "And for future reference, I never have anyone get me coffee. I make it here or get it myself. If I do ask you to get me one, I pay. You don't make enough to be buying me coffee and you're not here to fetch things for me. You're a Detective now. I appreciate the thought but now you know it's not necessary."

"Okay. Noted. Staff, are you sure you want me to go on this?" responded Jackson.

"Yes of course, why not."

"It's my first arson or any big case really," Jackson spoke quietly.

"This is your first arson. Well, sometimes they can be heartbreaking when it's a person's home. Sometimes gruesome if there's a body. Take it slow. Remember to think like you're doing a simple break and enter and do everything for the arson you would do for a break and enter investigation just bigger. Follow Tamara's lead. She's been doing this awhile. Make sure Fire does a thorough search in case there is a body. Something I learned the hard way early in my career."

"Got it Staff. Thanks," said Jackson as he heard his Sergeant call for him to go.

Enoch sat at his desk computer to call up emails and check his phone messages. Busy morning already. Coffee would help. The Detective Sergeant on the floor had emailed him everyone's plans for the day and investigations of interest. Enoch quickly sent an email to the Inspector of the Criminal Investigation Division and the Deputy Chief to update them on manpower and investigations of interest. He also updated them on the new arson investigation. With three suspicious fires now, that changed the game. More resources would have to begin to work on this as a series if this fire turned out to be similar to the other two. He grabbed his coffee from the machine and walked the floor to speak with all his detectives working today.

Enoch made his way to the Major Crime Unit office where there was only Detective Sergeant Andy Travis on duty. The office was a bit messy but that was par for the course. The white board was covered with todo items, photos on the wall for the ongoing cases and an easel with blank white paper ready for the next team briefing. It was a quiet room with good lighting. This had been a large briefing room at one time but with the large number of rotating major cases, it had become the unit's office.

Major Crime Unit Office Components

"How's it hanging? Last day right?" quipped Travis.

"Sure is. I may be moving a little slow but I'm packed for tonight and head out right after work," replied Enoch. "I'm staying at the Sportsman's Lodge tonight on Kukagami Lake. I start my solo trip in the morning."

"Remind me again what you do for fun? A canoe trip to look at painted rocks or something?" asked Travis.

"That about sums it up," said Enoch.

The canoe trip was Enoch's chance to get away from all the craziness of his job. Single and with few commitments besides his job, Enoch loved the outdoors and took any chance he could to be out in the woods. This was his chance to look closely and photograph pictographs on Lake Matagamasi.

Enoch spent most of his free time in the woods, dreaming of the woods or studying Anthropology something he took at University. University was quite a time for Enoch gaining his Bachelor's Degree in Anthropology after four years. He had been in the Canadian Armed Forces Primary Reserves (Militia) as a Corporal in the infantry. The Militia paid the bills through school and gave a wealth of adventure and knowledge to Enoch. He loved his time in the army. He was proud of his time and never failed to attend at a Legion on Remembrance Day.

Anthropology field work and the infantry gave him a love of the outdoors and exploring. His father had been a canoe instructor. Enoch got his first canoe with his brother when he was ten. Family camping from an early age gave him little fear of roughing it. This was how he enjoyed his down time. It was the only time he was able to leave work behind and concentrate on something else. Since his wife had died, Enoch did work and spent time alone in the bush. His was a solitary life but it was better than being around too many people.

He had settled in Sudbury, Ontario a city that had 167,000 population with an area the size of all the cities around the Greater Toronto Area, approximately 1400 square miles, with 220 lakes and hundreds of miles of logging roads within city limits. An outdoor sports person's dream with lots of places to explore. With the City's main workforce being in mining, lumber and medical care, policing was the career he chose. The job was different every single day and always exciting for him. Some days he felt the job was all he had.

Factors Defining the Protagonist's Life

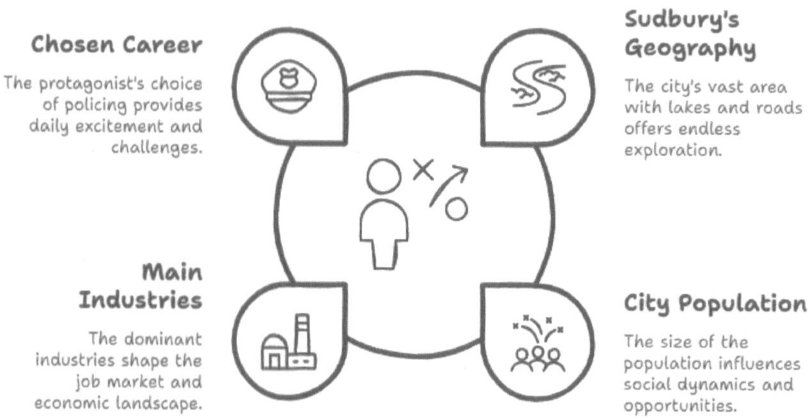

This excursion Enoch planned was to be a canoe trip on Lake Matagamasi to Algonquian rock paintings a short way up the east arm of the lake. He planned to photograph them in great detail for study. There were interpretations of the meaning by the indigenous people and learned scholars. Enoch had his own ideas and he wanted to write an article about those thoughts. It would not be his first time published for his hobby in anthropology.

When he got back to his desk, he started to read through officer reports for the last 24 hours to approve them. He took short breaks having his coffee and mentally reviewing his preparations. The canoe was on his truck, the gear was loaded in the back seat along with his food. He had to get some perishables at the grocery store before he left. He was loaded up and planned to drive to the Sportsman's Lodge to spend the night. He would leave from there by canoe. Before lunch on the second day he should make the paddle to the rock paintings.

<u>Chapter 2</u>

Enoch's phone rang. "Detective Staff Sergeant Brown in Criminal Investigations. How can I help you?" he bleated out the greeting he had been taught as a cadet

and continued to use to this day as being professional. It was informative to the caller with just a pinch of "customer service".

"It's Philips. I have an update on the fire," came the voice of Detective Sergeant Tamara Philips. "It's clearly arson with lots of accelerant in one spot. Forensics is photographing and taking samples, measurements, etc. The Fire Marshall is here and agrees."

"Did the firemen sweep for any bodies or anything of interest for us?"

"They did and we've done a quick sweep. It's the old garage near the graveyard. There are lots of signs of squatters using this place. This is not accidental though. Too much accelerant right up the wall. I'm leaving Jackson here with the Fire Marshal and Forensics for the experience. I have all I need. There are two uniform here who are going to do a canvass of the neighbours. I found the caller and did an audio interview here so I'll head back in. Uniform will guard the scene until Fire Marshall and Forensics are done. The two uniform we have here are enough. I've already updated the Uniform Staff Sergeant and Media Liaison. Media will call you about a media release shortly. Anything else?

"Nope," said Enoch. "Very thorough as always, Tamara. Make sure to keep in touch with Jackson because this is his first one. Talk him through everything you do. I'll see you when you get back to the barn," he told his top lead hand from the floor today. "I had a homeless guy burn to death in a garage fire when I was a rookie. I just don't want to miss anything. Come see me when you're in so we can talk about this and the other two fires this month."

"No problem. Cheers, boss," replied Tamara.

Enoch sighed and rubbed his temple. This would, he hoped, be the last case before his vacation started. He knew that work always found a way to follow him. Even when he was far away doing something else. It never stopped eating away at him. He should let it go knowing Tamara was good at her job but he could never let anything go.

Another arson at a homeless site. An encampment last month, a vacant shed downtown last week and now this. No one dead but if they are connected, it could just be a matter of time. That is, if the locations are escalating, as they seem to be and if this is a series by the same offender. Tamara will need to take these fires to the Crime Analyst to see about comparing the cases for similarities and maybe running up a geographic profile although they will need five scenes to get any kind of accuracy there.

The math for geographic profiling boggled Enoch's mind. That was the reason a computer program called Rigel was used. It was different from behavioural violent crime linking that he used to do on his two year secondment to the Ontario Provincial Police Behavioural Sciences Section when he was a Violent Crime Analyst with ViCLAS (Violent Crime Linkage Analysis System) trying to link serial cases of homicide, sexual assault and non-familial abduction.

Enoch knew arsonists came in a little variety. There were the thrill arsonists who loved the activity of the police, fire and people watching all around like a carnival. They were usually in the audience while the fire was being extinguished. Enoch thought the detectives will have to interview the firemen for anything suspicious. There were the arsonists who were hired to torch a place for insurance or revenge or a person doing it themselves for those reasons. There were the weirdly wired ones who just liked fire. Starting it, watching it, playing with it. It was a behavioural thing and usually sexual for them or at least some kind of gratification. Lastly, there were the "heroes" who found the fire or tried to put it out after starting it in the first place for the recognition.

Understanding Arsonist Motivations

He was going to need to assign them more help. He could pull another detective in that would give them a team of three to work this case plus Forensics and Crime Analysis from Intelligence. That should be good with his temporary replacement managing the case while he was on holidays. Enoch hammered out a quick memo to that effect and sent it to Tamara, the Forensic Unit Sergeant and the Intelligence Sergeant cc'ed to his temporary replacement, his Inspector and the Deputy Chief of Operations.

The phone rang as he finished. Jackson was calling, "Staff, Sergeant Philips is on her way in but I found a neighbour with video. It's pretty bad but there is a dark figure moving from the side of the garage just before the fire breaks out."

The video showed further up the road the figure cloaked in shadows and backlit from the fire's licking flames. He did not look back or seem startled when the flames broke out of the building like a billow of fog and fire. He was walking in a determined manner and looking around like his head was on a swivel as he moved. He was looking everywhere but back at the fire. His posture seemed calm when the fire began.

"Okay, let Tamara know. Tell the Fire Marshall. It may have taken the fire a while to start rolling or there may have been some kind of timer. He'll know what to look for. Once the canvass it done, go to the fire hall and interview the firemen on the call to see if they saw anyone suspicious around while they were working the fire."

"On it. Sergeant Phillips told me to get the firemen statements before they left but I forgot," Jackson muttered in a low stuttering voice.

"That's okay just swing by the fire hall. Get their statements. Make sure to ask them if they saw anyone suspicious while they were putting out the fire. Also get a copy of their report on this fire, it should be done. Take a breath, Jackson. We all have that first big case and the best thing is to learn as much as you can and do it right for the victims.”

“Sorry, Staff. I’ll do that. Thanks.”

“It’s okay. We all miss things and forget things. When we do we go back and get them. Don’t ever skip over anything in an investigation. And then head in and report to Tamara. I want to see you both after that.”

Now Enoch did more report checking and a second cup of coffee. No meetings today for a change. Everyone kept their head down on Fridays. A quick review and some changes to the media release. Enoch sent it back with an email to release this final copy to all papers, tv, radio, and other media outlets.

<u>Chapter 3</u>

Time for a quick lunch in the cafeteria. Enoch took the stairs to the 1st floor marvelling again at the powers that be who decided a police station should be seven floors high. A vertical building created physical barriers to communications, moving prisoners about, team building between units but it also did promote exercise with an ancient elevator system that was often not working. A horizontal building would be so much better but little choice was given to the police when it was built as it was a repurposed office building. They had been fighting for a new building for more than a decade but little progress was being made.

Leaving the elevator, he walked through the door into the City portion of the building. It was visually pleasing with an open concept atrium looking up at four floors with balcony styling rather than walls. A lovely glass elevator to give a great view on the ride up and many people moving around going about their business. Enoch made his way to the cafeteria through a long hallway into another building known as the Provincial Building with lots of provincial offices. It was kind of great in the winter to never have to go outdoors to do your meetings and business.

The cafeteria had great food and the staff were the friendliest. Enoch almost always took his lunch there as many people he knew did. As he left the cash register with his meal he saw the Regional Coroner wave him over. He knew the Coroner would want to talk about the opioid crisis and the deaths the last few years. He walked over to the table and sat down with his tray.

"Hey Enoch, I was hoping to catch you at lunch today. I'm in Toronto next week and you know what they want to talk about," said Doctor Samantha Wilson, the Regional Coroner.

"I know and I've been to a few talks lately from the Centre of Forensic Science and the Chief Coroner's office in Toronto." replied Enoch. "They're looking for an easy answer and it's not out there."

As he said this he started to see flashes of faces of people he knew who had died in the last year of an opioid overdose. He could remember the scream of a mother when he had to tell her that her daughter was dead. She completely fell apart. She tore a framed picture off the wall near where she was standing and fell to her knees sobbing, It was heartbreaking. He recalled telling a young man he had arrested many times not to take "purp", heroin with Fentanyl or Car-Fentanyl in it. It was new on the street then and there were many bodies dropping. He told the young man that he was tired of so many people he knew dying.

Enoch realized after that almost everyone he knew that had died had criminal records and he had dealt with through work. What a sad thing to hold that kind of connection with criminals and to feel their deaths so strongly. He always reminded himself that nobody was in as bad a place as when they met the police. They were just people who he always saw at their worst or most desperate time.

Enoch shook his head and continued, "Sorry, I drifted off there for a second. I'm putting together a report to my Chief about this and the laying of charges in an opioid death. I can send you a copy today."

Enoch's report looked at the problem with inconsistent statistics gathered from police, hospital, the health unit, ambulances, Stats Canada and the coroner's office. The fact is that none of them were the same. They were all pretty bad, all of the numbers were likely low compared to the actual number of deaths. This was because all the numbers gathered were not collated with the others. The opioid deaths had other contributing factors and often those factors were listed as cause of death rather than simply a drug overdose.

When a person died out of hospital and there was evidence of drug use, a toxicology report and the autopsy would tell the tale. A person transported to Emerg may have other medical issues. Dying under a doctors care in the Emerg meant it was unlikely to be a coroner's case and may be reported as a death from another cause. The same was true of someone admitted to hospital in longer care. Police were not always called to overdose calls. It may be an ambulance crew alone and never reported to police.

When police attended a sudden death, they called in the coroner but circumstances may mean that ambulances were not called to attend. The systemic problem was that multiple causes of death clouded the statistics. Multiple agencies collecting and submitting the data had different numbers. No one agency is able to collate the numbers. Stats Canada could only add up the numbers given to them. They often pigeon holed cases with set categories for better analysis. This all led to inaccurate and lower accounting of the true number of deaths.

How to improve death data accuracy?

Fragmented Data Collection

Leads to inaccuracies and inconsistencies

Unified Data Collection

Enhances accuracy and consistency

With this problem becoming known to agencies, reports were being developed everywhere to deal with each aspect of the problem. Enoch had been tasked with writing a report as to why there had been no charges laid in any opioid death by the police. There had in fact been two cases that had been submitted to the Crown's office where Detectives felt they had a case. One was rejected by the Crown. The other had seen charges laid but they were later lost in court.

The rejected case had the victim buying drugs from a friend who told him they were strong and to be careful. The victim consumed the drugs and other drugs with another friend. The other friend got sick but recovered quickly. Later the victim died. Toxicology revealed multiple drugs in his system. It was unknown which drug killed him and therefore it would not be solely attributed to that dealer.

In the other case there was a friend of the victim who witnessed the drugs being purchased and could identify the dealer. The witness stayed with the victim while he took the drugs and until his death. Toxicology revealed the drugs to be the cause of death. At trial the credibility of the witness came into question. The Judge did not believe the witness had seen what he said and the case was dismissed.

Enoch's report outlined these cases in great detail. The report mostly focused on the difficulty with statistics. It went into great depth on three cases in Ontario that created the case law with regard to manslaughter charges in these types of cases.

Enoch had found three cases that outlined what was necessary to prove manslaughter in the case of an opioid death in addition to the Criminal Code definition of Manslaughter. The accused person must have sold those drugs to that victim. As this is a crime that is often not witnessed or the witness may see the exchange but not the use of the drugs. It is difficult to prove this point. It must be proven that the drug was the cause of death and no other mitigating factors. There are often other health issues involved in the death. It must not be an intentional overdose (ie. suicide or death by misadventure - overdosing with a hope to be revived by Narcan or Naloxone). It must be the only drug contributing to the cause of death not mixed with other drugs or alcohol. As many addicts often take a cocktail of drugs this makes it virtually impossible to identify which drug caused the death.

Enoch explained this all to Samantha over lunch and promised her a copy of the report emailed to her today. Samantha was happy to hear so many people and agencies were aware besides her own. She was also glad that everyone seemed to be looking for answers beyond "just tell the addicts to stop taking drugs." An opinion that was ridiculous to anyone knowing anything about addiction. Or the "who cares if addicts die." Knowing those with that opinion are unaware that addicts are everywhere in society and almost no one has been untouched by opioid deaths of friends, family members or co-workers.

"I wanted to mention to you that my pathologists and coroners have noticed some burn marks on some of the victims. These are anti-mortem, happening after death. We're not sure what it means but someone must be with them when they died or shortly after. All these bodies came from homeless camps or abandon buildings people were squatting in. I picked up on it in a couple of reports then found it in several others. It is just mentioned as a small external burn on the leg or arm of the deceased. I wanted to make you aware."

Factors Leading to Mysterious Deaths

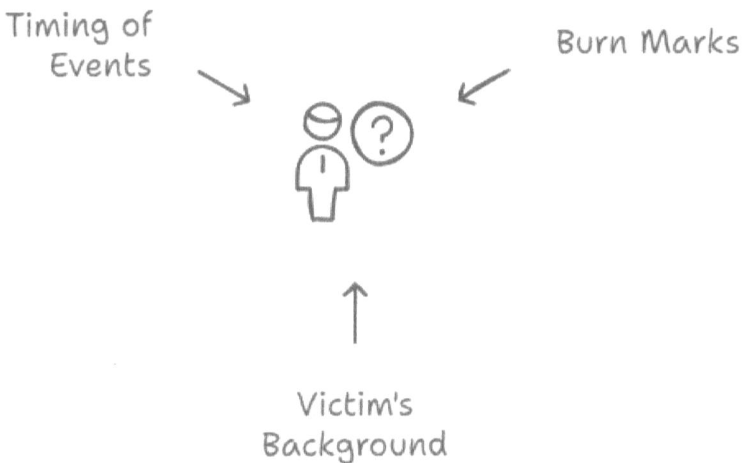

"Thanks, it wasn't on my radar but it is now. Can you email me those reports so I can match them to police reports?"

"Of course. Some were ambulance calls where police did not attend."

"That's okay, I have a couple of detectives out this morning on an arson call. I'll give this to the Crime Analyst in Intelligence to collate and have those detectives review all the cases. While I'm at it, I'll do case reviews on them myself so we triple check everything."

"As always Enoch, good talking to you."

"Same with you doc."

Walking back through the City building to the station, Enoch wished for some good old fashioned murders that were cut and dried. Something complex to sink his teeth into but something that could be resolved. Opioid deaths right now were the never ending story. Enoch always said he preferred homicide to any other type of investigation because it was the only time your victim couldn't screw up your case. That proved untrue with opioid deaths. The 21st Century's epidemic that was led by the medical community overprescribing pain killers. Now it was perpetuated by the science of chemistry adding designer drugs and mixing exotic drugs like Fentanyl and Car-Fentanyl that are commonly known now but not so well known 15 years ago.

Deaths had risen to unbelievable rates and were inclusive of anyone from all strata of society. Overdosing on drugs was no longer a street junkie only demise. It touched every family in some way, all professions, education and ages. No one seemed immune. It was the dirty little secret of using drugs that could not be kept in death. Drug overdose deaths were always sad but now they were surprising, sudden and indiscriminate. They were still sad. They made everyone feel helpless. The deaths had not seemed to slow or stop in the last 7 or 8 years.

Enoch believed that the Major Crime Unit would be overwhelmed taking on these cases and the Drug Unit was not equipped to investigate cases like homicides. The teams of General Detectives on the floor in CID took the cases now. Enoch had insisted on extra training and providing information to all those officers for a better skill set in these cases. The Crown Attorney's Office was always consulted now after the coroner's findings for cause of death and the investigation showed a link to the dealer or provider of the drug. This was a stop gap solution only to stem the tide but also move forward with cases to charges and convictions.

Enoch spent his walk to the office trying to reconcile that a special unit was needed for these deaths but there was, of course, no manpower for this. He tried to think of a better process and thought he would talk to his boss about a combined unit with two uniform officers, one community service officer, two detectives and a Sergeant. This would allow public education from one officer, supervision for all and give uniform officers experience and training in these death/homicide investigation while building expertise in CID. Getting that put together would be a battle and likely only allowed for a short time period. Enoch thought that 3 to 6 months might show a track record that would allow the success of such a unit to continue.

Chapter 4

As Enoch entered the building, he was approached by a rookie he had seen but did not know. An earnest look while doing the pee dance told Enoch that this officer had been waiting for him and nervous about something important to say or ask. He told the officer to walk with him as he headed to the elevator. Once on the elevator he said, "Speak."

"Sir…"

"Stop," said Enoch. "I am not a Sir, I am a Staff." He could tell by the way the young man stood and his eyes kept looking away that he was very new and very nervous.

"Staff. My Coach officer said to call you Ewok," he said quietly with a crooked smile.

"Ha ha. Yeah that would be correct," replied Enoch. "What's on your mind?"

"I have an interview to do this afternoon and I've never done one before. Somebody on Platoon said I should tell him I have the guy on video breaking into this house and that will get him to confess. My Coach said no and told me to speak to you. Do you mind or am I just bugging you and looking stupid?" said the young officer.

"Questions are never stupid and I love to share my knowledge as well as get some in return," Enoch told him. "I will say your friend is an idiot." Enoch placed his hand on the rookie's shoulder. "We never lie to a suspect. There are other things you can do like use props."

Enoch continued, "By saying you have him on video, you are lying about evidence you don't have. The courts will see this as a constitutional violation on your suspect's rights. They may see it as you fabricating evidence and committing a criminal offence yourself."

"Oh"

They walked off the elevator, down the hall, through the bullpen in CID into Enoch's office. Enoch took his seat behind his desk. When he looked up, the young officer was standing at the door outside the office. He was shifting his weight from foot to foot. "Are you coming in?" asked Enoch.

"Yes sir, I mean Staff," his voice barely above a whisper. He walked in and took the chair opposite Enoch. Both sat on either side of the desk to speak.

"The courts may have strict rules for us to follow but the lines are drawn very clearly for us. Be smarter and keep everything legal. We can't lie to a suspect about evidence we don't have. We can use trickery however and that's okay."

"I see. No, I'm not sure I see. I don't know what a prop is and when to use it."

Enoch lectured, "In this case, take a thumb drive, put it on the interview table on a big envelope that the suspect can see. On it put the word video and on the envelope put the address of the break in and the date if you know it. Place it in a way he can read it. Do not ever refer to it during the interview. If he asks about it, tell him it's nothing and put it away. Understand?"

"Yes… maybe?" said the young officer. "But no, I don't get it."

"Then you speak to him and interview him. At some point after he has looked over there at it, ask him if he had any concern about any evidence you may have on him. Likely this will not be necessary. This is a prop. He will think you have video evidence even though you don't. That is called trickery. The courts allow us to use trickery but not lying. If you hold it up and tell him you have video evidence of him committing the crime, that is a lie. Let his imagination do the work. Never confirm you have video evidence. Hopefully he will assume you do and confess to make himself look good with an excuse or explanation," lectured Enoch.

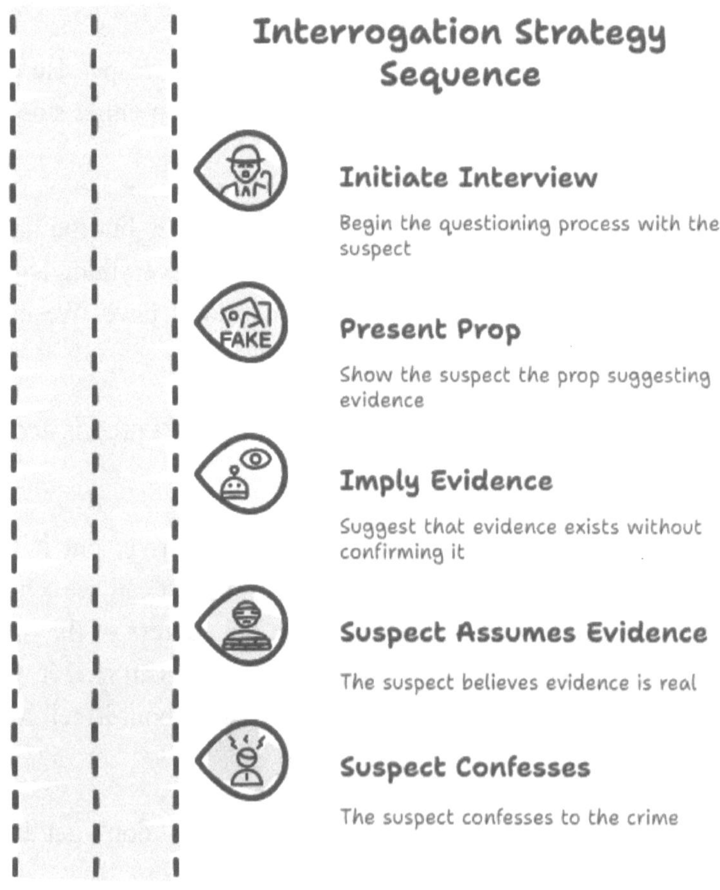

"Now I get it."

"There is another way to go without a prop and that is to bait him with a question like, I haven't checked the neighbours yet but I will be doing that. With everyone having video cameras these days, what are the chances someone will have a video of you near the break in or even doing the break in? This will cause a pause then a weak denial or silence. Be prepared though, sometimes suspects will confess there. You haven't told him you have a video only that you will be checking to see if one is out there," instructed Enoch.

"Ah I get it now. That's great."

"What's your name?" asked Enoch

"Constable Tom Wilson"

"No nickname yet?"

"No Sir… ah Staff."

"I think you can call me Ewok now."

"Okay Ewok, that's a weird nickname for a cop," said Tom.

Enoch laughed, "They're all weird. It could have been much worse."

Nicknames are a sacred thing in policing. You can't give yourself one. It is conferred on you by another officer and if it's picked up by others, you have it for life. Enoch had his from his first 6 months on the job when his coach officer started to call him a "wookie". He called him wookie because the coach and another officer were called the star fighters. They got these nicknames for arresting a bad guy with a gun. They then proceeded to take out little toy laser sound makers and pretend to shoot at each other. The bad guy told them it was not funny and who did they think they were, star fighters? It caught on.

On an early call, the coach went to speak to a caller who was "trapped" in their house in January by a "vicious dog". The dog was a big puppy and cold. He was just trying to get in the guys house to get warm. The coach told Enoch to get rid of the dog. Not entirely sure what to do but pretty sure he wasn't suppose to shoot the dog, he opened his door on the passenger side and the dog jumped in then over to the driver's side. Wanting to impress his coach, Enoch began to write notes with the dog happily sitting in the driver's seat.

Enoch looked up at the driver's side to see his red faced coach with his winter hat earflaps pulled down and heavy cloud breath steaming from his mouth glaring at him with a not happy look on his face.

"Get that fuckin' dog out of my seat. Now," yelled the coach.

With wide eyes Enoch said, "Yes sir." He opened the door and pulled the dog out of the car through his side. He opened the back door and the dog happily jumped into the back of the cruiser. Closing the door, Enoch looked up and saw his coach looking angrier if that could be possible and the coach said, "Not in the back, out of my car."

Enoch pulled the pooch out of the car and said, "Do we just leave him here?"

"No we don't leave him here", yelled the coach. "We do police work and solve the problem. This dog lives up the street." The car moved forward slowly. "He follows us to his house we beep the horn or use the siren until someone opens their door and lets him in. We do not put the dog in the driver's seat, my seat, and we do not chauffeur it home."

He finished as he drove in the driveway and he whelped the siren. The front door opened. A woman in a pink fuzzy bathrobe yelled sorry and that she had spoken to the neighbour. Won't happen again.

"See?" said the coach. "Police work is investigating and solving problems wookie. No not wookie, Ewok. You're too stupid to be a wookie yet."

That may well have been the end of it but a few weeks later it was Enoch's first call where he was to do everything on his own and the coach would just watch. It was a woman calling that her husband had run off to kill himself. Enoch had to get information from her at her home. She was very upset and crying. She and Enoch were sitting on her couch facing each other. The coach was sitting on a chair behind the woman. Enoch was calming her and trying to get information to go look for her husband when he noticed his coach making laughing faces at him and pointing to the coffee table. On the coffee table sat a video tape of "The Ewok Adventure."

Enoch calmed her, learned his parent's address, sister's address and some of his friends. Told her to stay where she was and to call the station if he came home or she heard from him. They found him at his sister's place and took him to hospital for a psych evaluation. Nothing about the video tape had been said.

They went for coffee at Tim Hortons on Lorne Street and the coach quietly said, "You did a good job. That was quite an adventure. A real Ewok adventure. You know what this means now, Ewok?"

The next day in lineup everyone heard the story of the dog, the video tape and Enoch had been wearing that moniker ever since. He wore it with pride as there is no other way to wear a nickname forged in fire as this one had been. Over time it tweaked just a bit as people would call in or come to the station looking for him saying, "I don't remember the cop's name but they were calling him The Ewok."

Enoch thanked Constable Wilson for coming to see him, wished him luck and to let him know how it all turned out. As he left, Enoch reset his mind to everything he heard at the Opioid Crisis meeting over lunch as well as his thoughts walking back to the office. He looked around his desk piled with files, papers and books. Everything all over the place but with his keen ability to reach into an unrecognizable pile and pull out what he needed, he did just that.

Opening his computer, he pulled up a new memo document to work on. He wrote three long memos taking an hour of his time. He knew the Inspector, his boss, was back soon from meetings so he made a coffee, checked messages and emails. Then he set his voicemail advising he was on holidays, when he would return and who they should call for quick assistance. He did the same with an automated email response for the dates he was gone.

Mid afternoon, Inspector Frank Townsend walked through his office to the door opposite that was a back way into the Inspector's office. "Anything new Ewok?"

"Just the arson this morning. I expect a briefing shortly I'll send you an email update before I leave. I did the opioid crisis meeting with the Regional Coroner over lunch. I have a memo updating that meeting. I also have a memo suggesting something." said Enoch. He handed the Inspector both memos. He took them and went into his office. Enoch gave him a couple of minutes and then followed him.

"Opioid memo is good I'll bring this to the Chief and the Deputy's attention in tomorrow's meeting. This other memo is bullshit. You know we'll never get a unit to deal with this. There's no manpower," said the Inspector.

"Here," quipped Enoch and handed Inspector Townsend the third memo. As he read it he began to smile.

"Son of a bitch," laughed Townsend. "This is better. Supervision by a Sergeant part time. Two uniform guys to be mentored and learn to take back new knowledge to the uniform division, someone to do media, presentations and deal with upcoming issues in an investigation with family, the press and the public and finally only two detectives off the floor to create new investigative techniques, expertise and work with the Crowns office on case law. Haha. And only for six months. We'll be lucky to get three months."

"I only need three months," replied Enoch. "Give them the first memo, follow up with the second memo for six months and then accept their suggestion we try it for three months. That gives us a chance to get a leg up on these things and make a case or two. Then we can sell them on an extension."

"I love it," said Inspector Townsend. "When are you off? I thought you would be gone now."

Enoch looked at his watch and said, "I have a briefing on this morning's arson and then I'm off."

Chapter 5

The rest of the day flew by with a briefing from Philips, Jackson and Constable Janice Frieze from Forensics about the arson. Acting Staff Sergeant Sandy Morrow sat in as she was taking over CID until Enoch returned. They talked about examining the other two fires for similarities but all agreed they seemed connected. Jackson had interviewed all of the firemen and no one remembered anyone suspicious hanging around. They would be more vigilant if there were any other fires like this.

"I want us to take care in these cases. I get a bad feeling with fires like this. No one is dead yet but that may change. Tamara, I will send you some cases that were sudden deaths at homeless encampments and abandon buildings. The coroner's office has noted there were small burn marks on the bodies. The marks are anti-mortem and therefore concerning. Just keep it in mind. I have no idea why I think they might be connected but it is coincidental. I hate coincidences and don't believe in them," preached Enoch.

"On it boss. I'll review all the reports and we'll keep an eye out for new ones," responded the Detective Sergeant.

Briefing Inspector Townsend and the Deputy Chief on the way out the door on the arson, it was time for Enoch to head for the hills after picking up his groceries. He stopped for a moment on his way out. He was ready to head out and be offline for a while. Everything was in good hands but he just didn't want to let go. He sighed and said, "Time to take off."

Booking off shift, "10-7 Charlie 1," over the radio (10-7 out of service and Charlie 1 was his call sign). Enoch then called the Comm Centre to remind them that Acting Staff Sergeant Morrow was now in charge and on call. Enoch's vacation officially started. Walking to his truck felt fresh and carefree. Heading home, he changed and loaded his dog Jake an Alaskan Husky Shepard into his pickup truck. He headed out with a quick stop at the grocery store for perishables.

All of his equipment was meticulously packed in an organized fashion from experience knowing what he would need and the best way to access it. He used different coloured waterproof sacks for clothes - blue; cooking - green; tools - yellow; and, survival/medical supplies - red. These all went into his canoe pack with his tent and cot. He had a barrel pack for food and perishables. He had a stuff sack for dirty clothes and was well packed for several days and nights out in the bush.

The drive on Highway 17 East was bumper to bumper with commuters as it was at 5 pm everyday. So many people had moved out of the City of Greater Sudbury to live in the smaller surrounding towns and townships. His only stop after the grocery store today was the Kukagami General Store on Highway 17 East at Kukagami Road, the gravel road he would take. Pulling into the parking lot he saw Brad, the owner, standing at the doorway.

"What do you need?" asked Brad.

"I'm not too sure but I'm heading up Lake Matagamasi and Kukagami Lake area doing the Donald Lake Loop, so I want to just have a browse and get a coffee," spoke Enoch.

"Well your timing is great, I have some rain suits on sale that just came in. They're calling for thunderstorms in the next two days," Brad offered.

"No", replied Enoch, "I have frog togs but I can't remember if I brought my hat so I'll get one of those camp hats you sell."

They chatted for about 10 minutes then Enoch headed out with fresh coffee and a new green camp hat on his head. The satellite radio was playing Met Opera. Something Enoch had begun listening to in University on Sunday afternoons on CBC Radio while studying. It soothed him although he didn't understand German, French or Italian so the words were lost on him. It was more the feeling of the music. He played it quite loud on his drive in. His dog Jake was sitting in the passenger seat as navigator. He seemed to enjoy the opera music too.

After 30 minutes he reached his destination at the Sportsman's Lodge on Kukagami Lake Road. He had known the owner Jim for a few years and often rented a room before heading out on a canoe trip in the area. It was a safe place to leave his vehicle always thinking bad things as cops do about theft and vandalism. He would then time his trip to come in late about suppertime for a meal and renting the room for another night to decompress from his trip before heading home.

Enoch had an uncle who used to have a camp in the area on Lake Matagamasi. It's a lake that starts many different canoe routes. It is a short hop of four portages or two portages off Kukagami Lake depending on the route you take to Lake Matagamasi. This is the beginning of the Temagami area although few people canoe up to Lake Temagami from here, unless they are advanced paddlers.

Enoch's plan was to launch his canoe at the Sportsman's Lodge and paddle to the portage into Donald Lake. A short hop portage of 20 feet to get from one part of Kukagami Lake to the other. Then a 1 km portage into Donald Lake. Paddle to the northwest end of Donald Lake portaging into Colin Scott Lake, Gold Lake and then Lake Matagamasi. All well used portages and fairly easy. There was an island on Lake Matagamasi about a 45 minute paddle from the portage from Gold Lake that had a great camp site with a nice fire pit and a Thunder Box. What is a Thunder Box you ask? This is a box with a hole cut in the top and a cover that lowers onto it. A mini outhouse with no walls. A real luxury on a canoe trip.

Jim, the owner of the Sportsman's Lodge, met him in the parking lot. "Hey man, long time no see."

"Hi Jim. Yeah not since last winter. How's business?"

"Hey Jake," said Jim as he patted Jake's head stuck out the window with his tail wagging crazily. "Good season so far. Lot of weekenders during the spring and lots of week-long rentals to families this summer. Been a lot of canoe groups pushing off from here. Glad I have the room to park their vehicles for the week. I usually get one or two night rentals and a parking fee. Same as your deal. You're here in plenty of time for supper and man is it going to be tasty. I have some venison in requested by some of the fisherman staying this weekend."

"Sounds great. I could use a quick cleanup before supper. Mind if I take my canoe down to the dock with packs so I am ready to go in the morning?"

Jim replied, "No problem. Park over by the garage if you like, then you don't have to leave me your keys. Your truck will be out of the way there."

Enoch went to the dining room/bar and got his room key from Jim's girlfriend who helped him run the lodge. He unloaded his Swift Prospector kevlar 14 foot solo trip canoe. It only had one seat. Weighing just a little over 30 pounds, Enoch lifted and carried it easily down by the main dock. Laying it on its side so that it rested upside down. He put his small barrel pack of canned and dried food, his canoe pack with his tent and equipment all under the canoe. He brought his small daypack and grocery bag of perishables to his room then cleaned up for supper. Jake followed along sniffing everywhere with a discriminate pee here and there.

At supper Enoch sat with two fishermen, Ed and Mike from Toronto. They were up for the whole week and had brought their own boat. Enoch talked about his trip and the exploration he planned to do. Ed found it interesting. Mike was more interested in the fishing near there and the boat launch at Lake Matagamasi. They were going out on Kukagami Lake the next day but the day after that they told Enoch they might see him as they wanted to fish Lake Matagamasi. Ed wanted to see the Indian rock paintings.

They had a pleasant evening. Enoch gave a detailed map to Jim in case he didn't come back or texted him on his SPOT satellite emergency device. He could have 911 contacted by SPOT or he could text someone. If it was not a big emergency he could text Jim to come or send someone to pick him up. Again the cop thing, plan for the worst. Saying good night, Enoch went to bed early so he could get up early.

The following morning about 6 am, Enoch woke, showered with plain soap, brushed his teeth, packed his daypack and stopped at the dining room on his way out to give Jim the key. He talked with Jim for a bit about weather coming up and possibly a storm coming the next day. After some toast, orange juice and coffee, he went down to his canoe. Jake was jumping all around excited. Enoch loaded the canoe, put Jake's lifejacket on him. Then his own lifejacket and pushed off heading to the portage into Donald Lake.

The trip to Donald, Colin Scott, Gold and Matagamasi went great except for Jake swimming in swamp muck on one of the portages. Even after throwing him in the lake he was still black all through his white fur legs. Husky Shepards never stop being puppies and always want to play with energy to burn. Jake never met a squirrel he didn't chase. And he had never caught a squirrel.

Jake's Adventurous Trip

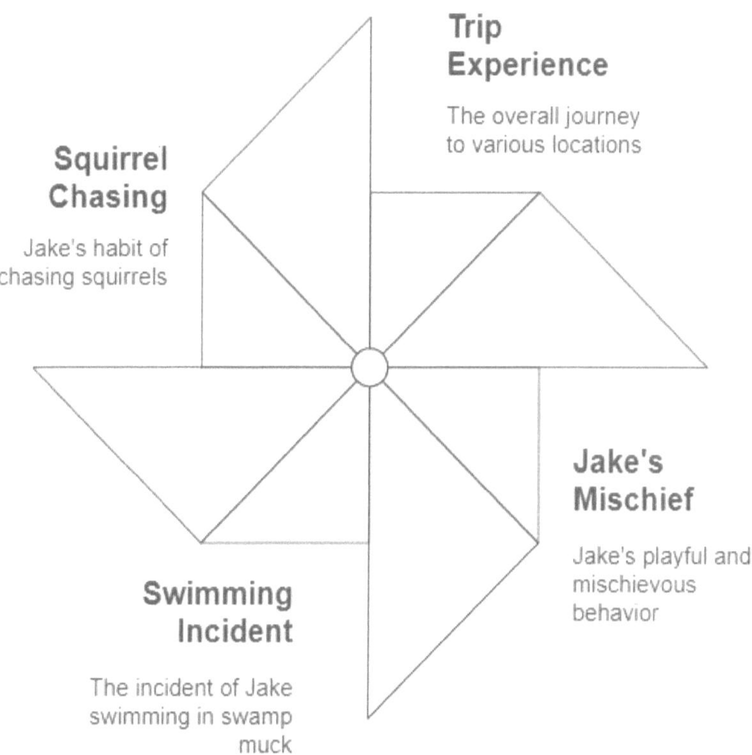

Paddling to the island campsite went well and they arrived at about 6 pm having made great time. Jake got scrubbed in the lake and rubbed down. Lunch had been on the go in the canoe. Now Jake got a bowl of dog food he wolfed down and Enoch made some chilli and had a pear. A small campfire rounded out the evening. Setting up camp and tent while the fire took was only a matter of ten minutes. Hanging the barrel pack was the last thing about 50 feet from camp in the air with all potential food and garbage in it.

A trip to the Thunder Box was a welcome respite. A quick jump in the cooling lake for a scrub and wash. Coffee in front of the fire telling Jake a few fish stories and singing some camp songs out loud rounded out the night. Anyone watching who knew how straight edged he was would have thought he had lost his mind. Opening the tent had Jake bounced in first away from the bugs he had been biting at. He jumped on the small cot Enoch had set up with his sleeping bag and laid down.

"Hey, what do you think you're doing? Jake get off there. You sleep on the sleeping pad over here," pointing to a nylon pad in the corner of the tent. "Every time we get in the tent you jump into my bed. No. You can sleep in a big bed with me at home, but not this tiny cot," Enoch muttered.

With that final speech, a pic burning in a holder to drive off mosquitos and a glow stick cracked to light the tent hanging from the ceiling, Enoch rolled on his side in the sleeping bag and quickly went to sleep. Breathing in the smell of the trees, wood smoke and listening to the frogs and leaves shaking in the wind like chimes.

Chapter 6

In the morning, Enoch woke with sleep in his eyes feeling the moist air. You could feel new weather was coming in. Checking the time as 7 am, it was time to get up. Enoch kept some comfort on his camping trips now that he was getting older. He had a nice sleeping bag on top of a small cot. The cot was very low to the ground causing him to roll out of it and then onto his knees to stand. He unzipped the tent and stepped out and stood up into a big stretch. Jake ran past him sniffing for the perfect spot for his morning pee.

The lake was still with the wind picking up having a cold bite. It was cool and he could see dark clouds coming. Grey skies were rolling in. The weather was not good but he was sure the rain would hold off for a while.

Enoch broke camp to spend a day at the rock paintings. The spot he was heading was about a 90 minute paddle away. These were a sample of just over two hundred documented sites of Algonquian rock paintings in Canada. This site showed hunters and prey. They also showed Manitou but a large piece of that painting had been broken away over time. The Algonquian paintings were always distinctive in their red colour and depictions. They are thought to be put in places of spiritual importance. This site had been documented and written about many times.

Enoch's goal today was photograph the pictographs from the water. Then to scale the small cliff away from the site to avoid disturbing it, photograph them in detail from above and then search the area above. It may have been scoured many times in the past but that was not documented. He wanted to see if there was anything else of archaeological importance in the immediate area.

Although a hobby, Anthropology had been Enoch's University Degree. It was still a passion for him. Once completed today, he would stay another night in the same campsite before setting out to complete a three day canoe trip known as the Donald Loop through several lakes including back to Donald Lake then Kukagami Lake. He would conclude his trip back at his truck at the Sportsman's Lodge, spend the night then head home.

This morning was for coffee. Once his small Kelly kettle, a stick stove pot that was hollow in the centre for fire, boiled his water, he poured it into his cup. A touch of creamer and Italian Roast Starbucks instant coffee tube completed the concoction. Steam rose. It smelled like mana from heaven but was too hot to drink yet. Time to enjoy the sounds of wind blowing through the trees, the smell of the burnt sticks and meditate to clear his mind for the day. He prepared (unwrapped) a breakfast bar. Blowing on the coffee, he sipped it slowly holding a bit in his mouth before gently swallowing. What a great taste.

He had his camera to prepare while he drank the rest of his coffee. Sitting looking out at the lake it felt like he was the only person on earth. He heard voices singing and shouting. Teenagers he guessed. There were a lot of high school groups doing the Donald Loop this time of year. Although sound carried on the water, he would be upon them soon as they sounded like they were coming from the spot he was heading. Grabbing his camera, daypack, life jacket and paddle he pushed off. Savouring the last of his coffee as he drifted away from shore, he drove the paddle forward to leave the bay using a J stroke to keep him moving straight and forward.

As he came out of the bay, he watched his paddle pull in the water leaving two tiny whirlpools in the wake. He pushed the paddle away from the canoe as the stroke came back to complete his J stoke. He noticed the leaves were showing their undersides in the wind. The small birds could be heard tweeting as the wind stopped. It was eerie and signs of an impending storm. The calm before the storm. Enoch gripped his paddle tighter.

There was the snap of a branch making Enoch pause in mid-paddle. He scanned the shoreline but all he saw were trees swaying in the wind. Still he couldn't shake the feeling that something was off. His mood had quickly changed from peaceful to being on edge. It took about 30 minutes to meet the canoe group of six canoes with 2 or 3 people in each.

As they passed, Enoch learned from one of the chaperons they had spent the night in a big campsite in the bay just before the Indian rock paintings. They pushed off at 6 am eating bannock on the paddle to the small cliffs. After a quick lecture at the rock paintings, they had pushed on. They wanted to get into Donald Lake by lunch if they could. Enoch described the portage conditions to them and they parted after all the kids made a fuss over Jake who loved the attention.

About 60 minutes later, there was a boat anchored with Ed and Mike fishing. "I never heard you guys," said Enoch. They laughed and told him they launched at the boat launch a 5:30 am. Once they got to the y split on Lake Matagamasi, they had trolled for while. They had just got to this spot and set up seeing the kids paddling up ahead of them. Mike said the canoes must have been high schoolers. They could hear them singing and yelling for the last half hour after they saw them.

Enoch replied, "I'm never going to be that young again. They went to the rock paintings I'm heading to. Gonna spend part of the day there then back to camp on the island up the lake."

Mike said, "We left early because a storm is coming and the sky is so dark. We plan to head back to the lodge after lunch. If the storm hits we'll just pull into shore and wait it out. We have a packed lunch and rain gear so no problem."

"With luck," quipped Ed, "we will make it back before the storm. Have a nap, supper then out on Kukagami for a fish."

"Tough life," responded Enoch. "Take it easy, I'm back at the Sportsman in 4 days for supper. I'll see you then."

Saying their goodbyes, Enoch paddled on with Jake to the indigenous rock paintings. He bobbed in the water for a few minutes while he pulled on his frog tog pants and jacket. No sense in waiting for the inevitable rain. He set up his camera and grabbed his writing pad. With a rain cap pulled over his camera strapped to his chest, he paddled forward to his goal.

The paintings were just as he remembered them. He had read up on them before he came. He took careful documenting photographs. He shot the paintings first with a 50 mm lens then with a macro lens to make as sharp and clear an image as he could. By then the rain was starting to filter drops here and there. Enoch paddled 50 feet up the lake before tying his canoe.

He carefully stood on a small rock shelf taking his and Jake's lifejackets off. Then he lifted and pushed Jake up so he could scramble over the top of the rock face. Enoch climbed the ten foot rock face to the top. He walked toward the paintings and could see the lake water begin to boil with drops of rain splashing down. It was a sudden torrent. Those are the worst but he was dry and his camera was covered so he carried on.

It was raining too hard to search or see much of anything. Enoch sat on the ground about 10 feet from the edge of the rock. The sky turned black, the wind whipped round in small circles, the air felt charged.

The thunder started first. A few minutes later he could see the lightning in bolts. It was quit a fireworks show. Enoch was enjoying the show until the thunder cracks were in time with the flashing bolts.

Too close for comfort. Enoch stood. His anxiety rose. He began to feel fear. Purple lightning, high winds, driving heavy rain. He leaned forward trudging through deep brush to return to his canoe. A blinding flash lit up the sky, and he felt his arm hairs stand on end. Then came a crack of thunder and a sudden searing pain. Everything went black.

<u>Chapter 7</u>

Ed and Mike from the other shore saw the lightning strike. They heard the ravenous thunder at the same time. Knowing Enoch was up there somewhere, they drove their boat across the lake. Ed steered the boat to his canoe. Mike climbed up the rock face squinting through the downpour. "I think I see him! Call 911," yelled Mike.

He could see Enoch on the ground smoking as though fog was drifting off his entire body. He ran up to kneel beside Enoch checking for a pulse. He had one. "He's alive," Mike yelled. "We've got to move fast," Barely believing anyone could live through that blast from Mother Nature.

Ed was making the call. He was lucky to finally get a signal for the call on his cell phone. He was told an ambulance was on the way along with the fire department to the boat launch. Fire had a rescue boat and would bring the paramedics with them.

Ed climbed up to peer over the edge where Mike was with Enoch. Ed's heart was pounding. It might already be too late. Mike shouted, "He's breathing. I don't know how."

"Fire and ambulance are on their way. Should we move him?"

"No. Come here and bring the first aid kit in my tackle box and my other jacket," rattled Mike.

"There's something in your first aid kit we can use?"

"Nope. Just bring it and hurry."

Ed grabbed the jacket, first aid kit and flew up the hill like a mountain goat. Running to Mike, he realized the rain was lessening and the storm was moving away from them. As he ran up to see Mike had used some pieces of wood to lift Enoch's legs. Ed lay the jacket on the supine body and handed Mike the first aid kit.

"Where's his dog Jake?" asked Ed.

"Over there," pointed Mike.

Ed ran to the dog and found he was still breathing. He began to rub Jake's belly and head. Jake let out a whimper and opened his eyes. "He's alive too."

"Ok, leave him and get back here. I have to monitor his breathing. You need to make a signal for the boat that's coming," said Mike.

"No problem. My old hunting vest is in my pack sack with our lunch."

"Bring the vest but leave the lunch."

"Sure, no problem."

Ed ran to get the vest to make a signal. Mike heard a loud splash. "You okay, Ed?"

More splashing and Ed replied, "Yep. Just a bit wet now. Missed the boat. All good."

"Careful climbing back up here."

Jake had limped over and was whining at Mike. Mike yelled, "Hey bring that lunch. Maybe we can feed Jake a sandwich to keep him quiet."

"Rog."

With Jake, the two men sat and waited getting a small fire going to help Ed dry off a bit. The rain had subsided to a light misting. The wind still whistled ominously in the trees. Enoch never became conscious but he did shake, tremble and moan. This was disconcerting to both men. Jake lay beside him letting out small whimpers now and again and licking Enoch's face.

Chapter 8

The Markstay Volunteer Fire Department was the first truck to arrive at the boat launch as they were the closest for response as per protocol. Markstay was a small community east of Sudbury just past Kukagami Lake Road. Not long after, the ambulance with two EMS paramedics arrived. Finally a Greater Sudbury Fire Service (GSFS) pickup truck pulling a boat started backing up the road to the launch. This was not the old "John" boat they had used as a rescue boat in the past or the RIB they still used for fast rescue.

This was their newest toy being a 16 foot aluminum deep hull boat with a 90 hp motor. It had what looked like a big roll bar on top with lights and siren. At the stern end of the boat was a mounting frame in front of the motor for a stretcher that was fixed to it. They were able to load 3 firemen, equipment, 2 paramedics with their bags of equipment and squeeze in comfortably. The patient would ride back in the stretcher. They tested their radio with the Comm Centre and were off. A Greater Sudbury Police Service (GSPS) cruiser was just arriving on scene as they pulled from the boat launch.

The boat ride seemed to take forever but they spotted the orange vest in a tree on shore with two men waving. There was a dog jumping and barking beside the yelling men. The boat landed on shore on a flat rock with one fireman and both paramedics running up the hill past the fishing boat. Then they ran past the tied canoe to the patient. The other two firemen secured the boat then carried the rescue stretcher up after the others.

The paramedics quickly unpacked equipment from their bags. They began monitoring vitals of the victim. Enoch's blood pressure was very low, his breathing shallow and they were concerned about moving him. One attached an AED to his chest high and low on both sides. Enoch violently shook then went still. All of his vitals plummeted. "We need to use the defibrillator now," said the triaging paramedic.

The AED indicated they needed to cardio-vert the patient. They did this once before his pulse and breathing returned. With the wind picking up, the rain, though light, was whipping around their face and hands. The one assessing quietly told the other paramedic, " We gotta fly man. Breath is shallow, blood pressure is way low and his heartbeat is almost not there."

The assessing paramedic shouted to everyone else, "We have to move or he may not make it. I'd call air ambulance but there's no place to land here. Once we get moving we can radio for a bird. There's a heliport on Kukagami Lake Road in their picnic area. I just hope they can fly in this weather." Everyone began moving in a well practised ballet with paramedics securing the equipment and the patient. The firemen prepared the stretcher. Together they all lifted Enoch onto the stretcher where he was secured. Lightning began to flash again. The rain began to grow heavy.

Ed and Mike could do nothing but watch and hold Jake who was starting to become more vocal. A firemen told the fishermen they had to go and couldn't take them on the boat as there was no room. Also it was against policy. They responded they had their boat and would bring Enoch's canoe, equipment and Jake back to the Sportsman's Lodge. Lifting and walking as one, they lifted the stretcher passing the fishermen and Jake without looking back.

One fireman had their personal details and where they were staying. One paramedic heard from them what had happened. As they loaded Enoch onto the boat, waves rocked them and they almost lost the stretcher over the back of the boat. The wind had greatly picked up.

They locked down the stretcher, one of the firemen said, "That's Staff Sergeant Brown. I've seen him on the news speaking for the police."

Another fireman responded, "Yeah it is. I know him. If anyone can pull through this, it's him."

The boat ride took 30 minutes. As they arrived they saw a fire truck from Markstay Fire Department, a police cruiser and the ambulance. Firemen were waiting to help land the boat and other firemen were keeping back a small group of gawkers who had arrived to see what was happening. The firemen were also positioned to ensure that the road was not blocked. The boat landed and Enoch was carefully removed from the boat to load on the ambulance. They decided to keep him in the rescue stretcher for the trip to the helipad. The Comm Centre had advised that the Air Ambulance helicopter was on its way.

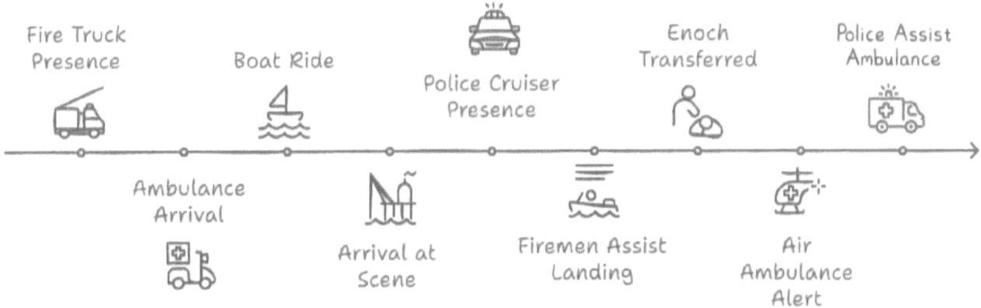

As they were pulling out, the ambulance radio came alive telling them that the storm had picked up strongly again and Air Ambulance was grounded due to lightning. As though a prophecy, rain began to pour from the sky that also lit with lightning. "Just great," said the driving paramedic. Then he rolled down his window and yelled at the platoon captain from the Fire Department, "Script change. We have to go by road now. There's no chopper."

The ambulance was moving fast for a gravel, washboard road. They had to stop twice to use to use the defibrillator. The second time, a police car stopped coming the other way. The fire truck was behind them. The officer, Sergeant Tellifer, recognized Enoch and advised he would lead them through town. He told Fire the officer at the boat launch would speak to the fishermen to get their information and statements. They radioed that information back to the other fire truck waiting at the landing.

Sergeant Tellifer radioed ahead the victim was Detective Staff Sergeant Enoch Brown and asked for cruisers to shut down intersections as they approached. Sergeant Tellifer was the road Sergeant for the Uniform Platoon that day and advised he would set things up asking for a 10-3, meaning officers not involved in this call were to move their radio traffic to an alternate frequency. He asked units to advise what intersections they were close to so he could set them up.

Tellifer radioed the officer at the boat launch, Constable Jim Simon, to wait there, speak to the fisherman and take statements. One fireman from Markstay had the keys to Enoch's truck. Tellifer told Simon to have the fishermen take Enoch's stuff to the Sportsman's Lodge someone would come later to pick it up. Simon was to take Jake to Tellifer's house as he and his wife had looked after Jake before. His wife would take him. Then he was to head up to CID with his statements after he stopped and briefed the Uniform Staff Sergeant.

Cruisers were moved to cover Moonlight Ave at Hwy 17 East, Third Avenue at Kingsway, Falconbridge Road and Kingsway and so on for the route to the hospital, Health Sciences North (HSN). Officers at the station became aware and ran out to Paris at Kingsway and Paris at Van Horne some in plainclothes to direct and stop traffic in the pouring rain. Once the ambulance passed by an intersection the officer at that intersection was detailed to leapfrog to a further intersection to block it for the ambulance. The ambulance moved very quickly through town but Enoch's heart stopped before arrival.

The ambulance arrived at Health Sciences North Emergency Room with one paramedic doing chest compressions. A team was waiting at the door with two doctors and two nurses from the ER to take over. He was rushed through the entrance, lobby and into an ER bay. The real work now began to bring him back and keep him alive. Nurses hurried, their voices blending with the beeping of machines. Enoch lay still, his chest was now rising weakly with each breath. He looked small and helpless in this chaos.

Detective Sergeant Travis met Sergeant Tellifer in the waiting room along with several officers. Tellifer told him what he knew. Tellifer sent another officer to go to Markstay for the witness statements from the firemen. Then go to the Sudbury fire hall to get statement from the rescue firemen. Another officer took statements from EMS. Tellifer called the station and updated the Uniform Staff Sergeant while Travis called the CID Inspector to update him. Tellifer detailed two officers to go to the Sportsman's Lodge to get Enoch's truck and equipment. They were to take his truck and park it at Enoch's house bringing the keys to CID.

Tellifer began moving officers out back to the road for calls. Travis told Tellifer, "The Inspector sent me to advise any updates. I'm to stay here as long as it takes."

Tellifer brought him up to speed.

Tellifer told Travis, "Keep us up to date? The whole platoon worked the ambulance run and are worried."

"No problem."

Tellifer left shooing the last of the officers out of the Emerge. He put out on the radio that officers were to remain away from the hospital unless coming on a call. They would be updated of any news. Travis went to find someone for an update from Emerg staff. After his update, he called Inspector Townsend to bring him up to speed, called and updated the Uniform Staff Sergeant, then settled in the waiting room for answers.

Chapter 9

The Emergency Room looked like an unorganized disaster with people moving to and fro. Injured in medical bays, on chairs, in wheelchairs and stretchers in the hall. Nothing could be further from the truth. A ballet of nurses, doctors and personnel moved efficiently knowing where everyone was situated. The equipment and supplies needed were always nearby and on hand. Communications with other departments such as the X-Ray Department was perfection. It still looked crazy to the novice visitor.

Enoch was in Bay 5 for critical patients. He had been defibrillated once more and now seemed stable. Blood tests were run off to the lab. People were talking over each other with orders and repeating those orders. Everyone knew what had to be done. He presented as an electrocuted victim but he did not have the associated burn marks. He may have been grounded but that was only speculation.

A cardiologist was called in. Also a neurologist. More machines were brought in. It was felt his heart had been through the washing machine ringer but was beginning to settle. More tests would later show no damage to the heart. The neurologist frowned at his scans. "I've never seen brain waves like this," he said. "It's like his brain is running at double speed." These findings he translated as "his brains were scrambled,"and there's "a ton of activity and synapses firing."

The decision was made to put him in a medically induced coma until more tests could say what they were dealing with in Enoch. It seemed clear he had been struck or been close to the lightning strike the fisherman had reported. Enoch was eventually moved to the I.C.U. for monitoring. Travis was given the update and passed it on to everyone else.

Doctor Emerson, the emergency room doctor, explained, "The coma is induced by us until we have a better idea of what is happening. I can't give you a prognosis at this time. We need to notify his next of kin."

"Good luck," said Travis. "The police are his family. His parents are dead, his wife is dead, he never had kids. I don't know of any next of kin. He and I are pretty close so you can keep me updated. You need to know he needs to be okay. He's the lifeblood of CID. He holds us all together. Without him, things will not work out right. He's important to the Police Service, to CID and to me. Do your best doc."

"All right. Unorthodox but it will have to do and only because he and you are police officers."

Travis gave the doctor all his information with instructions to contact him 24/7 if there was any change or news. With nothing else to do, Travis leaned against the waiting room wall alone staring at his phone before updating the Inspector. "Damn it Ewok," he muttered. "You're the glue that holds us all together."

Chapter 10

Images of horses, old time streets and a street car. Gunshots. Voices speaking. Swirling images that made no sense. They seemed pictures of memories that had never happened to him.

Enoch found himself in a briefing about bikers. Lucifer Soldiers. An old m/c gang he remembered his parents talking about. He was in a hospital room taking a statement from a drug dealer about being shot. Sitting surveillance in a car near the old Prospect Hotel hearing on the radio someone had been stabbed and all units being dispatched with a 10-3. Anyone not going was to switch from channel F3 to F2. Being stuck in an attic all dusty and dark, waiting. Standing with a Fire Department Platoon Chief watching an old house burn in the Flour Mill somehow knowing this was the Lucifer Soldiers' Clubhouse.

Enoch continued dreams that began to become so vivid he did not know whether they were dreams or memories. They were memories of things that never happened to him. He was riding a horse with others. He was interviewing people about a dead police officer. He was kneeling beside a car and reaching for a standing man with his hand pulling as hard as he could on the man's shirtsleeve and ripping it down his arm. Watching as the man's body fell in slow-motion beside him. Knowing the man was dead when he saw a third eye above and just to the left of his nose. A wedding in cells at the OPP station that used to be on Cedar Street.

These images seemed to go on forever although they were not coherent, Enoch knew their meaning but did not know how he knew. Examining a crime scene in a house kitchen. Speaking to tenants in a rooming house about their landlady. Interviewing neighbours on a street about the nearby booze can. All of these things somehow related to each other.

Enoch was speaking to a woman in a restaurant. It was not a pleasant conversation. Suddenly he was in a kitchen covered in blood. He was standing on a bridge with a gun in his hand with bullets kicking into the wood all around him. He woke in a cold sweat, with a shaking body and pounding heart, he was drenched in his seat and his heart was racing. Enoch awoke screaming, "Stop."

Pain tore through him as he blinked at the light, his fingers twitching. Shadows shifted at the edges of his vision, morphing into familiar shapes. Was that the crackle of fire in the distance? Or just his imagination? He tried to move, but his limbs refused to cooperate, like his body was still catching up to his mind. From the corner of his eye, he swore he saw smoke curling into a familiar shape, a silhouette in the sky through the window, but it vanished as quickly as it appeared.

A nurse sitting beside his bed took his hand and said, "Everything is all right."

She pushed the call button as she made shushing noises. Enoch's throat was on fire. He was hungry, thirsty and exhausted. It was night out and only one light in the room was on. Another two nurses entered advising they had called down to Emerg for the Doctor.

In a calm voice, the nurse holding his hand said, "Everything is all right. There was an accident but you're all right. You're safe. The doctor will be here soon."

Enoch felt he had heard this before. He tried to speak but his throat hurt. Another nurse came in with a styrofoam cup with ice chips in it. They brought it to Enoch's mouth telling him to be careful not to swallow the ice. He was sucking on it for relief as the doctor came in. The overhead lights had been turned on.

The Doctor took his pulse, shone a light in his eyes. The nursed put on a blood pressure cuff. The kind that takes a blood pressure then cycles through a few blood pressure readings to provide an average.

The Doctor spoke to Enoch. "Can you hear me?" He received a nod yes. "Your throat is very sore?" Another nod yes. "Do you know what happened?" A shake no. "Do you know me?" No. "All right. You have been in a coma for two weeks. You were brought in after being struck by lightning. You were in bad shape so we induced a coma."

Enoch's eyes got heavy and voices sounded far away. The doctor told the nurses to let him sleep and continue with one on one monitoring with a nurse always with him. After some time, Enoch jolted awake with the sound of automatic gunfire still ringing in his ears. For a moment he didn't know where he was. The hospital room felt strange, unreal. "What's happening to me?" he whispered. He passed back to the realm of the unreal.

When he woke again, the nurse gave him ice chips but no drinking yet. His throat was too raw from the intubation tube that had been removed earlier when he was taken off the ventilator. Enoch slept. This recurred several times before he became awake and lucid.

Chapter 11

Enoch first told the nurses about his flashes of vision. They seemed real like memories rather than dreams. They persisted and there were always new ones every time he slept. Sometimes when he was awake he would see flashes of images. Often sudden and violent but not with a consistency of a memory or a dream. It was more like a partial event with no logical beginning or end. They seemed to be getting worse.

Enoch's family doctor, Doctor Hussain, came to visit a few times to speak about these images and his general health. He had been Enoch's doctor for over 25 years. Doctor Emerson the Emerg Doctor came a few times as well. Finally, after several days, two others visited. Doctor Vince Dhwalla, a neurologist and Doctor Sam Patton, a psychiatrist. They spoke to Enoch at length about his visions. They left him without any real answers but some new medications to "help with the visions", Doctor Patton said.

It was clear to Dhwala and Patton there was something troubling here. Going back to their medical school days, both doctors often practised Problem Based Learning (PBL). In the medical community, it was a way of attacking a problem through different experts to work through the problem from different angles brought together for input to come to a solution for the patient. They did their reports and called for a PBL session on this patient.

Invitations were emailed out with an urgent RSVP to select professionals connected to Health Sciences North and the Northern Ontario School of Medicine (NOSM) at Laurentian University. With the meeting set, they met at a board room at the hospital. Cindy Thompson, an Administrative Assistant at HSN, arrived first to ensure coffee had been delivered for the meeting. She set up her seating area near the head of the table. She was here to take minutes of the meeting. The next to arrive was Doctor Sam Patton, psychiatrist, and Doctor Vince Dhwala, neurologist, who had examined Enoch and called this PBL meeting. The others all began to arrive including Janet Mack, nursing supervisor, Doctor Hussain, Doctor Emerson, Doctor Hakkala, neurosurgeon, and Doctor Heather Martin, psychologist.

Doctor Patton called the meeting to order and everyone went around the table to introduce themselves. More for Cindy's benefit and her notes as they all knew each other well. Doctor Hakkala chaired the meeting. After giving an update on the patient, he asked for everyone to go around the room.

Doctor Emerson said, "Well, I saw the patient in Emerg when he was brought in. I have followed his progress and treatment. You all have my report on how he presented. His heart stopped 3 times on the trip to HSN. It stopped again in Emerg. Cardio-vetting with the defibrillator brought him back. I was concerned for the strain on his heart. He also became semi-conscious after a while. He was mumbling about a horse, being shot, in a bar fight. He murmured something about bikers. I didn't get it all but they did sound like incoherent ramblings. He was never completely lucid. As a result we place him into an induced coma and sent him to ICU for monitoring to give his body a chance to heal."

Doctor Hussain spoke next, "I have had Enoch as a patient for 25 years. He is very intelligent but not given to ramblings. He is in excellent health as of his last physical 4 months ago. There was no sign of problems with his heart so I believe that he did not suffer from a heart attack other than that brought on by a massive electrical source. As we know from our reports here, witnesses stated it appeared he was struck by lightning. I have also been monitoring his case closely and I cannot explain Doctor Dhwala's findings as being related to anything in his past."

Doctor Dhwala picked up this conversation thread, "The findings I have are difficult to explain. His synapses appear to be firing at a very accelerated rate. On the rMRI, we can see various parts of the brain are lit up like a Christmas tree. I cannot explain this activity."

Doctor Patton spoke up, "I have, through the police liaison, Sergeant Travis, an IQ test the patient did when he first joined the police department. I administered the same IQ test to him on one of my examinations. His results were very close. With margin of error I would say his IQ has not increased or decreased since this event. I have spoken at length with him about his dreams and visions. They are consistent with what we know as flashbacks in PTSD survivors. They are very real memories to him but he insists they are not his memories. He does not present with any other psychopathology that I can see. In short, I don't think he's crazy."

Back around to Doctor Hakkala, "I have also looked at the rMRI and other scans. I do not see anything surgical at this point. Tons of brain activity but I don't know the source or where to operate. I also don't know if it's harming him. He presents as normal in every other way."

Doctor Patton advised, "The police have reported to me that there is a lightning strike on the site he was found. It may not have hit him directly as he has no physical signs of a lightning strike. There are no burn marks. His memories or intrusive flashbacks, as I said, are very real to him. I think he would benefit from treatment through counselling. Cognitive Behavioural Therapy (CBT) to dampen the effects of these flashbacks as we do with PTSD survivors. Cognitive Interviewing to see if we can make the flashbacks more complete first, then having him go over and over the events until they no longer distress him."

"I have a suggestion about who should be involved in this and was going to consult with her until we decided to call this PBL session. Doctor Nancy O'Brien has recently semi-retired and moved to Sudbury. She holds a teaching position in the Psychology Department at Laurentian University. Up until recently she was the go to hostage negotiator with O.P.P., Metro Toronto Police and several other police services. She has treated many police officers for PTSD in her practise before leaving Toronto to come here. She has over 30 years in the field. If she will do it, I think as far as my recommendation, it would be to ask her to come in and consult, or even better, treat the patient."

Doctor Hakkala added, "From my perspective until I have something to examine, there is no place for surgery in this case at this time."

Doctor Dhwala said, "I would like to continue to monitor the patient and track his progress to see what effect the treatment is having and to see if the brain activity we are noting does not change, gets worse or returns to normal over time."

Janet Mack raised a hand to indicate she had something to say, "I have all the nursing reports. The patient is clearly distressed from all these memories for want of a better term. The treatment you described could do him a world of good. I would also say that he has been given many tests and other than the activity in the brain, everything presents as normal. I would suggest he remain under hospital care until he starts his therapy so he may continue to be monitored in case there is a change in his health."

Doctor Hakkala added, "I think we all seem to agree with calling in Doctor O'Brien to see what she thinks of Doctor Patton's course of treatment. If there are no objections or concerns or anything else to add, I will step back from this case and leave Doctor Patton and Doctor Dhwala as his primary doctors while he is at HSN."

All agreed and the meeting was adjourned. Everyone filed out except Doctor Patton, Doctor Hakkala and Janet Mack. Doctor Hakkala pronounced, "Well, he's in your hands now Sam. Please keep me informed. It's a fascinating case. Never seen anything like it before. I may suggest some tests along the way to see if we can determine anything we've missed."

"No problem. And thanks for your support Janet. Without the nursing staff we would be much further behind in this case. Please pass on my thanks and ask them to continue to note anything unusual and any memories he may repeat to them."

"I can do that," said Janet.

With that they also left the room to go their separate ways. Doctor Patton went to his office to call Doctor O'Brien.

Chapter 12

Patton called Doctor O'Brien at work. She picked up on the first ring telling him she was in her office. "Hello."

"Hello Nancy, I have an interesting case for you," started Patton.

"Sam. It would be you to start off that way. No 'how are you?' 'What are you up to?'" quipped Nancy.

" Yep. Right to work. I have a challenging case I think is up your alley. Can we meet on it this afternoon?"

"Sure. I finished my morning class and was just grading some papers. I can be in your office in 30 minutes. I could use an interesting case. I may have retired too soon. The pace in academia is much slower," said Nancy.

"Haha. Regret nothing and this involves a police officer injured off-duty but his current problem does not appear to be physical. We can't explain his brain activity and psychological issues the patient is having. I believe we can address the one problem, hoping the other goes away or dampens on his own," stated Sam.

"Okay Sam. See you in 30."

"Bye."

Sam hung up the phone looking out his window with a view of the golf course behind Health Sciences North. It was a good view. Not a great view like the offices overlooking Lake Ramsey but better than Regent St. He sighed as he wondered if they were doing the right thing. In light of nothing physical to fix then it fell to his realm. Nancy had a great deal of experience with PTSD survivors and police officers. Hopefully she could get to the bottom of these images and sort them out to something the patient could understand and then deal with.

Nancy arrived right on time with 2 Timmies. "You were still double double right?" asked Nancy.

"Oh yeah. I needed a coffee too. Thanks," said Sam.

"What have we got?"

"What no how are you? What are you up to?"

"I thought we were beyond that."

"We are. This is an interesting case. It's a police officer struck by lightning or standing near a lightning strike. His brain activity shows too many synapses firing to be explained. There is activity all over his brain. His IQ is the same as when he joined the police. No change there. There is nothing physical we can find to explain this other than accelerated brain activity. He is also having flashbacks, intrusive images and memories that are not his. There's no explanation for this. I've run him through the usual tests and find no psychopathology to explain what he's experiencing. I'm out of my depth for treatment.

I believe he needs Cognitive Interviews on each memory, for lack of a better word. He then needs Cognitive Behavioural Therapy to help dampen the traumatic events he is experiencing. He may even need hypnosis. To bring cohesion to these memories and context. That's it in a nutshell."

"Okay," responded Nancy. "I guess we need to eliminate hallucinations. Determine fact from fiction to break it apart like an onion. I would like to meet with him to unpack everything. I will need all his files on this so far. I am going to guess you already talked to a neurologist?"

"Yes and a neurosurgeon. They're also monitoring this case."

"It may not be a quick fix. So let's start with my reading the files and then meeting the patient who is…?"

"Enoch Brown. Detective Staff Sergeant, whatever that means, with Greater Sudbury Police."

"It means he's middle management, experienced and probably well-dialled in," responded Nancy.

"Here are all the files. When can you meet with him?"

"Tomorrow morning so I can read these files tonight. Like studying for a final exam," quipped Nancy.

They said their goodbyes with Doctor O'Brien leaving with the files. Doctor Patton thought to himself, that was quick and painless. I hope she see this challenge and takes it on.

Chapter 13

The following morning, Doctor O'Brien went to Enoch's room and introduced herself. She noted he was only a little on edge talking with a shrink. For a cop that was good. She told him about her background and the plan to unpack his memories, flashbacks and intrusive images to make them understandable. During her interview phase of bonding with the patient, she discovered Enoch was also a trained Crisis Negotiator. They had some other common threads and Nancy got them on a comfortable first name basis. Nancy left telling him she would see him the following day.

Nancy called Sam to arrange a private room suitable for her to counsel Enoch meaning two places to sit and quiet with nothing distracting in the room. Nancy then went home to study the files more thoroughly. In the files, Nancy learned more about Enoch's background and his event with the lightning. She learned about the threads of visions he was having. There seem to be several that were distinct. She thought it best she start there.

In the morning, Nancy was summoned to a meeting of the PBL group. Not everyone was there but Sam, Doctor Dhwala, Doctor Hakkala, Doctor Heather Martin, a psychologist on HSN staff and Cindy Thompson to scribe the minutes of the meeting. This time Doctor Patton chaired the meeting. Nancy gave them an outline of what she planned.

She would conduct Cognitive Interviews first. These would require little information from the counsellor and gather the most information from the subject. It began by having the person place themselves back to the event thinking about how they felt, the sounds, sights, smells, everything. Then the counsellor would require the subject to recall in detail the event with an example like what did you do when you got up this morning? This would then be challenged by the interviewer with a more detailed example that there was more to report and every detail was important causing the subject to report everything.

She went on to explain that she may ask the subject to remember the details in reverse or start and stop at different points of the story. The interviewer may use pneumonic cues to help with specifics like remembering a name by suggesting the subject see the alphabet flash in their mind hoping to latch onto the first letter of the name. Or remembering things like numbers, were they high or low numbers going through each one. Finally the counsellor may ask the subject to place themselves in a different location in the memory to see what they see from a different angle or point of view. This was a very accurate means of enhancing recall for the subject.

Once she had a cohesive version of events to work with, she would use Cognitive Behavioural Therapy as she would with a PTSD survivor. She would help the subject unpack the memory of the event. Then she would have the subject tell the memory again a few times. The subject would be asked to do some homework and write the event out several times. This would enhance details of the memory. The more remembering and retelling of the event, the more the effects of the event would be dampen.

Doctor Martin asked, "What about Neuro-Linguist Programming? (NLP)"

Doctor O'Brien responded, "While that is possible, it will put the person into a light suggestible place. It is really a post hypnotic suggestion. In this case I may consider using hypnosis to enhance the memory. I am a trained Forensic Hypnotist. Studies show that the Cognitive Interview produces the same and often more information of events from subjects than hypnosis. However, they are really just different ways to access the same thing. The memory. If one does not do it, perhaps the other will. The hypnosis will be last and should we not develop anything new at that stage then it will not be a real memory."

"What will it be?" breathed Cindy Thompson who was caught up in recording the conversation with notes.

"It may be a hallucination. Then we look for the cause. It may be confabulation with memory hardening or cementing. This most often happens to small children. An example of confabulation is the child who comes home from shopping with their parents, they wake up in bed. When asked how they got there, the child has a memory of their father lifting them and carrying them to bed. It is the most logical thing to have occurred in their mind. The true event is the mother lifted the child and carried them to bed but the child has no real memory of this because they were asleep. The child creates the most logical memory. That is confabulation. Every time they recall it, it becomes more hardened to the point they would pass a lie detector test on their version of the event because they believe it is real. That is if a child could be tested on a lie detector but of course they can't be." responded Nancy.

"What about using a lie detector?" asked Dr Hakkala.

"Well if it is confabulation we won't know because he will pass the test believing it was a real event. I know some forensic polygraphists so we could look at that down the road. Should the subject fail the test, it would show he did not believe the memory was real," answered Nancy.

Doctor Martin queried, "What about Epigenetics?"

"Not this again," said Doctor Dhwala, "There is no such thing as remembering past lives. This is a fairy tale. No studies have ever proved there is a genetic memory passed down from our ancestors."

"There is no study to show it does not exist," responded Doctor Martin.

Doctor Patton piped up, "There is anecdotal examples of epigenetic memory. The idea of environment coupled with an inherited genetic memory or responses. The Australian Shepard born and isolated from others. They will still know how to herd sheep, lie flat and hop to see better under the other animals, running using their barks and nudging with their nose to guide the sheep. We call it instinct for lack of a better term but it has been thought this could be a genetic memory."

Nancy spoke up, "I have read the studies and I agree there is nothing to support the theory and nothing to refute it. We will cross that bridge when we get there. A sample of the patient's DNA before the lightning event and a sample after may be coded for its genome and see what differences there may be. It would be a good experiment anyway. I will get his informed consent first. In the meantime, if we can all agree on this course of action, I will go ahead with the Cognitive Interview and Cognitive Behavioural Therapy (CBT). After that I may consider hypnosis. I have that training and have been listed in the courts as an expert witness on this subject. It will mean we will skip using NLP as they are too similar. Hypnosis will take the subject deeper and that is what we want. I would expect better results from hypnosis than NLP.

With everyone in agreement the meeting broke up. Cindy apologized for speaking up. She was told that was nonsense. The goal of a PBL session was to get the maximum points of view from different perspectives. Her perspective had produced results. Sam said goodbye to Nancy and wished her luck. Nancy headed to the counselling room to meet with Enoch.

<u>Chapter 14</u>

Enoch was waiting for Doctor O'Brien in a wheelchair in the office. The office had a great view of the golf course. There was a desk with papers on it. A bookshelf of professional psychology books mostly. There was a leather couch, two comfortable chairs on wheels and a round office table. The standard coat rack was behind the door. Doctor O'Brien had picked up two Tim Horton coffees with some sugar and cream on the side.

"Do you drink coffee?" she asked Enoch.

"Very funny Doc. I'm a cop, we all drink too much coffee. Thanks. I just take it black," he replied.

Doctor O'Brien took off her coat and hung it on the rack. She passed Enoch a coffee then sat across from him after placing her book bag on the table and removing a digital recorder with a pad of paper and necessary pen. She used a pen with black ink to make cops comfortable because that was what all cops used. She used a yellow writing pad because it was easier on her eyes.

"Do you mind if I record our sessions?"

"This is a session?"

"No, today I am going to outline our course of action. What I plan to do and how you may participate to see if it helps."

Nancy explained to him the concerns of neurosis and psychosis to him. She paraphrased to him the famous example: neurotics build castles in the sky and psychotics move in by Jerome Lawrence a famous playwright. His words are used in every basic psychology course taught everywhere. She included the final quip from Lawrence that psychiatrists collect the rent. That was received with a grin by Enoch who was now sipping coffee and starting to relax.

Nancy went through much of what was talked about at the PBL session. When she got to the polygraph test, Enoch asked what was the purpose of the test. Nancy explained, "If you are telling the truth we know you believe what you see as memories are real. Should you fail, we will know that you know the memories are not real."

"Hah. I can never get my younger detectives to use polygraphs in their investigations. Most cops don't believe in it and many more don't think it's admissible in court. It has been admitted as evidence in Civil Court and Family Court in Canada. Everything about the test is admissible in Criminal Court except the results. The rest of the test is treated as any other police interviews and must hold to the same rules. If it stands up to that test, it is admissible."

"What do you think about doing the test?" asked Nancy.

"Well, as I am a true believer in the polygraph, I would take that test. Do we do that today?"

"No, I have to set it up and we should leave it for this week. I'll call an OPP polygraphist that I know who owes me a few favours and set it up. Meanwhile, I think we should do some cognitive interviewing of one memory to get the most details we can," replied Nancy.

"Sounds good. Where do we start?"

Nancy advised, "Best if we start with memories or flashbacks we believe are connected. You spoke about a police shootout where the police had an apartment building surrounded."

"Good one Doc. I have dreamed a lot about that one. Lots of flashes of images too. I know it was on Ontario Street and it was July. I'm not sure of the year but the cars were old like from the 40's."

Nancy instructed, "I know you know about Cognitive Interviewing as do all police officers. So I would like you to try and place yourself there in that time and place. You may close you eyes while we do this."

"Okay," said Enoch as he placed his coffee on the table next to hers. Enoch sat back and began to remember.

"I was on the street in uniform behind a car. There was a man in an old suit beside me. I could hear shots and grabbed the man's sleeve to pull him down. His sleeve ripped and he fell backwards. I could see his third eye. Right in the middle of his forehead above his nose. I wondered why he had a third eye and then realized it was a bullet hole. The shooting had stopped. There were women screaming nearby and men shouting. People scrambled to get further away from the street. I saw a Sergeant in uniform down the street from me also behind a car but he was behind an old police car.

The shooting had come from the upstairs apartment initially, then there were shots from officers around the building. There was a quiet lull after the madness reaction to the shots. I yelled out to the Sergeant I had a man down. He asked how bad and I told him dead. He told me to leave him for now and run to him so I did.

Things before and after that are just jumbled and images. I can't make sense of a lot to it."

Nancy paused for a moment and said, "Tell me what you remember again but with more detail."

Enoch repeated what he had said but this time he knew the make and model of the police car. He knew the gun he used was a revolver. He described more of how he felt and could remember feeling the sun on his hands.

Enoch was speaking faster this time and his hands were shaking. He was also sweating. Nancy told him to stop and relax. It was enough for today.

"We will have a session again tomorrow. In the meantime, try to think harder about this memory and maybe write it out a few times. That will help with bringing out more detail. Remember, you are in the hospital and you are safe," Nancy told him.

Chapter 15

Enoch went through physiotherapy for the week to take the roughness out of his body for walking, lifting and stretching from his time in the induced coma and hospital stay. The sessions with Nancy continued much the same with more of the story of the barricaded persons coming out. Nancy told him a polygraph examiner from the OPP would be coming to test him.

During Nancy's phone conversation with Sergeant Jean Guy Degagne, they discussed the type of polygraph testing to be done. Sergeant Degagne was concerned that confabulation may have occurred with the barricaded person memory. He also felt they needed a different answer than yes this one was true. It would mean several tests. Instead he suggested what they call an informant test that would test the truthfulness of broad knowledge.

"This will be trickier," advised Sergeant Degagne, "because informant tests cover broad information and many informants are gifted liars, they can "rationalize" things in their minds as truthful. If they do this they may have a false negative and pass the polygraph test. The test often holds no large risk for them because of this type of test. They won't go to jail if it doesn't go well. That means they don't take the test seriously. There needs to be fear generated during the test in order for it to not fall in the inconclusive range."

Nancy asked, "Remind me of the results again?"

"Yes. Well a false positive is coming up as deceptive when you are truthful. A false negative is coming up as truthful when you are lying. There are three ranges in the numerical score, those being truthful, deceptive and inconclusive. Inconclusive is a range of 11 points.

Anything scored at over +6 is truthful. Anything scored below -6 is deceptive. Anything in-between is inconclusive. About 30 percent of tests come in as inconclusive. Reasons for this may include not taking the test seriously, use of drugs as a countermeasure, physical countermeasures, asking the wrong questions or the examiner not setting the psychology for the test appropriately."

"The psychology…"

"Yes. The polygraph examination is the most complex psychophysiological test ever devised by mankind. It is based on the principle of psychology being set during a lengthy interview process of between an hour and a half and two hours. The testing itself takes about 20 minutes. It includes a practise test to see the subjects physical reactions. Then three tests in a row with a short break, about a minute, between each test. This is testing on the issue at hand. There may also be a knowledge test of three tests in a row. The issue test is whether they did it. The knowledge test is whether they know who did it, helped someone do it or other knowledge they may have withheld.

This could lead to as many as 7 tests in a row. The more tests you do, the more time on the instrument you rack up. Over time, the subject will begin to flatten their responses on the tests. You risk losing the last few tests to inconclusive if the responses are too flattened."

"To prevent rationalizing the test. You mean such as I was the getaway driver but I didn't rob the bank?"queried Nancy.

"You got it. In this case we would only run the knowledge test to save our chart minutes, time during the testing, and it's modified to what we call an informant test as that is when they are usually done. The Canadian Security Intelligence Service (CSIS) runs this test often on its agents to ensure they are still loyal to Canada and not a foreign state. It is mandatory testing for agents. They also use it overseas with informants to test the truthfulness about the information they are providing. I did an internship with them last year for two weeks doing informant testing. I am very familiar with this type of test. But remember it is only 60 percent reliable."

"What about the other tests?"

"The issue test is 96 percent reliable."

"Wow that's pretty good."

"It still means it's wrong 4 times out of 100. The benefit we get from testing is to bolster our confidence in a case, getting a good and detailed statement cooperatively from the subject who is almost always a suspect and sometimes getting a confession during or after the test. While the results of the test cannot be used in court, everything else about the test may be used. We have found that confessions in the polygraph examination lead to a 90 percent conviction rate."

"I like those odds,"murmured Nancy.

"I will remind you again, in this case I can only do an informant test and it is 60 percent not 90 percent. But… the interview may give you more information as it always does. The subject, if he is making everything up, may confess he has been untruthful. It may bolster your confidence if he passes. In other words comes up as truthful."

"What do you think Jean Guy?"

"I think for this, it's worth the testing. I have tested cops before and find them to be black and white people. They stay between the lines. Therefore, very good test subjects."

"How do you score the test?"

"Haha. Take the polygraph examiners course and find out. It's taught once or sometimes twice a year at the Canadian Police College (CPC) where you spent 11 weeks at the college and write an examine every week plus numerous polygraph tests on practise subjects. Fail one exam or a practise test and you are out of the program. Then you go in the field for an internship where you run tests of live issues in real cases where an experienced examiner monitors you. All of your tests are sent to CPC and should they fail you on one of them, you are out of the program. Then you go in the field for 5 to 8 months running first 5 tests then 25 tests. Once your tests are done, the first 5 go to CPC for grading. Fail one and you are out. Of the next 25, CPC randomly selects 5 tests and grades you from those. Fail one…"

"And you are out. I get it."

"Someone once said to me it was like being on the battlefield. The shot could come from anywhere. Pass everything and you join an elite few in Canada of about 70 Forensic Polygraph examiners and maybe 50 civilian examiners. In police circles, they sometimes call us a cult," quipped Jean Guy.

"I think I'll pass on the course and trust you know what you're doing. When can we do this?"

"When did you tell him about the test?"

"On Monday."

"Okay today is Friday and I have nothing booked for this Monday so tell him today I am coming to test him and I will do it on Monday. I also need a quiet place to do this in the hospital. I can't test him at the police station. He works there it would be too distracting. I need a quiet room with two chairs and a table. One chair only should have wheels. I will set up the room when I get there. Will he let me video and audio record the test?"

"Yes I will tell him about that but he has no issue with me audio recording him. He is very cooperative. He wants to get to the bottom of these dreams or memories or whatever they are."

"Great. This should be an excellent test. Plan on two to two and half hours for the test. No one else can be in the room. As barren a room as you can find with no windows would work best. Usually I like it no smaller than 8 x 10 feet and no bigger than 14 x 16 feet," instructed Jean Guy.

"I will work that out and tell him during our session."

"Also set the test for 10 am as morning testing works best. I need a list of the meds he is on the morning of the test. He should be told to get a good nights sleep and have breakfast. No exercising before the test."

"I will make sure of all that. Glad I took notes."

They said their mutual goodbyes. Nancy ended the call on her phone and looked out her window at her office at Laurentian University seeing the students walking here and there. She was thinking that after this, she may decide to switch gears and go into hypnosis therapy for answers. Neurolinguistic Programming (NLP) was like hypnosis but did not dig as deep or directly as she could under hypnosis. The Cognitive Interview was relaxing the subject with a gentle post hypnotic state making that the reason not to add information in questioning what the subject tells you. NLP would be similar to that. Best to move forward with hypnosis rather than repeat what has already been tried. It may also bring answers faster.

Nancy knew that the case law in Ontario was 50/50 whether a hypnosis interview was admissible. It was on a case by case basis. It would have to stand up to a "voir dire" or a trial within the trial to test its admissibility. Better than other provinces like British Columbia where it was never allowed. In this case, she also took into account they were not going to court with any of this so it really had no legal impact. Time would tell her how wrong she turned out to be.

Chapter 16

The day of the polygraph examination, Enoch, Doctor Nancy O'Brien and Detective Sergeant Jean Guy Degagne of the Ontario Provincial Police, Polygraph Unit met in an interview room that Sergeant Degagne had set up with a table beside a chair. He had his computer set up attached to the interface of his Lafayette model 4000. Attached to the interface box were two Pneumographs, Galvanic Skin Response spoons, a blood pressure cuff and a chair sensor. There had only been a slight holdup to find a chair with arms on it for the subject to rest his arm on during the test with small pillows under his arms.

After a brief introduction, Doctor O'Brien left the room. Sergeant Degagne began with his formal introduction. "Hi. As you know I am Sergeant Degagne. I am a police officer and a polygraph examiner but you can call me Jean Guy today and what do people normally call you?"

"They call me Enoch," was the response.

"Okay Enoch, today I am going to administer a polygraph examination to you. First I need to go over your rights with you. If anyone told you that you had to take this test, they were wrong. This test is completely voluntary. Do you understand?"

"Yes."

"I want you to know I am recording this with video, see the little camera on top of my computer pointed toward you? Also I am recording you with audio."

"Okay."

"Now you should know that besides this being a voluntary thing, you do have the right to speak to a lawyer before speaking to me about anything. I can tell you that there is a 1-800 number I can give you that will put you in touch with a legal aid duty counsel who is a free lawyer you may speak to right now. Do you want to speak to a lawyer now?"

"No."

"Okay, just so you know you may ask me at any time to stop the test or our conversation so you can speak to a lawyer and I will stop the test and let you call a lawyer."

"Okay. But I'm good. I don't need to speak to a lawyer."

"Now I want you to know that if anyone has told you to say anything to me or threatened or promised you anything to say anything to me, I don't want to hear what they told you to say. I want to hear what you have to say and nobody else. Can we agree on that?"

"Yes."

"Now before we begin, can you tell my why you are here today?"

"Yes. I'm here to see if I'm telling the truth today."

"Essentially yes. I want to know if you are telling the truth about the memories you are having that don't seem to be your own. Can we call these echo memories so we both know what we are talking about?"

"Yes. I like that. Echo memories."

Sergeant Degagne went on to speak to Enoch about truthfulness. "It is important you be truthful today."

He spoke to Enoch about nervousness explaining that nervousness has nothing to do with the test and will not affect the results. He explained about the fight, flight or freeze response. That is what the polygraph reads during the testing. He tells him how the test is the most complex psychophysiological test ever devised by mankind.

There is the physical component read by the instrument that is the fight, flight or freeze response. This response takes place as an autonomic response meaning it is a reaction that is not controlled. It happens when the body responds to a threat like a lie. The adrenal gland secrets adrenaline. Adrenaline is like a natural speed. When this happens, it causes the heart muscle to beat more quickly pushing the blood through the body. Blood carries oxygen. Oxygen is what the muscles burn. In other words, getting the body ready to fight or runaway. It's like when you are out picking blueberries and you run into a bear. That sudden rush you feel is the fight, flight or freeze response. You can't control it.

There is a psychological component as well to the test. You may have a fear of something else coming up in the test that may interfere with what you are responding to. This is avoided or at least reduced by using safety valve questions. These are about other things that may have happened that are similar. There must be no confusion.

"Therefore we will devise some safety valve questions to take this away from our issue questions. Also there are some normal truth questions that I will ask you so I can compare your normal responses. We call these control questions. "

Degagne summed up what he had to say on the test questions by telling him there were 3 safety valve questions, 3 issue questions, 2 known truth questions and an intention question to show Enoch intended to tell the truth today. The questions were devised by both the examiner and the subject and practised before the test even began. The questions decided on by Enoch and the examiner were:

1. Is your first name Enoch? - known truth question

2. Do you live in Canada? - known truth question

3. Do you intend to tell me the truth today? - intension question

4. Have you ever told a lie? - safety valve question

5. Have you told the truth about your echo memories? - issue question

6. Have you ever committed a fraud? - safety valve question

7. Do you believe your echo memories are real? - issue question

8. Have you stolen anything? - safety valve question

9. Have you made up these echo memories? - issue question

Once the questions were agreed to and practised, the instrument was attached to Enoch. First were the pneumographs. There was an upper pneumograph placed around his chest. It was a long tube in the front with some elasticity and a small chain like on a drain plug in the bathroom to fasten around the back to hold it on the chest. Then came the lower pneumogaph around his belly. Jean Guy explained, "Some people are belly breathers usually men and some people are chest breathers. So we measure both."

Next came the Galvanic Skin Response spoons or GSR spoons. They are small silver plates slightly rounded to curve against the inside of the finger with velcro straps. There are two with one on the ring finger and one on the index finger. Finally, there is the cardio cuff the same as a blood pressure cuff. It gets pumped up to about 80 mm and helps measure the rise and fall in blood pressure. Then Jean Guy explained about the chair sensor sitting under the chair legs being used as a counter measure for a subject who tries to move or push thumb tacks into his foot to catch them.

"I will take measurements that are very minute in nature and will score the readings to all of the questions," lectured Jean Guy. "There will be an aggregate score at the end that will tell me if there is no deception indicated meaning you are truthful, deception indicated meaning you have not been truthful and inconclusive that is a range where I cannot tell if you are being truthful or not."

After reviewing all the questions again, Jean Guy ran a practise test using numbers. He began by telling Enoch to say no to all the numbers, even the number he picked from a stack of numbered cards that Jean Guy could not see. This would have him lying one time. Jean Guy would then pick out that number based on the readings of his physiology. It would calibrate the instrument and at the same time demonstrate that it worked to the subject. They did the demonstration test and he was able to see a good response from Enoch and pick out the number he lied to. With the instrument calibrated, they began testing. There were three tests run that were essentially the same questions each time. Every answer could only be yes or no. There could be no coughing, movement or talking by the subject during the test.

After the test, Jean Guy took his computer to go and score the test after removing all of the accoutrements from Enoch. "How did you do on the test?"

"Good."

'Did you tell the truth?"

"Yes."

"I'll be right back," said Jean Guy.

Jean Guy went to another office nearby where Doctor O'Brien was waiting. Nancy asked, "Well, how did he do?"

"I was scoring a bit during the test and it will be no deception indicated meaning he is telling the truth. It took some time to hammer in to him what he is experiencing we will refer to as echo memories. That way he knows strongly what we are talking about. There were some problems with his control questions but that is not abnormal. Give me a few minutes to measure the charts I took, score them and add them together," requested Jean Guy.

Nancy left for a few minutes to check on Enoch. He was happy it was over and starting to relax. Jean Guy entered a few minutes later and asked him how he thought he did on the test.

Enoch confidently said, "I passed for sure because I told the truth."

"You did pass with a high score indicating that there was do deception indicated. Can you tell me if any questions bothered you on the test?"

Enoch responded, "Yes the one about stealing and maybe the lie questions."

"Yes, I could see that on those safety valve questions but fortunately it was not enough to interfere with what we had to do today. Do you have any questions or comments for me?"

"Nope. It was interesting."

"Nancy and I will step out for a few minutes and then we will be done," said Jean Guy.

In the hall Jean Guy went over the results with Nancy and she thanked him for coming by. In asking him to lunch, he told her he had to go. He was catching a flight to Thunder Bay for a test the next day. "The life of a polygraph examiner is an adventure that never ends," quipped Jean Guy. They said their goodbyes. Nancy returned to the office to check on Enoch and they decided to meet in the morning for another session.

Chapter 17

"This morning we have some time so I would like to explore the use of hypnosis with you in regard to the "barricaded persons" incident as you called it. I think we can get much more detail from this echo memory with hypnosis," stated Nancy. "Can we use that phrase now? It gives us clarity to what we are talking about."

Enoch replied, "Fine with me. I know you were a hypnotist for police witnesses. It's on your Curriculum Vitae."

"Been looking me up online?"

"Yep and a few phone calls to cops down south I know."

"Doesn't hurt. I know a lot about you so why shouldn't you know things about me. Do you have any questions about my professional history?" asked Nancy.

"No. All good. I feel I am in good hands so let's do this and see what I can learn."

The room they had today had a large leather bed like those found in high school nurse's offices. It was bare with one end elevated to make lying on it more comfortable. There were no windows in the room and nothing on the walls. There were the two chairs Enoch and Nancy sat in but nothing else. Nancy had her notepad and an audio digital recorder. She had Enoch lie on the bed on his back and get comfortable.

"Let's start with some relaxation first," instructed Nancy.

Enoch trusted Nancy. She had been direct and forthright with him. He had looked at her background and discovered there was a lot of respect for her work in the policing world. He had high hopes she could help him. He had only a little experience with hypnosis on a witness. They were able to gain from them a license plate number they needed under hypnosis to crack their case open. He had a strong belief this would aid him.

She led Enoch though exercises designed to relax him. She then began to deepen his consciousness into an even more relaxed state. When she had him where she needed him, she began to probe for the echo memory. With his eyes closed, Enoch began to tell his echo memory for Nancy and the digital recorder.

Chapter 18 - 1948 - Bank Robbers

I remember it was a warm July morning. I was in the station on Elgin Street getting ready to go out on foot patrol when I was asked to take a complaint with Officer Scott Wilkins. Scott was grinning ear to ear holding up the keys to one of the two new D25 Deluxe Plymouth P15 cars with the Dodge badge and Dodge grill. Since the tragic death of Danial Dodge on Manitoulin Island, the Chief had been partial to buying Dodge cars and the fleet of 6 cars were all Dodges. Young Danny Dodge was injured in a dynamite explosion. His wife tried to rush him to hospital by boat but the waves overwhelmed the boat and Danny was lost in Lake Huron. His body was located a few weeks later. It became international news because he was an heir to the Dodge Brothers Company but also because it happened on his honeymoon.

The D25 cars were new to them but slightly used 1946's. They had just been painted and given a hand siren on the driver's side below a multidirectional spot light. It also had a new two way radio installed to speak with the police station without having to look for a phone or a police call box. Both of which were often difficult to find. Only the D25's had the new radios. The other 4 cars were Dodge D10 4 door sedans. They were all 1938's and due to be retired when the police budget allowed.

Scott's grin was from ear to ear because as a rookie with only 1 year as a policeman, he had been told he would always be on a foot beat. I didn't have the heart to take the keys from him and told him, "You can drive but no accidents."

"Yes sir," he replied with a cheery hop, heading to the door.

I took the paper from the Sergeant with the address for the complaint. "Don't let him fuck up," swore the Sergeant.

"I won't. Had lots like him in my regiment in the war. You learn to look after them a bit."

"Well your wartime experience aside, you only have 3 years working here so take care of both yourself and your partner lad," barked the Sergeant.

I laughed and told him we were a long way from Europe now. I took off after my new partner for the drive. It would be his report as junior man so this should be easy. The details were given to me on the ride by Scott who was very animated and excited. I had to tell him to settle down and drive. There was a car parked on Ontario Street with a broken window near Regent Street. The owner wasn't known and the car had not been seen there before. A neighbour walking to work had seen it and stopped at the police station to let us know.

I hoped this would be simple because I had lunch plans that did not include sitting with a car trying to find an owner. I didn't want to dampen Wilkins' spirit. I remembered the exciting new times when I first joined the army in training and my rookie year with the police. The army had dulled my shine at Juno Beach and beyond. Seeing death up close and personal will do that to a man.

I pointed the parked car out to Wilkins. It was parked on the northwest side of the road with the passenger side window smashed out. A 1946 Ford Deluxe Tudor in slate grey. A real beauty other than the window. Wilkins parked directly behind it. I got out to cross the street to the houses and a two story brick apartment building across the street from the car. I told Wilkins, "Check the window and the glove compartment for information on the owner. Don't cut yourself," I warned.

A woman peeked out her front door and told me three men in the upstairs apartment next door had come in late at night and parked that car there. She did not know them and had never seen the car before. I walked to the side of the building that had an outside staircase leading to the second floor door. As I reached the top, Wilkins caught up to me and passed me on the landing to stand in front of the door. He said, "There was no glass."

"What?"

"I said, there was no glass. You said not to cut myself but there was no glass in the car or on the ground," he said as he knocked on the door.

"Get away from in front of the…" was all I got out as gun shots blasted through the front door.

Wilkins went over the railing falling having been hit. I started down the stairs hearing the door kick open. Shots toward me. A burn on my shoulder. I fell hitting the ground face first scrambling around the corner. I flashed to being back in the war with Gerry shooting at us as there was a mad scramble for cover. A few more shots my way and the door slammed closed. I had not even drawn my gun. I reached across my belly to open the widow make holster I had been issued taking out my Mark IV Webley top break open .32 revolver. I heard foot steps coming down the stairs.

I heard a rifle shot from the top landing. I was laying on my back with my legs and knees locked in triangles and the revolver in my hand pointing at the corner. A young man's face came around the corner. I fired hitting him in the face and he went down on the ground at the bottom of the stairs.

"Shit. He got Joey," said a man's voice.

"Get in here," said another man's voice.

I heard a loud stuttering rat-tat-tat and the world on my corner of the building exploded with pieces of brick, noise and dust. It felt like my world was ending. Turning over and turtling up was all I would think to do for a few seconds. Then training and experience had me doing a fast leopard crawl to the other corner of the building. Silence. Smoke and dust hanging. I know that hell. It was a machine gun. A Thompson from the sound of it. I had to move before they came for me. I had to leave Wilkins.

I desperately ran zig zag across Ontario Street to our prowl car. My safe place. My trench. There were single rifle shots but no more barrage of bullets from the Tommy gun. He must have had a 20 or 30 round mag and emptied it at me on the corner of the building. I could see what looked like a Browning Hi-Power 9 mm automatic lying on the ground near the boys body. He couldn't be even 20. The rifle I saw as I slid around behind the car. It was one of the much treasured Lee Enfield No 5 Mark 1 that we started to get toward the end of the war. I had one. Very accurate and lighter than the Lee Enfield's with the full fore stock. The No 5 had a much shorter fore stock with a nice flash eliminator on it in .303 calibre. A very smooth bolt action that was battle tested. Who was I at war with?

"Still alive copper?" yelled someone from the apartment window.

"Yeah and you're not going anywhere," I challenged as I pulled out my knife and crawled to their Ford. I punctured both passenger side tires and crawled back to my prowl car. I heard my two way radio crackle with the Sergeant yelling for me and Wilkins. I opened the door and reached in. Pressing the mike I yelled as though yelling back to the station house downtown. "Under fire. I have cover behind the prowl car. Wilkins is down. He was shot through the door and fell. Over."

"Where the fuck are you? Over," squealed the radio.

"Ontario Street across from…" I took a quick peek and was rewarded by a shot from the Lee Enfield my way. "Ontario Street number 373 near the corner of Regent. Over."

"Help is coming. Stay behind the engine block and don't move or stick your head up. Over," came from the radio.

I composed myself and pressed the mic, paused and spoke clearly. "I was hit in the shoulder but seems just a graze and some blood. I'm ok. I have…" A quick top open of my Webley showed 6 rounds with 3 dimpled. Giving me 3 left unfired. I had 6 bullets still in my pocket. "I have 9 rounds left. Wilkins revolver is still in his holster. I shot one guy who is lying dead at the bottom of the stairs. Head shot. Wilkins isn't moving. He was shot through the door and fell. Then I heard a rifle shot I think was down at him in a coup de gras. They have a No 5 Lee Enfield and a Thompson Machine Gun. Over," I was rambling. So much for radio etiquette giving no air time to anyone else.

"Help is coming," came the radio. "Hang on. Over."

"Roger. Out."

I yelled at the apartment, "We have you surrounded. Drop your weapons and come out."

This was met by a hail of bullets rapidly into my car. Clearly I was going to be in trouble as this car was not going anywhere on it's own again. Full of holes and a flat front tire. Thankfully behind the passenger side wheel and engine block, I was not hit. I could hear sirens coming my way wailing. One prowl car went onto Regent Street by the alley. Another 1938 Dodge D10 4 door sedan, black with Sudbury Police Department on the doors, came in from the

Martindale Road side of the alley behind Ontario Street. Both parked out of line of sight from the apartment building. Seeing those cars, I knew I might have a chance after all.

"Anyone comes to those stairs is dead," yelled the voice inside the upper apartment.

Chapter 19

I could still smell cordite and brick dust. The metal of the car I leaned against was hot. My shoulder ached but it wasn't bleeding much anymore. As I looked around I could see people standing above me across the tracks on Lorne Street that ran parallel to Ontario Street. I yelled for them to get down and take cover. Most did. Some stayed. Stupid. Then I realized there were people standing and walking on Ontario Street.

A man walked right up to me asking what was going on. He stood then turned to the apartment at the sound of a shot. I reached up and grabbed his shirt sleeve. I heard another shot as I tried to yank him down. I ripped his shirtsleeve off as he seem to hang in the air for a moment before crumpling to the ground beside me. I yelled, "Mister, mister." As I took in the third eye above his nose. A trickle of blood from that eye told me it was a hole and the rest of the tale was told by the gore behind where he had stood. He was dead.

I screamed, "Everybody down. Get out of here. Right now."

I heard a new voice on the radio. Constable Jock McRae. A seasoned veteran. "Calm down Rick. Station we need the fire department to bring their wooden barricades they use for fires to Regent Street and Ontario Street. Set them up on the east side of Ontario Street. Another set up on Regent Street at Wembley Street. On the west side of Lorne Street before the hill crest we need another set there and Ontario Street on the west side and Ricardo can show them where. Far up Ontario Street Enzo. Over."

"Roger, out," replied Constable Enzo Ricardo from his place in the alley to the west of the apartment.

"We're gonna need some further up Regent Street by Lorne Street on the east side to stop traffic coming up on Regent Street. You got all that? Over."

"Roger," came the reply, "We're on it. Out."

Man I was sweating. I was also breathing hard. I did not want to be shot at anymore. It had been too much in the war and it was too much now. I radioed to McRae, "What about Scott? Over."

"Leave him for now," came the Sergeant's voice on my radio. I could hear the siren wail in the distance and on the radio. "Where the Christ are you McDonald? Over."

"Right in the thick of it in front of the house. I have a dead civilian with me. Over."

"I see you. Can you move? Over."

"No. Car tires are flat and the engine is shot to shit. Over."

"Right. I'm coming to you. If they shoot at me, you send in cover fire. Out."

I heard the roar of an engine coming fast. Siren off. The other new Dodge D25 squealed to a halt behind my car. No shots fired. The passenger door opened and the Sergeant bailed out onto the ground pulling a tan duffle bag with him. "Help me with this," he ordered.

I rolled over to him to grab the bag pulling it behind the engine block.

"Chief's gonna have out asses for destroying his new beauties. Probably both of us will be on the beat for the rest of our time on the job. You got some blood on you, Rick."

"Just a graze Sarge."

"Good. How did he buy it?" The Sergeant indicated the man dead on the ground.

"He walked over to find out what was going on. I grabbed his arm to pull him down but they shot him. I ripped his sleeve off pulling him down."

"I see. Good shots. You said they have a Lee Enfield 5 and a Tommy Gun?"

"Yeah. There's a Browning 9mm on the ground by that boy."

"Rick, that's not a boy. That is a dead killer and don't you forget it," preached Sergeant Tom Makela. "Are you good?"

"Yeah Serge. I've been in this shit before."

"No blaspheming young Rick. Only I get to do that," grinned the Sergeant.

Sergeant Makela began to pull out two Tommy guns with 30 round mags. .45 caliber Thompson Machine Guns the Police Department had bought surplus. He loaded them both and gave one to me. I ran the bolt loading a round and checked the safety was on.

"I have J.J. taking side by side barrel coach shotguns to Enzo and Jock. Then he will sneak up above Lorne Street to high ground," said Makela.

I knew Constable John Jenkins was well known to have been a sniper in the war with a stellar record. The men in his unit called him Angel because whenever he had their backs, he would pick off the enemy like an angel saving them from on high. Somehow, as the odds evened,

I started to feel better and calm myself more. Maybe I wouldn't die today.

Chapter 20

Sergeant Makela pulled a bull horn out from the front seat and began hailing the men inside the apartment. He wanted them to put their weapons down and come out with their hands high. No response. The radio crackled from the station advising that the vehicle plate was on a bulletin just delivered to the station. Yesterday a Toronto Dominion Bank in downtown Toronto was robbed by three men who drove off in this car. It had been stolen a few blocks away just before the robbery. The bulletin was sent to Northern Ontario because one of the bank robbers had been identified as Joey Maxwell who had an older brother in Northern Ontario somewhere. It was thought they may head there. They were considered armed and dangerous. Shots had been fired in the bank but no one had been hurt.

The Chief Constable was on the radio reading the bulletin. He added, "I spoke to Toronto Police, these are suspects up from the Buffalo area. Thomas Gregson and Michael Reubins who have done several bank robberies in Buffalo and headed to Canada to hide out. They are thought to have met Joey Maxwell whose brother is Paul Maxwell. A call to Inco confirmed he works there but is out of town this week on a holiday and they can't reach him. His brother Joey is 18 years old. Gregson is 32 years old and Reubins is 45 years old. Both served in the U.S. Army overseas during the war. Over"

Sergeant Makela responded, "I read you clear. They are heavily armed. From what we can see, it's Joey Maxwell who is dead. Constable Scott is also dead and we have an unknown civilian dead. We need to end this now. Over."

"Can you wait until I get there Tom? Over."

"No. I think we should go now. I have J.J. up on a hill behind Lorne Street. I have Enzo and Jock at the back of the building with coach guns and revolvers. I have Rick with me. We have the station Tommy guns and our revolvers. Over."

"All right. You are there so you know best. What else do you need? Over."

"Nothing just got to time this right. Out."

Sergeant Makela handed over some loose .32 calibre bullets to me as I had broke open to reloaded my revolver.

"Jesus," exclaimed Makela. "Why don't you have the new Smith and Wesson Model 10's we issued?"

"Not enough to go around. Besides, I'm used to this one."

"Okay. Holster it and pocket the rest of these bullets. We have two mags of 30 rounds each for the Thompsons. When we are ready to go we will advance forward shooting at the windows. Below the windows I will throw this baby up and through the window," said Makela showing me a tear gas grenade. The latest toy for the department. We had never used one before.

"We have no gas masks."

"That's why we'll wait outside below the stairs with the Tommy guns. When they come out we take them out. Understand?"

"Yes Sergeant."

"Good. I'll let McRae and Ricardo know what they are to do." With that Sergeant Makela got on the radio ordering McRae and Ricardo to use the side by side short barrel shotguns, and to get to the opposite corner of the building from the stairs so each could cover the south side and the west side of the building. He radioed J.J. to make sure he was in position. Makela told his men to move on the sound of our shooting.

"Ready?" asked the Sergeant.

I looked him in the eye, took a deep breath and told him I was. We stood on three firing at the upper windows. We moved forward quickly firing bursts from the Tommy guns to the upstairs windows of the apartment building. As we reached the bottom, we were both out of ammo and reloaded. I took out my revolver as Makela pulled the pin on the tear gas and threw it into the upper window. Bullseye. We could hear the hiss and then saw smoke. We moved to the bottom of the stairs.

They didn't come out. Then yelling and more smoke. Real smoke. Someone inside yelled, "Fire." Finally we could see flames in the window. The door suddenly kicked open and two men came out. One jumped off the porch and rounded the corner with a Lee Enfield. There was a deafening boom as the other man raised his Tommy gun. I saw the drum under the barrel and knew it held 100 rounds. I ducked back around the corner, Makela was in the open and began firing. When his gun emptied he jumped under the stairs. The bad guys gun was still firing. He paused. Without a thought, I twisted from behind the corner and opened up with my Tommy gun now in one hand and my revolver in the other.

My shots were more true than Makela or the bad guy. In their haste and confusion, they poured lead at each other but both had missed with bullets flying everywhere but their targets. My shots were more measured and sure into the torso of the bad guy who fell the rest of the way to my feet. McRae came up from behind me grabbing my Tommy Gun as I turned toward him. "Easy lad. It's done."

My hearing was almost gone from the barrage and I yelled, "What about the other guy?"

"Enzo's with him. Shot him with one double blast of the coach gun, he did. Where's the Sarge?"

"Right here," spoke Makela for the first time limping from behind the stairs. Not all the bullets had missed after all. He had been hit several times in the leg, arm and shoulder. Once he saw us he collapsed but was alive.

I remember it was a clear beautiful day and suddenly with nothing changed in the sky, it was ominous.

"You are relaxed. As you count backwards from 10 slowly you will feel safer with each diminishing number," instructed Nancy.

Enoch could feel himself swimming away from this memory. Back to the present with Nancy at Health Science North. He felt safe but was still panting with his heart pounding. He was sweating profusely. It took a few minutes before he could speak.

Nancy asked him to describe how he felt. He told her he felt like he had been run over by a train, hit by a transport truck, fallen from a cliff and had an anvil dropped on his head. In short, he felt like Wile E. Coyote. They both had a little laugh at that. "It was all so clear. I remember it. Not a dream. A memory," commented Enoch.

"It was pretty detailed. But how do you feel?"

"I feel wrung out. I can still remember it all vividly. Not a very nice memory," replied Enoch. A small tear falling from his eye. He wiped it away. He whispered, "Scott."

Then he looked at Nancy. "This did happen. My grandfather was Scott's partner. I remember him telling the story. Not as detailed as that but I remember. I remember him talking about Makela. He never walked right again and lost the use of his left arm from his wounds but he stayed on the job. They called him the house Sergeant. He just worked at the station. He still did lineup every morning during the week. My grandfather always talked about him being a hero that day. I never realized the firefight that they went through. How lucky Makela was that day. It was a miracle he survived. My hands are still shaking."

"That's the adrenaline. It just takes time to settle."

"What do I do with this now?"

"You will likely experience effects from this for a while. It should get better over time. If it doesn't or it gets worse, we can talk about strategies," stated Nancy. "I think we should do some Cognitive Behavioural Therapy on this event. I would like you for the next week to write out what you remember happening. More of the memory should present itself and the impact should lessen with each time you write it out. Maybe do it three times a day."

"All right. Nothing else to do around here anyway."

"Well, on that note, you're being discharging tomorrow. I will see you in a week for another appointment. I want you monitored tonight but I see no physical reason to keep you here. Your physio has gone well and there will be followup appointments for you as an outpatient. We will talk about this session next time we meet. Maybe we'll do another hypnosis session next week. How does that sound?"

"Great but I may not have much time to write out what happened with work and all."

"Haha. You're funny. No work for you. I'm not signing you back to work until we get a better handle on what is going on with these echo memories. Next week we will unpack what happened today and look at another memory. Maybe."

"All right. I'll just be glad to get home tonight and see Jake. Next week then Doc."

"Yes, next week. When they discharge you tomorrow you will have information to follow for physio and the next appointment. Also my cell phone number. Call me anytime 24/7 if you need me or experience anything weird."

"What do you call weird?"

"In your case I'm not sure but you'll know when you need to call me. I'm going to have someone speak to you about Critical Incident Stress Management (CISM). It will help with managing the repercussions from today. It will also help with your mental health generally. It will educate you in coping skills and offer you a way of self triage for your mental health."

They said goodbyes and Enoch headed back to his room after a side trip to Tim Hortons for a coffee. Nancy began making copious notes.

<u>Chapter 22</u>

"How have you been?" asked Nancy once they settled into the same room as a week ago.

"Good. Well… some restless nights and a few nightmares. Everything is getting better. I have the written memories with the date and times I did them. You were right, I remembered a lot more detail. It was getting easier to write about it by yesterday," said Enoch.

"That's what should happen. We hope by doing that exercise and exposing yourself to the trauma, you will begin to dampen its effects on you and allow you to live with it. We can't erase it but we can make things better."

They went on to discuss the memory in depth with Nancy asking lots of clarification questions, feeling questions. Just generally unpacking the whole event. Then they discussed the week with regard to the nightmares, some shakiness of hands, loss of appetite, not wanting to be around others and insomnia. Nancy had lots of strategies to help with these symptoms.

"Just to be clear, these are all normal reactions to an abnormal situation. As a police officer, you're used to traumatic events others aren't exposed to but sometimes there are things that happen outside your training and experience. This memory is that kind of trauma. For you it's an abnormal event. Your body should be reacting to it. These are the mental and physical manifestations of the reaction. How you deal with them will help you get better and move forward."

"So heed your advice Doc?" asked Enoch.

"Absolutely. If any of these things we talk about get more frequent or worse instead of better or new symptoms start, let me know and we will find some other strategies. How did you cope with it this week?"

"With lots of love from Jake," responded Enoch.

"Jake?"

"My dog. He was a maniac when I picked him up from Andy Travis. I put him in the truck. He was so busy trying to lick me and jump on me it took me 5 minutes to get into the driver's seat. He's never left my side since I picked him up. I also did a lot of walking and thinking about the memory. It doesn't really feel like someone else's memory. It feels like something that happened to me. You know?"

"I understand."

"I also did what you said when I had trouble sleeping. I would get up. Go to my living room or office for an hour and do something not sleep related. Then back to bed and it broke the cycle so I could fall right back to sleep. My shakiness went away after a few days. I read science fiction books and some biographies. No mysteries, thrillers or police procedurals that I usually read. All in all, the week got better. Better than I thought it would at the start of the week."

Nancy reviewed a report she had. "They reported you having nightmares and bouncing around on your bed, talking in your sleep the night before you left hospital. Also you seemed angry about everything. Are you still angry?"

"Not so much but I was at first. Everything that happened. Scott's death. Makela being shot up. I still feel guilty about the civilian who was killed. His name I remembered was Joshua Tillman."

"You remember that?"

"Oh yeah. I'm not sure how but I must have learned his name after it happened. Anyway, if I had pulled him down quicker, maybe I could have saved him. It all happened so fast. I also feel guilty for running down the stairs for cover when Scott was shot. But I couldn't have saved him. That impulsive reaction to get down and get safe saved my life. Same with Makela. Ducking back behind the brick wall saved me from being shot to hell."

"Anything else you remember from before or after what you recalled during our session," asked Nancy

"Yes. I remembered that the money was partially burned up in the fire. It was all turned over to the Toronto Police and the bank's representative. Between the burned papers in the leather bag and the bills still tight together in stacks singed but that didn't burn, they were able to account for all the money."

"What else?"

Quietly spoken, "I remember killing that boy. The one at the bottom of the stairs. He looked so young. I killed the other bank robber with the Tommy gun. In both cases it was them or me. I had killed before in the army but I expected to have to do that. I became a cop to help people. I thought my killing days were over. The boy bothered me more. He was so young. He reminded me of the German soldiers I had to kill."

"Thank you for sharing that with me. I will state the obvious. You had no choice in either case. It was you or them. They made decisions that day that put them in that situation. You did not put them there. That boy had just killed your partner. He would have killed you."

"Yeah, Doc. Thanks. I think I needed to hear that from someone. It's still hard."

Probing questions continued from Nancy. They reviewed the latest write-up of the memory by Enoch and one of the earlier ones. The later one did contain a lot more detail. It also had some follow-up information like the civilian's name and the burned money included that Enoch had remembered during the write-up but he was not sure how he knew these things.

After an hour, they took a break for Enoch to go get some lunch while Nancy wrote up notes of their conversation. Enoch had indicated he was ready for more and had the afternoon free. It was decided they would do another hypnosis session when Enoch came back from lunch.

Chapter 23 - 1923 - Train Robbery

My name? I am Town Constable Joshua Brown of the Coniston Police. Born in 1899. I joined the army and saw the last two years of the Great War in Europe. Fighting mostly in France and I was wounded. I came home with a bit of a limp but all of my other parts intact. I was hired two years ago to be a policeman. I tried mining, lumbering and even worked in a bakery in Sudbury. Nothing interested me until I found the police. I love my job. Talking to people, doing something different every day, solving problems and even breaking up the odd fight.

I got to work at 7 am on a Thursday. The Chief Constable, Tom Thomas who many people called Tom Tom, was already in the office. He seemed a bit frazzled.

"Everything good Chief?" I asked.

"No, everything is not good. The night man is not working out. I had another complaint last night about him. One more complaint and I'm going to fire him."

"Easy Chief. No need to get upset."

"You should be upset. I don't know where I'll find a night man on short notice. If he goes, I'll be the day man and you'll be the night man.

"Aww, c'mom. I did my time on nights."

I was moving backwards to nights but we needed another Town Constable so it shouldn't be for long. I guess I could adapt if I had to for this job. I hoped it wouldn't be for long. I was not surprised to hear the night man was not working out. I liked him well enough but he was overconfident, careless and arrogant. Not great traits in our job.

"Just until I find someone. I'll talk to him today but I haven't heard anything good about him. I should have checked him out a little better. Now I have a copper who is gambling and going to booze cans on the job. Last night I heard he was over visiting the Snake Lady."

"The Snake Lady. That's funny. How did you hear that?"

"It's not funny. Someone saw him sneaking into her back yard. A bit of a peeping tom who says he only heard noises of pleasure and joy but I think he saw it too. I can't have my men with reputations like that."

"Chief, why do they call her the Snake Lady?"

"She keeps a snake in a big glass jar."

"Why do we never raid her place?"

"Because she helps me with information from time to time. And I'm afraid we might catch the Town Reeve in there or the Fire Brigade Chief or the Anglican minister or someone of importance from town. Can't have that on my watch. She does more good than bad. Don't you be repeating any of that and stay away from the Snake Lady on or off duty. Understand?"

I chuckled and put both hands up, "Not for me Chief. I'm a good lad. Have we got anything on today?"

"Yes. A booze can. I need you to stay a bit late. We're going to raid it at 7 pm. Sudbury is sending us two men to help plus you, me and our stellar night man, Constable Lee Coulson. That should be lots. It's the afterwork crowd I'm after to send a message to. I'll ride over in a carriage with the two Sudbury men. That are being sent to help us. We'll dump the booze halfway back to here. You can ride our horse. Damn Lee can walk there and back."

I wondered out loud, "Where are we hitting?"

"That old lady in Garson on Pine Street. She hasn't been touched for some time and I am hearing talk about protection. That talk is gonna stop," said the Chief. "What do you have on today besides foot patrol?"

"I was going to check with the school on truants. They were concerned the other day about some brothers not coming from Garson. I'll look into that tomorrow if they still aren't here. Maybe take the horse this time."

"No you won't take our horse. We have one for emergencies. Being a truant officer is not an emergency so you can walk tomorrow but I'll let you ride tonight," scolded the Chief.

"Okay okay. I also have to check with the rail station. They said there were some gypsies on the train Monday. If they're in this area, they're making the rounds. No complaints yet but they may have just been looking. I've dealt with them before. It's probably that bunch that come up from Toronto from time to time. I'll run them out if I find them. Also I need to check on the payroll delivery for the Mond Nickel Company tomorrow. I'll do escort duty with their guards when it comes in. With the horse if that's okay."

The Chief shook his head, "Not an emergency but I guess if you get robbed it will be so you had better take the damn horse."

The Mond Nickel Company came to Coniston in 1911. They began buying local farms. They had a railway station there already. They built streets and infrastructure including drawing water from the Wahnapitae River. In 1913, the company opened up a smelter in Coniston. They also built roasting fields to burn logs under the ore to smelt it. They had stopped using roasting fields by this time but still had the smelter going strong with ore from Victoria Mine. The area was bare of trees used in the roasting fields and the rocks were black from all that smoke.

I told the boss I was off for breakfast at the Colonial Inn. Best food in all the North. He said he had a meeting this morning with the Reeve and the Fire Brigade Chief. There was talk of the King of England coming for a visit so they had a lot to talk about. Then he was headed home to bed for a nap in case this was a long night.

Chapter 24

I knew the Chief's meeting would be short as he would be taking the train back to Sudbury to rest at home. He would probably ride back with the Sudbury men in the wagon. To save time I was sure that Lee would get a ride on the wagon, at least one way. I checked out the log book and signed myself on duty with notes of my plans to check the train station, the paymaster at the Mond Nickel Company and the catholic school. It was quite a hike to Public School #1 in Garson so I would check their attendance rolls tomorrow if I went to Garson to charge the parents of the absent children from the Catholic school with breaching the school act by neglecting to send a child to school.

The teacher at the Catholic School was Miss Molly McGuire. With me being single and her being single and oh so pretty, I tended to take my Truant officer duties very seriously. I still didn't have the gumption to ask her out. I had thought about church this Sunday, so today might be the day. We had both come over as small children from Ireland and been fostered out. She was fostered to a family in Toronto. I was fostered to a family in Ottawa. Due to her education and my military service, we found our way to this place in these jobs. I had high hopes and long term dreams with Miss Molly.

I went to breakfast at the cafe in the Colonial Inn as I did to start everyday. I met Doc Mantha. He had a notice for me to post on a house in Polach Town for a polish family that had recently moved here. I did not know them but felt bad for them. It was my job to post health notices on homes. Today was the usual bad news. Scarlett Fever was in that house. Not a great start to my day. Doc Mantha was the town doctor but also the Medical Health Officer. Where and what he told me to post, I did.

I spoke to the Pay Master at the new refinery for Mond Nickel Company above the town. He was sure they had enough men to guard the shipment and I would not be needed. I agreed mostly because I would be working late tonight and I had to walk to Garson tomorrow. We spoke for a while and I passed on the news of Scarlett Fever in Polach Town. He knew the family as the husband worked for Mond Nickel Company and he would let his boss know. I said my goodbyes after trading gossip and headed to the train station.

I arrived with the train's arrival. I saw a gypsy man get off the train looking all around. I had dealt with him before. I walked up behind him tapping him on the shoulder. He looked at me, smiled and said, "Hi copper."

I replied, "Hi gypsy. You're nicked."

"What for?"

"Being of loose idle character having no visible means of maintaining yourself. Unless you have some money or a job."

"This is harassment," cried the gypsy.

"Not if it's true," I argued.

I cuffed my new found friend and walked him back onto the train for the ride to Sudbury telling him it was his lucky day as we were going to see the Judge in Sudbury right now. That meant he didn't have to spend time in my cells or another minute in my town. I also told him to pass that on to his family telling him I knew they were about. He would get out today probably and this favour I was doing him would only cost him to make sure no gypsies came to Coniston.

"What about Sudbury?" he asked.

"Sudbury, Creighten, Copper Cliff, Levack. I don't care about, but the coppers there might. Time to maybe head back to Toronto. And none of your malarkey about how Jesus Christ himself promised the Roma people they could steal all they want because they stole the nails to be used on him on the cross," I scolded.

I put handcuffs on in front of him. I put him back on the train. The train ran all day to Sudbury and my turnaround time was only 1 hour. Then back in Coniston.

A quick stop at the pool room, I spoke to the owner. I told him I heard a rumour he was open past midnight all week this week. Sam Chapel, the owner of the Mond Nickel Company Boarding House and Pool Hall, told me he had paid Lee for the privilege.

"That is not to happen again. If he comes looking for money, tell him to see me. You close at midnight. That's the prescribed time for closure of a pool hall. Next time I charge you," I lectured.

Damn Lee. If the boss hears of this, that will be the end of his job. I knew I would give him a warning not to let it happen again and about the thin ice he was skating on. I could not understand someone being so obviously stupid. I would tell him before the wagon showed for the raid tonight.

I checked the abandon houses for squatters until lunch. I ate at the Colonial Inn. They gave me a copper special for two bits. Soup, sandwich and coffee. My afternoon would be spent collecting fees, fines and rents from people for the town of Coniston and the Mond Nickel Company. I walked into a cow on East Street. I encouraged the cow to go home where I found the fence down. I found the owner of the cow, helped him fix the fence and issued a ticket for "cow at large." This was becoming a weekly occurrence. I talked to the owner about better fencing.

A boy ran up to me about a man gone crazy the next street over. It was Tony Renzi from Polach Town. He was visiting at his brother-in-law's house and things got out of hand. When I arrived he had a 2x4 and was swinging it around like a club with everyone staying out of his way. I knew he never drank but he did get his dark times. Everyone knew he had melancholy since his wife had died last year of Scarlett Fever.

"Tony, put the board down. Now," I ordered.

"No. Leave me be. My brother-in- law's an asshole and he's gonna get it. The whole world are assholes. I want to kill you all and then die," Tony raged.

I waited until his bother-in-law spoke and Tony turned to him. I ran straight at Tony. I tackled him high above the waist trapping both arms and dragging him to the ground with me. His brother-in-law and some other men nearby watching helped me wrestle the 2x4 from him and cuff his hands behind his back. I said in a loud, clear voice, "I arrest you for suspicion of being mentally deranged and dangerous to the public at large."

Two of the men helped me take him to the station and put him in one of our two jail cells. Another man was in the other cell. "Who are you?" I asked.

"I'm Jerome. Chief Thomas said I could stay the night. I have no money and no place to go."

"Have you eaten?"

"Yes, the Chief gave me a sandwich for lunch and a sandwich for supper. Said you would be busy tonight and he would let me out in the morning."

"Okay. This is Tony. Just talk to him but don't rile him up. He needs rest now. He's had a bad time of things."

"No worries, sir. I don't want any trouble. I'm looking for work. A fella at the Mond Nickel Company gave me a letter for the manager at the Victoria Mine and a train ticket. They have a job for me after tomorrow. I'm going on the train tomorrow to take the job."

"Good for you. I'm back in the morning so I'll let you out if the Chiefs not here, about 7 am."

"Thanks."

I got out our log book and wrote passages of all of the work I did today. I left out the comments made about Lee at the pool hall. I would talk to him when he came in which would be soon. I filed my tickets, fines, rent collections and town fees for the Chief for tomorrow morning. I walked home for supper.

Chapter 25

After some beans and toast at home, I headed over to the stable to check on our horse, Charlie. I fed him a carrot I had brought and spoke to the kennel manager and dog catcher who ran our stable. We gossiped about the day and other things. I learned that Lee had been showing off a new gun he just got. I wondered how he got the money for that as he just started. I carried a medium barrel Iver Johnson .32 calibre 5 shot revolver. It was a used gun but all I could afford and it was a perfect police weapon. I also had a lever action .30-.30 Winchester rifle that I bought also used after I left the army. I would probably take it with me tonight as I had a holder for it that fit the horse saddle.

After saddling the horse, I stopped back at my house for the rifle and rode back to the station tying Charlie up outside. There was a wagon outside as well. I saw Lee coming toward the station. I walked over to him to talk before we went into the station. "Tom Tom's on the warpath. He had another complaint about you last night. One more and you'll be let go."

"Don't worry about it," responded Lee.

"I do worry. He doesn't even know about the pool hall. I told them no more payoffs and they close at midnight. You see them open you give them a ticket. Do you understand?" I growled.

"Yeah, yeah. Don't worry about it."

"Why aren't you worried?"

"I got big plans. This is just a short stop to a bigger world."

"Well while you're at this stop, do your job. I don't want to be covering for you. I like this small world. What's that on your hip?"

"You like? It's my new Colt Army Special .32-.20. This is a real revolver. I got the matching lever action rifle too. They use the same ammunition. Bought at the store in Sudbury brand new. You're not the only one with his own gun and rifle now."

"How did you afford that?"

"All part of the grand plan."

"I know, I know. Don't worry about it."

"That's right. What's with the horse and wagon?"

"Chief will tell you. We have a raid tonight in Garson."

Lee Coulson the night man whined, "This is going to ruin my plans tonight?"

"What plans?"

"The Italians in Polach town are having a wedding tonight at their social club. I was going to stop by for a drink or two."

I glared at him, "No drinking on the job. No drinking at anytime. You ticket people for that. You're not suppose to do it yourself."

"Don't worry about it."

Lee Coulson the night man was only 20 years old. He had missed the war. He had come here from Peterborough from a farm looking for better things. He could read, write and he spoke well. The Chief hired him but he had regretted it ever since. Nothing but bad rumours and he got no work done. I was counted on to do all the rounds collecting during the day shift. A few weeks ago the Chief started a night time short shift on Saturdays where I walked with Lee from 9 pm to 1 am. Just to keep a lid on the town.

It worked out okay except I quickly learned he was a bit bent and loved to brag. He did more than covet the odd neighbour's wife. He drank and gambled. He had no issue with looking the other way. When we were together, he always had my back in everything. He let me take the lead as long as I was making the arrest or writing the ticket. I liked that part of him. But he was lazy and full of himself. We would never be friends but I could work with him. I was more concerned with what he got up to on his own.

We went into the station where the Chief said, "At last we can go. I'll brief Lee on the trip. The other men have their orders. You bring your rifle Josh?"

"Yep. Holstered on Charlie."

"Okay. We have one shotgun I'll carry. You men all have your revolvers. Josh has the rifle so he comes in last. Anybody runs, Josh will order them down. Warning shots are okay but for gods sake nobody shoots anybody. Got that Lee?" instructed the Chief.

"Got it Tom Tom."

"That's Chief to you and we will be having a chat when we get back here. Let's get going."

Chapter 26

At least for the ride over to Garson I didn't have to listen to Lee and the Chief. The two men from Sudbury Police were both Constables named Grange and Cooper. They were often sent by the Chief Constable of Sudbury Police when we asked for assistance. Both good lads and big. Cooper was an Englishman. Grange was a Frenchman from Paris. Both had seen action in the war. Too much action. Grange was missing his left hand pinkie finger. Cut off when the Gerrys got him and tortured him for information. Word was that he had many other scars not visible under his clothing. Cooper on the other hand was missing his left ear. Shot off by a German sniper while he was popping his head up from the trench. He could still hear but it did look ugly. Amputated after infection of the wound.

They were steadfast, quiet and tough men. They could be twins with their dark curly hair, blue eyes, always grinning together. Except when they spoke as both had thick accents. I was happy they were along. Chief Thomas was a great boss and happy to be involved in these raids. Eli I was not impressed with but like I said, he did always have my back when we worked together.

We met at the end of Pine Street. It was the house halfway up the street on the left. I had been here before and knew an older lady known as Ma Allen ran the place. We had raided it a year ago. It was a dirty little secret, everyone knew she had a booze can. Once a year we raided it, took her booze and shut her down. No charges. Her sons were more of a prize. They ran stills in different locations and kept moving them. We had never been able to catch them but the Chief said one day we would and they would be charged.

Not everyone agreed with prohibition. Actually, it seemed not many agreed with it. But it was the law of the land. If we didn't enforce it, they would sent in the federal police to do it. We did not want them coming to take over our patch. They had been the North West Mounted Police until after the Second Boer War when many had been sent and fought overseas. Upon returning to Canada they were re-named the Royal North West Mounted Police. Then recently in 1920 they were re-organized and named the Royal Canadian Mounted Police due to rising concerns of Bolshevik conspiracies and other political concerns. They were our federal police now. They were still new enough we were not sure what all they were going to take over.

The Complexities of Prohibition Enforcement

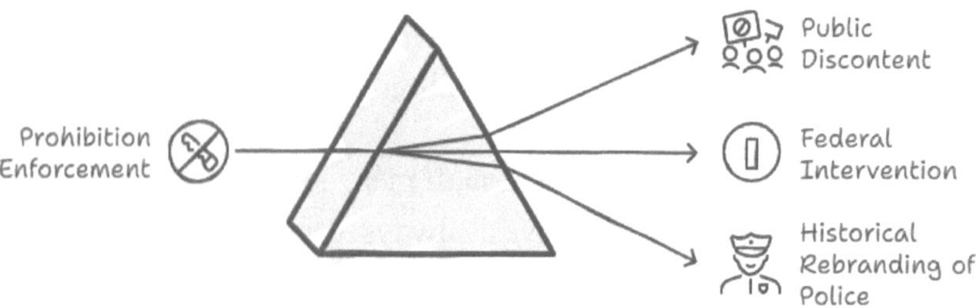

The word the Chief had about tonight was that there would be Ma and all three of her sons there. Tonight we would be laying charges under prohibition as well as destroying all of the liquor. The Chief had heard that they had set up a still in the shed behind the house. It was so brazen a move that he'd had enough and we were taking Ma to court this time. With her sons there, he was hoping the Judge would see the still and booze can as proof of a conspiracy taking the charges more seriously. If not it would be a fine for all four of them plus losing the still and booze.

Grange and Cooper went to set up in the back ready to hit the shed and back door. The Chief and Lee went to the front door. I stayed on

Charlie with my rifle in case anyone ran. It was something we had all done before. Even Lee had raided a still and a couple of booze cans with us before. I expected no problems. And there were none. Everyone left with their ticket. Ma and her three boys were arrested and transported by wagon to Sudbury Jail. We destroyed the booze in the back yard. The still we took with us to scatter pieces in the dark off of the wagon on the ride to Coniston. Charlie and I took another trail to beat the wagon to the station.

I put on a pot of coffee and filled out the log book. It was 9:30 pm. After a little meeting, Grange and Cooper headed to Sudbury with the prisoners to see the Judge in the morning along with a written report by me of the arrest circumstances and destruction of the whiskey and the still. The Chief caught a ride with them back to Sudbury where he lived. He would attend in the morning to see the Judge as well in case testimony was needed. Likely it would not be needed. This was fairly routine. A bit of a game with bootleggers and coppers.

I headed home for sleep. Lee was anxious to go rattle door knobs of businesses and abandon houses, he said. I knew otherwise. He wanted to get over to that wedding. A bit of hypocrisy where we raided a booze can but left a wedding party alone with home made beer and wine. There would likely be spirits too. Once I got home, I had a few moments to think about Molly and how I would ask her tomorrow to go to church with me on Sunday. We were both catholic so that worked in my favour. We were both from Ireland and had been relocated as children. She always smiled when she saw me. She was so pretty. Her face was the last thought I had as I drifted off to sleep.

Chapter 27

It was morning. The sun was up and I was late. The Chief would be angry. I got to the station as quickly as I could. Jerome was gone from his cell. So was my deranged man. The Chief told me he had released him to his brothers this morning. He was calm. They took him home. There was a car parked outside.

"That damn Simpson is charging me $6 to and from town today instead of the usual $5 because he knows I'm in a hurray. Did you read the logbook?" sniped the Chief.

"Not yet. Sorry I'm late."

"Forget about that we have bigger problems. I have to meet with Sudbury's Chief Constable. Lee was found at the rail station this morning passed out drunk in uniform while on duty. I hear that's where he spent most of last night. When we got back from the raid, he went to that Italian wedding. He's had it. When he sobers up and comes in he's fired. I'm going to see if an Inspector From Sudbury Police can be spared to help me with that this afternoon."

"What do you want me to do?"

"Work today on your usual rounds. Get that school off my back over those Garson kids not coming in. Go home early and get some sleep because tomorrow you start as the new night man until I find someone else," instructed the Chief.

After the car left, I walked over to the school. Molly was waiting for me and we went outside while the children were settling into their lesson. I could hear them stage whispering "Ooooooowww." Then a chant of constable and teacher sittin' in a tree. Molly said very loudly, "Enough children. Get on with your lessons quietly." We both shyly smiled at each other.

"Did the Bremen boys come to school today?" I queried.

"No and that makes over a week since they've been to class. Their family lives in Garson on their farm and none of the other kids have been over there or seen them. Their names are Timmy, Tommy and Seamus."

"Okay. I'm going to head over there today and speak with the parents."

"I don't know them well but this is not normal for them so I am concerned."

"No problem. I wanted to ask you if you had any plans for Sunday?"

"Why Constable. Of course I am going to church. Why do you ask?"

"I wondered if I could escort you to church Miss McGuire."

"Why that would be lovely."

We both broke up in quiet laughter as though she knew the question was coming and I knew the answer she would give. We smiled shyly at each other. I told her I would see her this afternoon about the Bremen boys. Then I headed off.

Having to walk to Garson was not unusual given we only had one horse. Still I had hoped after last night and because I would be moving to nights, I might get a break from the walk. But I was not asking the Chief for a horse this morning. He had enough on his plate. It was a beautiful sunny day for a walk. A brisk wind kept it from being too hot. I would take the walking trail instead of the road so I could take off my tunic until I reached houses on the Garson side.

It only took me an hour and a half to reach the Breman farm. They had a field of gardens, a few fields of hay, some cows and chickens. It was a healthy small farm. I had never met the Bremans before but I had my speech all prepared. A few days without school meant a warning the first time but over a week would be a ticket under the School Act where the breach was "neglecting to send child to school." I would let the Justice of the Peace decide whether they should receive a warning or a fine.

A husky woman met me on the porch. Her dress had dirt on it and she wore no apron. She had clearly been toiling but not in the kitchen, more like in the fields. Maybe in the large vegetable garden they had. I introduced myself and she spoke with a Finn accent saying she was Mrs. Martha Breman. I asked after her husband and she looked around and down as though not wanting to tell me. "Is this about the boys and school?" she asked quietly.

I replied, "This is about the boys not attending school."

"I see. You better come in for some tea. The boys are out working and not here right now."

As I walked into the house I could see a makeshift bed in the front room. She introduced her husband George who had an English accent. I learned George had badly broken his leg and was unable to walk while it healed. The boys had been kept home to help their mother work the farm. They could not afford to hire help. Martha assured me she could work the farm with the boys help but they couldn't go to school then.

I had heard this tale before and knew the truth of it. Clearly they were just trying to get by and keep their farm. I had my tea and spoke with both of them. They seemed like a very nice family. I spoke to the boys when they came in. I told Martha that this was only a warning but I thought if she could walk to the school and speak with Miss McGuire. Something could be arranged. I suggested the boys go to school one day a week and bring home their lessons for the rest of the week in order to keep up. This way they may not end up a year behind their peers.

After our conversation I thanked them for their hospitality and a sandwich Mrs Breman made for me to take on my walk back. I stopped at Garson #1 Public School and used their new telephone to call the Coniston Separate School. I spoke with Molly and explained what I learned. She agreed with me. She told me that the siren had been going from the Mond Nickel Company for about 20 minutes. The children had been outside and thought they heard gunshots just before the siren. She had all the kids in the school and would keep them there for the afternoon. There was no answer when she called the police station.

I tried to call and received no answer at the station. I started back to Coniston on the path as it was faster than the road. Not twenty minutes down the path I met Lee Coulson in uniform and riding a borrowed horse leading Charlie already saddled. "Come on," said Lee.

Without thinking much I mounted Charlie. "What's going on?"

"The payroll was robbed at the train station going to Mond Nickel. There were four men on horses. They shot a guard and one of the conductors from the train and rode off. They were seen heading on the road toward Garson. I was at the station with Tom Tom and Inspector Peck from Sudbury. Can you believe next week I have to go before the Police Council to be fired? I was suspended but Tom Tom changed his mind with the robbery and me already in uniform.”

“Why are you here?”

“Chief sent me. He took a car with three men from town, Dewer, Suosalo and Reinhart. They are heading toward Hagar to meet more men and Hagar’s Town Constable Miller. Inspector Peck headed in his car to Sudbury to bring reinforcements. They called for Grange and Cooper to head from Sudbury on horseback to Skead Village. We will meet them as they work down the Wahnapitae River from Skead toward us.

“Why?”

“Tom Tom thinks they’ll use the rail line to get away with the railway bridge over the Wahnapitae River. No one will be around and they have a clear run all the way to Hagar. He’s going to set up there and he wants us to chase them into the trap in Hagar.”

“Why didn’t they take the bridge in the town of Wahnapitae. There’s not that many people in town and they could cross the railway bridge there quickly before anyone was on them.”

“That was probably the plan before the shootout with Mond security and they killed the guard. That’s when they headed to the Garson Road.”

We started to ride. That’s when I realized that Lee had my scabbard from the station on his horse with his new fancy lever action Colt .32-.20 rifle. I didn’t say anything but I wished I had my rifle as well. We rode fast on the narrow trail past Garson all the way to Happy Valley north of Falconbridge. Then on from there to the rail line. The horses were getting tired when we met with Grange and

Cooper. They had seen nothing from Skead and no sign horses had past that way. We could see clear signs of horses from Happy Valley on the trail. They headed down the rail line to the river.

The Wahnapitae River rail bridge was high off the river by about 60 feet. It was built with an intricate series of railway ties. I had walked across it before and it was daunting looking down between the rails at the rushing water below. I knew I would be walking Charlie across. Grange and Cooper said they would wait until we were across then come across themselves so we could cover each other.

It made sense. As we got to the bridge, I dismounted but Lee kept riding. "The trick is to go slow and trust the horse," explained Lee as he started across.

The mad bastard was going to die from the fall before he got shot. I dismounted and walked Charlie across carefully. Lee moved slowly on his horse but was across while I was still halfway. He rode out of sight. There was some whooping yells and gunfire. I ducked, then began to run forward. Suddenly there were shots all around me. The noise was deafening. I saw splinters fly from the rails. I heard Charlie's whiny turn to a scream and felt his reins pull hard. I let go and fell flat on the rail ties. Looking down I saw Charlie hit the water in a mighty splash.

There was a lull with complete silence. A moment passed before the shooting began again. I realized it was coming from both sides. I had no where to run but forward or backward. I was rushed to a decision between the noise and the flying splinters of wood around me. I ran forward knowing there may be a chance Lee was alive although not likely. I was almost to the end of the bridge when I felt a punch to my chest. I flew forward onto my face. The pain burned right through me.

My head fell forward into darkness. I had flashes of Grange and Cooper dragging me off the bridge. I could hear them saying "Lee's gone and so is his horse. Maybe he was okay and still after them."; "We can't leave Josh."; "He's been shot. We both see that. He'll never make it."

Next I could see the ground bouncing past as I was strapped over a horse. Cooper was riding his horse in front with Grange on his horse holding me over the saddle. We were riding way too fast for the good of these horses, I thought. Then passed out again.

The next time I awoke I was in Doc Mantha's office hearing him telling the Chief how lucky I was to be alive. Something about the bullet ricochetting off a rib then lodging in my back. Too dangerous to operate further but not near anything too vital. For now it should be left alone.

I passed out again and found myself being washed by Miss McGuire. "Molly," I gasped.

"Oh so it's Molly now is it? One sponge bath and I am no longer Miss McGuire."

"No, I mean yes. Miss McGuire. I… I… what happened?"

"You got shot. I'll let the doctor know you're awake." She kissed my forehead smiling as she left the room. That was the best medicine I could get.

Chapter 28

I heard from the Chief that Lee Coulson was dead. His body was found half way down the tracks toward Hagar about 3 miles from where I was shot. He had been killed by the robbers who continued on. The four men were all killed in the gunfight from the ambush waiting for them. The Chief, the three men with him from Mond Nickel Company security, Hagar Town Constable along with seven farmers who joined them were the posse at the ambush. All of the payroll money had been recovered.

Grange and Cooper had ridden hard to get me to Doc Mantha's office. It was closer than going to town. It was decided I would rest best at his office then home. There had not been much damage by the bullet. Mostly just its trail into my chest. By hitting the rib, it diverted down away from doing damage to the lungs or heart. It rested against my spine. A car trip to the hospital on Elm St West near Pine Street had confirmed with their new fangled x-ray machine where the bullet lay. It was decided that it was too dangerous to remove in that spot.

With a broken rib and time to heal the wound, I would soon be able to return to work. My toes had feeling and my heart was soaring for Molly who became my nurse in the evening. The Chief had to bring in some Fire Brigade men for a while to help police until finally hiring Suosalo, the big Finn from Mond Nickel Company Security who had been on the posse. He was the new night man for Coniston Police. Lee Coulson who had no family was given a hero's burial and a town parade. I did recover and a few months later I was back to work as the day man for the Coniston Police with 2 new officers making a rotation for night man by these 3 officers. I was steady days with Chief Thomas. A few months after that I married Molly McGuire.

Chapter 29 - 2024

Bringing Enoch out more slowly allowed for some follow-up questioning to get answers to what happened in the aftermath of the shooting. Dr. O'Brien felt this session, being longer than the last session, had been a much longer memory. She began to wonder if the longer the session, the longer the memory.

"How do you feel Enoch?" asked Nancy.

"I'm good. Very relaxed. I know who I was. That was my grandfather on my dad's side. I never knew him. He was a cop with Coniston Police and later with Sudbury Police. He was Sudbury's first detective."

"Did you know your grandmother?"

"No they both died before I was born. My father used to tell me stories. They had him later in life. In fact, I have that bullet from the shooting. It became a complication for my grandfather and it was later removed. My dad gave it to me when I was a kid as a display I did for school. I still have it somewhere."

"I think we need to follow the same Cognitive Behavioural Therapy as before. Write out this memory as often as you can. A few times a day at least. You seem less bothered than last time."

"I am. Happy thoughts of Molly and even though I was shot, it was the start of a happy life together."

"We will unpack this in a week's time."

Nancy made an appointment for Enoch for a week later. After he left, she began to write up her notes. She had written a lengthy report that was sent to the others in the PBL group for their input. The consensus from the group was that he had a confabulated memory from his time in his medically induced coma. Although there was no clear direction, there was a concern that the hypnosis was cementing that memory. The PBL group was to meet a few days after the next session. When they would have three reports to look at and decide if this was in the patient's best interest to continue this course of treatment. In the meantime, he continue to take tests every few days and scans by other departments after his physiotherapy sessions at HSN.

Nancy reflected on how real his memories seemed. The most logical conclusion was that it was confabulation but she wondered if another theory fit. She would bring that up with the group at their next meeting looking for another theory. She was definitely not in support of the epigenetic theory of remembering a past life or ancestral memories. She was sure there were only one or two in the group leaning that way from the content of the emails by the group she had seen.

Enoch left HSN with his usual Timmies coffee and an apple fritter. He paid the parking machine his requisite 8 dollars then walked to his truck. In his head he was thinking about the cost of parking and how on physio and testing day he got free parking in the physio parking lot on the other side of the hospital. He was scheming whether he could stretch these sessions to be counted as physio. All cops hate to pay for parking.

When he got to his pickup, he began to think about his echo memory. He cringed at the thought of those bullets hitting the bridge. He could almost feel when he was shot. The worst thing that bothered him at the moment was seeing Charlie hit the water knowing he was dead.

After driving from the hospital, he had another faint memory of his mother telling him that Lee Coulson's handgun and rifle had been donated to a museum down south somewhere and later returned when the Sudbury Police Museum formed in 1996. On the drive home he stopped at 128 Larch Street. The Sudbury Police Museum had opened there last year after being re-located from the third floor of Police Headquarters on Brady Street.

A quick cell phone call to Heather Petrin, the curator, arranged for her to meet him at the museum with the key. The new police museum was on the first floor and more accessible to the public. The displays were very much the same as when it was in Police Headquarters. Part of this building was a new secondary site for some non-operational police services. The museum displayed a collection of uniforms, equipment, a functioning cell and even weapons connected to policing in Sudbury. The museum represented all police in Sudbury not just Greater Sudbury Police.

Enoch knew there were log books from Coniston Police that were partially filled in by his grandfather's hand at the museum. Also some of the weapons from Coniston Police. He had seen the .32-.20 revolver belonging to Lee Coulson on display. That was of interest to him today. He had the bullet from his grandfather and a suspicion after being in the gunfight. The round that hit his grandfather had come low at an upward angle as though someone was shooting from the ground. The other bullets seemed angled down as though from a person on horseback.

Enoch was also now suspicious of Lee having money to purchase his new gun. It might have been graft money but this seemed like more. Along with the cocky attitude toward the job, He also didn't like Lee's cavalier attitude toward everything. Enoch and Lee were not friends as his grandfather had been with Lee. Not even co-workers.

Enoch was suspicious that the inside man they had speculated about from the train station, on the train or with Mond Nickel Mine Security may have been Lee himself.

Heather met Enoch at the door of the museum asking how he was doing and was he back to work yet. He told her he was still off but he wanted to see the pistol from the 1923 train robbery belonging to Constable Lee Coulson. She took him to the display.

"I'm always amazed that guns just sit here on display in museums," mentioned Enoch.

"Oh its okay. All these guns have been deactivated," responded Heather.

"What do you mean by deactivated?"

"Well the firing pins are welded over. Cement is poured down the barrels. With the revolvers, the cylinders are welded shut. None of these guns will ever fire again."

"So the barrels are basically destroyed?"

"Oh yes. They're not really guns anymore. It costs us about $100 to deactivate a gun to government specifications for a museum display. That's so they can never be used as a gun again."

"What about rifles?"

"Yes, rifles too. Well…"

"Well what?"

"We don't have many rifles on display. We only have so much money. Some rifles we get we may keep off site until we can afford to deactivate them. They're in a secure lockup at another location that's alarmed."

"What about Lee Coulson's rifle?"

"I'm not sure but I can check the records. I don't remember a rifle with that display."

Heather opened up the computer. A quick check of the database showed that Lee Coulson's rifle had also been donated to the museum but was in storage as it had not been deactivated yet so it could not be placed in the museum on display.

"Can you get that rifle for me?" queried Enoch.

"Well… I'm not suppose to. I don't know especially with you being off work and all."

"No problem but don't deactivate it."

"Not likely. It's expensive and the rifle is too big for the train robbery display."

"I will send a Forensic officer over to seize it for testing with an incident number for you that can track it until we can return it."

"That would work."

"Thanks Heather"

Enoch's next stop was to Forensics to see Sergeant Bobbie "The Bear" Whessal. He explained to the Bear what he needed and told him about the bullet he had. The Bear had lots of contacts at the Centre of Forensic Science.

"Normally, as you know, all of our exhibits go to Sault Ste Marie Centre of Forensic Science (CFS) but for ballistics they have to go to Toronto CFS. I will make an incident number and text it to you. If you could do a General Occurrence Report, I can send it down. I'll make a call to see if I can get it expedited but no promises. Gun testing is a busy thing right now with all the shootings in Toronto and all around that area. I know a guy there who might stay late without overtime to do it out of curiosity," the Bear explained.

"That would be great. When can you get the rifle?"

"Frieze is done with a couple break and enters she was processing. She is heading in now for lunch. I'll have her stop by and see Heather on the way in and seize it."

"Thanks, I really appreciate it Bear."

"No problem Ewok. I'm interested in the results now too."

Chapter 30

The ballistic results came back 4 days later due to the curiosity of the old case and because it involved the wounding of one officer and the death of another. It was a positive match. The bullet from Joshua Brown was fired from Lee Coulson's rifle. A rifle he had with him minutes before the shot was fired. He was ahead of Joshua and had dismounted before the shooting started. It all fit. Enoch needed to confirm the angle of the shot. Enoch knew where the entry wound was and where the bullet had lodged. He also knew which rib had been hit. These were in the Chief's notes in the logbook. Given his grandfather was average height at 5'8", they had an approximate angle.

The Bear had a day off so he borrowed the laser mapping unit they used that had replaced the Total Station survey sighting system that was previously used at fatal motor vehicle collisions and homicides. It would map and create a 3 dimensional image of the scene. They could then recreate the scene, study it at a later time and show it in court. Enoch and the Bear went out to the old rail bridge over the Wahnapitae River. "You rode a horse over this?" asked the Bear.

"No, not me. My grandfather walked a horse over this. Lee Coulson rode his horses over this. The bridge was in much better shape a hundred years ago."

"Well somebody has to go and stand out there so I can point the laser to get our measurements. Are you the same height as your grandpa?"

"Yeah. I'm 5'8" too."

"Good. Out you go. Do you know where he was standing?"

"The logbook said about three quarters of the way across was where they found him."

"Walk out one quarter of the way or crawl out if you're nervous and then stand up. This will all be approximate anyway. We just want the general angle. We know the others were still on their horses and a little further back from the edge so their shots will be angled downward. If the angle is upward it must have come from the ground."

Enoch groaned, "Here I go." There was a light wind that felt heavier than it was. He could hear a slight whistling from the bridge. The water of the river was rushing below he saw with the one glance down he took before he said in his head, "Don't look down. Don't look down." He moved very slowly and made sure each foot was firmly planted before the next step. The timbers all looked old with large pitted holes in many of them. He started to hear creaking noises as he walked out further. Finally he heard the Bear yell that he was in a good spot. He turned around.

"Hold still," the Bear told him. He had a measurement started between the approximate entry wound and the approximate rib location. Now he extended that angle back to where he was off the bridge. He moved to the right and then the left. He crouched down. "I have it. Come back. Slowly."

"Oh yeah."

Enoch made the perilous walk back to the end of the bridge. He didn't look down or back the whole walk trusting the footing of his feet to find his way. He exhaled upon reaching the end. He hadn't realized he had been holding his breath. "What do we have?" asked Enoch.

"We definitely can say the shot was first, at an upward angle. Second, it was likely from the left side of the bridge on the ground. We know it was from the .32-.20 lever action rifle we tested. Other than that, I don't think we can say more. Everything we measured is approximate. We can't recreate the measurements exactly. I believe it is enough based on what we know from the museum logbooks with witness information like the Chief who also noted what the doctor told him from the examination to say that Lee Coulson is the likely shooter in this case."

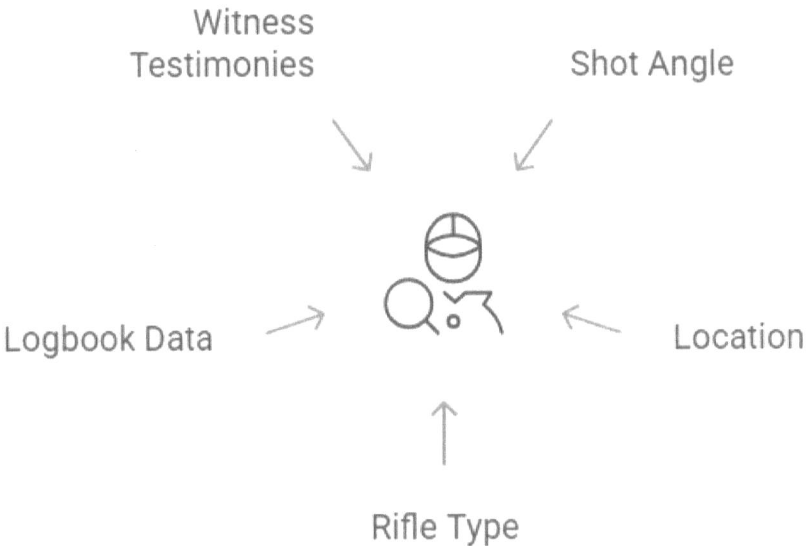

"That is what I had suspected."

"Let's walk further back while we map the scene in three dimension so I can recreate these measurements later if we need them."

"Thanks Bear. This solves a very old mystery. Two in fact."

"Two?"

"Yeah, who shot my grandfather and who the inside man was on the train robbery."

146

Chapter 31

Enoch walked into the bullpen of CID heading to his office. Phillips raised an eyebrow as he entered saying, "Shouldn't you still be on bedrest?"

Enoch grunted, moving past her desk, "I'm fine."

"Hey boss, on that happy note," chirped Phillips. "On your desk is a photo of a message we found scrawled on the back wall of the burned garage. It said 'I'll light another soon.'"

"I'll take a look," said Enoch as he hurried past.

"Just so you know Staff, Jackson is out with a receipt we found in the grass beside the garage from a store that sells paint solvent. That was the accelerant used here. He is speaking to the store owner now for a description. No video and the man paid cash the day before the fire."

"Okay, keep on it."

Enoch looked at the photo on his desk and other messages then decided to wait for the Inspector.

Sitting in the Inspector's office in CID, waiting for Inspector Frank Townsend to return from his morning meeting to update the Deputy Chief, Enoch thought of what he was going to say. He was not sure if he was going to get an attaboy, great job, you're in it deep now for using police resources or who cares. Time to beg for forgiveness likely. Looking around the office, he saw on the 4 x 8 white board that there were some new additions. More names under opioid deaths and a list of some old cold cases.

Along with the cold cases was that damn painting. A Tom Thompson, group of seven, painting had been stolen from the Copper Cliff Library in the early 1970's. It was quite valuable. There were no alarm systems installed in the library back then. It had never been recovered. About every five or ten years, the newspaper ran a story on it and word came down from the Chief's office to investigate. There was never anything new to go on. Enoch wondered what poor detective had gotten stuck with this case.

Inspector Frank Townsend came quickly into the office closing the door with a slam. Enoch jumped and looked at him sideways. "Sorry," said the Inspector. "Just another morning meeting that did not go my way. It would have been worse without your solve."

"My solve?"

"Yeah, closing a case 100 years old where a police officer is shot and finding the inside man on a train robbery is a big deal. Although it would have been better if I had known what you were up to. No more freelancing okay?"

"No. I'll keep you up to date. Speaking of up to date, am I back to work?"

"Not full time but if you can get a note for light duty, I have a little job for you."

"Not that fuckin' painting again."

"Haha. I need someone to start a cold case unit for missing persons that are suspected homicides and unsolved homicides. You can work with Major Crime but I will give you a detective and uniform will give us an officer. If it works out I will have you run that and the Major Crime Unit. I'll get another Staff Sergeant to run the floor."

"What about that fuckin' painting?"

"Okay okay. Yes you will have to take on the painting too but no one expects that to be solved after all this time."

"Well it sounds too good to be true."

"It was that or they were going to stick you in Professional Standards. I know how you would have loved doing internal investigations."

"Don't even joke about that Frank."

Inspector Townsend began to change. This was normal for a meeting with him. Very informal Frank and Enoch were. Taking off his tie while he talked, jacket and shirt. Going to his locker/file cabinet, he opened it to take out a uniform shirt. He changed his pant pulled out a tie, shoes and his jacket to complete the outfit before he picked up his forge cap with gold on it.

"I have to go to this presentation for the Deputy today at the YMCA. He wants me to say a few words on behalf of the department. I love doing these gigs when there is a dinner or at least a snack table. I've been to these fund raisers before. Hand over a giant cheque, say a short speech thanking everyone and present it to the charity. Have our photo op with the paper. Then out the door."

"I expect you can find your way to Timmies on the way back. Large dark roast black, thank you."

"Ha ha. Always an angle Ewok. You want to come to this thing with me?"

"No, I think I'm due for physio at HSN."

"Say, before you go, how did you get CFS to jump the queue and do your ballistics testing?"

"It was a friend of the Bear. He did it after hours for no overtime to keep us all from getting into trouble."

"Well it worked. CFS is quite happy with this win. They're sending someone up tomorrow afternoon for a short media conference with you, the Bear and I, if you can be back to work on light duty."

"I'll get my back to work light duty note today and have it in Human Resources tomorrow morning."

"Sounds great, Ewok. I have to go. See you tomorrow. Think about who you want on this team. Poach whoever you want from Uniform Division but we will have to talk about who you get from CID."

On his way off the floor in CID, Enoch ran into Jackson who stopped him. He had a detailed description of the suspect for the arson case. Jackson gave him the description and then muttered, "What if I miss something, Staff?

Enoch patted his shoulder, "We all do. The trick is to learn from it. You'll do fine. Go brief Phillips."

Enoch left headquarters feeling much better and lighter. He had a win. He was going to get some press. The best news though was he was coming back to work into a meaningful job.

Chapter 32

Enoch got his back to work note from Dr. Hussain, his family doctor, who was up to date on his recovery and agreed this was a good way to ease back into the type of work he did. A quick stop into Human Resources with his note and an agreement of what he could do and what his limitations were going to be. He was back to duty.

They had a positive media conference with everyone looking good on this one. Except for Town Constable Lee Coulson. He did get the uniform officer he wanted, Greg Bouchard. Greg was a younger, experienced uniform officer but he also had a year as a detective under his belt from an internship post he did. He would fit right in and could hit the ground running. He had been on loan to CID for a year some time back. The Inspector dubbed the new unit, the Cold Case Squad (CCS).

The detective from CID was a more difficult sell to the Inspector and the Deputy Chief who waded into the conversation. There was a detective on light duty, Detective Constable Sharon Lavric. She had only been a detective for a short time when she had been injured. She was on light duty inputting data into the Major Case Management computer system called Powercase. All sexual assaults and attempts, all homicides and attempts, all non familial abductions and attempts, all found human remains and all missing persons with suspicious circumstances had to be inputed and managed from this system. It was linked across the province to all police services in Ontario.

Powercase would link cases in a number of ways such as through names or vehicles. It also was set up with triggers that would alert the manager of a case if there was some connections to another or other cases. It also alerted the Serial Predator Unit. The Serial Predator Unit was originally set up near the end of 1997. It had an experienced detective assigned to the unit to conduct training, examine triggers and had the ability to order multi jurisdictional major case management investigations. This was to prevent another Bernardo case from ever happening again. The Paul Bernardo case was reviewed demonstrating many deficiencies and systemic problems within major criminal investigations. It also showed how difficult it was for different jurisdictions and police services to coordinate with or even learn about similar cases in other jurisdictions.

Ontario, in 1997, had made many changes to how Police Services did business on these types of cases after a Judicial Review of the Bernardo cases was done that came with many recommendations. They were all very constructive changes. ViCLAS, where Enoch had been assigned for two years, was another of those changes in addition to the Serial Predator Unit and Powercase. The Violent Crime Linkage Analysis System (ViCLAS) Centre in Ontario had begun in 1994 with a Sergeant and 4 Constables in the Ontario Provincial Police. They did Behavioural Science training for officers and detectives, analysis of cases typically entered into Powercase and linked up cases by descriptions, Modus Operendi and, most importantly, by behavioural features.

The analysts were trained and had access to a Forensic Psychiatrist and two Criminal Profilers trained by the FBI. Most importantly, it was written into the Police Act of Ontario and became law in February, 1997 for all officers in Ontario to fill out ViCLAS booklets when they had a designated offence case. The booklets had to be submitted to the ViCLAS Centre within 30 days. These were the same designations as Powercase. This created additional ways of triggers being made for cases.

Ontario did not want to have another serial case like Paul Bernardo without being ready this time. Ontario wanted to have the tools and abilities to identify and investigate these horrendous multi-jurisdictional nightmares. It had taken years to get these new processes up and running. ViCLAS was increased in 1997 to a 40 person unit of officers and civilians to handle the influx of all mandatory cases. By the end of that year, the first person for the Serial Predator Unit had been selected. By 2000, all detectives received training across the province on Powercase. It was a massive effort but it paid off.

Sharon Lavric was the first member of the new Cold Case Squad that Enoch interviewed. He started by telling her she had the job. He was clear with her his concerns were about her lack of experience but her limitations were not a huge issue. She had some mobility issues because she walked with a cane. More to the point, she could not pass her use of force testing because of these limitations. That meant she could not carry any weapons including her gun. She also was limited in not being able to leave the station or go on the road. She could do the job of File Coordinator and that would be her role in all of their cases.

In a major case, there were three main roles that make up the investigative triangle at the top of major investigations. There is the File Coordinator who takes in all papers, interviews, evidence, officer notes, everything to be chronicled in Powercase and keep track of original documents and evidence for court. They also keep a running synopsis of the investigation as it proceeds and a million other things. Commonly referred to as "the paper bitch."

The investigative triangle also included the Case Manager who was Enoch. The third position was the Lead Investigator. Greg Bouchard would fill that role. This triangle would follow the case right through to the end. There were many other position like investigators, forensics, media relations, family liaison, civilian clerks, surveillance teams, warrant writers, etc. One person could fill more than one role. These positions were filled on an as needed basis. The triangle positions were considered permanent to the case.

Detective Lavric was thrilled by this prospect. "I can't wait to start this. I thought I would never get to do any investigating."

"Well, you will get a lot as there are only three of us and I expect you to use the phone as much as possible. You will also be doing witness interviews here at the station as well as writing warrants for us. It's the job of three people but I only have you to do all that. Are you up to it?"

"Up to this challenge? You bet," Sharon said enthusiastically.

That meeting had gone well. Enthusiasm sometimes trumped experience. He had spoke to Greg Bouchard by phone the night before. Greg would start in a few days. He would help Sharon set up their desks in a corner of the Major Crime Unit. That was starting to look like a mini bullpen with 8 desks in there. A bit cramped but Enoch felt it may engender some assistance to both teams. Fresh homicides always pulled everyone into them at first. All hands on deck. During lull periods, the Major Crime detectives may become interested and lend a hand on some of the cold cases.

Enoch had a simple philosophy he had learned from his homicide mentor. Homicides are like octopuses. In the beginning you reach out and grab everything you can to sort out later. Often there are arms reaching out from the main body of the case. They may be witness statements, tips or forensic followup. You deal with all of those and pull them into the head of the case where they belong. If they are red herrings or not relevant or belonging with the case, they still must be disclosed to the defence. In those cases, you follow them up and hack the arms off showing that there is no connection to the case. This prevents the defence from exploiting them as avenues not pursued by the police. It was a simple and good system everyone seemed to understand.

Sgt Phillips interrupted his thoughts bursting into the room excited. "There's been another one. This time there is a witness with a good description. I understand there is also another tag on the wall of this old house that's burning. The firemen saw it but aren't sure whether they can save it. It says, 'stop me before I do it again.'

"Get out there with your team and start a canvass. Get the description out to uniform right away in case they can spot this guy. Keep me informed and media relations. Go. Go."

Great, another arson. With likely the same suspect. With that taunt to police in the graffiti tag, Enoch knew it would not be the last. Very concerning.

Enoch's replacement Detective Staff Sergeant leaned in and said, "Thought I was you while you are here."

"You are. Sorry. Forgot my new role. Remind Tamara that you have the case and to call you. I would like to be updated. This one is a bit personal."

"No problem, Ewok."

Thinking about Greg Bouchard, Enoch knew he was a steady hand. He had 9 years in uniform and been a coach officer training rookies for 3 of those years. He had another year as a detective. Although he had been back in uniform for 2 years, he had worked a few major cases when he was in CID. He had been temporarily assigned to CID as a mentoring position for the year he was here. He would be a welcome addition to the team. Enoch had fought for and got him the treasured "clothing allowance" of $1000 per year to buy suits. This meant he wouldn't have to wear a uniform while he was assigned to the Cold Case Squad.

Enoch spent the rest of the morning going over a supply list with Franklin, the CID Administrative Assistant. He was very good at his job and had anticipated what the new unit would need. Computers, phones and supplies were already on their way. Enoch would work from his old office with the new CID Staff Sergeant as the room was large enough for two desks. They should be able to juggle the room when they needed privacy. All in all it had been a good day.

Enoch's next session was that afternoon with Dr. O'Brien scheduled for a little longer than usual. They spoke about the solved case. Enoch talked about later remembering feelings in those memories at the time of suspicion of Lee all along. But nothing tangible he could put into words. They decided to move on to another echo memory.

"You spoke about flashes of a school and a wedding, let's try that." stated Dr. O'Brien.

Following the same procedure as before, Enoch was placed under hypnosis and taken very deep with instructions to seek out that memory. At first as he remembered things he was very uncomfortable and mentioned being "unfamiliar in his skin." Getting to the bottom of that through a process of questioning, it was finally learned that Enoch was having an echo memory from Jane McDonald, who would later be Jane Brown, Enoch's mother. Jane was a Constable with the Ontario Provincial Police at this time.

Chapter 33 - 1969 - Hippies In School

I am Jane McDonald. I have lived in Sudbury all of my life. I am one of the first Ontario Provincial Police (OPP) officers who was a woman assigned to work uniform patrol out of the District of Sudbury OPP headquarters on Cedar Street at Paris Street. My dad was a cop, Rick McDonald, with the City police force. I always wanted to do this job. I was always a bit of a tomboy and did not take no for an answer when I wanted to do something. My dad was very proud of me. I had only been with the OPP for two years.

I was dispatched to a call in Waters Township across Highway 17 West from Lively. I was patrolling alone when I got this call and proceeded to drive though the City of Sudbury from Highway 69 South. The call was a break-in at Waters 1A Public School. I had been to the school to give talks to students about safety but I had never taken any call there before.

Driving into the parking lot beside the school, I observed it to be an all brick brown building. I knew the Principal's office was in the centre of the building at the front just left of the front doors. There were classrooms on both sides of the building with the gym in the centre toward the back. I had met the principal, Mr. Buchanan, a few times in the past. It was his first position as a principal having been a teacher for a few years before this job. He seemed nice and was easy to get along with.

I walked to his office. He met me at the door telling his secretary he would show me what they had. His office was small but had a desk with two chairs in front of it. There was a scent of pipe smoke in the air. His desk had a large ashtray and some files on it. There was a small bookshelf with several grade school text books and some history books. I noticed a picture of him, his wife and two small children. He saw me looking and smiled, "My wife and kids. Jordie is the oldest and just started Kindergarten here."

He told me the janitor had discovered the break-in this morning and called him. A side classroom window had been smashed out with most of the glass on the inside. I asked him if anyone had touched anything in that room and he told me no. The children in that class were in the gym. The people who did it had been in the classroom but also the rest of the school. Some basketballs were on the floor in the gym that had not been there the day before. The teacher's lounge was the real mess.

He walked me down to the classroom first. I noticed what could only be described as hippie slogans on the blackboard. "Down with pigs"; "Save the Earth"; "Suits Are Square"; "Kilroy was here". Well maybe the last one was just a regular slogan. There were rainbows from multi-coloured chalk drawn on the blackboard. There were a few other crazy pictures as well. I asked him to keep this room locked. Someone would come to take photographs and check for fingerprints.

Then he took me to the teacher's lounge. We met the janitor, Mr. Pukara, just outside in the hall by the lounge. He was quite upset someone had done this to his school. His sanctuary breached. The damage in the lounge was worse. Cans of paint had been thrown on the walls. The couch had been tore up by some kind of knife. More slogans on the wall about pollution and "Damn the Man." I told him this room needed to be locked too.

Mr. Buchanan explained to me that he had moved one item from a table in the teacher's lounge. It was in his office. "This is what I moved," said Mr. Buchanan as he pointed to a cassette player on his desk. "It has their voices on it."

He then pushed play and several voices could be heard talking and laughing. They sounded high. Lots of laughing and speaking nonsense. I lit an Export A cigarette as we listened with the office door closed. I started to differentiate the voices and identified a young woman and three young men at least. From the questions they were asking each other, the woman and one of the men knew each other while the other two were new acquaintances.

"You can see it was hippies by the way they talk," exclaimed Mr. Buchanan.

"I can. Have you had problems with young people or hippies before?"

"No. Just that time they had a protest over Meatbird Lake being polluted. They came here first to protest before they moved on to Meatbird Lake. They took their signs and left after a newspaper reporter got here and before the police arrived. I understand they did the same thing at Meatbird. Just looking for attention."

"Your grades go up to grade 8?"

"Yes."

"Any older kids in the classes? Maybe held back?"

"No. And before you ask there may be a couple of women teachers whose skirts qualify as mini skirts and are shorter than I would like and a few men teachers with side burns and longer hair, none of them are hippies," he huffed.

I extinguished my cigarette in his ashtray. He had opened a small window behind him and had his pipe lit.

I told him, "Just making sure I cover the basis. Can I take that tape with me?"

"Yes. Of course."

I used a cloth lying there to take it out and place it in an envelope Mr. Buchanan gave me. I asked him to speak to his students maybe in an assembly and should any of them have any information, to call me and I would follow up with them. At this point no one had reported anything to the teachers. I wrote my name and the report number along with the Sudbury O.P.P. phone number. I reminded him to keep people away from the classroom and teacher's lounge until the Identification Officer had been around to clear those two areas. Damage, mischief, a break-in and nothing taken.

The students were assembled in the gym. I stood on the small stage with Mr. Buchanan. The teachers were all there as well. I explained what had happened and that police were now investigating. If anyone had any information they should report it to Mr. Buchanan who would call me. I asked if anyone wanted to speak with me now, I would be around for a few minutes at the office. I told the students whoever had done this were gone now and not likely would they return. I told them this when I could see some of the younger students were upset.

After the assembly, I got into my police car. This was a strange one. Usually I would first consider students from the school or the local High School but the voices on the tape sounded older. I would head into the district office and write up my reports. I would speak to the Sergeant and see about extra checks on the school at night. I radioed I was heading to the office and pulled out onto the highway toward Sudbury.

I wished for the millionth time that our cars had AM/FM radios to listen to while we drove. Never mind the new air conditioning you could now get in cars. That would be great for the summer. My 1968 black and white Plymouth Fury had plenty of power and was a great car. It was getting near the time to change it over to a new patrol car.

They lasted 18 months maybe two years but by then they were finished, put up for auction and replaced. For now, I was used to driving it. It just lacked some newer comfort things. No extras for police. I heard the O.P.P. paid extra to have the AM/FM radios removed so we couldn't listen to music on patrol.

I was heading through Copper Cliff on Hwy 17 West when I saw two hitchhikers. A man and a woman. Young. Both sporting long hair and peace signs on their denim jackets. I stopped to check their I.D.s. The girl had long hair tied back in a ponytail. So did the boy. They were both 19 years old. He had a denim jacket, tie dyed t-shirt and blue jeans with running shoes. She wore a denim jacket with a short denim mini skirt and a white peasant blouse. She also wore running shoes.

"Hi, I'm Provincial Constable Jane McDonald with the O.P.P. Can I see some I.D.?"

"Did we do something wrong?" asked the young man.

"Well you shouldn't be hitchhiking but other than that no. I'm just checking up on you."

"We're okay," said the girl.

They both gave me some I.D. I ran their names and dates of births 10-28 and 10-29. I was looking for wants and warrants also to see if they had criminal records. His came back with a record for breaking and entering. She had no record. Nothing was outstanding on either of them.

I went and spoke to them for awhile and learned they were both from Waterloo, Ontario. They had been to Thunder Bay and were hitchhiking home. They had been in Salt Ste Marie a few nights ago. Neither wanted to tell me where they stayed last night. As we talked the voices got more familiar to me until I realized they were two of the voices on the tape. I stepped back to my police car and radioed for backup. Another car was already on its way to me. As the other police car pulled up, I spoke, "I am arresting you both for breaking and entering and mischief to Waters 1A Public School last night. Are we going to have any problems?"

"Aww man," said the young man I now knew to be Todd Drapper.

The young girl I now knew to be Tracey Hunter asked, "Can we get a lawyer?"

"Yes you can call a lawyer from the station."

I searched Tracey, put her in handcuffs and placed her in the back of my car. My backup searched Todd, handcuffed and placed him in the back of his car. We started to head in to the District Office. On the way, Tracey began crying saying they were just trying to find someplace to get married. It had to be the most beautiful spot in the world. They went to Thunder Bay because of the sleeping giant and Kakabeka Falls but they didn't like those spots. They went to Sault Ste Marie to the locks but it was too dirty. Now she didn't care where they got married. It had been a long trek.

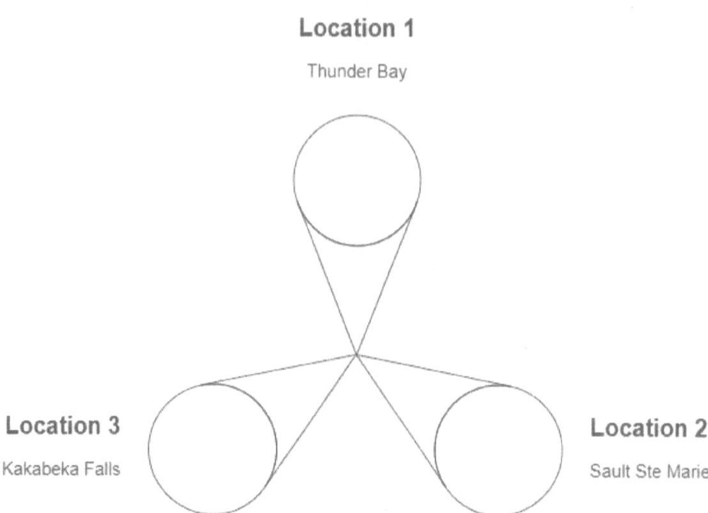

Tracey told me about the break in with two guys they met on the road. They were just going to stay the night to sleep but they got writing on the chalk board. Then they found the teacher's lounge with a couch and a couple comfortable chairs. They turned record on the tape recorder because it was such a "gas, man". After they played with it they must have left it on and recording. They talked all night and got high with some pot and LSD those other guys had. It was the other two guys who went crazy throwing paint on the walls and ripping up the couch she told me.

They left at dawn. They were still tired so they walked a little ways up the road to a playground. From the description of the streets they walked, it was the playground in Mikkola Subdivision. They lay down beside the clubhouse there and slept some more. They found a restaurant across the highway and had enough money for breakfast. They must have eaten at Anna's Restaurant as it's the only restaurant there. Then they had walked trying to hitch a ride until I stopped them.

It all came tumbling out. By the time we arrived at the OPP district office parking lot, my backup officer had radioed me he had a complete confession too. We got out of our cars and spoke. I told him what Tracey said. He told me that Todd had the same story and was also crying just wanting to get married. What a mess. We walked them both inside and paraded them in front of the Sergeant before we placed them into separate cells. They were yelling I love you to each other the whole time and both crying like babies. I think they might have still been a bit high.

I talked to the Sergeant about it then began my reports. I wrote on forms that had 8 copies for the Occurrence Report and Arrest Report knowing 5 of the copies would be ripped off and go in the garbage. My hand always hurt by the end for all the pressing on the pen I had to do so the writing would go through to all the copies. There must be a better way. I called Mr. Buchanan at the school. The Identification officer had been there and gone. The janitor was repairing the window. Some parents were donating paint to re-paint the teacher's lounge and a used couch would be coming as well.

I explained to the principal what I had. He did not know the names. I told him they did not know who the other two people were and we had no other information or witnesses. After a lengthy conversation, it was decided that I would just release them and chalk this up to youthful shenanigans. And no, he did not want them to come back to the school to paint the room. They could just go ahead, get married and get on their way.

I went to see the Sergeant who was with the Justice of the Peace. He was ready to remand them to the District Jail or release them on bail if I should recommend that. I told them what Mr. Buchanan had said. It was decided that we would let them go unconditionally. The Justice of the Peace offered to marry them. After checking with Todd and Tracey, they loved the idea.

I called over to City Hall and picked up the marriage license request. They were both ecstatic and filled out the forms. I paid for the marriage license and the Justice of the Peace waived his usual fee. They were married in front of their cells. The Identification officer had come in by then and took a polaroid photo for them. I was Tracey's bridesmaid and the Sergeant was Todd's best man.

They left us the short form marriage license to frame in the police station. The long form license they took with them. Once they were married, we sent them on their way. Mr. and Mrs. Todd and Tracey Drapper. It was my weirdest day yet as a police woman. I knew we would all take a ribbing for this but still, it made me feel good that something had come of the day that was positive. Sort of. I still didn't know who the other two were or how to find them.

Chapter 34 - 2024

Being brought out of his hypnosis state by Dr. O'Brien was like swimming up from the depths. Light got brighter, pressure ease. As Enoch awoke, he felt warm and happy inside. "Not so bad this time. No shakes. No sweats. No feeling like I just ran a hundred yards," he told Nancy.

"A much better memory. Not so exciting for sure. Almost routine. Did anything stand out to you?"

"Yes I did not feel right in my skin. It's hard to explain."

Nancy suggested that was because the echo memory was from his mother.

"From the personal history we did, I thought your mother was a Sudbury Regional Police officer?" noted Nancy.

"She was but before that she was with the O.P.P. I remember her telling this story at a barbecue and laughing about it. I remember my dad was more somber saying it was not so funny because the two that weren't caught had robbed a bank."

The Toronto Dominion bank on Frood Road had been robbed the day after the wedding in 1969. Two men who came in with a rifle and shotgun robbed the bank and fled in a stolen car parked around the corner. The man with the rifle had shot a teller in the leg to show they were serious. The teller lived but lost the leg. The guns turned out to have been stolen the night before in a house break-in that happened in Little Britain. City of Sudbury Police handled the investigation.

The two men not identified in the Waters 1A break-in were prime suspects.

By the time the investigation put together the break-in connection in the week after the robbery, the young newlyweds were long gone. They were not located again to speak with although they had already said they just met the men and did not know their names. The cassette tape was listened to in detail but no names were ever mentioned. It was very clear to anyone listening that the couple did not know the other two.

"I wonder if we could find the couple now?" mused Enoch.

"How old would they be?"

"Not sure. Let me turn on my phone for the calculator."

Nancy quipped, "Sad we can't do math in our heads anymore?"

"Can you?"

Guiltily she replied, "Not so much."

When he finished, Enoch said, "They would be 75 years old give or take a year. Not outside the realm of possibilities that they could still be alive."

"Are you going to follow the trail on this one too?"

"Yeah, I have to see how real these echo memories are for myself."

Nancy cautioned, "We still don't understand what is happening. There is another PBL session with myself and the other doctors happening next week. Have you been following your testing and scan appointments?"

"Yes Doc. And my physio but the therapist there said I could stop the physio now."

"Physio yes. But tests and scans no," ordered Nancy.

"That's about as much as we can do today. As with the other session, write out what you remember a few times a day until we meet again. You memory should recover more detail. This is more an exercise. It isn't a critical incident so much as a funny story."

Enoch headed to the office. Walking into the office he hung his coat at his desk and sat to check his messages and emails. After responding to some emails and returning one phone call, he told Franklin he would be in the Major Crime Room. Looking out at the bullpen seeing all the desks with detectives working, it made him feel great finally being back to work.

He walked across the hall to the Major Crime room. Now set up like a mini bullpen with four desks together facing each other in the centre of the room for his Major Crime Unit. Two desks at the back of the room facing each other for his Cold Case Squad. Two more desks facing each other at the front of the room for Enoch and Julie Cross, his civilian Powercase data entry clerk.

The Powercase data entry clerk worked closely with the File Coordinator to log and track everything coming into the case. They also worked on a running log of the investigation, notes from all meetings and synopsis of all statements. Plus a million other organization items and recordings. Enoch had always believed the Powercase data entry clerk should be the File Coordinator but the Ontario Police Act stated that the position of File Coordinator had to be a sworn officer. It was the File Coordinator who would assist the Crown Attorney at trial with the organization of the case, finding things and assisting with witnesses.

Enoch noticed his big 4' by 8' white board lay empty on the side wall next to a 4' by 8' bulletin board. While he was looking at the board, Detective Sergeant Andy Travis came in with a coffee. "Early bird, Staff?"

"Something like that. Where is everyone?"

"Julie's on her mail run. Sharon is down in HR to get some paperwork straightened out. Greg Bouchard for Uniform is here but in uniform. I told him to go change. He's in the new Cold Case Squad with Sharon?"

"Yes. That ok?"

"Yeah I worked on Platoon with him. He's a steady hand and knows what he's doing. Natalie is running a little late. Nick went out see the Crown before court." Natalie Lefebvre and Nick Torlone were on the Major Crime Unit.

"Well that explains the ghost town. I need a meeting with everyone. Can we do 2 pm?"

"Sure. All of us?"

"Yeah and also get the Bear and Janice Frieze down here. They are part-time assigned to us for Forensics."

"No problem."

"Say, did you hear about the O.D.s with the burn marks?"

"Yeah I talked to the regional coroner before my accident."

"No, I mean since then."

"No what about them?"

"We have 4 more cases. Now that we know what to look for we are finding them at the scene. So far, nothing. It doesn't look like homicides but someone is putting burn marks on the bodies. Three were in encampments and one was in an abandon building."

"Who is working these?"

"Tamara, she thinks it links to her arsons although she has nothing tangible to prove that."

"Okay. I am sure that she and the Staff Sergeant are on it. I will let them do their thing unless they ask for help. Hard not to jump on board something like this but they know what they are doing."

"I have to see the Deputy and Inspector before our meeting for a short briefing. Then we can have our meeting and everyone can get started."

Travis took his seat as Enoch began writing on one side of the white board, "Cold Case Squad" and "Major Crime Unit" on the other. Under "Major Crime Unit", he put "Groulx", a solved homicide they were still gathering information about, "Bertrand", an unsolved, unknown, masked suspect on a violent sexual assault that hospitalized the victim, "Thompkins", a missing person with suspicious circumstances from last year they were treating as a homicide. Under "Cold Case Squad", he put "Waters 1A".

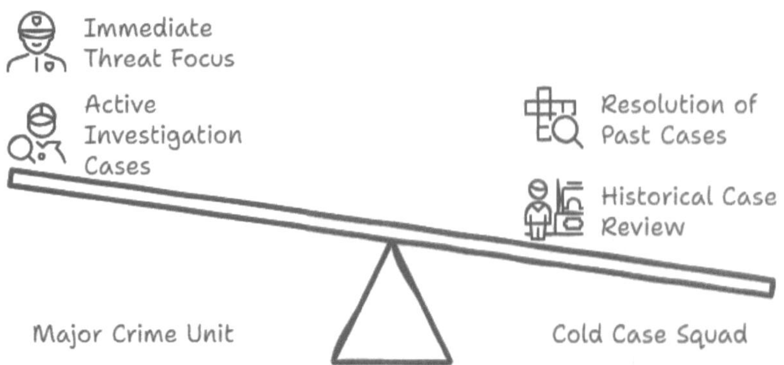

Comparing Current and Historical Crime Investigations

"New case already, boss?" asked Detective Constable Sharon Glass from the doorway as she entered the room. She rounded out as the fourth person in the Major Crime Unit.

"Yes I'll explain at our meeting this afternoon."

Travis asked if Enoch knew who their new File Coordinator would be as Jamie Scott had left on maternity leave. That would be Sharon Glass, Enoch informed him. Enoch finished then left for the supply room. He preferred to get his own supplies of pens, paper, etc. He also picked up some necessities from his old desk and brought everything to his MCU desk. He preferred a click fine point black pen for his notes. Always he used a yellow pad because he found the colour gave less strain to his eyes when he was spending a day writing on it. For his notebook he preferred the 8.5" by 11" police notebook issued to Detectives.

Enoch then went to see Inspector Townsend in his office before they're meeting upstairs. "Frank, how's it going?"

"It's going. How bout you Ewok? Ready for your first day?"

"Yeah. I want to hit the ground running. I have a project to start the Cold Case Squad on today. I have to go through some of the old unsolved homicides and suspicious missing persons. We have cases going back to 1972. I am hoping to narrow down to a few. If I see something that is essentially solved but needs more work before a charge may be laid, I'll give it to Major Crime like we did in the past. Right now I don't see one yet. The others are all the whodunits and will go to the Cold Case Squad (CCS) to see if they can organize and build on the past investigations. It's a lot of work but now I have a File Coordinator for Major Crimes, that helps. Thanks by the way."

"Don't thank me. The Deputy suggested it and he is giving me another officer for CID so it works out. My CID floor would have been striped. But this way I only lose one detective and fill out both new teams."

"MCU will help your detectives when we can. Newbies and walking wounded like I have for Cold Case is fine. They just need to be dialled in a bit with common sense. Both of them are. Julie will teach them and guild them into what they should know. The File Coordinator doesn't have to go out on the street. Travis can mentor young Bouchard. It will work out."

"That walking wounded, I'm already getting grief from the Association for having one."

"Sharon came from our floor so they can't complain about where we put her as she isn't taking anyone's spot and we aren't replacing her."

"Let's head up to the meeting."

Both men walked from the Inspector's office into the hall to the elevators heading to the fifth floor where all the magic happened.

174

<h1 style="text-align:center"><u>Chapter 35</u></h1>

The meeting with the Deputy Chief went about like Enoch expected. Happy with the resolution to an old case. Hopeful for future results on other cold cases. The teams being set up as they were provided some satisfaction for the accommodation of a light duty officer and a temporary detective.

Everyone was in the MCU room including the two Forensic officers for the briefing at 10 am. Julie Cross was assigned as scribe to take minutes of the meeting and create tasks from the meeting into Powercase. Enoch started with a quick introduction of everyone and their role. He advised the Cold Case Squad that all of their work would be done in Powercase only and not in Niche that was the report management system (RMS) for Greater Sudbury Police and that many other police services used. Powercase was used by all police services in Ontario. Normally case reports went into Niche RMS first and then into Powercase. For the cold cases they would skip that part and go straight to Powercase. He got a review from Travis on their outstanding cases and their actions moving forward.

Then he came to the Cold Case Squad. The CCS in the MCU. Everybody loves an acronym. "Waters 1A" was described as being a short case to start with that was the 1969 bank robbery of the Toronto Dominion Bank on Food Road. A teller was shot in the leg. The teller lived but lost the leg. Both robbers escaped. They were also suspects in a break-in at Waters 1A Public School where two other people had been caught. There were no available police reports or case files on the school but the bank robbery had a thin file. It was to be placed on Powercase so they all would have access to it. He also had a written report of historical information he had gathered, he didn't say how, about the break-in at the school that would be entered on Powercase. The two caught in the break-in were to be located and interviewed.

After the morning briefing, Enoch went back to his office to check his mail and speak with the new Detective Staff Sergeant who was taking over the floor. He found Staff Sergeant Stephanie Rheaume sitting at her desk on the other side of their shared office. "Stephanie, I'm glad you're here," said Enoch as he presented his hand for a shake.

"Happy to be here, Ewok. I was not happy to get the call to move up but it's worked out good so far. It may not be as temporary as I thought it would be."

"It won't be. CID is suppose to have two floor Staffs and an Integrated Crime Unit Staff for Drugs, Intelligence and B.E.A.R. (Break, Enter and Robbery Squad). We have been down since your predecessor was promoted and the ICU Staff retired. There will be two promotions in the next month.

"Where will they go?"

"Both uniform. We get you and Staff Sergeant Glenn Thibeault. He has experience in all three ICU areas as a Drug officer, Intelligence officer and BEAR Sergeant. It will mean more work off our plate. I will do Major Crime Unit and Cold Case Squad. In speaking with the Deputy this morning, I will also take Forensics and Cybercrime Crime/Offences Against Children. That leaves you with the floor, General Investigations, Sexual Assault Unit, Fraud Squad, Missing Persons and High Risk Offenders. When you get a homicide, assign a team from the floor and we will supplement them with Major Crime and Cold Case. Usually homicides are all hands on deck, especially if they are whodunits."

"We should grab lunch tomorrow and go through some of the personnel and the civilians? Who handles those?"

"I have the Powercase clerk and Forensics. You have the rest. They are all pretty good. Oh yeah and you have the Crimestoppers liaison. You don't have to worry about Intelligence analyst, that falls to the ICU Staff Sergeant. His office will be in the Intelligence office. Knowing Thibeault, he is usually with one of the units and on the street but if you need him, he's always a phone call away."

"That sounds well organized."

"Thank the Inspector for this division of labour. By the way, I wanted apologize to you, I butted in a bit on your arsons. They are personal to me since I was here when they were first coming in. I will try to keep out of them now but I would like to know what's going on and any help or advice I can give are yours."

"I appreciate that. We have just linked them with the O.D.s with burn marks. A note was found near one of the bodies. It was wet from the weather but they were able to bring it up so it could be read. It says, 'I have to mark the dead. Stop me from lighting the fires.'"

"Wow. Yeah, that would link them in my mind. Do you need help with that?"

"Not right now. We have a handle on all of it but maybe in the future. I may also need to tap your brain about this from time to time."

"No problem. I want to see this solved and stopped before someone gets hurt in the fire. Very weird, the burn marks. Something to check with ViCLAS for similar cases that may have been homicides. Also a good case for a Criminal Profiler and Geographic Analysis."

"The Intel analyst is doing the Geographic Analysis on the Rigel system. We had talked about the Criminal Profiler but wasn't sure. I will call the OPP and speak to one today. We hadn't thought about ViCLAS but I will have Tamara call them. Thanks Ewok. This is going to work out okay."

After some personal chit chat, they agreed to meet for lunch the next day to go over things in more detail. Enoch went to his desk and began a memo for the Inspector on the TD Bank Robbery as a first case. He also pulled up an old project file that had been shelved a year ago without result. Project Remembered was to open all historical missing person cases that had suspicious circumstances and were believed to be homicides to work them as cold cases. He wrote another memo to resurrect these cases and assign them to the Cold Case Squad. That was a start.

The briefing for ongoing cases with Major Crime brought Enoch up to date on their current cases. He gave out some assignments on Powercase but they were generally well in hand. He explained Project Remembered to both teams by way of an email. Cold Case would take lead with the investigations and Major Crime would assist when they could. He also outlined the TD Bank robbery in 1969. He assigned Sharon Lavric to find any paper files on the robbery. Sharon was to also liaise with OPP on the break-in at Waters 1A for any paper records they had. Julie Cross, the Powercase clerk was to add everything in to Powercase and create electronic files for the Cold Case Squad. Greg Bouchard was tasked with locating Todd Draper and Tracey Draper.

TD Bank
Robbery

Paper Files

Electronic
Files

Locating
Individuals

With everyone having tasks to do Enoch left them to their work to check with the Sudbury Police Museum to see what they might have for records or artifacts from the TD Robbery. Heather was able to check their database and learned there was nothing from the TD bank job.

"Would you have anything on the Waters 1A break-in?" Enoch asked Heather.

"No, we have some OPP stuff for Sudbury area but nothing like that. Did you say something before about the wedding?"

"Yeah just kidding. Well, two of the accused were married in cells by the Justice of the Peace after they were released."

"That rings a bell. I have to check in our storage room upstairs but there was a wedding certificate that was framed like a picture. I think it came from the old OPP District HQ. It was donated by a retired OPP officer who had worked there and had kept it when they moved to their offices on Highway 69 South."

"Could you look? It would be helpful."

Heather called an hour later when she found the wedding certificate. It had Todd Draper and Tracey Hunter as the names. Enoch gave those names to Greg Bouchard to help his search.

Greg reported that he had located a death certificate from the office of vital statistics in Thunder Bay and they were faxing a copy to him. He had confirmed the wedding. Todd Draper had died in a car accident in Winnipeg, Manitoba in 1975. There was no record of a death for Tracey. He called Winnipeg but they had no paper records for that time and nothing on their system for Tracey Draper or Hunter. He had called Waterloo to see what records they may have but there was nothing on their system. They were checking for paper records from 1969 onward but that would take time. They were advised it was in relation to a bank robbery.

Sharon Lavric found there were no records for the break-in with OPP or Sudbury Police. Sudbury Police Force did have paper records for the TD bank robbery including and an old occurrence report and several witness statements. No followup reports or police notes. Enoch had expected less. He knew that in those days investigators kept the file on follow-up reports with them. When they retired they took with them, their notebooks and files. Policy had tightened up greatly since then with officers not allowed to take anything with them when they retired but in those days retiring officers were told to clean out their desks and take everything not re-assigned with them and their notebooks in case they were needed for court. The file

Sharon had found was much more than had been expected. It was given to Julie Cross to put in Powercase and converted to digital files for the team.

Greg Bouchard located Tracey Hunter through Waterloo Police who had located her sister. Tracey now lived in Barrie, Ontario. Greg had her address now and a request to go interview her cold. Cold interviews are done with no advance warning, just a door knock. Enoch approved the interview and told him to take Detective Natalie Lefebvre from Major Crime to assist with the interview.

"Down and back in one day." Enoch ordered.

"Yes Staff," Natalie and Greg both replied.

They would leave tomorrow and call if they got anything significant. Until then everyone was to continue to plug away at their assignments.

Chapter 36

A call came at 2 pm from the interview team. They had an audio interview with Tracey Harper who had re-married. It turns out she did know the names of the two men they had been with in 1969 but didn't want to share that information with police at the time. Victor Unger about 22 years old then and Jude Parkinson also about 22 years old then. Sharon was assigned the names for background checks.

Victor Unger had been arrested for robbery on 4 counts for banks in the Ottawa area. He was convicted in 1975. He died in 1996 in Kingston Prison. A phone call to Ottawa Police learned that he had shot tellers in two of the robberies. He was suspected of having done more robberies out east and out west but they never had enough evidence. He received 18 years for his crimes. In 1984, he killed another inmate and received a manslaughter conviction for 10 years. He died of a knife wound having been considered a very violent prisoner.

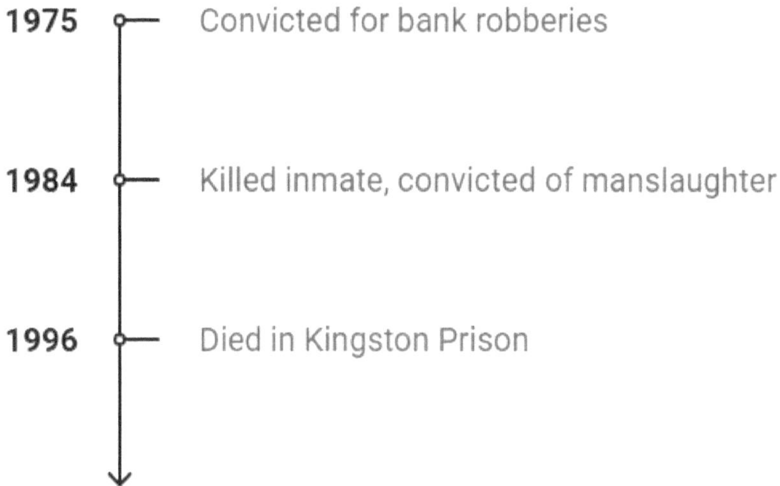

Jude Parkinson was found to have been charged in Quebec during the FLQ crisis for having bomb making material. He was convicted for two years less a day. When he was released at warrant expiry, there was a notation he intended to move to the United States. There was no further information.

"I have a call in to the F.B.I. to see if they have any files. I am waiting back on N.C.I.C." (National Crime Information Centre equivalent to Canada's federal C.P.I.C. - Canadian Police Information Centre). "I spoke to Intel and they are checking to see what they can find," advised Sharon.

"Okay," Enoch said, "Call those two in Barrie to hoof it home. No overtime but they can come in at noon tomorrow. Schedule a briefing for 1 pm tomorrow with our Cold Case team and Intel to see what everyone has learned about Mr. Parkinson."

"Anything else?"

"Yeah, Kingston Pen used to have the OPP Penn Squad. They investigated inside the prison and developed a lot of intelligence for police. Have Intel check with C.I.S.O. (Criminal Intelligence Service of Ontario) to see if we can access any of that information that may be there about Mr. Unger."

"Copy that."

"Then knock off and we will get together at 1 pm. I will see you in the morning."

Enoch finished checking reports on Niche RMS the police reporting system and new reports put into Powercase. He allocated tasks from the meeting or that he had given out during the day. He went to the gun room. A small room that had lockers like mail boxes in the post office. There was a counter in there with gun cleaning equipment. There as a gun proving station. This looked like a tube at an angle. You placed the muzzle of your gun in there and unloaded your weapon. There should never be an accidental discharge but if one should happen the bullet would stay in the proving station. You were doing this and thus proving the weapon safe when you placed an orange tag that went into the muzzle from the breach leaving a small orange piece sticking out. Anyone who picked up that gun would know it was safe.

Enoch put his trigger lock into the trigger guard, locked it and put it in his box. When the small door opened, a box was pulled out like a safe deposit box. The gun and ammunition were placed in there and it was all locked away. He did a quick check of the gun cleaning book to insure all his officers were doing their monthly cleanings while he had been gone.

Jackson walked in, "Sorry Staff."

"It's okay just checking the cleaning records. Maybe let everyone know I was checking so some of them might clean their gun."

"Sure thing. I have to tell you that these notes this arson guy is leaving are getting spooky. He says he wants us to catch him but he doesn't stop."

"He's taunting you. It's a behaviour that he will repeat with his crimes now for the attention."

As Enoch said this, he remembered back to his first arson death. The smell of charred meat. Puffs of ash everywhere he walked. He destroyed his dress shoes walking the scene that day. It was terrible but that was what he remembered. He also remembered he wanted to cry he felt so bad for the victim. But that was not going to bring the victim back so he didn't.

"You will get your guy. Leave no stone unturned in these cases. He will slip up and you will have him."

"Thanks Staff."

Enoch headed out to the elevator. He went out the headquarters side door onto the sidewalk for his 5 block walk to his truck. That was the closest free parking. The walk gave him fresh air, exercise and time to reflect on the day. Things were moving quickly. That was good. Some positive information from CISO and the Penn Squad may help them.

Chapter 37

The afternoon meeting the following day in the Major Crime room saw both teams sitting and waiting for it to start. There was some excitement in the room. Enoch went to the large white board and started the meeting announcing the start time as 1302 hours for the scribe minutes of the meeting. Then they went around the room. Greg Bouchard spoke first about the interview with Tracey Harper.

"Mrs Harper is a widow twice over. Her first husband Todd Draper died in a car accident. Her second husband, Chad Harper, died of a heart attack. She lives alone in Barrie but has children nearby. She was reluctant to speak to us at first. Then she opened up a bit. She told us about meeting the other two men involved in the break-in. She maintained that they did the destructive things like cutting up the couch and throwing paint on the walls in the Teacher's Room."

"But she gave you the names," stated Enoch.

"Yes, Jude Parkinson and Victor Unger. She gave a little more saying that she had run into Victor Unger some time later and he told her that the TD bank was robbed by him and Jude. He told her it was him who shot the bank teller. She was too afraid to come forward."

"Anything else?" Asked Enoch.

"No those are the high points. The statement is being transcribed from the audio recording and our notes have been uploaded to Powercase."

"Okay Sharon, you're up," said Enoch.

Sharon squirmed a bit in her chair as she looked at her notepad of information she had. "I called CISO first. They had an old intel report from Sudbury Regional Police Intelligence Branch about Jude Parkinson. It's a bit of a long story."

"That's okay. Take your time," said Enoch.

"In 1996, Jude Parkinson was located in Sudbury staying in an apartment with another man and two women. The man was a gun dealer in Michigan and friend of Jude's, Timothy Grant. He sold guns to Jude. Maybe I should back up a bit."

"Okay."

"I spoke to Michigan State Police who knew Jude very well and they supplied old reports they had on him. I also spoke to the F.B.I. and the R.C.M.P. They also had reports they have shared with us about Jude."

"Maybe tell us chronologically about Jude," suggested Enoch.

"Right. Well we have the Waters 1A break-in. Then we have the TD bank robbery. He is suspected in bank robberies out west. I am waiting for those reports. He made his way to Quebec where he was originally from. He joined the Front de Liberation du Quebec (FLQ) during the FLQ Crisis. I had to google that one. A bit before my time. They were a left wing terrorist group who set off bombs and kidnapped two men. One of the men was found in the trunk of a car strangled. It was a large group with different cells. Jude is believed to have been one of their bomb makers. Something he learned from his father who had worked in the mines in northern Quebec until he had an accident. Then he ran a small watch repair business.

Jude stayed with the FLQ until after the kidnapped man was killed. They call that Black October. He was arrested and spent two years in jail. He then fled to the United States. That was the last the RCMP had on him until reports he was in Sudbury in the 90's. The trail picks up in the U.S. where Jude seems to have hired himself out as a bomb maker for many different radical student movements against the Viet Nam war and other protests that turned militant. In Boston, he had an accident that blew all his fingers on his left hand off."

Andy Travis interrupted, "Was he right or left handed?"

"Right handed."

"Thank goodness."

Everyone laughed. Sharon continued. "He went quiet for many years. They believe he was underground doing whatever but in 1988 he emerged as the leader of a right wing religious cult. They had a compound in the Upper Peninsula of Michigan. The area is policed by Michigan State Police and a small Sheriff's Office, Clearwater Sheriffs Department. At this point, I finished with the FBI as they had little information but a footnote that Jude had moved back to Canada where he maintained his citizenship in 1996 and since then he has never returned to the U.S."

"The Michigan State Police had been aware of the cult known as the Mountains of Christ. They had assisted in a raid of the compound that included the Church, a quartermaster stores, some housing, shooting ranges, and underground bunker filled with all kinds of weapons including machine guns. These weapons were supplied by Timothy Grant. He fled to Canada with Jude in 1996. He returned to Michigan in 1997 and was arrested for the sale of illegal weapons. He spent 7 years in jail until he was killed in a prison riot. He did not give up any information about Jude."

"I spoke to the Clearwater Sheriff's Department as they were the hands on investigators of the raid the State Police conducted. It was due to an informant inside the compound providing information on the weapons they had. The informant was becoming fearful of Jude as he was beginning to sound more and more unstable. Before the raid, the informant disappeared. Jude and Grant fled to Sudbury with Sarah Somers who was the cult's bookkeeper and girlfriend of Grant. Also with Tina Wash an 18 year old follower. Tina was alleged to be Jude's girlfriend although as leader he was suppose to be celibate."

"Not so much though, eh?" added Travis.

Another round of chuckles. Sharon continued, "Sarah Somers returned with Grant. She was also arrested on warrants outstanding for theft and fraud as all of the cult's money had been taken when they left. She was arrest in 1997 and received 5 years in jail. When she got out she seemed to follow the straight and narrow. She died in a car accident while impaired about 3 years after she left jail."

Sarah Somers' Troubled Journey

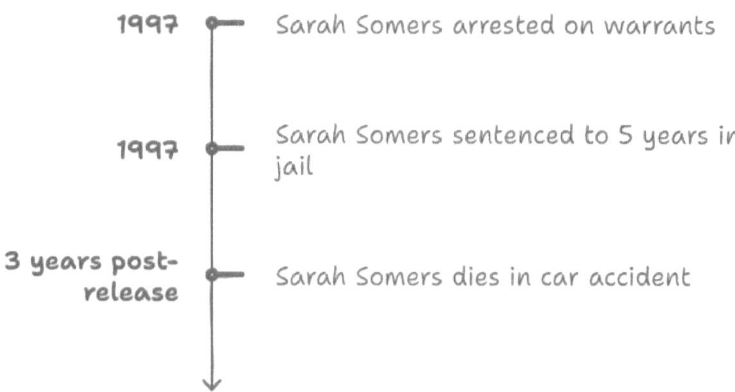

"That brings us to Tina Walsh. Tina's parents were part of the cult. They never heard from their daughter again. The last time she was ever seen was in Sudbury in 1996 by a police surveillance team. I have a call in with RCMP, Surete du Quebec and Surete de Police de la Ville de Montreal to see if any of them can locate Jude Parkinson for us."

"In 1996 when they fled Michigan and came to Sudbury, the landlord of the apartment was concerned as the group was strange and called police. The vehicle was flagged by Michigan State Police. The State Police were contacted and the Clearwater Sheriff's Department. It was decided Sudbury Regional would put them under surveillance. CISO has those reports as it was the Intel Branch that did the work and put their reports into the ASIIS 2 system for CISO. An officer there is getting the reports together for us to put into Powercase. He gave me the highlights. There was not much movement. The men stayed in the apartment. The vehicle never moved. The women walked to a nearby grocery store on Notre Dame to get groceries."

"Where was the apartment?" asked Natalie Lefebvre.

"On Kathleen. Not far from the grocery store."

"How long were they there," asked Jim Simon.

"Only a month and then they left at night by bus to Ottawa where we lose track of them. The car was left behind. It was towed and Forensics went over it for the Sheriff's Office but nothing other than their known prints were found."

"What happened to the car?" Asked Enoch.

"Not sure. It was towed by us. There was a note in the report that the car was treated as abandon when no one from Michigan wanted to come and get it."

"How the hell did they get an MLAT that quickly?" asked Greg Bouchard.

"No MLATs back then. We wrote a warrant to search with the information provided to us by the Michigan State Police and Clearwater Sheriff's Department. That's how it was done back then," responded Enoch.

M.L.A.T stands for the Mutual Legal Assistance Treaty. It allows for gathering of evidence from another county in a form that will allow the evidence to be legally admissible in the country making the request. At this time, MLATs may take up to a year to go through their processes. However, it makes sure the evidence has been obtained legally and will be admissible in the country that needs it. The old days were quicker but due to differing laws and rules of admissibility, often evidence was lost because of how it was collected.

"I'll have to figure out who has the records, if any, from the tow company at the time. They're no longer in business," said Sharon.

Enoch spoke, "Okay. Sounds like some great work with a ton of information for us. Let's keep fanning the flames and see what else we have."

"One more thing," added Sharon. "There were other disappearances besides the informant. The Sheriff's Office has 7 open missing person cases all linked to the Mountains of Christ cult. They believe most of them may have just left but none have popped up anywhere. The informant though, they believe is probably dead because of how quickly the four left before police raided the compound."

"Something to think about as we move forward. Anything we find that can help the Sheriff's Office, make sure we pass it on to them. Sharon you are our liaison to those agencies. Anything else? Any house keeping? No? Okay you all have new assignments given to you so check the assignment screens on Powercase. Meeting ends at 1415 hours."

Chapter 38

Enoch had meetings for the rest of the afternoon scheduled until 4:30 pm. He spend most of the time in those meetings thinking about Jude Parkinson. When he was getting ready to leave after booking off with the Communication Centre and locking away his gun, Sharon and Greg stopped him in the hall asking him to come to the Major Crime Room. Everyone else was gone for the day.

Sharon started, "I heard back from the OPP that they have some intelligence from the Penn Squad. There was a report that Victor Unger's cell was searched after he died. Inside they found notes about some bank robberies including a TD bank where a teller was shot in the leg. The other notes were about banks out west and in southern Ontario. The Sudbury bank job was not connected to it at the time as they did not know where that robbery had taken place. Now his notes seem to fit the Sudbury one. They are sending us everything. It looks like he was maybe going to write a book."

Greg added, "This leaves us with a stronger belief that Jude is the other robber. I called the Crown's office. They said unless there was tangible evidence like DNA, fingerprint, identifying video something they could use tie everything together, it was just a strong circumstantial case. You may lay charges with overwhelming circumstantial evidence and in this case we have reasonable and probable grounds, that is our threshold to arrest. The threshold they use to prosecute the case is higher than ours. They may proceed with an overwhelming circumstantial evidence case but not it cases of violence. There has to be something tangible they said. But they also said if Parkinson confessed, they would prosecute. His confession would tie it all together."

"Make notes of that consultation because we will hold them to that. What about Unger's notes?" Asked Enoch.

"Too vague they said but it would help corroborate any confession from Parkinson."

Enoch and the team knew they had to find Parkinson and alive if they had any hope of laying charges. Enoch said his good nights and told the Cold Case officers to knock off for the night. They had done a great job for two days work. He returned to his office to write an update memo for the Inspector to leave on his desk for the morning.

Enoch headed home. On the way home, he reviewed everything he knew in his head. He knew he could close the TD bank robbery case now without charges as "enough to meet reasonable and probable grounds" but not enough to reach a "reasonable expectation of conviction." The whole thing was frustrating to Enoch. These cases were so old that it seemed next to impossible to find evidence to link the crime to the criminals. He had to push for his team to follow whatever leads they could get. He felt responsible for his mother not taking the original break-in more seriously and his father not solving the bank robbery.

Now they knew it would not be good enough to just close the case. They had to try and get a confession to tie it all together for a charge. He would not lay a charge unless he felt they could get a conviction. That was his threshold. The decision to lay a charge or not was always in the realm of the police. They took advice from the Crown's office but the police made the decision. The decision to prosecute the charge lay with the Crown's office. The Crown could withdraw the charge if their threshold was not met. Enoch always made that clear to victim's when explaining why a charge would not be laid that it was his decision. When he made that decision to charge, it was when he knew he had a likelihood of conviction at trial.

In this day and age of 90% of cases being deals made between Defence and Crown, Enoch did not play with the adage, they're going to plead anyway. His cases had to stand the test of a trial. Otherwise, if the evidence was not a high enough standard he did not charge to go to court and lose or have the Crown withdraw the case. Any case could go to trial and he wanted to win for the victims, for the public, for justice. He did not close cases until every avenue of investigation had been exhausted. Even closed cases were never really closed as they could move forward if new information came to light. It was a tough standard but every detective in CID knew it and followed it as well.

Over the next three days, Sharon Lavric continued to gather information from different sources. She learned from the Surete that they knew that Parkinson had moved to northern Quebec in 2015 and then across the border in 2016 when his uncle died to take over a farm there. It was no longer a farm just a nice home and property. He had no visible means of support but seemed to live well. OPP in Matheson detachment had never had any problems or issues with him. RCMP had lots of early information on Parkinson but nothing more recent than 1972 when he left for the U.S. other than a footnote from the U.S. Border Services that he had returned to Canada and another report from SVPM that they had been requested to confirm he had moved back with his father in 1996 alone.

Lavric also learned from the SVPM that Parkinson had taken over his father's business in 1999 and that he ran the business until he sold it in 2015. It was mostly a jewelry store and pawn shop at that point. He had then moved out of the Montreal area. The farm in Matheson, Ontario was his last known address. A check on phone records showed a landline at that address in his name. He had a valid driver's license for Ontario at that address. He was now 79 years old with no living relatives as far as they knew.

Reporting all of this it was decided that Sharon brief Travis and Greg to go on a road trip. Enoch gave them permission to go to Timmins, stay in a hotel to prep for the interview and then attend the farm the next day to interview Jude Parkinson. They were to try and get Parkinson to the local OPP detachment but brought a video camera and audio recorder just in case. It would not hurt to use redundant recording devices in case one failed.

Travis and Bouchard left at noon to head to Timmins. It was a 3 or 4 hour drive depending on the weather. Enoch warned them that it could be a treacherous highway given it was more narrow than most highways. He also suggested they stay at the Super 8 by Wyndham on Algonquin Boulevard. It was outside the downtown but near the Timmins Square mall if they needed anything. He reminded them to check in with OPP when they got to Matheson and to call them now so they would know they were coming tomorrow.

In Enoch's mind, this had to work. It was the last lead they had on this bank robbery. Without a confession, this crime would go unpunished. He couldn't walk away or let his team walk away without at least trying to get a confession.

The drive to Timmins was uneventful save for watching a moose cross the road. A regular event on Highway 144. They picked up a 6 pack of beer and got their hotel room. Travis complained about having to share with a Constable as he was a Sergeant but Enoch told them if they both wanted to go they would have to share or he would find a Constable to go with Bouchard. It was a good night with a dinner out on the Police Service's dime then back to the room. Like studying for a test in College, they sat with the files on Parkinson and drank Corona beer as they planned how they would handle the interview. This time it was Bouchard complaining because he had no lime for his beer. By midnight they had their plan.

In the morning, driving in the cruiser, Greg Bouchard kept asking questions of Andy Travis who was driving about their subject, the case files and strategy for interviewing. Travis asked, "Greg, have you taken Forensic Interviewing at the Canadian Police College (CPC) yet or Strategic Interviewing at the Ontario Police College (OPC)?"

"I took Strategic Interviewing but not the other. Why?"

"Because I think you should do this interview. It's your case, you have done more homework on it than I have and it needs to be a one on one interview. I'll monitor and if you're not comfortable just step out and I'll step in."

"Really? All right."

"First big interview?"

"First international bank robber."

"Yeah well, just remember if he starts talking don't interrupt just follow his flow. There's lots we don't know about this guy. Who knows what he's going to tell us."

The rest of the drive was peaceful to the Matheson OPP detachment. They were met by a Constable on duty who showed them to their video interview room. They were still using DVDs but that was okay. Travis suggested Simon use his audio recorder too just in case. They were given the security code to get into the detachment in case no one was there when they came back.

They had a 20 minute drive to Parkinson's farm as it was called. There was a long driveway to the house with a barn in the back, a two car garage and some sheds. "How would you like to shovel this driveway?" asked Travis.

"Not on your life. He probably has a plow or has someone do it for him."

As they pulled up, an elderly man stepped out on the porch. He watched them park and approach the stairs to his two story white farmhouse with wrap around porch. The man was tall and thin. You could see fingers missing on his left hand. It had to be Parkinson. "Mr. Parkinson?" asked Bouchard.

"Yes, that's me?"

"Jude Parkinson?"

"Yes sir. You would be a couple of cops. I can tell from a mile off between your suits and that car."

"Yes sir. We are with Greater Sudbury Police Service and we came to speak to you about an old case of ours."

"You may as well come inside."

"Would it be possible for you to come with us to the OPP detachment. They have an interview room," asked Travis.

"Am I under arrest?"

"No, we thought it would just be easier. These days we use audio and video to record our interviews. You're not under arrest. In fact you can drive your car and meet us there," said Travis.

Parkinson looked to the sky and seemed to be thinking. Then he quietly spoke, "I guess that would be alright. I need to tell you I am not a fan of police. Never have been."

"We understand and appreciate your candour. We'll meet you there in 20 minutes?" asked Bouchard.

"Let me wash up so give me 30 minutes."

"See you there," said Travis.

They left and discussed whether he would show and if he showed whether he will have called a lawyer.

"If he calls a lawyer, he won't come. If not, he might. At least to see what we have to say," said Travis.

They arrived at the station. No one was there. They set up the interview room and checked the recording equipment. There were three chairs in the room so Travis removed one chair while Bouchard pushed the table into the corner placing a chair beside the table. He took out the other chair and brought in an office chair on wheels to be by the table. They made sure that there was a clear path for the subject to the door to allow him to relax. Everything was taken out of the room but a large file folder marked Toronto Dominion Bank Robbery 1969 was placed as a prop on the table so the subject could read the name of the file. The audio recorder was placed on the table. Everything else was removed from the room.

Bouchard was feeling very nervous as though this was his big test for CID and the Cold Case Squad. He caught his hands shaking and held them until it stopped. He remembered back to the first time he ever interviewed anyone. It had been a disaster but he had learned so much since then. He just wanted to do everything right.

Travis was happy to see that Bouchard knew how to set up an interview room. He would stay in the monitor room unless needed. Bouchard saw the car coming into the parking lot and yelled, "It's showtime," at Travis. He then walked to meet Parkinson at the door inviting him inside. "Right this way Mr. Parkinson"

"Okay."

Bouchard led him to the interview room pointing to the chair without wheels. Parkinson sat down. Bouchard picked up and turned on the audio recorder. He then said, "Thank you for coming. My name again is Greg Bouchard and today you can call me Greg. What do people normally call you?"

"Jude is fine."

"All right. Just so you know, I am a police officer, a detective with the Greater Sudbury Police Service. This room is video and audio recorded."

"Okay."

"I also want to make it clear to you that you are not under arrest. You are free to leave at any time. In fact, whenever you decide you want to leave you just let me know, get up and leave.

"Yeah, alright."

"I need you to understand that you can also call a lawyer at anytime. In fact, here in Ontario we have a toll free number that will put you in contact with a legal aid duty counsel lawyer who is free. Do you understand?"

"Yes."

"Do you wish to call a lawyer now?"

"No."

"I also want you to understand that everything is recorded and that anything you say may be used in evidence. Do you understand?"

"Yes."

"I want you to know that you don't have to say anything to me that someone else has told you to say because of threats or promises. I only want to hear from you today what you want to tell me."

"I understand."

"The reason I am here to speak with you is because of a break-in at Waters 1A Public School with Todd Draper, Tracey Hunter and Victor Unger in 1969. I also have some other matters to speak to you about but I thought we would start there."

"Yeah, I bet Tracey gave us up. She was a bit rattled over the break-in. Not a big deal. I did it and I'm an old man now so I'll pay any damages. I was the one who broke the window. Tracey and Todd drew stuff on the blackboard. Victor threw paint on the walls of another room and I cut up the couch with my knife in that room."

"Anything else?"

"Isn't that enough?"

"Well what about a machine of some kind."

"A machine? Oh yeah, there was a tape recorder Tracey was playing with. Don't tell me it was recording."

"It was."

"So many years ago. You guys are like the Mounties, always get your man. What am I looking at here. A fine? Pay for damages?"

"That's not up to me. I just gather evidence."

"Okay. Is that all?"

"No. Just give me a minute," said Greg as he moved the file around so that Parkinson could read it but it was out of his reach unless he stood up. Greg walked back to the monitor room and asked, "What do you think?"

"I think that he wasn't worried about a break-in back in 1969. He's done much worse. He's giving you the little things to seem honest and not hiding anything but he is hiding something. Better get back in there."

Greg walked to the interview room, entered and sat down. Now he moved his chair around to be facing Parkinson but still a few feet back from him. Greg started, "There is something else we need to talk about."

"Yeah, I read your file there. Toronto Dominion Bank 1969. That was Sudbury. Fuckin' Unger. I thought he was a stand up guy. Guess not."

Greg said nothing just let the silence hang until Parkinson spoke again, "Yeah we did that but Unger shot the teller. I told him after, that was a dick move. I guess I'm not getting a fine for that, eh?"

"Again I have no control over what will happen when it comes to something like that. If you want to call a lawyer about this bank robbery you can. This is a different event than what we were originally talking about. This changes the information we were talking about. It also changes your jeopardy, in that you will now be charged."

"No. I don't need a lawyer. Okay well you might as well get it all. We did 4 bank jobs out west and 1 in Ottawa."

Parkinson continued given exacting detail on the bank robberies. He explained them in depth. Each time it was a new case and his jeopardy changed for new charges, Simon would stop him and ask if he wanted to call a lawyer. Each time he said, "No."

Once Bouchard had all the details about the bank robberies he asked him about the Front de Liberation de Quebec (FLQ). He spoke about making mailbox bombs and pipe bombs. How they often targeted soldiers in scoped rifles but then didn't shoot them. Just to practise getting close and not getting caught. He talked about having been at the place once where they kept Laporte who was later found dead in the trunk of a car. His details were more hazy like he was almost bored. Again, Simon asked him after each crime if he wanted to call a lawyer. Each time Parkinson gave a clear no.

When he described getting to the U.S., Parkinson was much more relaxed and spoke in general terms of helping different militant groups by making bombs. His only time tensing was when he spoke of the accidental explosion that took the fingers on his left hand. He teared up a bit on that. He was much more detailed as though he had relived it many times. He found God at that point and moved forward with the Church. He joined a congregation of young people in a church called the People's Church. He stayed with them many years becoming a lay minister and then a minister. He got restless after the 80's. Their group had become more militant and self reliant. They had compounds in different states.

In the early 90's, he left and started his own church called the Mountains of Christ. He was the prophet at this point. He trained up a few lay ministers. They set up on a farm beside a State Park in the Upper Peninsula of Michigan at Clearwater. They recruited many people with money. This led to the Compound being built. There were bunkhouses, smaller homes, a store, a large church and sheds. The best part was they were secluded enough to have a firing range and built an underground bunker with an armoury.

Some followers lived at the Compound but many did not. They all kept to themselves about their religion that had a status as a cult. Many affluent people in the area belonged so money came in large sums. A friend of Parkinson was Timothy Grant. Grant was an arms dealer who supplied the church with guns. He was a shady character who always said he could get anything in Detroit. He had a store in Ypsilanti, Michigan but spent much of his time at the Compound.

Parkinson described how a married woman was their bookkeeper who started an affair with Grant whom she found exciting. When questions were being asked about the finances at the church, Parkinson knew it was time to move on and decided to head back to Canada skipping out on police, FBI, Bureau of Alcohol, Tobacco, Firearms and Explosives (ATF) and the Internal Revenue Service (IRS). He spoke to Grant who got them both fake ID's. Sarah Somers got wind of the planned exit and she insisted on leaving her family and coming along. Parkinson was sleeping with several women and girls in the Compound including Tina Walsh who was 18 years old. Tina found them as they were leaving and insisted on going along.

They crossed the border in a car registered to Grant with Michigan plates. They had two fake IDs and the women had real driver's licenses for Michigan. They travelled to Sudbury where they rented an apartment to figure out where to go next. In truth, Parkinson wanted to ditch the others and go back to Quebec where he was originally from to lay low and maybe retire from crime and church. He had the money to do that.

Parkinson talked about separating from Grant and Somers who he presumed had returned to the U.S. He said he didn't know about

Walsh. This seemed to be an untruth to Greg. He questioned him on it asking, "What can you tell me about what happened to Tina Walsh?"

"Nothing." Then silence of Parkinson who looked down at his lap.

"You have told me a lot today and I believe you. Now you seemed to have changed and I don't think you are telling me the truth. All I want today is the truth. I know more than you think but this is your decision to tell me the truth of what happened to Walsh."

Parkinson had tears starting and he began to weep openly. "I killed her," he blurted out.

Greg stopped to remind him they were talking about the murder of Tina Walsh now and if he wanted to call a lawyer he could. He said no and waived his right to counsel. There was a long silence then Parkinson began to speak low, "She just wouldn't go home. She wouldn't leave. I told her too much. Of course she knew about the money but she also knew my plan to go to Quebec and ditch the others. I don't know why I told her but I did. She was in love. I knew she would never leave. One night I had enough and just strangled her. The others were out. I had the car. I carried her body out in a rug from the apartment. I put her in the trunk. It was dark out."

"I had read a book once where a body was buried in a grave yard. I thought that would be good. There was one on the highway through Lively. I saw it when we went out that way. I remembered it because I saw it after we left the school all those years ago and Unger and I joked about it. There is a back road in and no lights. I had a shovel in the trunk I had taken from the landlord's shed. When I got to the cemetery there was a fresh grave. I could see the mound.

Convergence of Elements Leading to a Grave Digging

It was pretty easy digging. I buried her a few feet down. I even remember it was a woman's name. Fran something. Something like beer. I know it was Heineken. I was filthy when I got home. The others were still asleep. I washed and changed my clothes. I grabbed my stuff and all the money and took off. I didn't take the car. I walked to the bus depot on Notre Dame not too far away and caught a bus to Ottawa.

I made it home to Quebec and my father welcomed me home and into his business. After Sarah, I stopped doing anything remotely criminal. I really did love her. I was sickened over what I had done. It was worse because I was off the drugs and feeling more emotional about everything. I saved the money and cashed in a little at a time to make sure it wasn't all old bills. Eventually my father died. I kept the shop. His brother died. I inherited the farm and moved here. Now, I'm going to jail."

"Yes," stated Simon. "You are going to have to come with us to Sudbury where you will be charged with the break-in at Waters 1A, the TD bank robbery in 1969. You will be charged with the other 5 bank robberies by those jurisdictions. You will be charged with the murder of Tina Walsh. Is there anything else you can think of that I haven't asked you about but I should?"

"You didn't ask about the other bodies."

"What other bodies?"

"Never mind."

"You mean the missing persons in Clearwater affiliated to your church?"

"Yes. You might as well know I killed them as sacrifices and buried them in the State Park beside the Compound. There were 7 of them. All young with no real ties. Drifters."

"I have to remind you that this changes jeopardy for you again and you may speak to a lawyer."

"No. They will be easy to find. There was a pavilion and a hill above that. From the top of the hill you can see a big stone cross I had my people put there. The bodies are buried around that cross. I drugged them then strangled them. I did it as sacrifices to God. I was really messed up back then."

In shock, Greg asked if he wanted to add anything more. Parkinson said no and went completely quiet. Greg knew it was over and went to the monitor room after locking the interview room door. Greg was exhausted. At the monitor room there were three uniform constables and Travis. He had been in there for 4 hours interviewing Parkinson. It was quiet. "What now?" asked Greg.

"Now we take him home. I'll drive. You can sit in the back with Mr. "Sacrifice to God". Sanctimonious asshole," replied Travis.

While Parkinson was searched and allowed to call duty counsel at the 1-800 line, Travis called Enoch and caught him up on what they had. Enoch was stunned. He called the Coroner who had him call a Forensic Physical Anthropologist at Laurentian University to meet them at the cemetery in Lively. Enoch sent Natalie Lefebvre out to the cemetery to look for the grave marker. She called as they were on their way with Forensics to advise she had found Fran Heikkala not Heineken who died in 1996.

Tina Walsh's body was located about the time Parkinson was delivered to Greater Sudbury Police Headquarters where he spoke to a local lawyer and was lodged in a cell pending a bail trial in the morning at the Courthouse. Bouchard and Travis headed out to the cemetery where a tent had been erected around the grave. Inside the Forensic officers and the Forensic Physical Anthropologist were working to uncover the bones. And there were bones. A skeleton in fact only a few feet down into the grave.

Enoch spoke to them and they advised they would be here a few days at least. It was decided the bones would go to the Osteology lab at Laurentian University where the Coroner's Forensic Physical Anthropologist would come up from Toronto to assist. Also they were trying to get dental records and had a Forensic Dentist standing by to identify the remains if possible. All in all a great job. Enoch reminded the two to get their Crown Brief, bail sheet and other paperwork done before they left and to dictate their reports. He advised them to send the audio file of the confession to the transcribers so they could start working on it overnight. He told them he wanted them both in bail court in case they needed to testify but he had teed up the head Crown Attorney already and they were going to ask for three days to put it over for the bail hearing.

There would be lots of work still ahead including the Forensics, contacting foreign agencies, other Canadian jurisdictions to see what charges they wished to lay. He had called the Michigan State Police and Clearwater Sheriff's office. They were going out in the morning with the FBI to try and find the other graves. Sharon Lavric was about to have a very busy week, loading Powercase, handling filing for this case and keeping everyone up to date.

Enoch called Detective Staff Sergeant Stephanie Rheaume and Inspector Frank Townsend to update them on everything. Enoch received a call from the Deputy and then the Chief with questions. Everything was in hand and would progress by the book. The head Crown called back to ask to see the DVD in the morning as that was now the vital piece of evidence that would lead to everything else.

It was all for nought, Parkinson was remanded into custody to put over his bail hearing for three days. While in District Jail, he suffered a massive heart attack and died. There was solace for the Walsh family in Michigan as well as other families when the graves were discovered in Michigan. Both the Forensic Physical Anthropologists went to Michigan when the bodies were found to help with the recovery of the remains. A local dentist who had testified before on identification was able to identify Sarah Walsh from her dental records. Many cases were closed with the death of Jude Parkinson.

Enoch thought about all that had spiralled over time from a break-in to robberies, fraud and many murders. He felt sad that at so many points someone could have worked harder to catch these guys to prevent this domino effect leading to this tragic end for so many people. He felt guilty for his part. Even though it was an echo memory, it still hit him hard that it was treated so lightly with a wedding at the time.

Chapter 39

Enoch had missed several sessions with Doctor O'Brien and some of his brain scan appointments. During this time another PBL session had taken place. Cindy Thompson, the Administrative Assistant was present ready to take notes again and the first to arrive. Doctor Nancy O'Brien came in with a curt "good morning" as she sorted out her papers. Doctor Patton, Psychiatrist and Doctor Vince Dhwala, Neuologist arrived together. Both enthused to be there and went to the side table to get coffee offering a coffee to both Nancy and Cindy. Nancy declined. Cindy was happy for a cup. Doctor Hussain, Family Doctor arrived wearing his customary prayer cap and took a seat. Doctor Heather Martin, Psychologist came in very bubbly looking forward to hearing more of this case. Finally Doctor Emerson, Emerg Doctor and Doctor Hakkala, Neurosurgeon.

Doctor Sam Patton began the PBL session with a quick review of who was present and their specialty for Cindy's notes. He gave apologies for Janet Mack who was unable to attend. "I see everyone has the reports from Doctor Hakkala and Doctor O'Brien. Maybe we will start this session with Doctor Dhwala."

"Certainly. As you can see from the activity on the brain scans as we progress forward, there is an ever so slight slowing in the patient's firing neurons. This is still much too fast to be considered normal. His brain wave is still being seen as abnormal as well with some slight deviations. The parts of his brain lit up are still a kaleidoscope of light and colour we cannot explain. It does appear to be dimming. I think we are seeing his brain as processing at a slightly slower rate meaning he may be slowly returning to normal presentation," lectured Doctor Dhwala.

Doctor Hakkala spoke up concurring with Doctor Dhwala. They had spoken and were in agreement on this point although they were not sure this meant the patient was returning to normal, it did seem to be a likely prognosis with caution. Doctor Hakkala added he did not see anything in any of the cat scans, rMRI or dye tests they had run that would point to any need for surgical intervention.

Doctor Emerson asked if there was any way to accelerate the progress of the brain toward a normal presentation. "Not at this time," answered Doctor Dhwala. "It is just wait and see for now. We will continue to monitor in case intervention or some treatment is warranted but Doctor Hakkala and I agree the best approach from our perspective is to monitor."

Doctor Hussain asked, "Are there any treatments at all you would consider?"

Doctor Dhwala responded, "Have you a suggestion?"

"No I only wondered if there was anything else to look at from your perspective. In my experience, what you describe sounds positive and monitoring the patient who is progressing seems the best practise."

Doctor Dhwala nodded to Doctor O'Brien to go next. Nancy reported, "The patient, Enoch Brown, has been subjected to a number of tests including I.Q. tests, psych and behavioural tests even a polygraph examination."

"Did he pass?" Cindy quietly spoke as her eyes darted around the room still unsure if she was allowed to speak.

"Yes," grinned Nancy. "Detective Sergeant Jean Guy Degagne of the OPP, Polygraph Unit administered the test. He passed."

Dr. Heather Martin, Psychologist asked, "What was he tested on with the Polygraph?"

"It was whether or not the echo memories were real. Sergeant Degagne decided to use that term to give weight to what the patient is experiencing as the patient believes these are not his memories but memories of others. I have continued using that term with the patient"

"Who are the others?" asked Doctor Hussain.

"His recent lineage. So far, his grandfathers on both sides and his mother. There are other echo memories as well but we have not explored them yet. Perhaps I should explain how his treatment has progressed. Following the polygraph, Enoch went through Cognitive Interviewing and Cognitive Behavioural Therapy. This did help lessen the impact of some of the memories however, there was not the level of detail sufficient as there is with real memories. Next we tried hypnosis. This led to an extraordinary level of detail and recall on the memories. It was done on one memory at a time."

"Still, his memory you have read about in the paper of the 1923 shooting of his grandfather after a train robbery. It resulted in the patient searching for evidence and gathering the same to locate who shot his grandfather and who the inside man was for the train robbery."

"He remembered this?" queried Dr. Emerson.

"No, he had his memory of the time but it was through investigation of forensic ballistics today that he was able to determine it was another officer who shot him. This lead to their conclusion this was the inside man who had not been uncovered at the time. He did have a great level of detail but the solving of the mystery was done with today's investigative techniques and after the hypnosis session."

"His last session has led from a break-in at a public school in 1969, to solving several murders and bank robberies. Again he remembered the details of the investigation on the break-in but it was through following the thread of information that led him to discover these other crimes and who was responsible. As I am sure you are all aware of those cases in the news, we will dispense with discussing them."

"His level of memory during hypnosis is very detailed and always told by him from the first person stand point. If it wasn't experienced by the patient who is giving the echo memory, then he does not remember it except from conversations repeating what someone else has told him. The Cognitive Behavioural Therapy has helped lessen the PTSD and he does recover further memory after the hypnosis session as I would expect with a true memory."

Doctor Heather Martin spoke, "I have some thoughts on this after reading your session notes and everything else in the patient file from all of you."

"Go ahead," stated Doctor Dhwala.

"I think what we may be dealing with is a version of the "Clever Hans" Theory.

"What's that?" asked Cindy as she stopped writing in interest.

"For your notes, Clever Hans was a horse in Europe in the 1800's that was trained by his owner to do arithmetic. He could be asked complex mathematical questions and stamp the answer with his hoof. The horse became famous however, when studies were done on the horse and it was found that the owner did not have to be visible to the horse. However, someone who knew the answer to the question had to be visible. Clever Hans was very special as he picked up on physical cues ever so slight and when reaching the correct answer he stopped stamping his foot.”

“Today we know this as the “Clever Hans Effect” and it is seen with police dogs being trained for drug sniffing. If the trainer knows where the drugs are, the dog will read the slight cues of the trainer and stop at the location of the drugs. This is different but combine this with the confabulation of created memories, memory hardening theories we talked about before then it may be similar. The cues he is reading are from his experience and knowledge as a detective. Cues he has from stories he has heard from family and others for most of his life.”

“As a child, we know from his history taken when Doctor O’Brian and Doctor Patton first examined him that he comes from a cop family. The echo memories may be stories he has in his head and forgotten that now manifest as memory but may not be echo memories. They may be fabricated. He takes a cue from something he remembers as a child or teen, that then comes forward during hypnosis. He extrapolates the memory now and legend becomes fact for him.”

“Does it matter if he is solving the cases today?” asked Doctor Hussain.

“I would say no,” said Doctor Patton, “not really. He is finding forensic physical evidence to prove what his echo memory has told him.”

Doctor Hakkala asked, “Do we tell him this theory?”

“No, not at this time,” responded Doctor Dhwala. “I don’t mean to sound mercenary but this is an important research opportunity of something we have never seen before. It’s only a theory. Something we may prove or disprove depending on how he progresses and what our treatment and study of him show.”

Doctor Heather Martin weighed in, "I think you have to tell him something. Tell him we have a theory but we would like to keep it to ourselves while studying and treating him. If he consents, we move forward. If he does not consent, we stop. If he is okay with moving forward and not knowing our theory at this time, we are ethically okay."

Everyone agreed with this assessment. Nancy would move forward with this hypothesis in mind for her notes. Also looking for anything tangible the patient dredges up from the past memories. The meeting adjourned with everyone a bit excited now they had a working theory that may explain things.

The DNA sequencing lab was still working on the patient's DNA and had not gotten back to them. It was a U.S. company and it would take time. So far nothing supported the epigenetic theory of an ancestry gene. Nothing could be shown in the neurology except that whatever was causing the massive activity in his brain was minutely slowing.

Getting back to her office, Nancy called Enoch to schedule another session. He had been busy and had not attended the last two sessions they had planned. This was a bit of a worry for her. He advised her he would make time this week. She told him there were things she needed to discuss with him. Over the phone she explained they had a working theory. Due to their study of him, they would like to continue without him knowing what it was yet to prevent skewing the results. Enoch was okay with that and wanted to continue considering the success he was having in solving old cases.

They met two days later. The session began as all the others. The echo memory selected was one of fire, explosion, bikers, shooting and being trapped. It was very discombobulated compared to the other memories. Early on, Dr. O'Brien realized they were dealing with two memories one from his mother and one from his father in the same time period. She separated them for him while he was under hypnosis focusing first on his mother Jane McDonald and later they would discuss having a session with his father's memories.

Chapter 40 - 1975 - Biker War

My name is Jane McDonald, I am a police woman with Sudbury Regional Police. I was an OPP officer but I changed jobs in 1973 when the Sudbury Regional Police was formed. I recently joined the Grubbies really known as the Old Clothes Detail (OCD). I was partnered with another officer and they still considered this my training. I would stay for 2 or 3 years then back to Uniform. I would sometimes work with other Units like the Intelligence Branch and the Drug Unit. We sometimes even worked with the RCMP and OPP.

I was working an afternoon shift from 4 pm to 2 am with my partner and 2 Morality Squad detectives doing bar checks. Looking for underage drinkers, people smoking and selling drugs, checking licenses and capacity numbers for the fire department. A call came over the radio of shots fired on Durham Street downtown. We were on Lisgar Street heading up the alley toward Durham Street when I saw someone crawling around the corner. It was a guy I had arrested a few weeks before selling weed. He had blood on his leg and hands. He was fast crawling like an alligator for his life.

As we got closer I saw he had nothing in his hands. My partner was driving so I jumped out drawing my .38 Smith and Wesson Chief snub nose revolver. I ordered him to stop. He yelled at me, "They fuckin' shot me. Help."

"I said to stop. Don't move. Let me see your hands."

My partner called for an ambulance and a Sergeant to attend the scene. I passed the wounded druggie and peeked around the corner toward the Coulson Hotel. I saw no one on the street and no vehicles.

"Hey stop crying," My partner told the guy. "Who shot you?"

"I don't know," he replied. "But it was two guys and they left on foot toward Minto. I ran around the corner then fell down and crawled to the alley. I never saw them before and I can't describe them."

A likely story.

He was Tony Vincent, date of birth August 12, 1954. Currently on charges for trafficking for selling me weed in the Ledo Hotel bar. He had a criminal record or CNI (Criminal Name Index) under CPIC for break and enter, theft and drugs. A stellar citizen to be sure. My partner, Joe MacDonald, used Tony's t-shirt to stanch the blood on his wound. Tony was crying and appeared to be in shock. Joe gave out on the radio what little description we had and suggested since we came from Lisgar that they either ran all the way up Cedar Street or more likely into Memorial Park which was dark and not well lit. Uniform units attended there.

I stayed at the corner of the alley with my gun out to cover my partner and the victim in case the shooters returned.

"Hey Mick, you have quite the maternal instinct there," said the Sergeant as he pulled up in his marked station wagon Sergeant's vehicle with his window down smoking a cigarette. My short time as a Grubbie working with Joe has led to us both getting new nicknames that stuck. McDonald and MacDonald. They called us Mick and Mack. Too cute. I wanted to barf but you don't get to pick your nickname when you're a cop.

I said, "With respect Sarge, fuck you."

"Haha. You're too much Mick. The ambulance is coming. I'll have a car go to the General Hospital or Memorial Hospital as soon as they tell us which Emergency Room they're heading too," the Sergeant responded.

"It's 10 pm. Memorial stops taking new patients and closes their Emergency Room at midnight," I replied.

"Well they can tell us anyway before I send a cruiser."

"Speaking of time, pretty quiet for this time of night here. Like everybody left before we got here," said Mack.

I winced at what he said. "Why the fuck would you say the Q word?"

Sheepishly, my partner looked at me saying, "Sorry Mick."

Now we were jinxed for the rest of the shift. No good ever came from the Q word in any context. I just shook my head. Mack and I had been cops the same amount of time but all his time was with City of Sudbury Police and when they became Sudbury Regional Police Force, he became a Grubbie. So he had two years on me in Old Clothes and was training me. We worked well together and got along great.

He also knew my secret. I was seeing a Detective in CID.

Well… more than seeing. We were living together. Sergeant Francis Brown. Youngest to become Detective in the City of Sudbury Police. He was a Detective Sergeant when they became Sudbury Regional Police. We started dating right before I left OPP. By dating I mean I kept following him to the Frood Hotel. a well known cop bar at the time. It took me a while to get him drunk enough to take me home for a tumble. Then I snared him with my charm and good looks.

Our age difference had him sweating with him being 12 years older than me and divorced. He suffered more when I left OPP and joined

Sudbury Regional Police. He had a complete fit when I slowly over two years moved into his house. Members of the Sudbury Regional Police are not allowed to marry. We had to live in sin. An older man, divorced and a cop. I felt like such a modern woman trapping him. Hear me roar. He was a bit more settled now but he didn't want the powers that be to know we lived in sin.

Mack was great at helping me cover it but I think everyone knew just no one was saying anything. Not to protect me for sure. I was a girl stealing a man's job. But everyone respected Francis. He was a good man and a great cop.

"Here comes the cavalry," I pointed out the ambulance arriving. The attendants got out and loaded our guy up.

"We're going to the General. The Memorial is slammed and not accepting any more patients," the ambulance driver told us.

That meant everything tonight now would go to the General. I passed that on to the Sergeant who was talking to my wonderful non-husband, Sergeant Brown. Francis had been in the CID office when he heard us take the call and came out. Uniform officers were on their way to the hospital. It was one of the two doubled up cars downtown. That would leave a double officer and a single officer cruisers patrolling downtown.

I heard dispatch calling another cruiser in to assist downtown. Everybody else available working downtown was cruising around Memorial Park and past our alleyway. Ident arrived to take some photos and headed to the hospital. I walked the blood trail with Francis, never Frank, always Francis.

"He was shot here in front of the side door to the Coulson Hotel," Francis pointed out. The door was closed and locked. With a stripper bar, even on a Tuesday night it should be hopping. Francis banged loudly on the door. No answer.

Brick and Styles, two older detectives who formed the Morality Squad showed up to assist. They banged on the door yelling and the bouncer let us in. The detectives stayed to get statements. I told Francis I would see him later. I came out and my partner was there to pick me up.

Mack laughed, "Well, he'll survive so I guess you still have to go to court." I loved that cop gallows humour.

"I guess so. I haven't even got my pink court slip yet."

"We should get a bean. We deserve it. What do ya say Mick?"

"I say maybe a traveller. I want to cruise around for a while. There was no shell casing found so Francis thinks it was a revolver. Do we know anybody with a beef on Tony with a revolver?"

"Nope. Let's pick up coffee at the Tim Hortons on Lorne Street then do a drive around through Little Britain, the Donovan and over to the Flour Mill area. We can cruise past the Lucifer Soldiers Clubhouse and see who's parked there."

"Why them?" I asked.

"Because I think Tony was pretty open with his selling. He didn't know any bikers that I know of but he does know some guys in the Network."

The Network was a group of affiliated drug dealers who worked together to bring drugs into the city. They trickled drugs down to the dealers. They also provided muscle for their members. They didn't have a name but we called them the Network. Lucifer Soldiers was a local biker gang with 12 members. They were tough and we were always looking for ways to jack them up with tickets. They brought in a large amount of drugs for their affiliated dealers. Lately there had been chirping that the two were bumping into each other. Sudbury was getting too small for them both. The word around the station was that one might try and squeeze out the other.

Drug Distribution Cycle

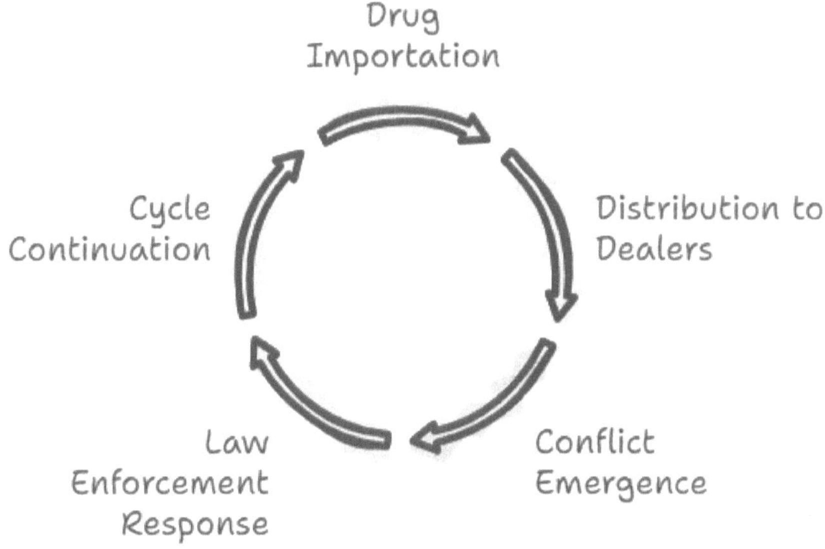

"Do you think this is the start of something?" I asked.

"Yep. He didn't shoot himself and Tony has been moving up since his drug charge. I hear he has runners now selling in the bars so he doesn't get popped by someone who doesn't look like police. And that means you, haha."

"Great so my big arrest gets Tony a promotion."

We picked up our coffee travellers then drove around until we ended up near the biker clubhouse in the Flour Mill. It was an old two story house they had converted into a booze can on the main floor and basement with bedrooms and an office upstairs. We had raided the clubhouse once since I got to Sudbury Regional Police for the booze can. It was a pig sty. Why anybody wanted to party with these guys was beyond my imagination except for the drugs and booze.

"Up the street the quaker is backed into that driveway across from the clubhouse," stated Mack.

He parked us around the corner and we went through some back yards to the driveway and knocked on the door of the van known as the quaker. It was a surveillance van with tinted windows and equipped with a tracker, cameras with long lenses, tripods and roomy in the back for 3 or 4 people. The side door opened opposite the side of the clubhouse.

"Mick Mack. What ya doing here?" asked Montel Halpern the Intelligence Officer who was also the techie for surveillance gear and specialist at bugging phones and places.

"Just passing by," replied Mack "What are you doing?"

"Got a call from Francis to come and set up on the clubhouse. See who goes in and out. They have a party going. I saw two guys come in from the alley on foot when I got here. There was some yelling and whooping when they went inside. It's been quiet since. It seems to be a church night for members only. I couldn't see anything other than dark shapes but I don't think these two were members."

"Do you think they're the shooters?" I asked.

Halpern said, "On a guess I would say yes."

"What did Francis think?"

"I talked to Francis on F4, portable to portable, Francis said there wasn't enough for us to go in but if they came out, everybody gets searched."

"Want us to stick around?" asked Mack.

"Yeah, my Sergeant is coming with all the drug guys plus horsemen and provincials. That should give us enough guys. Can you go and cover the other end of the alley near Notre Dame?"

"No problem."

"Is that coffee I smell on you two? You stopped for coffee? Where's mine?"

"We didn't know you were here," I advised. "Want us to go get you one?"

"No we better stay set up. The druggies will bring me one as they set up. No tailing. Everybody gets stopped and searched. No gun then Francis will try for a warrant to search the clubhouse. Church should be ending by midnight."

At midnight, they started to come out as a group. We had 5 unmarked units and a cruiser in the area by then. We stopped them all including two with new striker patches on. It looked like they were brand new and they were known to be dealers for the Soldiers. Strikers were probationary members who had to strike for one year doing scut work until they became full club members. Everyone was searched. No one was inside. That information was passed on to Francis who drove out to Copper Cliff to see the Justice of the Peace at his home to get a search warrant signed.

The RCMP offered to use a writ of assistance that allowed a search with grounds to then be written up after the search for the J.P. to sign. But it was only to be used for drugs and not guns. We were only looking for guns. We all had faith in Francis as a warrant writer and his creativity so no one doubted the warrant would come. The Soldiers' President offered us the key. Halpern declined telling him we would call him to come fix the door when we were done.

We searched the place top to bottom. We found a bar with lots of booze, small bags of weed, a little cocaine on the bar top. No one was inside and no gun was located. One of the drug officers issued the President a Provincial Offences Notice ticket under the Liquor License Act of Ontario for selling booze inside. We seized all the alcohol. The gang members were snickering the whole time. No one seemed upset about the search or to be jacked up. Halpern filled out Contact Cards on everybody and said he would put in Intelligence Reports on the new strikers. He photographed them with their small patches with a polaroid camera.

We cleared out. Francis had come to help with the search. When no gun was found he left for headquarters upstairs to the CID office at 200 Larch Street. I rode with Mack to the station to book off. I headed home wondering if I would see Francis tonight. I drifted off to sleep after a rum and coke. Tomorrow was another day.

Chapter 41

As predicted, I woke alone. Francis never made it home. I headed into the station with a coffee for him about 10 am. I dropped off the coffee to learn there was nothing new on the suspects. The victim was not talking, of course. They had taken the bullet out so we had that for ballistics. Francis was busy with reports and briefings with the Inspector in CID, the Deputy Chief and the Chief. I headed down to the Old Clothes office. No one was in yet. I finished notes in my notebook that I didn't finish the night before. There was a flurry of activity in the hallway with uniforms heading to the exit.

I asked what was happening. Another shooting with two people shot. Both in the drug Network. I went to my locker in the Old Clothes office. I grabbed my gun and cuffs. I headed out in one of our unmarked cars to Kathleen Street where the shooting happened. I was told by the Sergeant on scene to drive around to see what I could see so I did that. About an hour of driving I called it and headed to the station booking off there. Francis was in the Uniform Staff Sergeant Office.

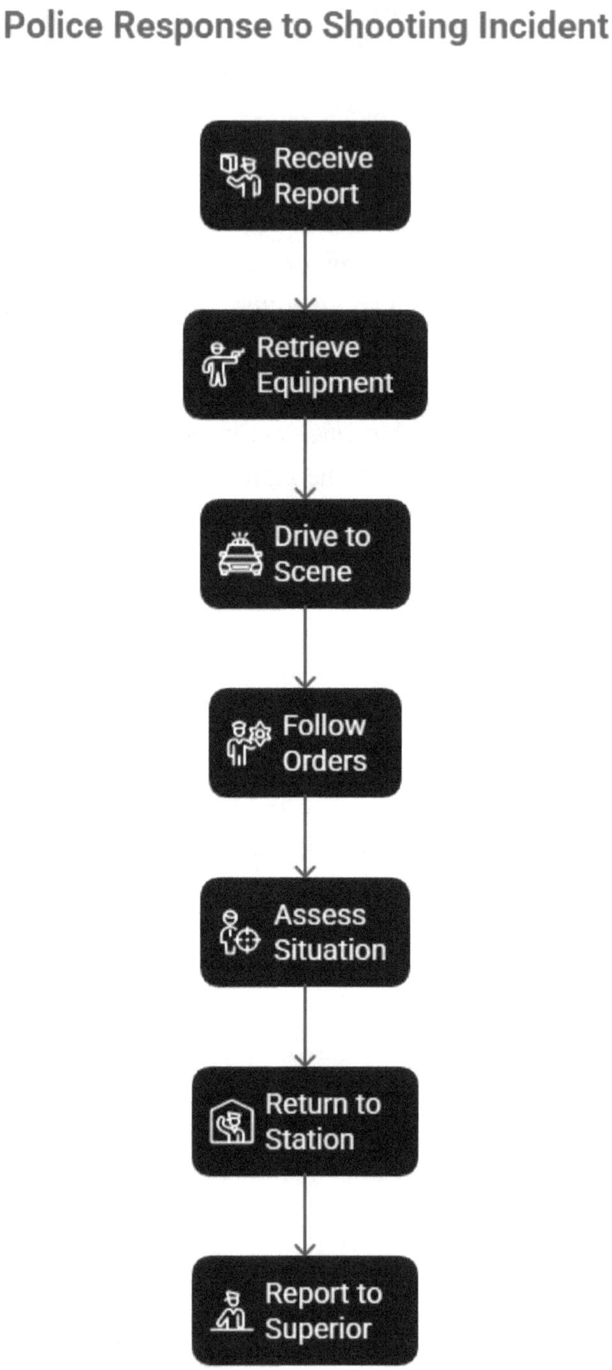
Police Response to Shooting Incident
Receive Report
Retrieve Equipment
Drive to Scene
Follow Orders
Assess Situation
Return to Station
Report to Superior

"See anything?" he asked.

"Nope. Nobody is moving around now. I checked the Clubhouse all in darkness. Need anything else?"

"Yes. Breakfast and a ride home. I'm too bagged to drive."

"Fuckin' boy scout," I said to the amusement of the Staff Sergeant. "The rest of us would just drive home and fall asleep at all the red lights until someone wakes us with a honk."

"Take him home Mick. He's had a long night," chirped the Staff Sergeant.

"Who's doing this one?"

"Nobody. Who cares?" proclaimed the Staff Sergeant.

"I'm doing it but neither of them will tell me anything. Ident is doing the scene. The doctors will seize the bullets for me and of course there are no witnesses. Pretty easy case. It would be better to find one of these guys dead. A dead victim can't fuck up my case," spewed Francis.

I could see he was tired and angry so I drove him home after a quick breakfast. He headed straight to bed. I headed back to work. My Sergeant was in the office when I arrived.

"You book on this morning?" he asked.

"Yep. Been to a shooting scene already."

"Anything?"

"Nope."

"Okay, book off at 8 tonight. Understand?"

"Yes sir."

"Brief me on the shit show last night and this morning."

So I did. As I finished, he was called to the Chief's office muttering, "This can't be good."

When he returned, he had news from on high. There was a project starting now to go after the bikers. Mack and I, 2 drug officers, 1 Intelligence officer, 2 uniform officers in plain clothes and my Sergeant are the SPIN team (mobile surveillance). Francis will be the CID officer with a detective yet to be named. We are to catch them at all costs doing something criminal and hopefully get one to flip on the others for the two shootings. Not much, I think to myself. A briefing was happening at 4 pm today. He was calling the others to come in for it.

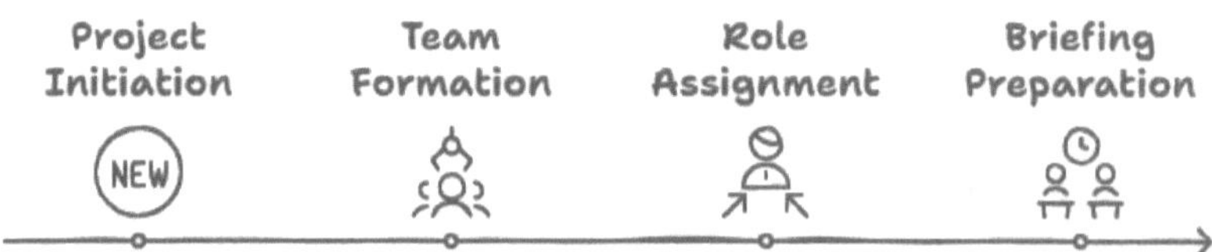

I took off and headed to the Clubhouse to set up static surveillance in my car. I brought the office binoculars to take note of who goes in or out. Halpern showed up about an hour after I got there with the Intelligence Unit's 35 mm camera with a 400 mm lens for me to get shots of people. Checking plates and taking pictures seemed like a fun day alone.

At 3:30 pm I pulled it and headed to the station. I had no photos and no plates. No one had been around while I sat there. The Old Clothes office was packed. Small to begin with it was now standing room only. I was assigned to work with Mack and the SPIN team with the 2 drug officers. We had the names and addresses of the new Lucifer Soldiers' strikers. We were to set up on them first. They were two peas in a pod apparently. I didn't know them but others did. They lived together in the Flour Mill not far from the Clubhouse. We set up on their neighbourhood with 4 unmarked cars.

At 4:00 pm, they left in an Oldsmobile station wagon with fake woodie paneling on the side. I had the eye being closest to the driveway and called it out. I followed for two blocks then turned off for Mack to take over. We kept changing who was following and the others staying far back, paralleling on other streets or taking them by the nose and leading them until they turned. By doing this they never got used to any one car behind them. They weren't doing any "heat checks" for police though. Just driving, talking and laughing. They parked on Elgin Street in front of the Prospect Bar. Our SPIN captain, one of the drug officers sent me in as the "dancer". That's a surveillance officer on foot. To follow them in and see what they were doing. I am the least known officer but it's still a risk.

I took a spot across the bar from their table with one chair at my table in a dark corner and ordered a Molson Canadian. I specified no glass. I don't like to drink out of a glass that has been washed in the same dirty water that's been in the sink for 2 or 3 days. It gives the beer a soapy, dirt taste. Never mind the germs. I prefer just the bottle. I sipped slowly knowing this one bottle had to last me the whole time

I'm here. One bottle is okay. Coming back to the office piss drunk is not.

The Prospect is well known as a biker bar, a wannabe biker bar, an "I'm an asshole who wants to show off and fight" bar. A large room with a bar on the side opposite the main door running half the length of the room. No fancy "Men Only" entrance and "Ladies and Escorts" entrance signs on this joint. It was dark, dingy and smelly. Stale cigarettes and spilled beer. There was a stripper on a small stage in one corner and it's her music we're listening to. One dance down to undies and high heels, one dance to panties, one dance on a small rug rolling and posing on the stage floor. Standard operating procedures for stripers. I hated the jokes I would hear as the "dancer" at the debriefing tonight.

I watched as our targets had supper delivered. Good. I hoped they died of food poisoning. One of them headed into the men's room. Well I was not following him so I stayed with the other. He was gone a long time. The other went to check on him. He ran out of the joint through the front door. This was not good. I went to the men's room and pushed the door open. Our target was on the floor bleeding. I tinned the bartender and told him to call for an ambulance. I ran out the front door. Mack pulled up. I told him target 2 was down. He told me target 1 peeled out of there and the others were on him.

"Who had the back door?" I asked.

"No one. We had two on the front and two floaters. There's no alley directly behind there to tuck in. Besides who uses the back door in this place?"

"The bad guy who stabbed our target. Tell the others, then radio for some uniform cars. Bring the ambulance attendants into the men's room when they get here."

I ran back inside. Holding my badge high I yelled, "Regional Police. Everyone step back. No one leaves. Clear out of the bathroom. There is an officer at the door so just take your seats."

"I have to get home for my sitter," the peeler tells me.

"Not today sweetheart. Today you're gonna be late."

I ran into the bathroom with towels from behind the bar and started packing the wounds. He was still conscious but crying now. He was slashed on his forearm, his leg was stabbed in the thigh and the knife I saw now was buried in his gut. I told him to stop moving.

He yelled at me, "Pull it out. Pull it out."

"No," I yelled back, "it has to say in. They'll take it out at the hospital."

The ambulance arrived to do their thing and load him up telling us this one was going to the Memorial and probably headed to surgery. Mack told me that target 1 went straight to the Clubhouse and had not come out. Members had started arriving there. Francis had been told and was headed to the hospital. Uniform officers had arrived. Five of them to take statements from everyone. Ident was on the way. I started taking statements too.

About an hour later, Francis arrived as we finished with everyone in the bar. Names, dates of birth, addresses, phone numbers and a brief statement. None of the statements were longer than a page except for the "ripper" who complained about that "cop bitch" who was making her late for her babysitter and what that was costing her. Pillar of society.

With Greg Joncas in surgery, that left Ian Harvey at the Clubhouse. Halpern went to the Clubhouse with Sergeant Urich to get Harvey who came in. He gave them a statement. I finished my reports during this and was sent home for some sleep. I was dayshift on the Clubhouse tomorrow for the day. I was not expecting much excitement but I was wrong.

Chapter 42

I pulled out of the station parking lot at 8:30 am to go to the Clubhouse. There were fire engines rushing by, lights and sirens. I tried to book on and was told 10-3 meaning only people on a designated call could use that radio channel. We had 4 channels. F1 was the Provincial channel to speak to OPP. It never worked but we could use it for the Comm Centre to see if the ladies needed coffee. It was not recorded. F2 was for District 2 that was in Valley East and another station where they had their own lineup Sergeant and patrolled outlying areas of Rayside Balfour, Valley East, Hanmer, Capreol, Azilda, Chelmsford, Dowling, Onaping and Levack.

F3 was the main channel for Sudbury, Walden and Nickel Centre. F4 was a channel to use with portable radios that we carried and from car to car. It had a limited range.

I switched to F2 and heard regular chatter. I booked on again as Oscar 3, my call sign. I was told to switch back to F3 and head to the Clubhouse for a fire. I stepped up my speed to get there quickly. I didn't want to tie up air time by asking what has happened. I could guess. Sure enough as I round the corner there were cruisers, fire trucks and an ambulance in front of the Clubhouse which was burning. There were people standing around and watching. I saw Sergeant Urich, parked and headed my way.

"Did you do this?" I asked.

"Don't even joke. Someone already said it was a Molotov cocktail thrown from a police car. I found the guy who said it and he was joking but that rumour is already started. Uniform have an eyewitness who saw a Molotov cocktail thrown from a pickup truck. Thankfully, none of our police vehicles are pickup trucks. Uniform is taking a quick statement of fact from him now."

"Anyone inside?"

"Not that we can tell. Comm Centre called Ian Harvey so we know he wasn't there. He was at home but said he is leaving to visit his parents in North Bay. We have their address if we need it. I think his striking days may be over. They called the Pres and he said no one should have been there overnight. Firemen haven't been inside yet but they will check for bodies."

I stayed around for a while then headed to the Park and the National Hotels, two bars on Notre Dame. The Network members often met there and discussed business. Both places were full of familiar faces. I know the Lucifer Soldiers haunt the Prospect and the Coulson Bars downtown as well as the Sorrento Hotel. Amusingly, they were all strip clubs. The Frood Hotel in the Donovan was a cop bar but sometimes there were Network people and bikers there. A neutral spot. The same with the International Hotel on Kathleen Street and the Laurentian Hotel on Lasalle Boulevard. Neutral spots. I checked them all and there were no bikers to be found but lots of Network dealers. Conversation stopped everywhere I entered.

I headed back to the station where I spoke with Francis. The fire was deemed arson. He had one witness who didn't see much other than someone throw a Molotov cocktail from a pickup truck that was dark blue or black or maybe green. Not much help there. Halpern came into the CID office to tell Francis that they had an informant who told them the Lucifer Soldiers were already set up in a new clubhouse using a two story house on St. Anne's Road near the police station. It was the President's house with lots of room. All the members were there now.

"Up to no good I'm sure," said Francis.

Halpern advised, "I'm meeting the project team now to make plans. Sergeant Urich is going to brief everyone on the fire and the new clubhouse."

I went along with Halpern and I briefed the Sergeant on what I saw at the bars. Within a half hour everyone was present and we were given our orders. Surveillance on the new clubhouse on St. Anne's Road and moving surveillance on all the bars where there might be Network people. We all expected the Soldiers to retaliate.

Chapter 43

Drug officers Desjardin and Salo were to be in one car. Myself and Mack in another car. The two uniform officers covering downtown would be in a plain car but in uniform. We would drive around monitoring the bars. Sergeant Urich and Halpern would set up on the clubhouse in the quaker. We would be on until 2 am that was one hour after last call. I told Mack he could drive tonight as I had a long day already.

Nothing happened all night. It was the Q word when we booked off. Everyone headed for home and sleep as we had orders to do this again tomorrow starting at 4:00 pm. I was happy to head home and find Francis already asleep. I made a sandwich for myself in the kitchen and ate it over the counter. As I headed to bed about 3 am my phone rang.

"Goddamit. Is that you Jane?"

"Yes who's this?"

"It's the Chief."

"What Chief? My Chief?"

"Have you been drinking McDonald?"

"No sir."

"Get Francis on the phone. I know he's there. You come straight in right now."

"What happened?"

"They blew up a goddamn cruiser is what happened. Just get in here but first get me Francis."

I woke Francis and told him what the Chief said. I got my shoes, jacket, gun, badge and handcuffs and headed out the door hearing a lot of yes sirs from Francis. As I got near the station and round the corner I saw flashing lights everywhere. In the side parking lot I saw a cruiser smoking. The fire had been put out and it was only the one car. Yellow police line tape was all around the parking lot. I saw the Chief and went to him.

"Sir."

"Jane. You awake now?"

"Yes sir."

"Good, take your unmarked car and check all the Network bars, the clubhouse and as many addresses for Soldiers and Network dealers as you know. Sergeant Urich is coming with the rest of your team but they'll be a while getting organized. I need to know who is throwing a victory party right now. Got it?"

"I got it. No problem."

I headed out checking all the bars first. All were closed. Nothing in the parking lots. I checked the new clubhouse and only the President's car was parked in the driveway. The lights were all out. I started checking Soldiers addresses first. By the time I had half of them done, the team was out and about. I let Sergeant Urich know where I had checked. He told me to continue after I picked up Mack at the station. The others would check Network dealer addresses.

That took all night. Everyone home in bed. Every light out. Nothing amiss and no parties held by anyone. It was dawn when I got back to the station with Mack. As we entered there was a flurry of activity near the Comm Centre door. The Uniform Staff Sergeant came out.

"You two. Get back out there. Head to Terry Fletcher's house. Fire Department is on their way there now. A car blew up in his driveway. Someone was inside. An ambulance has been dispatched."

"Okay," we both replied at the same time.

As we got there the fire was out. The car had the passenger door blown open. The driver's door was closed. There was someone going into the ambulance. A Uniform cruiser was on scene. I got to the cruiser.

"What happened?"

"Some kind of explosion. Terry Fletcher was in the car heading to work at Inco. A neighbour saw him get in and then a loud boom. The passenger door blew right off. He saw Terry crawl out the driver's side. He's burned up a bit on his right side. He can't hear anything right now. That's about all I have so far."

"Okay, give me the witness' information."

He did and then headed back to put up police line tape around the car now that the fire was out. The Fire Department was packing up. This car did not look as bad as our bombed cruiser. I heard another call on my portable radio. Another explosion at Brandon Tarkin's house. Another Network dealer. I radioed asking for details. Sergeant Urich responded that he had Salo and Desjardins heading that way.

I saw Francis pull up. "Another one just happened at Tarkin's house. That's two Network people."

"I heard," responds Francis. "You be careful Jane. These guys aren't fucking around."

"You be careful too."

"You and Mack head in and write up a quick report for me. Leave it on my desk then see Urich. The Chief has already decided what the plan will be for your project people."

"Aye aye." I yelled, "Hey Mack, let's go."

We both jumped in our car and headed to the station. I did our report up because of the two of us, I'm the only one that could type. I left it for Francis and we both headed to the Old Clothes office. It was packed again with people but this time the Chief and the Deputy Chief were there. The Chief was convinced it had to be the bikers. No big shock there. He had someone in CID writing a warrant to wiretap the phones of all Lucifer Soldiers homes and their new temporary clubhouse. He also wanted a probe in the new clubhouse to get conversations.

Halpern was the Intelligence Branch techie. He would do the physical taps with a bell employee. Mack and I were to sit on the clubhouse. Once we were sure it was clear, Sergeant Urich who used to work in Intelligence would come over to plant the probes. It sounded like a good plan to me. They were already calling in some officer's wives to listen to the wires as soon as they were set up. The Bell Canada building had a special room we could use for the wire taps. The probes would go to a voice activated reel to reel Marantz tape recorder hidden somewhere in the house. The tapes had to be changed regularly at least once a day. That would be hit and miss depending on whether anyone was in the clubhouse. We'd have to sneak in or break in without anyone knowing. No easy feat once. Even harder the more times you had to do it.

Mack and I were sitting up the street from the clubhouse. Sergeant Urich pulled up behind us. He jumped into the back seat of our car.

"Anyone inside?"

"No, the President and his girlfriend left and we've seen no movement," I told him.

"Okay we go in."

Mack asked, "What do you mean we Kemo Sabie?"

"I mean Jane and I. You watch for anyone coming and call us on F4. Okay?"

"Okay."

I got out of the car and met Urich on the sidewalk. We walked casually up the street to the front door. Urich used what looked like an electric razor with a short wire attached. He placed the wire in the lock and it buzzed until it unlocked. We both looked around with a touch of guilt and went inside. Our warrant granted us surreptitious entry to plant the probe. Urich planted the probe mic in the living room where we thought they would have their meetings. Then he ran a wire down the vent. He headed to the basement to hide the recorder. He told me to look around.

I walked around the main floor. Lots of beer in the fridge. Not much food. Lots of pizza boxes. I found some small bags of pills, powder and spliffs in a drawer in the kitchen. I headed upstairs. There was a bathroom and 4 bedrooms up there. Only one bedroom looked used. I checked the closet in another room and saw the hatch to the attic in the ceiling above a chest of drawers pushed into the closet. I wandered back to the hallway when Urich yelled upstairs "Jane."

I realized my portable was off. I heard a door slam. I looked out the back bedroom window and saw Urich climbing the back fence in the yard. I turned on my portable. Mack was on my portable saying, "Get out of there. They're walking to the front door."

I answered quietly, "I'm hiding inside the house."

I shut off my portable, jumped on the chest of drawers, pushed up on the hatch and climbed into the attic. I heard the door open and arguing between a man and woman about which one of them was to have locked the door. It was the President and his old lady. I was really scared now. I really needed to pee. I really felt alone.

The attic was like any house attic. Not finished with just the joists and insulation bats in brown paper stuffed between them. There was a little light from vents at the front and back of the house but not much. It was hot up here and dusty. I imagined rats and bats up there with me. I panicked and breathed rapidly. I talked myself down and got back to regular breathing. I knew I couldn't move around much or they would hear me. If I was quiet, I should be safe.

Chapter 44

Late afternoon, I heard the front door slam. I had been in the clubhouse attic for 6 hours now. My portable had been turned off. About 10 minutes later I heard a stage whisper, "Jane. Jane."

It's Urich's voice. I opened the hatch and climbed down replacing the hatch. "I'm up here."

"Did you hide under a bed. Why are you so dusty? You're covered in dust."

"I hid in the attic."

"Let's go we have to get out of here. I was already finished in the basement when they pulled up. I thought you were right behind me until I got over the fence. Mack told me you were hiding."

"I was always good at hide and seek. Not so good at sitting alone in a dusty attic balancing on the trusses. Ya know?"

"You gave us a fright. Halpern was down by the four corners. He drove through traffic like a madman to get here. There was nothing we could do but wait it out. We were about to have the Fire Department come over and pretend there was a gas leak in the neighbourhood to get them out of the house."

"That would have been okay. That attic was terrible. I could use a drink."

"I have a bottle of rye in my desk at the station."

"Did we get the probe in at least?"

"Yes. It should give us some information about their plans. We hope. Do you want to be the first one to go in and retrieve the tape?"

"Not a fuckin' chance."

I was trying to hide my hands but Urich could see them shaking. We got back to the station and he pulled a bottle of Crown Royal out of his bottom desk drawer. Mack brought down some cokes from the vending machine in the lunch room beside the lineup room. We all booked off and had a well deserved drink in the office. It would be a bad idea to go to a bar to let off steam in case someone overheard what we were talking about. The office was a safe space.

The Uniform Staff Sergeant stopped by to check on me.

"You should all be doing that in the sauna in the locker room upstairs. But I guess Mick needs it most and she shouldn't be in the men's locker room so… I was never here. Glad you got out okay Mick."

"Thanks Staff. Just a couple of drinks and I'm headed home."

I finished two drinks, told them I was okay to drive and headed home. I didn't like rye that much but I didn't want to mix drinks so I raided Francis' rye bottle when I got home. A few more drinks and I went to bed. First night with the wire room up and running with listeners taking in conversation on the phone taps. Francis would be there until there was no more chatter to listen to. I drifted off to sleep.

Francis woke me in the morning with breakfast. He was very happy. As we ate in the kitchen, he told me they had identified the bomber in a phone call. Manny Quint, a member of Lucifer Soldiers, was the bomb maker. He had been in the Viet Nam war and came back an asshole. He joined the Lucifer Soldiers as soon as he came home. He had been trouble ever since. It figures he had the know how to make a bomb.

Francis told me they also learned he used mercury switches so the bombs went off as the person got in the car causing the car to move which moved the mercury to close the contact. In the first bombing, the bomb was placed under the passenger seat and blew straight up. In the second bombing, the driver was only half in the car and was thrown from the vehicle. That's why both victims survived.

They also had chatter last night telling of a brawl planned for the Laurentian Hotel. Word had come to the Network that Lucifer Soldiers were planning to celebrate at the bar tonight. There was talk on the Network lines that they were going in there to stir things up. The Chief was aware. We were going to have night shift called in early for 8 pm instead of midnight and the paddy wagon available nearby. Once things kicked off, we would swoop in and arrest everybody. I thought it was a great plan.

I didn't need to be at work until 4 pm today so I had some free time. Francis did not. He was in for the planning session as was Sergeant Urich, and the Inspector who would be in command. The Chief and the Deputy Chief would be there too. I needed a little something from Francis after last night. I made him late and he had to take another shower before he could head off to work. I felt better and had drained my adrenaline from the day before.

When I came in for my shift, Mack, Desjardins, Salo, Halpern and I were told by Urich to report to the lineup room for a briefing. The surveillance team was to set up around the Laurentian Hotel to see who went in and out and to look for weapons. I was to go inside with a portable turned off in my purse. Mack would go with me so we could advise when things kicked off. I did not love this plan after yesterday. The room was large in an L shape with pool tables on one side and a long bar in the middle. There was only the one exit.

The uniform officers would be parked behind Apollo Terrace, a housing townhouse project on Lasalle Boulevard just west of thee Laurentian Hotel. They would have the paddy wagon and everyone would have a police car. The officers would double up with afternoon shift officers. There would be 2 two man trouble cars downtown that would take priority one calls only until we were finished. Our channel was to be F2 for all communications. We were to maintain radio silence in case someone had a police scanner, these new devices that could listen to our police radios.

Mack and I had a simple job. Watch inside the bar and call if a fight broke out then keep our heads down until help arrived. At least they weren't asking us to break up the fight alone until help got there. Small miracles.

I asked, "Can we have some beer?"

Everybody laughed. Sergeant Urich looked serious and said, "One beer each. That's it. Just for shade. And you're lucky I'm not making you share a beer."

Halpern yelled out, "Mack, don't forget to take Jane through the Ladies and Escorts door. Hahaha."

"Fuck off," I fire back. "I'm no lady."

More laughs from everyone. The tension was broken. The briefing ended. I went to our office with Mack and Urich to get ready for the night. Urich wanted us in the area from 6 pm but not to go in until some Network people or Lucifer Soldiers were seen going in. As soon as anyone from those groups went in, we were to be dropped off to go in. Why not drive up you ask? Well they didn't want to risk damage to an unmarked cruiser. Now that was funny considering we would be in the bar when things kicked off.

Chapter 45

I heard from the team that two Lucifer Soldiers had gone into the bar. Mack and I went in and saw them playing pool. It was Manny Quint, the bomb maker and Vern Cormier, the President. I had never had dealings personally with either of them. The same for Mack so we were reasonably sure if we stayed in a dark corner no one would make us. We had never done bar checks here. The drug unit usually did that as it was on their list of target bars where they might find someone holding a spliff or two.

"I'll get us a couple of beers," said Mack.

"No glass for me, just the bottle. I'll get us a table."

He got 2 bottles of Molson Canadian. I picked out our table and moved the other two chairs away so no one would try to join us. It gave a great view of almost all the bar. The bikers were playing pool and laughing. The place was not very busy for this time of night. That started me wondering. It wasn't long until more Lucifer Soldiers arrived in groups of 2 or 3, until the whole club with 12 members were there. They grabbed tables near the pool table. They were all wearing their colours.

About 10 pm, I saw members of the Network come in. They stayed standing by the doors. Two of them walked over to Vern Cormier to speak with him at the pool table. All the Lucifer Soldiers were watching what would happen next. Whatever was said, Cormier swung his pool cue across the back of one Network guys while the other Network guy picked up a beer bottle from the edge of the pool table slamming it over Manny Quint's head. There was a surge of colours as the Lucifer Soldiers ran forward grabbing the two. The one hit with the pool cue was yelling at Cormier who put his arms up for everyone to stop.

I ran to the ladies room with my purse. Inside I called on the portable, "Fight has broken out".

I shut the portable off and took my snub nose .38 Smith and Wesson Chief revolver out of my purse to tuck in the back of my jeans. I had a rubber band looped several times around the butt to keep it from sliding down my pants or falling out.

Back in the bar, I could see Mack hadn't moved and it was quiet as Vern and the Network man talked. Then Vern said, "Make a path."

The two Network guys walked out of the bar. Vern shouted, "Anybody not part of this should leave now. There's gonna be some trouble here tonight. Don't hang around the parking lot. Just fuckin' leave."

I looked over to Mack and he signalled with a nod of his head to the exit. We both headed out. Outside, cars were quickly leaving. On one side of the parking lot there were about 20 guys standing with chains, bats and pipes. There were a few bystanders from the bar who had walked across the street and but didn't seem to want to leave. We got into the lot between two cars and I turned the radio on again. "Fights gonna be in the parking lot I think. There are 12 Lucifer Soldiers in the bar getting ready to come out. There are about 20 Network guys armed with chains, bats and pipes. Mack and I are in the parking lot. Should we wait or leave?"

Radio Information

Mack's Signal

Presence of Network Guys

Presence of Lucifer Soldiers

Urich's voice came over the portable, "Get out of there."

I shut off the portable stuffed it back in my purse and we walked quickly to the opposite side of the road where there were others standing around. I saw the Lucifer Soldiers come out as one, with pool cues, knives and beer bottles. I didn't see any guns. The next moments were sudden. There was a pause as the two groups stared at each other. Then they begin to run at each other into battle with weapons held high. The fighting began.

I had nothing except my gun. Mack had a blackjack he inherited from his coach officer when he first started. He had that in his hand. I knew his gun was in a shoulder holster and was a full size Model 10 Smith and Wesson .38 revolver. The two groups were beating the shit out of each other. Swinging in close contact led to some hitting of their own people. I saw a few with knives on the biker's side slashing and stabbing. Some Network guys fell to the knives and didn't get up. A few bikers got head shots with bats and chains and also didn't get up.

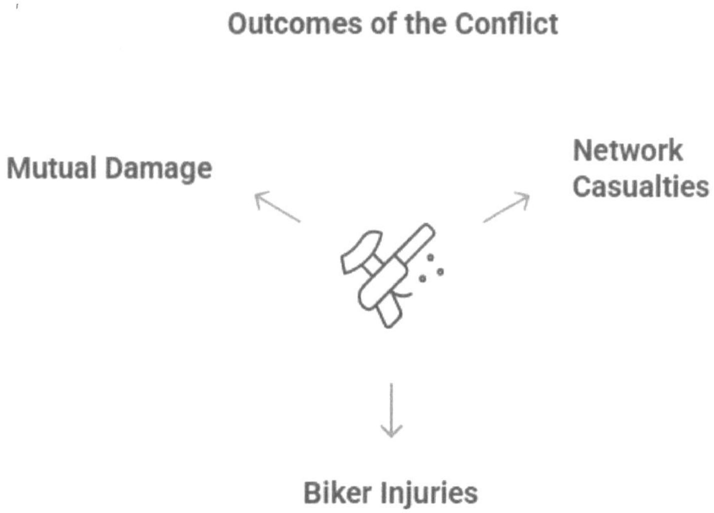

Outcomes of the Conflict

Mutual Damage

Network Casualties

Biker Injuries

Suddenly there was a gun shot. Then another. Manny Quint had pulled out a .45 automatic Colt 1911. I knew this would have 7 shots. Two Network guys grabbed his arm and the rest of his shots went into the air but his first two had found targets who were all down. Sirens were coming. Mack drew his gun and I held my gun up crossing the street we were both yelling,

"Regional Police. Stop what you're doing. You're under arrest." It was jumbled because we were saying the same thing just not in time with each other.

I saw a bat come down on Manny's head and he didn't move. I fired one warning shot in the air. That got attention. The lights and sirens of police cars pulling off Lasalle Boulevard onto Montrose Street got more attention. Those that could run did. Many were on the ground not moving much. I called on the radio, "District 1 this is Oscar 3. We need ambulances."

"How many Oscar 3?"

"All of them. As many as we have."

Cruisers had stopped on both sides of the Laurentian Hotel on Montrose Street, Lasalle Boulevard and behind the Hotel. Officers were jumping out and grabbing people to arrest. I told the Uniform Sergeant who pulled up to us that the people on the sidewalk were just witnesses.

The paddy wagon pulled up and officer's started chucking prisoners into the back not caring if they were Lucifer Soldiers or Network just as long as they were cuffed before they were thrown in. Mack and I ran over to help. The next wave of prisoners were going into the back of police cars. Both trouble cars downtown were advised on the radio to head to the station to assist with searching and booking in.

Ambulances could be heard coming from different parts of the city. They pulled into the parking lot and started to address the wounded. I could hear one of the ambulance driver's say that the Memorial Hospital Emerg was staying open past midnight for them and the General was opening a second Emerg for the overflow.

It probably had lasted no more than 5 minutes but what carnage. I could see two shot. A few with stab wounds. Lots with head trauma and the rest holding arms, chests and legs. I heard the radio advise those of us on scene that Sudbury OPP officers had been called in to go to the Emerg at both hospitals. Anyone still violent was to get an escort officer for the ambulance ride who was to stay at hospital. The rest were to 10-19 (return to headquarters).

Mack and I were detailed to take some statement of facts from witnesses on the side of the road and get everyone's information it case it was needed for later. About 2 hours later we were finishing the last of the witnesses who stayed. Mack said, "I guess we need to call for a ride."

I radioed headquarters, "District 1 this is Oscar 3. We need a ride to 10-19."

I hear the dispatcher say, "10-4."

Chapter 46

Arriving at headquarters it was like controlled chaos. Police cars everywhere. Cops standing around with coffee and cigarettes in the hallways, upstairs in the lunchroom and lineup room. The booking in area was clear. I was told by the Information officer at the front desk who was in charge of prisoners that it was a first for lodging prisoners the way they did it.

The police station was built in 1967 to accommodate the City of Sudbury Police. Then in 1973 it became the headquarters of the Sudbury Regional Police Force with the combination of all the police forces in the Region of Sudbury. When the cell block was built, it was recognized that with Inco having some pretty big strikes and other times of unrest, we may need to hold a lot of prisoners. They could not go to the District Jail until they were remanded there by the Justice of the Peace. Three J.P.s were coming in to do that and also do some bail releases as the D.J. did not have the staff needed to intake all these bodies. Some of the prisoners would be kept to go to a bail hearing at the court house in the morning.

The cell blocks were set up in two blocks with one block for men with 8 cells of 2 beds each. The other block was for women with 2 cells of two beds each. But the cell doors could be left open and the door leading to the cell blocks could be locked closed giving more room for more prisoners. There were 7 Lucifer Soldiers in the women's cell block and 12 Network guys in the men's cell block. It was loud with yelling, threats and taunts from both sides.

I was told by the Information officer that we were to write up a General Occurrence Report (GOR) and leave our statements from the scene. Then Mack and I were to go home. There was to be a debriefing tomorrow morning at 10 am and we were both to be there. I finished the report in record time and I left the mayhem to go home for a shower and a snooze. Mack stayed to shoot the shit with the Uniform guys. Officers on Nightshift were being rotated out onto patrol for the night as they cleared up their arrest reports with Crown Briefs and Bail Sheets.

No one had considered the Records staff. There were only two clerks. One dispatcher and the CPIC operator had all been pressed into typing service to help get ready remands and recognizance of bail for the prisoners. Remands went to D.J. and recogs got released. I didn't get out of the station fast enough. Sergeant Urich saw me. "Mick, you can type. Go into Records and help out until they don't need you."

Fuckin' great. I hated that I learned to type in high school. I hated that I'm a woman. I hated that I didn't haul ass out of the station faster and head home. I walked into the Records section, grabbed some briefs with notes on them as to whether they were recogs or remands. I started to type.

I crashed in my car for two hours sleep a block from headquarters. Mack woke me as he came in to work. We got to the debriefing just as it started to a round of applause. "Was it Mick or Mack who started the brawl last night?"

"Who do you think?" said Mack who pointed at me. He laughed as did everyone but me. I smiled and did a curtsy.

The debriefing went quick. I was asked to tell what happened from our perspective. Other people talked about their perspective. What went right. What went wrong. It was clear we could have had a better plan. But since no innocent bystanders were hurt and the damage minimal, it was still considered a win.

I then went to our office where Urich, Desjardins, Salo and Mack were sitting around. There was a "what now" vibe in the room. Halpern came in with his big voice booming. "Good news for us."

"Why?" asked Urich.

"You didn't hear? Dennis Hayes who was shot by Manny Quint just died. We have Manny our bomber for murder. The listeners in the wire room have Manny on the phone from the hospital to Vern Cormier who got released on a recog this morning talking about the two bombings and how Vern owes him. Manny wants to get out of town."

"Is there anybody with Quint now?" asked Urich.

"Yep but Francis just called me. He wants us to head out and arrest Quint. If he can be released from hospital we bring him here. I talked to the officer with him. Quint has a concussion but the doc said he could release him."

"Why the fuck didn't your boyfriend call us?" stated Urich glaring directly at me.

"How the fuck should I know," I fired back.

Halpern spoke, "Easy guys. You were all in the debriefing as we were getting these calls. We're all tired but who wants to come and show me how to make an arrest for murder."

"I'll go," I blurt out.

"I'll go," my partner Mack backs me up.

"No. I'll go with Mick," stated Urich. "I'm the one with his foot in his mouth that needs to apologize."

Enoch slowly swam to the surface and recovered from his memory. Nancy asked how he felt. He was okay. He was drenched in sweat again. It had been a roller coaster this time. He didn't know how to put it all into words. They agreed to leave it until the next session. They called it a day.

Enoch had a restless night. A bad dream about being stuck in the attic. Another dream about being hit in the head by a baseball bat. It was a restless night. He tried to remember more details that he could write out. He remembered the arrest of Quint at the hospital and Cormier at his house. They were both convicted in the bombings and Quint for 2nd Degree Murder after a lengthy trial that came down to bringing a gun to a knife fight. Cormier had died in prison of a prison fight. Quint had died of cancer also in prison but he lived for 30 years after the events of that night. Cormier's girlfriend had disappeared after they were arrested but she was not reported missing for a month.

It was a notorious case with a ton of speculation that the bikers had killed her because they were afraid she would testify against them on the bombings. The only evidence that existed for Conspiracy to Commit was against Cormier and Quint on the phone call. Sheila Jenkins could change that with testimony. It was a case that had gone unsolved since 1975. Enoch decided to look into the file.

As he arrived at work, he stopped at records to ask for the file on Sheila Jenkins. It was pretty thin. He was given an incident number for computerized records of followup information from the 90's and 2000's. He walked up to CID, told the Admin Assistant Franklin to hold down the fort. He picked up his mail and shut his office door. He began to read.

There was not much to go on. Sheila was home when police arrested her boyfriend Vern. They went back later to take a statement and she was gone. The neighbour saw her leave in a station wagon. She had a bag with her. There was a couple in the vehicle. The only distinct thing about the car was it had Manitoba plates. Sheila Jenkins was originally from Winnipeg. She had been married once before and had a daughter who lived with her parents. Francis Brown was the detective on the case. Despite all the rumours he concluded after a two year investigation that Sheila Jenkins had gone out west to re-invent herself or gone somewhere. He found there was no evidence it was murder. She would also have been charged with the Conspiracy and was unlikely to testify against her boyfriend. The couple in the station wagon were never identified.

There were many followups through the years with detectives taking up the case based on new information that was always just a hunch or a rumour. Nothing led anywhere. It was suspicious but many people testified against Manny Quint in the murder trial and none of them disappeared or were even threatened. The Lucifer Soldiers ceased existence in 1977. Over the years members had been interviewed who either said nothing or said they had no idea but it wasn't club business. The Network people were scattered and many still remained drug dealers but they were no longer united or organized. They were interviewed and had nothing to offer.

Inspector Franklin stuck his head into the office. "You're back?"

"Yeah, looking over the Sheila Jenkins' case."

"Why? Bikers did that. Is this a new case from your head?"

"Maybe but I don't have anywhere to go with it. I'm just going through a case review. Manny Quint and Vern Cormier were both in jail. I don't see the benefit to the others to commit murder. This couple she left with bothers me. There is nothing solid since she disappeared."

"You lost me with half of that. What are you going to do?"

"At this point it's not a case for my team. I don't even have enough to say it's a murder but I'll review it to see if anything has been missed."

"Good stuff. Anything for me to take to the afternoon meeting?"

"Nothing new on my end."

"How about the arsons?"

"We have had two more bodies with burn marks. Not homicides but overdoses. Another shed used to crash in was burned down. Same accelerant. The team has a sketch from a witness. It's tough going. I want them to write an ops plan for some surveillance rotating around the areas of the previous fires. My latest echo memory gave me that idea. We'll see if that gets any results."

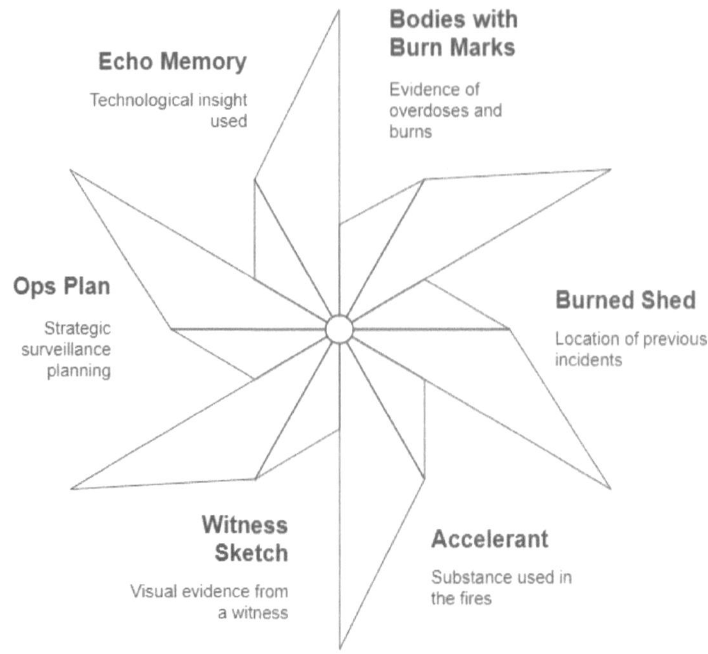

"How are you doing with all this?"

"The arsons are bothering me. They seem more vivid since the latest echo memory. I keep flashing to fires I hadn't seen before. I am just praying we don'e get someone dead in the fire. It's bad enough bodies are being mutilated by the small burn marks."

"I know what you mean. Kids play around some of those areas too. Get me the ops plan for surveillance and I will push it through."

"I will. Thanks."

"Okay. Keep going. These echo memories are turning into a gold mine for us in closing old cases and we're all looking good. I don't know if I believe it but as long as you're making cases, I'm all for it."

Enoch finished reading all the reports. Everyone left him alone that day as they could see he had sunk his teeth into something. The fires bothered him thinking about his first fire where he found that body. He didn't understand why he was smelling his first burned body at the biker clubhouse from 1975. He could feel the heat of hot smouldering metal from a burned car. It seemed to have ramped up his dreams and he took on these extra memories as though they were his. He reacted to them as though he had really been there. His hands shook as he thought about it.

At that end of the day, he went and spoke to the Missing Persons Investigator about the case. Enoch had a an idea about using family DNA. It was something that should have been done but he didn't see any reports indicating any DNA had been taken.

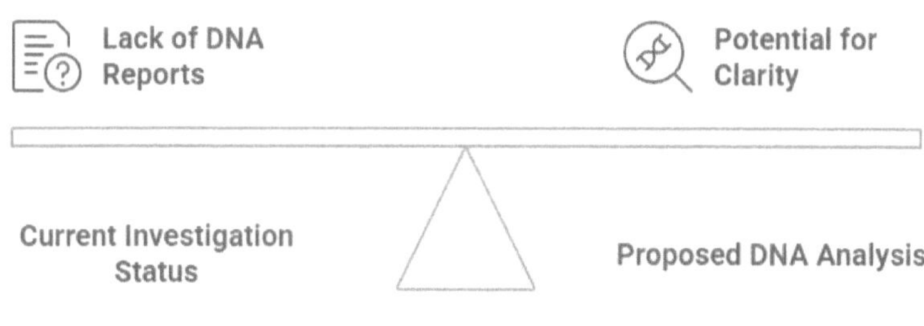

Evaluating Investigation Strategies for Missing Persons

"Nothing new on my end boss. You hear rumours but nothing pans out. I did put her on all the missing person social media sites I could find. My predecessor did lots of followup but that also went no where."

"What about DNA?"

"DNA? I don't know. I can check. We have collected it on some historical cases. We always collect samples with today's missing persons. I have a database that will tell me if it was collected."

"And was it?"

"Just a sec. Yeah my predecessor collected samples from her mom and her daughter in 2008. They were both still living in Winnipeg at that time. The daughter is still there but the mom passed away."

"Did the DNA go to the Missing Persons DNA databank that was started in 2017?"

"Ummm. No. Looks like we still have the samples."

"Damit. Call Forensics to have it processed in Sault Ste Marie at the Centre of Forensic Science there and then have the results uploaded to the databank at the CFS in Toronto. It will automatically cross reference with found human remains. Was she put on ViCLAS?"

"Yep. Looks like 2007. Put in by you."

"I remember now. It was when I got back from working at ViCLAS. I put one in for all historical missing persons. It was bare bones. Maybe call them tomorrow and check what they have. You can do an update if there is anything more than what is on there."

"Okay boss. Done and done. I'll send you an email after I talk to Forensics."

"Thanks. See you tomorrow."

Walking to his parked truck, Enoch reviewed what he knew about the missing person case and decided that it would be wait and see if it triggered on ViCLAS with any new information or triggered with the DNA databanks. He felt elated as there was a possibility of solving something so old or at least finding Sheila Jenkins to put an end to her missing for the family. Time to go home for a good night sleep. He had another session this week.

Chapter 48 - 1932 - Borgia Market

I am Sergeant Joshua Brown working for the City of Sudbury Police Force. I was a soldier in the Great War, a policeman with Coniston Police and now I am a Uniform Sergeant working dayshift. I am married to Molly, the love of my life. I love my job but there are bright days and dark days. Today was going to be a very dark day.

I came into the station and it was in turmoil. An officer passing me said the nightshift man did not come in. I asked who. It was Eli Walsh. A very dependable officer.

"Where's the Chief Constable?" I ask.

"In his office," came the answer.

I walked to his office. I poked my head in to tell the Chief I was about and had heard. He thanked me and said, "I told everyone to get out and look but they're just milling around. I'm sitting here trying to not be pissed at this circus but it's not working."

"I'll get them moving. He just didn't come in or is there anything else?"

"Nothing else."

"I'll get the boys checking the Borgia Market and the hotels downtown. He wouldn't have gone farther than that alone. Where's the other night man?"

"He went out after he reported it and now we haven't heard from him. Why did we put in these damned call boxes downtown if they don't use them."

"I don't know but we'll find him too."

I left the office and called everyone in the station together. I briefed them that I wanted them in pairs, with their whistles and to check in every hour by call box. I sent two to Borgia Market, two to check hotels, two to check boarding houses and cafes. I sent out our only car with two to drive the Donovan and Flour Mill neighbourhoods. Another two to grab a cab and do Little Britain then over to the new Gatchell neighbourhood.

"Talk to people," I said. "Someone must have seen or heard something. People don't just vanish. Tate was on nightshift as well. I understand he went out alone. Find him and send him to see me here at the station. Get out of those cars and speak to people. Those on foot, rattle door knobs and talk to people. I will be here or in the Borgia Market trying to talk to Lioness Marge. Off you go."

Lioness Marge was the woman who effectively ran the Borgia Market neighbourhood. She knew everything that went on there. If something bad had happened last night, she would know. Would she share that with me? That would depend on what happened and who was involved. She was not a friend of the police but she would help us if it was useful to her. Having a bunch of policeman scrutinize her neighbourhood was not useful to her so I hoped she might be of help here. That was how I would put it to her.

Four more men off duty came in to help. I put them on police bicycles to rove around the neighbourhoods on the outskirts of the downtown. Everyone was out but me and two men who were off today. No doubt they would show up when they heard. I had the map of Sudbury out and was ready to check off areas searched when the men started to call in.

It wasn't long until I could hear police whistles. More than one. That was not good. I ran out of the station with the Chief running behind me. The whistles were heading to the Borgia Market. As I got closer they were coming from behind the hotel and on Elm St. It was the alley beside the Regent Theatre on Elm Street between Lisgar Street and Durham Street. The Chief followed me in. The south side of Elm Street West.

Behind some garbage cans and boxes at the side door to the theatre was our Constable Eli Walsh with his throat cut and very dead. The second thing I noticed was that his gun was not in its holster. "Get the owner of the Regent Theatre out here."

"No one's in the Regent. It's locked up, Sergeant."

"Go find the owner and get him here now. I want that building searched and everyone working there last night brought to the station," advised the Chief.

The Chief began issuing orders to get the coroner out, put officers at either end of the alley. I suggested we put some more on Elm Street West to keep people back from even the edge of the alley as there would be a lot of curiosity.

"Do whatever you need to do. Use all the manpower you need. This is bad Joshua. This is terrible. He has no wife or family here but we have to notify someone," the Chief told me.

"There's a waitress he's been seeing at one of the boarding house cafes. One of the lads will know her. She should be told. I can do it."

"No Joshua. That's my job. You stay here. I think it's time we had ourselves a detective like the big city. That's you. I've been thinking about it for a while. This is your case. Whatever you need. Catch this son of a bitch. I don't care how. Understand?"

"Yes Chief. But what about someone else for the job."

"No you have experience and rank. You'll need both. Jameson is coming along fine. I'll promote him to Sergeant to take over your station duties. Your only job as of now is find this killer and bring him to justice."

"I appreciate your confidence in me Chief. I won't let you down."

I positioned men where I needed them. I sent a man to the local paper to get a photographer for us. I sent four men around to start talking to people in the nearby buildings across the street. I told the men standing post on Elm Street to start talking to the bystanders in case any of them knew anything. Then I started to look around the body as I waited for the coroner. There was a lot of blood.

The photographer arrived first. I pulled him aside to tell him he was working for the police right now. I needed photos of the body, the alley, around the body and some closer of the wound on his neck. I told him if any of these photos made their way into the paper, I would pull off his balls and feed them to him and the same for the editor. I told him he could quote me on that.

"No problem Sergeant. This is just for the police. I got it. I should have them developed by later in the afternoon," said the photographer.

More sedately I said, "Thank you. Tough day for everyone."

I let him carry on with his photos. He was done by the time the Doc arrived. He came with his black leather bag. He looked at the body shaking his head. "What the hell is wrong with the world?"

"I don't know Doc," I replied. "What do you think?"

"Well, he's dead. Bled to death. His throat is cut. No blood on the wall beside the body or blood trail in the alley."

"I noticed that too. Could he have been on the ground?"

"Very likely given the amount of blood. It should have sprayed out like a fire hose when the jugular vein was cut. Were you in the war?"

"Yes sir."

"See anybody with their throat cut?"

'Bad memories Doc but yes and I'm ashamed to say I cut a few."

"Get any blood on you?"

"Lord yes. Lots."

"Even if this was done with the man on the ground and the killer straddling him, there would be a lot of blood on the killer. If that helps."

"It does."

"I'll examine the body better at the funeral home. I'll go there with him directly and do that. I can say he has a big bump on the back of his head. It may have happened in a fall or he may have been hit by something."

"Like what?"

"Don't know. That piece of wood laying a few feet back from the body would do the trick. Let's see it."

I picked up a 2 x 4 about 3 feet long and handed it to the doc. He pointed to one edge. "See here? Hair and blood. I think your man was unconscious when his throat was cut. He wouldn't have moved around much then."

"Damit." I whispered. "He didn't have to be killed if he was down."

"Probably unconscious or stunned enough for the killer to climb on him and cut his throat. This is very bad Sergeant. Who do I give my report to?"

"To me Doc, it's my case. I'll brief the Chief or we can do it together if you like."

"Together would be good as I'm sure he'll have questions. I saw that photographer leaving. You got photos?"

"Yes but not the bump on his head or the piece of wood."

"Get him back for those photos and photograph the spot after the body is moved so we can see what's under him. Okay?"

"Yes I'll send someone to fetch him back."

"Mortuary men are here. I told them they would be needed on my way. I'll go with them and start right away. You want to be there for the post mortem?"

"No but should I be there?"

"Hard to say. I'll leave it up to you. I know you have your hands full with everything. Maybe send the photographer over when he is done here. You should really get a camera and someone who knows how to use it on your payroll."

"Good idea. I have a man now that can gather fingerprints. Maybe he can learn."

"Yeah ain't modern science wonderful."

"Thanks Doc. I'll stop by in a while at the mortuary."

I left the alley and spotted Constable Jenkins who was our fingerprint man. We sent him all the way to Toronto to learn how to take fingerprints. He started a library of our local criminals when they were arrested. He still wasn't used much at crimes. Not everyone believed in fingerprints but I did.

"Jenkins," I called, "come here."

"Sergeant."

"Get your gear. I want you to look for fingerprints. There's a 2 x 4 in the alley. Take it but be careful it has blood and hair on it. I want that preserved. Don't lose any of it. Got it?"

"Yes sir."

"Then use your best judgement to look for fingerprints. I'm not sure where to look or what you'll find but do the best you can."

"Yes sir. Right away."

Off he went toward the station to get his gear. I detailed 5 men to cover the scene. One at each end of the alley and three on Elm Street West to keep people back. I saw Constable Tate running toward us. Tears streaming down his face. I caught him by the waist and pulled him into the doorway of the Regent Theatre. I shook him to get him to look me in the eyes.

"Steady there, Tate."

"They killed him."

"Who killed him?"

"I don't know. But he's dead I was told."

"He is. I want you back at the station now."

I detailed a man to take him back in the car that was there now. I looked around at the crowd and everyone was staring and somber. I didn't see anyone running or even moving away as I stared at them moving my eyes back and forth slowly. The guilty ran, I knew that. This was a terrible day. I started to walk to the mortuary on Paris Street.

In the basement of the mortuary I found the Doctor Puri and the mortician. They had the clothing off the body in a pile on a cupboard. "Those are for you," indicated Doctor Puri.

"Thanks Doc. Anything new?"

"No. Hit behind the left ear on the back of the head. Likely unconscious when the throat was cut but still alive. He died of exsanguination. Means he bled out. The thump to the head must have hurt but he was unconscious after that. Never felt the throat cut or bleeding out. Means he didn't suffer."

"How do you know he didn't become conscious and try to get up?"

"There would have been blood spraying everywhere he turned. No. He was unconscious and never regained consciousness."

"Anything else you can tell me?"

"No that's the short of it. I will write a report and bring it to the Chief's office this afternoon. You can take his clothes. There's a bag for you to take them in. His gun is missing from the holster, did you see that?"

"I did. We searched the alley for it and the trash cans but couldn't find it. I think it was taken by the killer."

"Better check his pockets and clothes for anything else missing."

"I will. Thanks Doc."

"I'll see you this afternoon, Sergeant."

I gathered up his things. I could feel change in his pants pocket, his whistle was on his lanyard over his shoulder and in his upper chest pocket. When I checked his right pants pocket, there was no blackjack. All the officers were issued one so I would have to search for it. We had his nightstick already. It had been on his belt and looked to have fallen out of the holder when he fell or during the struggle.

If there was a struggle it might have been two men. If no struggle then it was probably one. Hit from behind. No rips or tears for the clothing. Only his blood. No marks on his hands, wrists or forearms. No bruising or scraping on his knuckles could be seen. There was nothing disturbed in the alley except the 2 x 4 and Eli Walsh. If there was no struggle it was likely one man. The blow to the head seemed to have been from behind by a left handed man. The cut to his throat the Doc had told me was a left handed man in front of the body or rather on top of the body.

I had a little more information but I was still unsure how a detective would investigate this murder. I decided I would go back to the station and issue some assignments. I would just do what I think is right and hope for the best. At lunch time, I would pay a visit to Lioness Marge to see if she would talk to me. If she didn't, that would speak volumes and I would have to pressure her business enterprises to get her to talk to me.

Lioness Marge had gaming houses, brothels, some boarding houses and lived at the Nickel Range Hotel. She was known by everyone. I knew that the opium dens that had sprung up this last year were all hers. We had yet to raid them but now might be the time. Also some of her booze cans and pool halls. There would be hell to pay as she was a force to be reckoned with but if she wasn't helpful, that was the route I decided to take.

I updated the Chief. I learned that Eli had just asked his waitress to marry him. She went home distraught with another waitress. I learned she had no idea who would hurt him. He hadn't talked about any recent problems with anyone at work. She had last seen him last night when he went in to work.

I detailed some men to go out and see if they could find anyone on the beat route he would have walked that saw or heard anything. Then I went to see Constable Tate. "Tate, how are you doing?"

"The Chief gave me a shot of whiskey and my nerves are settled. I still can't believe it."

"Where were you last night?"

"I was on my beat. I saw Eli a few times in the night. We had a coffee at the cafe on Durham that stays open all night and supper there about 2 am. I didn't see him after that."

"Any problems last night?"

"Nothing. All was good. I rousted a few drunks to go home. I shut down that new pool hall in Borgia Market and issued them a ticket for being open after midnight. I moved along a couple canoodling in an alley. I know him, he's married and it wasn't his wife. They left. Nothing else really. When I came in to the station, Eli had missed our morning breakfast. I thought he was there with a prisoner maybe but he wasn't there. No one knew where he was. I reported to the Chief when he came in and then I went out to look for him."

"Who had Borgia Market last night?"

"I did. Eli was doing the Elgin to Paris, Van Horne to Elm beat."

"Was that normal?"

"Yeah. Well I mean we switched around every set of Nights. It makes the beat more interesting to change it up."

"You have anything out of the ordinary happen last night?"

"No."

"What about the last time you did the beat he was on last night?"

"No. Nothing. But…"

"But what?"

"Eli did have something when he was on Borgia Market last time. He warned me about a guy named Jari Punkari."

"What about him?"

"He had a run in with him that came to a pushing match. Eli had to pull his blackjack and cold cock him. Another guy knew him and helped wake him up and took him home so Eli didn't take him into the station even though he was drunk."

"Okay."

"The next night he ran into Eli again calling him a cheat and a coward for using the blackjack and said he would get even. Eli told him, the next time he saw him, he was going to arrest him. That was it. Eli said he was a blow hard but to just keep an eye for him because he was a trouble maker too."

"You need to go home and get some sleep."

"I have my second wind, Sergeant. I want to help."

"Alright. Grab somebody to go with you and hunt down this Jari Punkari. Bring him in so I can talk to him. If he doesn't come peacefully, arrest him and drag him here. We'll figure out why you arrested him after you get him here."

Tate left on his assignment. He seemed very focused. I only sent someone with him to have a cooler head there. Even though I wasn't sure there were any cool heads on the police today. Definitely Mr. Punkari was of interest to me with Eli's blackjack being gone and the sneak attack from behind with the 2 x 4. I asked around the station and a few of the lads knew him. Someone remembered he was left handed.

He had been brought in drunk about a half dozen times. He was a miner at Garson Mine but he lived in a boarding house downtown. I sent two men out to get him and bring him in if he was home. I sent two more men to Garson Mine to look for him at work. I ordered the alley be washed to clean the blood out and officers could then leave the scene. I learned they had searched the theatre with the owner. No one inside and no blood. All locked up as it had been left the night before.

I saw Doctor Puri come in and motioned him over to the Chief's office. We both went in. Doc had his report for me. The Chief read it first. Then me. "Anything new from this morning?" asked the Chief.

"No nothing new. Just the finished report. Whoever did it was good enough with a knife."

"Why do you say that?" I asked.

"Because there were no hesitation cuts where he started and no cuts where he stopped to start again. It was also very deep. Maybe he was in the army or is a hunter. I don't know. He was very determined to cut his throat."

"Thank you Doctor, we appreciate your help. Let us know if you think of anything else," spoke the Chief.

Doc left as the newspaper photographer was coming into the station. I waved him over to the Chief's office. He had the photos for us. I showed them to the Chief and explained what they all were. The Chief reiterated that none of these photos were to be in the paper or turn up anywhere else. He also told the photographer to send a bill to the police department that was reasonable and we would pay it. We thanked him and he left.

"We need to get us a photographer. These are helpful to anyone who didn't go to the alley and see what we saw. Something to take to court later."

"And for us to review what we saw later," I added.

The Chief agreed. He would ask Town Council for some money for a camera and developing equipment. "Hell they gave us more men so we have 16 now. They said money was no object to that. I need to strike while the iron's hot. Maybe a few more cars too."

"Great idea Chief."

"And you take that storeroom down the hall. There's an old desk in the basement. I'll have some of the boys clear the store room out and bring up the desk and a chair for you. We'll call it the detective office."

"Thanks Chief but I thought it was just for this case."

"We need a detective but if you don't solve this, it may not be you."

"Yes sir," I said blushing a little.

Chapter 49

I headed over to the Nickel Range Hotel where I knew Lioness Marge would be having her lunch. It would be the only time today I could count on her being civilized to a police officer. Lioness Marge was tough and smart. She could also be mean. She ran many of the legitimate businesses in the Borgia Market. She ran all of the illegal businesses in the Borgia Market. Everyone feared and respected Lioness Marge. The Borgia Market was most definitely hers.

I walked in and spotted her sitting at her usual table with three men. All local businessmen. I walked over to them. She looked up at me blowing cigar smoke toward me as I stood beside her.

"I don't mean to interrupt your lunch but Lioness Marge, if you have a few moments for me I would appreciate it."

"Oh, the great detective. Sudbury is surely growing up now. But you are the first detective I have ever seen in uniform Sergeant Brown. That must be a first or is it a new fashion trend for police you are trying to present."

"I haven't had any spare time to go home and change. Today has been a bit busy as you can imagine."

"I can imagine a lot. I was sorry to hear about Constable Walsh. He was a very reliable copper for the public. He will be missed. Much like yourself."

"Myself? I'll be missed? What do you mean?" my voice growing angry and loud.

"I mean Sergeant that you will not be on the street anymore walking a beat or otherwise available to the public. You are a detective now."

"I see. I still need to speak with you."

"Not alone. Not today. But I will tell you what you seek to know. I did not kill him, I do not know who killed him and I am not happy he is dead. If I learn anything of value to you, I will pass it on. Now good day to you Sergeant Brown."

I stood my ground for a moment but realized I must take the high ground for now. Too many people were watching. Besides, she did answer all of the questions I had for her. If she could be trusted, I might even be satisfied to take her off my list. Making an enemy of the police did not seem to be a move Lioness Marge would make. We may have to speak again but for now I was done. A slight nod of my head, I turned and walked out realizing that the whole restaurant had been watching with held breath.

I strode down the street back to the station when an officer rode up on a bicycle to tell me they had Jari Punkari at the station. He had been found at home and brought in. They were verifying his story that he had worked at the mine last night and was not home. I quickened my pace.

At the station, I found they had Jari in a cell. I went and spoke to him. He was angry at being arrested and clearly no fan of the police. I sent two officers by car to his home to search it. They were looking for bloody clothes, Walsh's gun and blackjack. I had him come to the bars and hold out his hands. No blood under the fingernails but also very clean.

"Why are your hands so clean?"

"What do you mean?"

"I mean you work in a mine. Why are your hands so clean?"

"I had a bath this morning when I got home from work."

"What time was that?"

"About 9 o'clock. We come up for 7, then change. I catch the train to Coniston and transfer over to the Sudbury bound train there. Fastest way home. Then I had a bath and some breakfast. I was fast asleep when your men broke in and demanded I come with them. I don't even know what for."

"For murder. Constable Eli Walsh was murdered last night on his beat."

"I didn't know."

"You must be the only one in town who didn't know. You'll wait here until we confirm you were working at the mine."

I turned on my heels and walked out of the cell area. I went back to my new office to see a desk and two chairs in there. I sat down to think about this some more. Jari Punkari was just a hunch. I didn't like him though. For someone who hated the police, he was not crying foul too loudly at his own arrest. If his alibi did not stand, he and I would be having words and it would not be a pleasant conversation.

The Chief came in. "Nice office. I love what you've done with it."

"I just got here."

"I know. We just got word from the mine that Punkari was underground on night shift all night. He's not our killer. There is paperwork and his shift boss who confirmed that."

"I don't like him. I want to keep him until we search his place. Paper work can be faked and witnesses can lie."

"I agree but if there is nothing there, it may be we have to let him go and look elsewhere."

"Okay. Anything else Chief?"

"No, just keep at it. I want all the boys doubled up tonight on the beats. I think we have 4 fresh men I sent home earlier. Two can take the car and two can walk Borgia Market and Downtown."

"Sounds good."

The Chief headed back to his office. I was back to square one. I reviewed with officers what they had learned today. Gossip but nothing concrete. Punkari's name did come up a few times. But so did a few other reprobates. The fingerprint man did not find any useable prints in the alley, nothing on the wood or trash cans. I studied the photographs hoping something would jump out at me. It did not. I was at an impasse as to where to go from here.

My officers came back from a thorough search of the Punkari home. His wife and child had recently left him and moved home with her parents. The neighbours said his drinking and beating her were bad. There was no sign of blood anywhere or any of the items they were looking for in the house. I reluctantly told them to release Punkari. I had to look at other people for the killer. I made up a wanted poster to have printed by the newspaper and for officers to place around town to see what that would generate.

Over the coming days, weeks and months, there was no break in the case. I circled back to Jari Punkari a few times until he felt harassed enough he left town heading to Timmins and the gold mines up there. I grew comfortable in my suit. Despite his earlier threat, the Chief did keep me on as his detective although I never solved the murder of Constable Eli Walsh or caught his killer.

Chapter 50 - 2024

Enoch came out of his hypnotic trance state slowly as he had in the other sessions he had done with Nancy. He told her he had more of a sense of who his grandfather, Joshua Brown, was this time. Similar to when he had recalled the second echo memory from his mother Jane. He was very disconcerted about the lack of resolution in Eli Walsh's murder.

"It was a cop killer who got away. I can think of a hundred things they didn't do that we would do today." It was frustrating.

Nancy frowned, "I don't expect you can find resolution to every echo memory. The bank robbers who were in the apartment was already solved. The biker echo memory was just an incident and no real case as they had already solved everything but the missing girl who may not have been anything criminal. She may have just left town to live somewhere else."

"But at least I could do something. I have her DNA to run in the databank and if there are no hits, it will stay in the databank until such time as we may get a hit on found human remains."

"This mystery has been unsolved for almost 90 years. Even I've heard of Constable Walsh. It was a murder that was never solved and now there is no way of gathering new evidence."

"We'll see about that. I just have to think on it," said Enoch resolutely. Determined to find an answer somehow.

"If you become despondent or depressed over this echo memory I want you to call me. Don't focus entirely on this case. It is what it is and there may be nothing you can do about it."

"All right."

Enoch headed from the hospital home. He felt despondent. It was to be a night where he had a shot or two of Macallan 12 year old single malt scotch. His once or twice a year drink night. He thought it may relax his mind and allow him to think freely. It did help. He began to think of the echo memories. Trying to put them in his own perspective. Scott's death at the hands of the bank robbers still bothered him. His own acts of taking lives that day weighed heavily on him.

Eli Walsh had been a good officer. Seeing him dead in an alley surrounded by his own blood from his cut throat was horrible. It made his face squint every time he imagined it. That was often. Lee Coulson was a colleague who he had worked well with even if he didn't completely trust him or believe him to be honest. It still stung that it was Lee who shot him. The reaction to the time spent in the biker clubhouse attic was still volatile with in him. It had been terrifying.

He could tell no one about these things. He knew he wasn't crazy. He was trying to do the things Nancy had suggested but it all felt overwhelming. A career of never wanting to be labelled crazy or looked at sideways kept him from speaking the truth of what he had been been feeling. It was all too frustrating.

By the time his mind had thought all this through, he had 5 shots under his belt and was feeling quite drunk. Lightweight, he laughed to himself. Time for bed. He was ready to face his current demons and also take on the demons of his echo memories. As he went to bed, he felt like such a failure in his inability to control what was happening in his head. He openly wept as he fell asleep.

Morning rushed at him like a wall of water. He had only woken twice during the night drenched in sweat by his dreams and breathing heavy with a pounding heart. Nancy had offered him medication but he wasn't taking the medication he had already been given so why ask for more. He had been around and seen lots of bad things in his life. He had friends killed on the job and worked through those. He remembered dead babies and children, teenage suicides, days old bodies, the cruelty of husbands to wives and visa versa. It was a tough job and any officer worth his salt had to be tough too. Pack it all away and forget about it. Ironically, this is not what he told other officers to do. He advocated for officers to reach out to others and get help when they needed it. But he was already behind the eight ball with the time he had missed and the scrutiny he was under since his accident. He couldn't ask for help or tell anyone what he was going through.

Everyone said they were supportive but he knew just one more little thing to question his sanity would have him removed from the job he loved. Since his wife's death, the job was all he had. He could not let it down or lose it. He needed this identity. He could work through this. The scotch had numbed things enough to let some of it out and let him sleep a bit better. Maybe it wouldn't hurt to drink a bit on his own in private. He had been a non drinker or tea totaler since he was in university. Everyone knew that about him. He had to maintain control. But alone, at night before bed, a few drinks wouldn't hurt.

It was a little rough getting up but after a shower and shave he felt much better. He picked up a Tim Hortons coffee and an apple fritter. They sat okay in his stomach on the way to work. By the time he parked his truck, his coffee was gone. It was a pleasant walk in to work for a few blocks. As he approached the station, in his head, he said the same thing he said whenever he went in to an interrogation. "It's showtime." And through the door he walked.

<u>Chapter 51</u>

Franklin was waiting for him when he got into the bullpen of CID. "I have your messages and mail on your desk but there is a homicide that came in over night. Detective Staff Sergeant Rheaume has been running point. Inspector Townsend has been in most of the night. They couldn't reach you last night."

"Is it a whodunit?" Enoch asked.

"No they have the man in custody. It was a robbery gone bad. They have an outdoors scene on Melvin Street and a house on that street sealed waiting for a warrant. I just wanted you to know."

Franklin was antsy and Enoch knew why. He had managed every homicide since he came to CID as the Staff Sergeant. He also headed MCU and Cold Case. Stephanie had her head down writing notes as he came in. He said a jovial way, "Good morning, Stephanie. How's it going?"

"Ewok, you're here. The Uniform Staff Sergeant couldn't reach you last night so they called me to come in. I tried as well. But no answer at your house or your cell phone. I didn't leave a message since I was already here."

"No problem, I was just catching up on some sleep. Do you want to bring me up to speed?"

"Yes."

Stephanie outlined a robbery by a crackhead who robbed a guy on Melvin Street at knife point. Then ran a half block home. Break, Enter

289

and Robbery (B.E.A.R.) Squad members who would in the past have been called Old Clothes Detail, had attended. They set up observation around the house. The victim knew who the robber was and told police. They pulled his picture up on the car computer and got a good look at him. Lots of b/e's, drugs, some robberies, assaults and clearly a long time druggie and loser.

When the suspect came out of the house onto the street, they arrested him for the robbery. No one else appeared to be home. They contained the house to get a warrant. While all this was happening, the victim on route to the hospital, died. He had a stab wound to the chest but he had seemed fine. Something near the heart had been nicked and when he moved a certain way it pulled apart and he was dead. That was when Stephanie came in.

The warrant had to be changed to a different offence from robbery to murder and the new information had to be added to it. It had been faxed off to the Justice of the Peace Centre to be reviewed, considered and hopefully signed. It should be back shortly.

"Are you taking over now?" asked Stephanie.

"No, it sounds like you have everything in hand. When we get busy with more than one murder, I see Major Crime taking the whodunits. The ones where the suspect is identified and arrested right away should stay with the floor detectives with assistance from Major Crime. It will help build homicide experience on the floor. Otherwise we are going to get overwhelmed at some point. Plus you're new up here and this is great experience for you. I'm here to help you with anything you need today."

"Will you tell the Inspector all that?"

"Yeah, is he in his office?"

"Yes, just getting ready to go to a morning meeting on this."

"You should go with him. I'll pop my head in the office."

A loud voice boomed, "I heard you, Ewok."

"Inspector. Good morning to you too. What did you think?"

"We talked about that a bit before but that was the best way to put it. I'm stealing that for the morning meeting. You coming?"

"No I have nothing to contribute. I'll wait til you guys get back. Take Stephanie."

"All right. We'll talk about your phone service later."

"Gotcha."

They left to go to the 5th floor to see the Chief, Deputy and Uniform Inspector about this murder. Enoch checked his messages, mail and with nothing pressing he called the Comm Centre and booked on as Charlie 1. He went and put on his gun, handcuff pouch/mag holder and belt badge. He walked over to BEAR to see how they were doing. They were very happy with the quick resolution and the warrant had just come in.

They asked about waiting for Staff Rheaume. Enoch told them no, to go ahead. He reminded them they needed a Sergeant for the entry as he didn't see the B.E.A.R. Sergeant. He was at the scene waiting. Forensics was also already there as they had finished processing the street scene. They would go in for the search for the knife, bloody clothing, money, blood anywhere, anything listed in the warrant and connected to the crime. He reminded them when they were done, before they left the scene, to call a couple of drug officers over to search. It had long been recognized that drug officers search differently than other officers and Forensics. They have an eye to concealment. It had been best practises since the 1990's to never clear a homicide scene until drug officers had done a search.

After they left, Enoch wandered into the MCU office. Andy Travis was there talking to Detective Constable Pam Pomento, also known as Pom Pom. He was reviewing her duties as a File Coordinator and showing her the case as it was on Powercase. She had the training but this was her first time doing File Coordinator. He was just being thorough and helpful with her. I interrupted. "Just popped in to say hey."

"Hey." said Andy and Pom Pom at the same time.

"This the new File Coordinator for this latest homicide."

"Yes sir," replied Pom Pom enthusiastically.

"Any questions or help you or your team need, we're here for you. You guys need anything?"

"Nope, we're all caught up I think," said Travis.

"Can I see you for a minute?"

"No problem."

As they walked into Enoch's office, Detective Staff Sergeant Glenn Thibeault who was in charge of the Integrated Crime Unit (ICU) was sitting in front of Stephanie's desk. He had the B.E.A.R. Unit under his supervisory umbrella but had just come in a little while ago. He wanted to get brought up to speed. Travis and Enoch briefed him on what they knew. Enoch added that they would need a couple of Drug officers to assist in the search.

"No problem," Glenn responded. "I'll go over too and give them a hand." Glenn had worked in Old Clothes Detail, Drug Unit, Intelligence Unit and the first ever Street Crime Unit before B.E.A.R. There was a wealth of search experience with this man. He left to round up some officers to go with him.

"This is kinda what I wanted to talk about." stated Enoch. "I had another session."

"Do tell."

"Not like the others. It was about Eli Walsh."

"The murdered officer? When was that. The 30's or 40's?"

"It was 1932 downtown on Elm Street. My grandfather was the lead on the case. Hell, he was made detective because they didn't have one just for this case. It was never solved. But there was a suspect."

"Yeah? What happened?"

"They didn't have much forensics back then. They did have fingerprinting but there were no prints found. Photographs were taken. There was an autopsy and report. They had a suspect but only circumstantially. He had a motive but he also had an alibi. One I would question today. They also searched his home and found nothing. It was only a few blocks from the crime scene."

"Yeah and I guess no DNA, Criminal Profiling, databanks to search, surveillance teams to monitor suspect behaviour after the fact, etcetera, etcetera."

"That's about it. But this search has me thinking. It was the uniform guys that did the search. My grandfather didn't even go over there.

The suspect left town soon after he was arrested and released. I wonder what our drug officers would find in a search like that."

"Have you got a time machine? How would that even work?"

"No time machine but they could search the building today. Hear me out. We are looking for a knife, gun and sap, what they used to call a blackjack remember those?"

"Yeah leather things with leaded weight at one end you held in your hand to hit people with. Not very big but packed a punch. We don't have them anymore because they accidentally often killed people right?"

"That's them but in the past they were general issue to police. Eli Walsh was missing his gun and his sap. The sap he had hit the suspect with in the past. He was killed with a knife. We have the gun serial number but no DNA or fingerprints. We still might have enough to link it to our suspect if we can find these things at his building concealed."

"That is a long shot. How do you even get a warrant?"

"You don't. You find the owner today and get permission to search. The suspect has no expectation of privacy at this point. He hasn't been a tenant there since the 30's."

"I would agree with that."

"What do you think?"

"A long shot but about the only shot you would have."

Enoch tasked Sharon Lavric in Cold Case to start tracking down where Jari Punkari was today if he was alive and all the old reports on the 1923 murder of Eli Walsh. He dispatched Greg Bouchard of Cold Case to go to Punkari's address at the time, find out who owns it and get a consent to search signed. He then typed up a memo for Inspector Franklin. Checking his home messages, there were five from the station and Stephanie. His cell phone had a dozen from the station, Stephanie and Inspector Franklin.

He would deal with the fallout from that later, if there was any. In the meantime he wrote up an Ops Plan for the search as was required with every search police conducted under warrant. No warrant here but it wouldn't hurt to do it because he had time and was using resources like Drug officers and Forensics. He called Forensics and learned two were out with the Bear at the homicide suspect's house. Constable Janice Frieze was in the office. She agreed to go, just give her a call when ready in the afternoon hopefully.

Sharon came into the office excited. She had found an OMPPAC incident number from 1999 that had a report of two detectives in CID going to Finlandia Old Age Home. OMPPAC was the first computerized police reporting system before Niche RMS used by Sudbury police. A man there had confessed to staff that he had murdered Eli Walsh. Police were called and officers attended. The man was in later stages of dementia. When asked what he had done with the officers gun, he said "Attack, attack." Which made no sense. The report was final as they had no evidence to charge him and he was not of sound mind. It was Jari Punkari.

Enoch had no idea what attack meant but he tucked it away in his mind. Sharon also had a sudden death report that Jari Punkari had died at Finlandia shortly after. At that time officers were attending to these calls with Forensics and body removal. Now the doctor on staff would pronounce death, call body removal and go straight to the funeral home unless there was a reason for an autopsy. Jari did not have an autopsy and was pronounced dead by the coroner who attended with police. Cause of death was dementia.

Enoch had an incident number on RMS created to link to the OMPPAC number and dictated a General Occurrence Report explaining the murder investigation of Eli Walsh. He then created assignments in Powercase for Sharon Lavric for all the background information she was doing and gathering. He created another assignment for Greg Bouchard to get permission to conduct a search of the residence from the current owners. He created an assignment for Forensics and Drug Squad to assist in that search. He created assignments for the Powercase clerk, Julie Cross, to load in all reports and statements from hard copy into Powercase as well as scan them into the electronic case file.

Stephanie came back with Inspector Townsend. Enoch followed Frank into his office. He gave him his memo and advised him what the incident number for his GOR with details of the investigation would be under. He called Stephanie in and gave them the study notes version of the Eli Walsh homicide and his latest session with the doctor. They had questions that Enoch answered.

They had nothing new on their homicide except the warrant had been executed and officers were inside now. The Chief and the Deputy were happy with the investigation to date. They had met with Media Relations and crafted a media release updating the robbery to a homicide. Upstairs was satisfied with the explanation from CID as to the response because it was not a whodunit. They liked that Frank was thinking ahead to future cases and the best way to utilize his detectives and others. Frank thanked Enoch for his thinking on that. Enoch apologized for missing all the calls. All was well in the world again with some bureaucratic pressure off all of them. Frank approved them going forward with the search in the Eli Walsh case.

"What happens if you find nothing?" queried Stephanie.

"That's it I think," responded Enoch. "I will review everything we have but I can't completely close the investigation without some proof. Likely Jari Punkari is our man but without something to prove it, his statement alone is useless because of his state of mind when he made the statement. Not to mention some of what he said made no sense."

"Attack. Attack," cried Stephanie.

"Exactly," stated Enoch.

Inspector Townsend spoke seriously, "It would be nice to solve an old case but if nothing is found, review the case and put it to rest. Not everything gets solved."

"I agree," echoed Enoch.

Enoch left the office and headed to the cafeteria for lunch. He met Andy Travis down there. Andy brought him up to date on the search at the accused's house on Melvin Street. They had found bloody clothing under the bed. The knife was under a dresser found by the Drug guys. Money was under his mattress. Not a great hider was Travis' conclusion. The knife might have been missed without the Drug guys but it's not like he hid anything in the basement or the attic to make it more challenging.

"The attic?" repeated Enoch between bites. "The attic."

"Why do you keep saying that?"

"Does attack and attic sound close to you? If said soft and horse, would it sound close?"

"I guess, why?"

"Jari Punkari was asked what he did with Eli Walsh's gun when he was confessing at Finlandia. He said attack twice. I wonder if he was saying attic twice."

"Shit."

"Yeah, shit. That better be the first place you search."

"It will be and I'll get the Drug guys in there first to search it. I wonder if the dog would find a gun after this much time?"

"Call K-9 and find out. They smell the oil and metal. It will still smell like metal after this much time I bet."

Enoch threw out the rest of his lunch and he was flying high. This could be an answer to solve this hundred year old mystery. For the first time in a while, he felt giddy with excitement. Anxious to get this search done.

Travis put a call into the K-9 officer on shift. He said not his dog or the other police dog with GSPS but the Ministry of Natural Resources (MNR) had a Labrador Retriever that was genius with guns. He could call and see if the handler and the Lab were free later today or tomorrow to help with the search. Enoch and Travis quickened their pace to the office. Bouchard had just returned from finding the current owner of the building. It had been renovated into two apartments on the main floor and the basement. He made a call and learned nothing had been done to the attic.

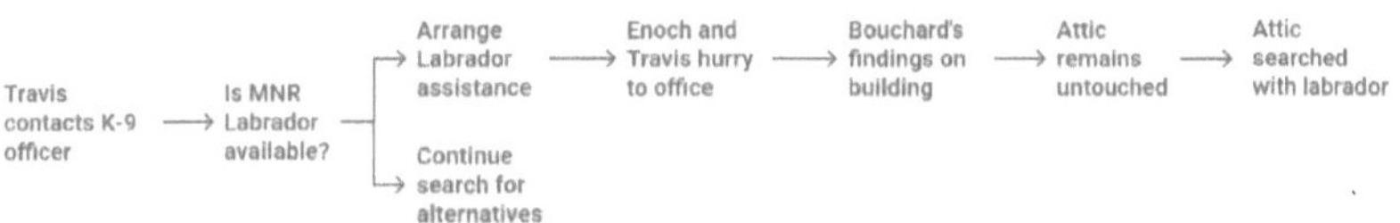

Phone calls were made to the MNR for the handler and dog, GSPS K-9 would be there, two Drug officers, Forensics Constable Frieze, Greg Bouchard, Andy Travis as the Sergeant and Enoch. The permission form was filled out and complete. It had been explained on video to the owner who had consented to the search. They were all set by 2 pm.

Entry was made by knocking. The tenants were aware and they had also signed a consent to search as they had an expectation of privacy. Once the formalities were cleared, two Drug officers brought in an aluminum step ladder and entered the attic hatch. They searched first and found nothing in the unfinished attic. The MNR handler brought in his dog on a special harness rig. The GSPS handler went up first and between both handlers they shoved the Lab up into the attic onto a piece of plywood they found up there.

The dog was suspended by harness between the two handlers and commanded to search. The handlers moved carefully like ballet dancers over the trusses carrying the dog so he didn't fall through the ceiling letting him sniff anywhere he wanted to go. The dog was a machine, sniffing everywhere until he caught a scent and signalled on a spot beside the outer wall of the attic far away from the entrance hatch. The GSPS K-9 officer laid down on his belly and crept forward lifting insulation bats as he moved forward. Against the wall he found a bundle in old butcher paper that was heavy. Wearing gloves he pulled it down and crawled backwards to where he could stand.

Like carrying a bomb he moved slowly following the MNR handler who was carrying the Lab back to the plywood. He held the dog who was quite excited until the MNR handler climbed halfway down the ladder then lowered the dog to him. The MNR handler and the dog went crazy with excitement. This was to reinforce to the dog he had done good and made a correct location hit. The officers in the room with him thought he and his dog had gone a little crazy. The GSPS K-9 officer climbed down slowly with his package for Constable Frieze

He handed the package to her, she placed it on a sheet of plastic she had laid on the kitchen table. Wearing gloves, she gently opened the butcher paper. Inside was a Webley break open .32 caliber revolver. She read off the serial number still visible. It was Eli Walsh's gun. There was also a leather sap and a folding barber's razor that looked rusty. It wasn't rust but blood, as they were to later learn. This confirmed the confession of Jari Punkari in Enoch's mind.

Forensic testing was to be done on all the items. A quick visit to the Sudbury Police Museum confirmed the sap they found was the same type issued to officers in the 1930's in Sudbury. Enoch wrote up another memo on the case and dictated a final report closing this case. Inspector Townsend popped in after his dictation. "We need a media release closing this case. The Chief said to make it brief. We will have a media conference on it tomorrow. You need to be there to answer all questions. I'll be there, the Bear from Forensics and the Chief."

"Great," moaned Enoch.

"You keep solving these old cases. By the way, Chief and Deputy both say congratulations."

The Bear walked in with Constable Frieze."I hope you are both are ready for this."

"We already know the good news," stated Townsend.

"About the DNA?" quipped Frieze.

"What DNA?" asked Enoch.

"The historical missing person case. It was a slow week at the Centre of Forensic Science and someone got interested in our case. They processed the DNA and added it to the database. They got a hit."

"Where?" asked Enoch.

"Thunderin' Thunder Bay," replied the Bear. "A body dug up at a construction site on the edge of town turned over a couple of homemade graves. Homemade is how they described them. Crude and not to grave normal specifications."

"What's normal?" snorted Townsend.

"Well, 6 feet deep anyway," said the Bear. "They have it as an open series of murders as the two bodies were laid to rest at different times. They said this made sense to them as they thought they were biker hits done in the city and buried here. One was identified as an Old Lady who left her biker husband and disappeared in the early 80's. The bodies were dug up in 2001. The Forensic Physical Anthropologist sent up by CFS was that guy at Laurentian University. He exhumed the bones. They were able to get DNA from the teeth for both. I guess in the tooth is the last place the body loses DNA."

"Here is an incident number. Put all your reports for that case in there," informed Enoch.

The Bear replied, "I have their incident number for reports as well. They are going to call you in the morning. They are just reading everything over. It's a Thunder Bay case now because of where the body was found but I'm sure they would appreciate some help."

"They are in luck, we just loaded everything into Powercase," said Enoch. "They will be able to access everything we have."

Townsend started, "Can we…"

"No," said Enoch. "We can't do media. Everything will come from Thunder Bay Police. We follow their lead now. Plus there are questions only they can answer about the body. In the morning when I speak to their case manager, I will ask if we can advise closing our missing person case and refer media to them. But I bet they're going to ask for some time before that happens. So don't get your hopes up."

"Gotcha. I'll update the Chief and Deputy. You should go home before you solve anymore old cases today," laughed Townsend to Enoch.

Leaving the office, Enoch saw Phillips moving fast across the room. He loudly said, "Anything new on the arson case?"

"Nothing new. We're busy right now helping with the murder on Melvin Street."

"Did you think about surveillance?"

"Yeah, I have an ops plan almost finished. I will leave it for you this week and you can look it over."

"Thanks, look forward to seeing it."

Enoch left the station and walked to his truck with a boggled mind. There was some satisfaction in solving two old cases. There were terrible memories in that alley. There was frustration in not having located Sheila Jenkins before she was killed. And at the heart of it all was guilt. Having not done enough at the time. Enoch got home and feeling no better, grabbed his scotch bottle and drowned his sorrows. Not even Jake's playful antics could bring him out of his doldrums.

Chapter 52

Nancy waited for Enoch who was 20 minutes late. Very unlike him to be late for a session. He mumbled an excuse saying he wanted to get going.

"I think we should talk first," Nancy said.

"About what?"

"Well I watch the news. How about the two big cases you closed?"

"They were just luck."

"Not luck or they would have been solved before by someone else. You're a keen detective. I'm sure that had a lot to do with it."

"Perhaps not luck but cheating. I know and have access to modern law enforcement tools and techniques they didn't have back then."

"Anyway you look at it, I would say they are both wins for you. How are you feeling?"

"Fine."

"That's a lie. No one is fine. It's a polite answer to the question. You were late today, you're speaking quietly, you haven't said anything about these cases you've closed. They must bother you a little after our sessions. You said they were vivid and real when we finished."

"I guess I am bothered a bit about them. I feel some guilt too."

"Let's unpack this a little."

Nancy proceeded to lead him through a Cognitive Behavioural Therapy session. They spend two hours at this. No session today but Enoch said he did feel much better. Nancy suggested some strategies for him to follow. One was no more drinking for now. That was a big behaviour change for him. She wanted him to self triage his mental health and reach out when he knew he needed help. She reminded him he could call her at any time.

Enoch left still feeling a little unsettled. He went home, picked up Jack and headed north to Falconbridge. Taking Jake for a walk in the bush for an hour, it did a lot to clear his head. Jake loved it and chased every squirrel he could find. Getting home, Enoch talked himself into just one scotch that turned into four and then bedtime.

He was late for work again but everyone was giving him space because of his recent success. Or maybe it was fear of the voodoo that he was making because they did not understand what was happening. Hell, he didn't understand it so why should anyone else. He felt at times he was going mad. He spent the morning quietly reviewing reports, returning messages and emails. The media conference mid morning went very well. He spent the afternoon going to one meeting and spending the rest of his time in his office staring into space and thinking.

He was not sure he could take anymore of this. His mind was jumbled. He had difficulty focusing on anything for long. He was not eating well or sleeping much. He had images flashing that were ones he remembered living, others came from the echo memories recovered during hypnosis while others still he could not place. They came when they wanted then flashed away. He had no control of them and that concerned him more than anything.

The next day he headed in to Nancy's office for another session. The longest session yet.

Chapter 53 - 1963 - Booze Can, Boarding House and Brothel

My name is Francis Brown. I am 28 years old. I have been a policeman since I was 21 years old. I worked in the mine after high school. I was very happy to become a policeman. My dream job. My dad was a cop. I had just moved into my other dream job. I was the new Detective Constable for the City of Sudbury Police. That position is really a Detective in training. Other detectives are either Sergeants or Acting Sergeants (Detectives). I would have the job for 1 year while they tried me out. I still received uniform officer pay but after a year, if I stayed, I would receive the Detective pay and be a Detective. I was the only Detective Constable in the office.

I had been given this opportunity because I foiled a car theft ring. The Chief was impressed. Now I just had to impress everyone else. I had no children, no wife, no life outside policing. I liked it that way. I knew many people but my only close friends were all police officers. I hoped to make a good impression on my first day.

I arrived just as the team of detectives were having coffee. One of them poured me a cup. I told him I take it black. He responded, "Wow, like a detective already."

He showed me around the office. I got a desk with a locked drawer to leave my gun if I wanted. I had a shiny new black leather shoulder holster. It felt like it sparkled when I took off my suit jacket to hang it on the coat rack. This got a round of "Wow!" from everyone in the office. I know I turned red with embarrassment but I sat down at my desk. The Detective Staff Sergeant came out of his office to tell us there had been a homicide. He gave a slip of paper to me. I looked at him blankly, looked around at every face in the office watching me and said, "Okay, I'm on it."

Everyone broke out laughing. A second round of embarrassment for me. The Detective Staff Sergeant Dennis Kitz took the paper from my hand. "I think I better send a couple of homicide detectives with you. Just to help you. You can show them how it's done."

"Uh, thank you Staff."

"Hanrity and O'Neal, go with young Brown here and he can show you how to solve a murder."

Detective Sergeant John Hanrity grabbed the piece of paper and gruffly said to me, "You sit in the back."

I grabbed my coat after a yes sir and followed them out of the station to an unmarked car.

I asked, "Do you want me to check the trunk, Detective Sergeant?"

"This is gonna get old fast. You're one of us now so just last names or first names. Never mind rank. I'm John and he's Mike or Hanrity and O'Neal. Got it?"

"Yes John."

Mike added, "We don't check the trunk or the back seat unless we've had someone in the back and we never have anyone in the back. I mean other than you. Hop in."

"What do we know?" queried John.

Mike responded while reading the paper, "We know someone is dead. It's at Walker's on Melvin Avenue."

"No surprise there."

"One surprise, the dead guy is Jason Walker, the owner himself."

"No shit?"

"Nope. And get this. It was a hunting knife to the chest. One stab. Right in the heart. No one else there. Broken back window. Maybe a break-in. Called in by his brother Mason Walker."

"I've heard of Mason but I don't know him."

"Neither do I but I heard Jason had a brother who helped out."

From the backseat I quietly asked, "Is that the booze can on Melvin Street?"

"Yeah, Walker's. You been there?" asked Mike.

"No but I knew there was one and Walker's sounded familiar."

"Okay young Frank. What do we do first?" said Mike.

"It's Francis. We'll want to make sure there's no one inside the crime scene who shouldn't be there. Isolate the brother and interview him. Call for the coroner. Call Ident to come. Have body removal on standby. We'll want photos of everything. Have the broken window checked for fingerprints and blood on the glass. Have officers set up to keep people out. Speak to three neighbours when we're done with the scene."

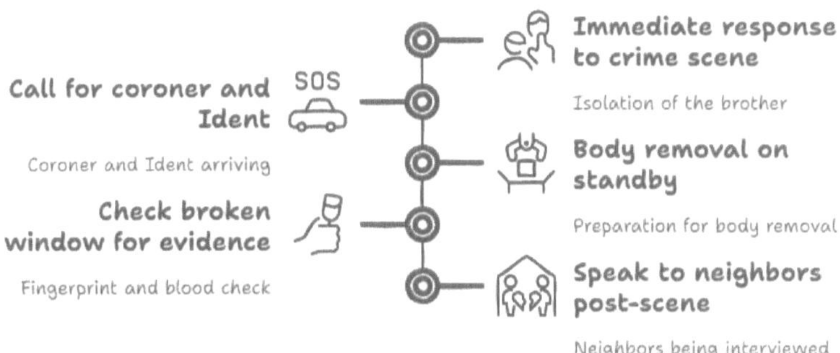

John interrupted, "Pretty good. Maybe he is going to show us how to solve a homicide. But maybe we'll talk to more than three neighbours. How about we talk to them all. You're right to think of a murder like a break and enter call. But remember it's bigger than that. So we do what we do at a break and enter investigation but more. Who told you three neighbours, your Sergeant?"

"Yes, if it wasn't in our report that we checked with three he would make us go back."

"Not a bad idea but we're gonna check with all of them. We're also going to check the cab companies because Walker's is after hours so some people don't get there until 1 am or even later. He's open usually until 5 am. I'm thinking this will be a fresh one. Don't puke in the crime scene and we'll let you go check the cab companies later. They keep trip sheets of all their rides. Just go in, flash your badge and ask to see the trip sheets from last night. But shadow us here first. No talking."

"Yes sir, I mean John."

We arrived at Walker's. It looked like any residential 2 story house in the neighbourhood. It straddled the Donovan and Flour Mill neighbourhoods. Both older neighbourhoods with working class families. I was familiar with both areas. They had reputations but that's all it was. They were safe places. You just had to mind your own business. They also respected police although they didn't like us around too much.

There were two uniform officers outside. John sent one to go and stand in the alley with instructions to both that no one goes in who shouldn't be there. We walked into the main floor. It looked like a regular house. We walked into a small living room. That led into a kitchen and dining room. There was a set of stairs going up beside the front door. Off the back door by the kitchen was a set of stairs to the basement. There was a door to the kitchen from the backdoor and stairs that was open.

Mike whispered to me, "They close this door for the booze can. Jason lived up here. The booze can is downstairs."

We went down the stairs. There was the patrol Sergeant with a notebook talking to a tall middle aged man. The Sergeant introduced him as Mason Walker. The victim's brother. Mason had a tear streaked face and was heaving a little with his breathing.

"You all right?" asked John.

"Not really."

"How bout you tell me quickly what happened then we can get a statement outside."

"I wasn't here last night. I came over to clean up this morning. It was just a party."

"Mason, let me stop you there. Your brother is dead. We need nothing but the truth. We don't care about illegal liquor sales right now. We're looking to find a killer, okay? Can we agree you're going to tell me everything you know and the truth?"

"Yeah, okay. Sorry. This is an after hours club. There's no license. We run it Thursdays to Sundays. Sundays we open early and close early. Usually opened by noon and closed by midnight. I work the bar on Sundays. Jason has a bartender for Thursday to Saturday. Those nights we open midnight to 4 or 5 am depending on whether anyone is still here at 4 am. I usually come over early on Monday to clean up from my shift. Lets me get home early."

"Is this time normal for you to come in?"

"Yes. Usually about 7 or 8 am. Today I came in at 8 am and found him like that." Mason pointed to another door leading to another room. As my eyes scanned that way, I took in the long bar, some tables with chairs, a juke box and an area cleared for dancing. There was wood panelling for the walls, drywall for the ceiling and shag carpet on the floor. It all looked pretty new. There were glasses, bottles and ashtrays full of butts on the tables. The bar had the same on it. It smelled like every dive bar I had ever been in with that stale alcohol and cigarette smoke smell.

We all walked to the door and looked in. It was a small store room. There was Jason Walker was on the floor on his back. The hunting knife was sticking out of his chest pushed in quite far. There was some blood soaked into the carpet beneath him. There was no smell yet that I usually associated with a dead body. This told me, he hadn't been there long. There was a broken window into the store room and some bottles of booze were broken.

John instructed, "Mike, take Francis upstairs and check it out. Then take Mason out to the car for a statement. I have forms on the front seat."

I followed Mike upstairs. As we got to the top of the stairs, Mike spoke to me quietly. "We want to check this without Mason. I'm sure he knows about his brother but you never know."

"Knows what about his brother?"

"He's a flaming homo."

"Really?"

"Yeah really. I bet you didn't know Sudbury had any. But here he is. His booze can is open on Wednesday nights from 5 pm to 1 am. The RCMP wanted to raid it thinking there might be Commies coming here with the queer fellas. They were hoping to do a sweep to identify both queers and Commies."

"Why doesn't the brother know?"

"He might but he said it was open Thursday to Sunday. I don't know much about him but I never heard he was a homo. Plus he has a wife. So you know, you can't fake that stuff when you're homosexual."

"I don't know much about them."

The upstairs had a bathroom and two large bedrooms. Both were very neat. Neither of the beds had been slept in. Nothing was broken or in disarray. There was no blood we could see. Mike told me that Ident would take some photos up here anyway and have a look. He was checking drawers. In the bottom drawer of one of the chest of drawers he found a manila envelope. Inside were photos of young men. All naked. Most were standing at attention if you know what I mean.

"I figured we would find something like this. They all have em. We'll take them now so the family doesn't find them. You go get Mason and bring him to the car."

"What do we do with them," I nodded to the envelope in his hand.

"Well we're not keeping them. We'll throw them out once we're sure they don't have anything to do with the murder. Just better the family doesn't see them."

Mike took the photos to the car and I went to find Mason downstairs. He followed me out to the the car and Mike directed him to the back seat. Mike had a clipboard with Statement of Fact forms. He told Mason that he wanted him to write out where he was, what he saw and what he did. He told him if he did all that then we wouldn't have too many questions to ask. Mike told me to go see John.

With Mason writing out his statement in the back, I saw a car pull up and the Ident car behind it. The coroner was here. I introduced myself to Doctor Friedman. I walked him into the house and down to the basement. John greeted him, "Hey Gerry. Happy to see you. Busy?"

"Not so much this morning but I have a packed afternoon with patients. I like to take Monday mornings easy. What have we got?"

They walked toward the store room. John telling him about the booze can, that Jason the victim was middle aged and a homosexual, there was a knife in his chest and he didn't think it was a heart attack. Doctor Friedman looked in and said, "No. I concur. Not a heart attack. Probably the knife in his chest did it. I think we are safe ruling this a homicide. I presume that broken window is related?"

"Yeah, we think it was a break and enter where he caught whoever was doing it. But given that he let queers and Commies drink here, there could be more to it."

"Okay. Take him to the morgue at the Memorial Hospital. I'll do the Post Mortem there tomorrow morning. Can you make it?"

"Sure no problem about 9?"

"Yes 9 is good."

"Okay to bring young Francis here? It will be his first."

"As long as he doesn't vomit on my corpse that's fine."

"I won't," I said earnestly. That got a laugh.

When we finished at the house and we drove to the back of the Chinese restaurant on Elgin Street. We went in the back door for the policeman special. For $1 they gave us a bag each of Chinese food. It was a lot. Mike explained when we got to the car. "They just charge us the cost of the food. They like us coming around because people know the police are watching out for them.

Chapter 54

Back at the station, John briefed Staff Sergeant Kitz on what we had found. He told him that the uniform officers would knock on doors to see if anyone saw or heard anything in the neighbourhood. Ident would be done soon. Body removal had got there just as we were leaving. There was nothing under the body but blood soaked rug. Ident was going to cut it out and take it. I was doing cab companies after lunch and then all the reports with Mike. General Occurrence Report, Sudden Death Report, Homicide Report, Supplementary Reports and review the statements and everything.

Mike would go back to the scene. He would check what uniform had found and do any followups needed. John was going to see the RCMP for what files they had on Walker. So far, it looked like a homosexual, Communist or break and enter artist. But that was just on first blush. He might have a boyfriend and when they found out who they would bring him in and sweat him.

Mike left to go to the scene for another look and to speak to neighbours that uniform had identified as knowing something. I went around to the cab companies to look at their trip sheets. Nothing from Walker's last night. I got back to the station before Mike. John was back and had learned that they had quite a file but they didn't have anything recent on the Communists. The Communist Party had held meetings there for a few months a few years ago. Jason Walker had been their informant at that time and told the RCMP what was happening on the inside. That's why they never raided him.

The also had him in their homosexual files but as he was not public about it other than his gay nights at Walker's, they let that pass too. He fed them names of all the local homosexuals so they could keep a list. All in all, he was a good informant for them. They were going to miss his information. They also advised that he gave information to the OPP and Sudbury Police Morality Branch. John had talked to both and learned essentially the same from them. He was a good informant and that's why he was never raided.

So we now knew he was a rat and that could be a powerful motive but it was a closely guarded secret. It seemed the Communists would have no interest in him now since they no longer had meetings there. From the neighbours, it was learned that Jason did not have a boyfriend, he kept his customers indoors and they were very discreet. There were no known local break and enters in the neighbourhood recently.

Mike showed me how to fill out all the reports and helped me with them. About 7 pm we called it quits and would meet at the station in the morning to go to the post-mortem. John also told us that the RCMP had a bulletin that they had a man trained in use of the lie detector. If we had any suspects and were interested, they could send a message for him to come. They were looking for tests for him to do.

The next morning we attended the autopsy. It was my first and I had to leave when he did the Y incision to throw up outside. Thankfully there was a door to the outside nearby. After I pulled myself together I went back in. Following the autopsy we had coffee with Doctor Friedman. He described the manner of death as the knife being thrust upward into the chest and going into the heart. Death was pretty quick but the heart must have pumped for a bit to have pushed blood from the body. He thought the time of death was probably between 5 am and 7 am. He was found at 8 am. Rigor mortis had not set in yet and the body was still warm to touch when he was examined at the scene. There was very little lividity, where the blood in the body would pool in the lowest part of the body due to gravity. All of this was new to me and a learning experience for sure.

We returned to the station on Elgin Street and went to the Identification room where the Ident officer walked us through the photos he had developed. Also measurements he made and sketches. He showed us the piece of rug he had cut out. The knife he showed us had blood on the blade but also on the hilt and handle. Possibly the murderer had shoved it so far in, his hand had slipped forward and he cut himself. They would know when they typed the blood if it was the same type or not.

We went out to lunch across the street at the cafe there. Detectives were allowed to eat in with the public while uniform officers could get take out but had to eat at the station. Over lunch we reviewed what we knew. I mostly asked questions more than provided insight. Mike and John were very experienced and whittled the case down to probably a break and enter artist because of the window or a homosexual because it happened in the store room after hours.

Chapter 55

The first week went by and we were no further ahead in this case. We had started bringing in rough kids from the neighbourhood and we were getting nowhere. Staff Sergeant Kitz suggested a reward to the Chief. It was approved. A Wanted and Reward poster was put up around town. The poster read:

WANTED

For the murder of Jason Walker on Melvin Avenue, Sudbury, Ontario

In the early morning of August 12, 1963, Jason Walker was murdered by being stabbed in the chest by a hunting knife in his residence.

The killer is considered armed and dangerous.

He is believed to have homosexual tendencies.

There is a reward of $500 for any information regarding this killer.

Communicate your information to the Sudbury Police Department

A lot of tips came in over the next few weeks but none of them led anywhere. The Ident officer, Sam Nichols, had provided us a report from the Attorney General's Laboratory at the Victoria Hospital for Sick Kids on College Street at Elizabeth Street in Toronto. They had typed the blood to two different blood types. There were fingerprints also on the handle of the knife but they were too smudged to identify. We now knew the killer's blood type was A positive because that blood type was the only one on the handle of the knife. Nothing else was new in the case.

We did a case review with the three of us and Staff Sergeant Kitz. There was not a lot of heat on CID over this case because of who the victim was. There was no public outcry. Even his family accepted that he lived a lifestyle with his booze can and proclivities that might lead to something like murder some day. During the review, John brought up the lie detector again. He had spoken to the RCMP about it. Sergeant Lester Proulx was the RCMP's first and only Polygraph Examiner. He had just been trained earlier this year at Chicago Police Scientific Crime Detection Laboratory. There had been a shakeup there in 1960 and many shortcomings were identified. One change was that John Reid and Fred Inbau were brought in to teach classes in Polygraph.

Evolution of Polygraph Use in Criminal Investigations

It was discussed at length and Staff Sergeant Kitz decided he would leave it up to the Chief but if we did it then the reward would likely be cancelled. After a few weeks with nothing but headaches from that reward, it was decided that was a small loss. Word came down an hour after our meeting to bring in the Polygraph Examiner. John would call and set it up.

Sergeant Lester Proulx was excited to come to Sudbury for this case. He was looking for a chance to prove himself. He showed up a week later. He had asked us to make a list of suspects and bring them in for him to polygraph. He was very careful about not using the word lie detector. He called it a truth verifier. He needed 30 minutes before the test for his instrument to warmup and then 30 minutes after the test before he was finished scoring the results on his paper graphs.

He was proud of his polygraph. It was a used 1960 Stoelting Model 22500. The RCMP had purchased it from the New York Police Department. They were manufactured between 1955 and 1960. It worked like new he assured us. It had 6 inch Kymograph paper, a 3 pen community inking system. This meant not much to us but we could see the pens and the paper. It had attachments for arm movements and thigh movements to catch people trying to cheat. It had sensors for respiration, galvanic skin response (sweating) and blood pressure. Much of what he said was lost to me. He described what he would do was the new Reid technique of comparison questions. He was very confident.

We had developed about 15 names of people who we believed were homosexual and with a criminal record for break and enters or robberies. He thought that was a great way to filter them out to the guilty party. He advised he would test them all and could test four per day. Two in the morning and two in the afternoon. The tests would each take about one and a half hours for the warm up, testing and scoring. He said he could stay for one week only but that should get them all done and time to write his report to us at the end.

The week was spent with John, Mike and I grabbing up our suspects and bringing them in for testing. Sergeant Proulx was able to get confessions to 5 unsolved break and enters and a robbery. That gave us six people charged but none for murder. It was disappointing although it was a good way to eliminate suspects and we solved some other crimes.

Chapter 56

On September 13, 1963 I was told to meet Mike to go to another murder scene. John was already on his way. It was 4 pm. This time it was on Kathleen Street. It was a boarding house. The landlady was the victim. Davida Scheffers. One of her tenants found her coming home from work in the main floor hallway. It was not a pretty scene we were told.

Constable Sam Nichols from Ident and John were already there with two uniform police cruisers. As we got to the door Doctor Friedman arrived and followed us in.

"Careful where you step," said Nichols. "There's a lot of blood here. Hardwood flooring is a mess. The neighbours are taking the tenants in and John is over now getting statements. Come through and walk where I walk to reduce our contamination. Doc I already have pictures of the body in situ."

Gruffly, Doctor Friedman said, "Thanks. That's the murder weapon? The scissors?"

"I think so. I'll take them after we move her."

"Okay I need her rolled on her side."

Mike told me, "Come on Francis. Get the lead out. This is your job."

I lifted the body and rolled it to one side for the doctor to look and then the other way.

"Never seen a body with this many stab wounds. Someone must have really hated this woman. There's an empty cash box through the closet door like it was thrown there. I'm going to take it for prints. I might pull up some of the floor boards and take some of the wall for the blood but I'm pretty sure it's all hers," informed Nichols.

"I agree," said the doctor. "You can have body removal take her to the General Hospital morgue."

As the doctor walked by Mike on his way out, he gave him some papers. "Here. So I don't forget again."

"What are those papers? I saw him give some to John at the autopsy."

Nichols laughed. Mike smiled and said, "These are coroner warrants pre-signed. When we need to get something or search something, we just fill them in."

"Really?"

"Yes really. He only gives them to policemen he trusts to not abuse them. Let's check around the house. You call for body removal. You okay here, Sam?"

"Yep, just doing my thing."

We then walked through the house starting in the basement and going upstairs. There was a bedroom on the main floor. The upstairs had 4 bedrooms and a bathroom. It appeared she was renting out the upstair's bedrooms. The basement was unfinished. There was a large living room with several chairs and a large dining room table with 6 chairs. The entire home was very neat and clean. The back door was unlocked and I learned from Sam that the front door had also been unlocked.

John came back from next door with his statements. "She was 58 years old, widowed. A very good neighbour. An amazing cook. All her tenants work downtown somewhere. We have two salesmen, a short order cook and a bank teller. None have criminal records. All in their 20's and have been living here from 6 months to a year.

James Mendes, the short order cook, found her on his way home from his dayshift. He works 6 am to 3 pm. She always got up to make him breakfast before he left. They're all pretty broken up. William Messier, the bank teller, has to go back to work. The other two are salesmen and taking the rest of the day off. They all have someplace else to stay tonight. So Sam, put crime tape on the door when you leave and lock up. There should be spare door keys on the wall beside the fridge."

John, Mike and I headed to the station. The autopsy would be at 9 am at the General Hospital the next day. Staff Sergeant Kitz was waiting for an update when we got in. John ran everything down for him.

"What do we think?" asked Kitz. "Connected to Walker's?"

"I don't see how Staff," replied Mike. "Other than they were both stabbed, this scene was gruesome. The worst I've ever been to."

"Multiple stab wounds," quipped John.

"Both sides of her body," I stated.

John looked at me, "Really?"

Mike answered for me, "Yeah. Francis turned her over for the doc. She must have put up quite a fight. Her chest was the worst though."

"Chief is gonna be pissed about this one. I'll take the Inspector and brief them both. You guys sit down and get busy. You interviewed the tenants. Go back and speak to neighbours. Find some family to speak to. You have to notify someone anyway. Check the cabs like last time.

Someone must have seen or heard something or knows someone who was mad at her."

Mike headed back to speak to neighbours. John had the name and address of her daughter so he was going to go there and speak to her. I got the cabs again. When I finished with cab companies I went down to the Ident office. Sam had come back from the scene.

"We have some fingerprints on the cash box. Some of it is in blood so that will be our bad guy. That's a lucky break. When's the autopsy?"

"At 9 am at the General," I responded.

"Okay, I'll take her prints then for elimination. I got the prints of the four tenants before I left so I can eliminate them."

I started on the paperwork that we had done last time. I made some notes for myself. By the time I was finished, Mike and John were back. Nobody in the neighbourhood saw or heard anything suspicious. The daughter, Mrs. Georgina Canton (nee Scheffers) was her only relative but visited her mother often. Mom was a widow who had no enemies, no boyfriends, no one in the world who would want to hurt her. John and Mike had decided that this murder and Walker's murder were not connected. We finished for the night.

After two weeks there had been a plea to the public in the newspaper by the daughter. There was a reward bulletin out for information leading to an arrest. The autopsy had shown she had been stabbed 27 times. The doctor theorized she had been on the ground and rolling while being stabbed in order to fight back or get away. She had defensive style cuts to her hands. The scissors were definitely the weapon. Many of the stab wounds were quite shallow and there were some hesitation wounds very small. The killing wounds were to her chest where there was a concentration of approximately a dozen wounds deep into her chest. That's what killed her. All of the others would not have killed her.

There just didn't seem to be anywhere else to go with this case. We were down to picking up petty thieves and break and enter artists to question them. We considered the polygraph but none of us were sure it had helped the investigation in the Walker case.. Then we became distracted. Another call. Another homicide.

<u>Chapter 57</u>

This one was on Eva Street. It was a large three story house. We all knew what this house held. It was a bawdy house. It had been raided in the past but not for a while now. Run by a 40 year old madam who claimed to be the granddaughter of Lioness Marg from the Borgia Market. That was thought to be a work of fiction but it did give her some air of mystery. She had several girls who worked for her. It was early morning. The girls were all late risers.

Madam Desire as she insisted she be called was in fact Louise Tremblay. She lived on the main floor of the brothel with a kitchen and dining room separated from the front room that was considered the greeting room, a place for the girls to meet their customers. They had a bar in the basement with tables and chairs if the client wanted to get to know a girl first or one of six bedrooms in the two upper floors.

Upon arriving, I thought the whole police department had turned up. There were several cruisers on the street parked haphazardly. John told the Sergeant to clear the cars out. We kept 4 officers. Mike spoke to the group who were now in the basement bar telling them we needed statements but they were not to talk to each other about what they saw or heard. He left one officer with them. John placed two officers out front and one in back.

Ident pulled up as did Doctor Friedman. I met them outside and we went in. Ident entered the kitchen first to take photographs. She was laying on her side with blood haloed around her body on the tiles. The back door was near her feet. There was a grocery bag on the floor with cans and food spilled out. The paper bag was ripped. A large kitchen knife lay on the floor beside her. It had clearly been taken from the kitchen counter knife block as the others had the same handle and there was one slot empty.

Ident seized the knife commenting he could see a hand print in the blood on the tile. It was mostly smudged but he photographed it with a special lens he called a Macro lens. Sam thought he could read the print from that. It was Doctor Friedman's turn. He had me get down and turn the body over for him. The wounds were straight to the chest that he described as a frenzied attack with the knife. That was the probable cause of death for now.

Doctor Friedman advised there would be an autopsy at 9 am the following morning. Being part time, he left his mornings free to do autopsies when needed. He worked his practise in the afternoon and it was difficult to get hold of him during that time. There was talk of taking on another one or two coroners and having them all rotate on call. That made more sense. He left some blank, signed coroner warrants with John. He authorized us to move the body. I called for body removal.

Mike came back from downstairs. "They're writing out their statements now but it all sounds the same. They always sleep late until lunch which is breakfast for them. Some customers in the afternoon but mostly at night. Some of the girls have what they call nooners and get up a little early but those are known in advance."

"Anyone see or hear anything?" asked John.

"Yeah. They all heard her screaming. By the time anyone got here, this was how they found her. One girl ran to the front. Then another looked out the back where the door was wide open. They saw no one. It took a few minutes until they came down because they were all afraid."

"Have an officer check outside for a blood trail. Use one from out front. If he finds anything, he gets Sam there right away. See if we can at least get a direction of travel," instructed John. "Francis, you call the Sergeant back here. He's to speak to his men and see if they saw anything on their way here. They all got here pretty fast. I'm betting they all rushed straight here but maybe someone saw somebody running. Tell him we need a man to drive around and another to go to the local stores that were open this morning to see if anyone came in. We need at least two more officers back here to start knocking on doors."

Finished briefing us, he spoke to Sam. We went about what we had to do. Mike and I did a search. There was a safe in the Madam's bedroom. On the floor beside the bed was an unmarked, empty envelope. "Want to bet it had money in it?" asked Mike.

"No bet. I'm sure it did. Do you think it's the same guy?"

"As the boarding house? Maybe."

"What about Walker?"

"No chance. Too different."

As we got to the main floor, John came up from the basement. "The girls are going to dress and leave. I have their statements. Have you done your search?"

"Yes," said Mike. "We found this envelop in the Madam's room."

"You picked it up?"

"Yeah but I know where it was if you want a photograph. I used my hanky to pick it up. It's not my first day," snapped Mike.

"All right. All right. I'm sorry. We just missed this bastard. We need to find something. I don't want anymore murders."

John told me to check the cab companies, I had a phone list for them and now they knew me well enough that I could call the taxi dispatchers to check the trip sheets for me and report back what they found. He also told me to help with the door knocks and take a statement from anyone who had seen or heard anything. I was to keep a list of everyone that we spoke to so if we had to come back and knock again we would know who had already been spoken to. Mike was to stay at the scene and make sure Sam got anything he needed. Mike was to call body removal. John headed back to the station to brief Detective Staff Sergeant Kitz and probably the Inspector, Deputy Chief and Chief.

Mike whispered to me, "This is very bad. John's rattled. That never happens. They will maybe put another pair of detectives on this."

The girls were all dressed and gone by noon. We had to turn away two nooners who left semi covering their faces. By 6 pm, we cleared the scene. Some people had heard the screams but no one had seen anything. There was no blood trail. There was no identifiable direction of travel.

The Chief was on the warpath but did not replace us as the investigators. He did offer for John to replace me due to my lack of experience. John said no. John and I attended the autopsy the following morning. Several deep stab wounds to the chest. There were also cuts to her forearms and hands. These were more defensive wounds like the last victim. She must have tried to fend the attacker off as he was stabbing her.

There were newspaper articles critical of the police. After a while, we were replaced on the latest two homicides. The only thing we had was a fingerprint in blood on a floor tile in the third homicide that matched the fingerprint on the cash box at the second homicide. Nothing to connect the first homicide at Walker's with the other two. None of these cases were ever solved.

Chapter 58 - 2024

Enoch came out slower than usual from his relaxed state to find his shirt was soaked from sweat, his hands were trembling. He felt like he was crawling out from inside a washing machine. This was the worst yet. Nancy asked, "You okay?"

Quietly Enoch replied, "Yeah but I need water."

She handed him a bottle and he drained it. She had a very concerned look on her face as he tried to shake himself out of things. He told her a little about his father and how he was as Enoch remembered him. Very detached. Always professional and proper even at home. He talked about how these cases haunted him as they were never solved. His mother once told him, he talked about them because he was sure they were the same person. The more experienced he became, the more certain he was that it was the same person. Until he died, he never shook off those cases and they did change him.

Nancy queried, "Do you feel any of that?"

"Yeah. I feel all of it. Anger, frustration, helplessness. I don't have any unsolved murders so I never felt this strongly before but I have felt it in other unsolved cases. Now I don't know what to do with this. Those cases are still unsolved but getting them solved would be almost impossible after this much time."

"Are you going to try?"

"Of course. Why do you ask that?"

"This session seems to have been more traumatic than the other sessions. I'm concerned that you may also be taking on the responses that your father had when he was the investigator. Maybe you should have someone else look at these cases?"

"No chance. I know how this sounds but I am the best homicide investigator we have. I'm also invested in these murders now so I'm best suited to look at them and see if there is anywhere we can go with it."

"Let's have a session tomorrow just to unpack what went on today and how you react to it. This may be more than you should take on at this time given everything else that has gone on since the lightning incident."

"I'll be fine Doc. But thanks."

"I mean it. I think it is necessary."

"Okay I can do Friday morning for an hour."

"Make it two hours and I will do Friday morning or afternoon."

"Morning for two hours is good."

"See you then but call me anytime you need to and practise some of the things we talked about to relieve stress."

"I will. Jake gets a long walk tonight."

His walk with Jake after supper turned into a three hour walk while he turned over and digested everything with this new echo memory. He was still not sure how to proceed to investigate but he did think of potential trigger places where he might latch onto more cases. One reason the killings stopped is that the bad guy may have died or moved. If he moved, the killings may have continued somewhere else.

For the next few hours, Enoch filled out three ViCLAS booklets on these cases for analysis by a Violent Crime Analyst looking for a link to other homicide cases that were similar in Canada. He noted in all three cases that these were not overkill. The amount of force used was just enough to kill each victim. With victim 1, the single stab wound to the chest killed him. With victim 2, there were hesitation and shallow, probing stabs that would not have killed the victim until the final stab wounds to the chest. Those were more determined and happened at the end of the struggle. With victim 3, the stab wounds went straight to the chest and were enough wounds to kill her. It was as though the killer was learning. That led Enoch to believe the offender was younger.

He also noted that the type of location was the same in all three. The were approached, attacked, and left at the same kind of scene. All of the scenes were residential workplaces for the victims. All the weapons were edged weapons. There was a sense of theft or evidence of theft in all cases. The weapons were all left behind by the offender who fled. All the scenes were locations where someone could have seen and heard what happened. They were all in the same neighbourhood close in time to each other. Enoch was convinced while putting the ViCLAS booklets together that this was the same offender.

They had no exhibits and only paper files. He had the files scanned into the computer and everything put on Powercase. Powercase could also trigger a case that was similar to these three cases from anywhere in Ontario or outside with agencies like the RCMP who also used it. He dictated all the reports and an update from himself on each case to open up each investigation. He created a memo for the Inspector of the three cases for a Cold Case project titled Project B. He then assigned all three cases to his new Cold Case Squad.

The Chief was impressed but came down to Enoch's office to speak to him after he heard. "I thought Cold Case were going to take older cases but ones that had a chance of being solved?"

"I think these can be solved Chief."

"They're pretty old cases that have seen no movement in over 60 years. When we find human remains that are 50 years old, the Coroner's office calls them historical and we don't investigate."

"That number of years should probably be higher with all the advances in forensic science."

"Maybe so. Can you suggest that to them? Send me a report and I will put it to the Ontario Association of Chiefs of Police to push to the Ontario Coroner's office. Maybe what? Anything after 1950?"

"That would be good. I will have your report to you tomorrow."

"You're not taking on too much are you? I know you were cleared back to full duty but it has been a crazy few months for you. It's been good for the Service but what about you. What's the toll on all this for you?"

"I'm okay Chief. I'll maybe take some time after we get moving on these cases for a little rest and relaxation. Right now I am in the zone and I don't want to lose momentum, you know?"

"I do. But take some time for yourself too. It can't be all high pressure all the time or we start to break down. Ask for time off when you need it. Someone else can take this on."

"I'm good Chief."

"You know you can call me on my cell at anytime day or night if anything is bothering you."

"Thanks Chief, I appreciate that."

Saying this but all the while, Enoch was thinking he would never need to make that call.

Chapter 59

All of the MCU and CCS were in the 5th floor boardroom. The room used for Chief's meetings and Greater Sudbury Police Service Board meetings. It was large with a huge table having 20 chairs around it. There was a large screen for powerpoint presentations. A podium that could be moved to different parts of the room. On the table was a conference call phone with surround sound. There was another smaller table to the side with 8 chairs around it.

Today this briefing was to accommodate the 2 Cold Case Squad officers, 4 Major Crime Unit officers, the Powercase civilian, Julie Cross, Inspector Frank Townsend and from Forensics, Sergeant Bobby "The Bear" Whessal and Janice Frieze. Franklin the CID Administrative Assistant was there to take minutes of the meeting. Julie Cross would be taking down any assignments handed out to put on Powercase to assign to the officers given the task.

Enoch was at the podium with his powerpoint presentation. He began seriously.

"We are starting this new project today called Project B. It is a project of three homicides in 1963. They happened at a boozecan, boarding house and brothel. Hence the project name, B. The Cold Case people are primary on this project but will receive help from Major Crime, Forensics and it will be run exclusively on Powercase. Nothing on the police reporting system on Niche. We will run this project out of the Major Crime office.

I am going to tell you about three homicide cases that I believe can be solved. These are not so much cases of whodunits. I don't have any idea who did them or even know for sure if they are all connected.

These are not cases we will solve with wiretaps, surveillance, canvassing, informants, video cameras or computer searches. I think we have everything we need to solve these cases. We need to turn these investigations on their head and look at 21st Century techniques that we can apply to them.

Innovative Approaches to Solving Homicide Cases

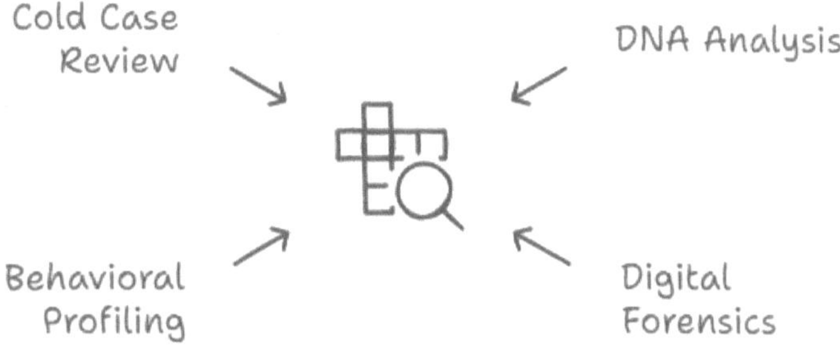

These are not whodunits because I know who did it. I know who did all three. Or rather, we have blood samples from one case where we should be able to get DNA. We have a fingerprint or prints in the other two cases that are identifiable and match. We have everything we need to convict a suspect or suspects except their name. That is our goal. To name the suspect or suspects, then tie them to the crime with the evidence already gathered. That way we may lay charges and get convictions in court if they are still alive.

I want each of you to review all of the files we have on these cases and turn your mind to what we would do today differently. What can we try that they did not have access to back in 1963 like DNA, AFIS (Automated Fingerprint Identification Service), running prints and DNA through databases in the U.S. and internationally, ViCLAS and their FBI counterpart, ViCAP (Violent Criminal Apprehension Program), Criminal Profilers, Geographic Profiles, anything else you can think of.

It is not too late to bring whoever did these murders to justice. For now only two are linked by fingerprints. The third we will treat as separate until such time as we can link it to the others. You have my full support as well as the Chief's and Inspector's. This is not to be a half assed job to say we looked into them and found nothing. I want us to look into them and solve them. Justice will not be defeated by time. Do you have any questions so far?"

Inspector Townsend spoke, "I just want to affirm my support and the Chief's support of this project. We believe in it and in all of you. We want these cases solved."

The Bear raised his hand, "Do we even know where the exhibits are?"

"Not right now but that will be a task for you and Janice."

"What about reports and statements?" asked Andy Travis.

"What we found is loaded or loading into Powercase right now."

"Powercase is loaded with everything," advised Julie Cross.

"So you may all start reviewing the written reports and statements."

Enoch then began a rundown on the three cases. The meeting ended at lunchtime. There had been a brief brainstorming session to cover some obvious points. Assignments were created to check the fingerprints against databases, extract DNA from the knife handle that was A positive and different from the victims, put in ViCLAS booklets on each case for analysis that Enoch had already filled out, call for a Criminal Profiler with the OPP to review the cases and see if they linked or not and what profile would they have for each offender.

Finally, have the Crime Analyst in the Intelligence Unit use the Rigel, a geographic profiling computer program, to analyze what they could with the geography of the crimes scenes. They usually needed a minimum of five scenes but they would see what they could do with three. The Crime Analyst was trained in geographic profiling and may be able to tell them things about the crimes, offender or offenders based on the geography that the investigators had not thought about.

The briefing broke up at lunchtime. The Bear cornered Enoch in the hall.

"What the fuck!"

"I know I should have talked to you first."

"I have no idea where those exhibits are. I'm pretty sure we don't have them. I'll check the database of evidence and tear the property room apart looking for them but what do I do when I can't find them."

"Think outside the box."

"Think outside the box. Fuck you Ewok!"

"C'mon Bear. You haven't even tried yet."

"All right. I'll put on a smile and try. This makes my day suck you know."

"Think ahead to the day we solve these, that day will not suck."

Enoch walked down one flight of stairs to his office and closed the door. He needed a little quiet time. Inspector Townsend poked his head inside to say he thought the briefing went very well. He asked if Enoch was all right.

"Fine. I just need to recharge my batteries."

"You're good though?"

"Oh yeah. For sure. I think we have the right team to solve these cases."

"Let me know if you need anything from me."

Enoch had worked with Frank Townsend for a few years and knew he was sincere in his support and would move mountains to get him any resources he needed. What the project needed was to find the exhibits. They would also need to find any officers still alive who were involved in the case and do KGB sworn video statements with them to preserve what information they could remember. R v K.G.B. was a case that involved taking sworn statements so that if the witness or victim was not available, the statement may be admitted into trial although it would hold a lower weight than other sworn testimony because it could not be cross examined.

Enoch's father was dead. He knew John Hanrity and Mike O'Neal had both died some years ago. He did not know about Sam Nichols the Ident man or the RCMP Polygraph Examiner Lester Proulx. He was not sure about any of the uniform officers. He knew that Detective Staff Sergeant Dennis Kitz was dead. So was the coroner, Doctor Gerry Friedman. He made a note to create assignments to locate all the people who were witnesses. Dead or alive.

Enoch decided to leave work a little early. He headed over to the Doghouse, a sports bar near police headquarters. He wanted some comfort food and they made the best chicken wings in town. He ordered a beer with his early supper. The waitress commented to him she had never seen him drink anything but ginger ale before. She had been working there for a few years and knew him well. He just felt like a beer tonight.

Hung over in the morning, Enoch dragged himself into work late. Franklin asked if he was okay when he picked up his messages. The Inspector told him to go home if he was sick. He motored through the morning checking reports and looking at triggers of other cases to their 1963 homicides. He was looking for any relevant similarities. He found none.

At lunchtime the Bear came to see him. "We have checked everywhere and we do not have any exhibits from any of those cases. No record of them being shipped out. But I had a thought. Back then it was the Attorney General's Laboratory. They became the Centre of Forensic Science in 1966. I called in a favour and they have looked in their exhibit database. There are no records. But he remembered a few years ago they found some exhibits at a warehouse in Barrie. They keep old exhibits there. Anything from the Attorney General's Laboratory that was left when they closed was moved to storage and it should have all ended up there. He's going to take a ride tomorrow and look for us."

"What about the print identification Nichols did back then?"

"We have his report in the file and the photo. It's pretty good photo making the print identifiable. The RCMP have agreed to load it into AFIS for us. I scanned it and emailed them a copy. It will cross reference with AFIS in the States with NCIC, Military and FBI databases. Internationally you will have to go through Interpol."

"Let's try that. Anything at this point. I was hoping we would have DNA on the Walker case. The other two have prints."

"No. We have prints on one of the cases for Tremblay where the fingerprint was in blood. The other print was done with dust and transferred. That transfer from the cash box and the tile with the bloody fingerprint are exhibits and we don't have them. We don't have the dusted print transfer from the cash box either."

"Great."

"Don't hold your breath on the Barrie warehouse. I doubt they will find anything. It probably looks like the warehouse where they took the Ark of the Covenant in Raiders of the Lost Ark."

"Okay well let's hope they find something."

Next to stop in after lunch was Sharon Lavric. "Everything is now loaded into Powercase and our electronic file. It's not much. Mason Walker is still alive but 88 years old. Torlone and Bouchard are bringing him in. We're going to have him sworn in, then read his statement and adopt it as a truthful statement. Then we'll see if he has anything new. It's a risk taking another statement after this many years but with the KGB statement, if he dies, we may still get the statement into evidence. All of the girls in the brothel have been traced and are dead. The tenants in the boarding house are all dead as well."

"Okay. Anything else?"

"Nope, I'm just a little ray of sunshine today, aren't I?"

That night was a repeat of the night before except 2 beers before he headed home. Then some scotch chasers at home like last night. Enoch was starting to worry in the morning he was becoming an alcoholic. He vowed to lay off the booze for a while. He spent the morning looking at Powercase triggers. In the afternoon, he spoke to a ViCLAS Violent Crime Analyst assigned to these three 1963 homicides. He was promised they would do the best they could but the system had only been around with the OPP since 1994 and the reports had only been mandatory for homicides in Ontario since 1997. There was a good chance anything from the 60's to the 90's were not even on the system.

Enoch went to an afternoon budget meeting with Detective Staff Sergeant Rheaume from CID. It was long, boring and left him with work to do to write up and justify what he needed for the budget. It was a process and probably the best they could come up with. Can't make the bean counters read my mind, thought Enoch. I have to tell them what I need, why I need it and how much it will cost.

Getting into the MCU office he saw the Bear and Frieze standing inside the door wearing huge smiles. "What?"

"They found the exhibits from us to the Attorney General's Laboratory from 1963. They have the knife with blood, the blood test to find A positive, enough of that blood to get DNA, they have the fingerprint card, they even have bloody tiles, bloody floorboards, bloody carpet and the cash box. Also an empty envelop."

"This is great news."

"I am sending Frieze down in the morning to go through it. She will leave what they need for DNA and bring the rest back here. We'll go through it and log it into our property room."

Frieze added, "Also I'll submit a report on where it was and how it was found for continuity."

They left after Enoch had called the Inspector in to break the news. There would be a briefing in the afternoon for the whole team to hear about the Forensics and the Bear wanted to have everyone to speak to CFS about something to do with DNA. He said they would conference call with CFS over Skype during the meeting.

Phillips poked her head in Enoch's office. "My people are starting to burn out a little with the surveillance detail on the arsons. They are discouraged and I can't say I blame them."

"Stay the course. Surveillance is tough and only works maybe 10 percent of the time but I am convinced it has a good chance with these arsons. He has to strike again. Maybe talk to the Integrated Crime Unit to see if they have any fresh bodies you can swap out with your detectives for a break."

"Okay."

"Listen, I know it's tough but hang in there. Be confident with your people. This will work. I just can't leave this where we might get another arson and this time there is a body. I have seen too much of that in my career. You can catch this guy, I know it."

"Thanks Staff, that does recharge me a little. I will get some fresh bodies and we will stay on it."

Enoch spoke to Andy Travis to make sure all the same people that were at the first meeting were invited to this next meeting for Project B. He wondered what the big deal with the DNA was. They had been using DNA for decades. He already knew about the databanks like the offender databank, crime scene unknown offender databank, missing persons databank and found human remains databank.

Chapter 60

The meeting was ready to start with everyone a little giddy over the good news of the found exhibits. The Bear had already got that rumour spread to wet everybody's appetites. Once everyone was seated, Enoch started the meeting and then turned it over to the Bear.

"I am doing a quick powerpoint because in 20 minutes we have a teleconference with CFS. As you may know, we found the exhibits from the 1963 homicides. This includes the cash box with fingerprint, the fingerprint card of the fingerprint taken from that cash box, the knife used in the Walker homicide with the offender's blood on the handle and photographs of the fingerprint in blood on the floor in the tile.

First the tile. We have looked at it. It has deteriorated over the years but you can still see enough of it to identify it as the fingerprint that Constable Nichols, the Ident officer all those years ago, photographed. From the photograph it is an identifiable print. An expert witness can testify to link all of that together if we can get the offenders fingerprint to compare with the two identified at the Scheffers and Tremblay crime scenes.

There were also floor boards, tile and carpet kept all these years. They have a limited value so we will hold off using them for any DNA testing. We are concentrating on the scissors found at the Scheffers crime scene, the knife found at the Tremblay crime scene and the knife found at the Walker crime scene. The Walker knife is of most interest as we know there are two samples of blood on it as they have already been typed as different. The knife was not identified at the time as Walker's knife. We believe it may have belonged to the offender. It gives us the best chance of helpful DNA.

Any questions? No? Okay. I spent a lot of time yesterday afternoon on the phone. The fingerprints we have from the two scenes are not on any North American database of known prints or unknown crime scene prints. The search was very thorough. We can link two of our cases by fingerprints and I am satisfied that an expert will get both into court as evidence and it should be evident to a Judge and Jury these fingerprints were left by the same person.

The reason we are speaking with CFS today is there have been new techniques to aid investigations with DNA. Once they extract DNA samples, we will be able to apply the DNA to the existing databanks but there is more that they may assist us with if we wish.

It's time to make the teleconference call, Franklin can you set us up?"

There was a blank screen replacing the powerpoint of the exhibits that Bear had been referring to. Then a squelch and a man sat down. He introduced himself as Doctor Yvan Matcher. He was in charge of the DNA section of CFS in Toronto where the samples were sent. Bear had explained earlier that usually it went to Sault Ste Marie CFS because we were in the North but CFS Toronto had held back the necessary exhibits for testing and placed it at a number one priority.

"First, I wish to congratulate you for taking on these cold cases. It seems like you will have a good chance at solving them. I am happy that the Centre of Forensic Science will have the chance to assist you with this. I am sure you understand that we will process the items left with us for DNA. We will also apply the sample to our existing databases. It will remain on the unsolved crime scene database until such time as the case is solved.

I wanted to speak to you about some other advances in DNA that the Centre is now able to offer. First, we are able to extract from the DNA certain genetic markers that will tell us hair colour, eye colour, facial features, abnormalities if they are genetic, age and race. It will not tell us things like hair length or whether the person has a beard or moustache. Then we can created an approximated sketch of your suspect at the time the DNA was left. It would be approximate because of all the unknown factors like hair length but it may be helpful to you. Even the general description of age, race, hair colour, eye colour alone may be helpful.

CFS would recommend you at least take the description although there have been cases in the U.S. where the sketch has assisted police investigations. There is a cost to doing these and I have given Bear all of the pricing that he can discuss with your case manager. It is a worthwhile investigative aid especially for such a historical cold case.

There is another thing we can do with DNA now. We can get markers in DNA that can be linked in genealogical DNA databanks. These are privately run companies that for a fee will put up your DNA submitted to them to find matches. The more common DNA genetic markers you have with someone, the more closely related you are to that person.

There are tests for paternal lineage and for maternal lineage. For paternal lineage we use Y chromosome tests. This is only done with men. The STR or short tandem repeat markers have a value given to them."

"Maybe for this crowd, the less science the better. Unless anyone wants to hear it. Maybe you have something you can send our Forensic people?" stated Inspector Townsend. "Sorry but I could see eyes starting to glaze over."

"Not a problem. I have a paper that explains all of this very well and I will email it to Bear. I won't get into Halogroups or mtDNA testing. I will just say something on Mitchondrial DNA. This test is for men and women and will show the maternal lineage. So depending on the sex of your DNA we will do two tests for male and one test for female.

Once the DNA has gone through this process and we know the markers, we will send it to the genealogical databases of which there are many with a lot of them already being connected to each other. We will learn the closest relative or ancestor to our sample on those databases.

From there, a genealogist takes over and begins to make a family tree using records. Records like birth records, adoption records, school records, immigration records, archives, newspaper articles, anything really to help create a family tree. They will bring it down as far as they can. Then an investigator goes through the family tree to find someone who may fit with what you know about your suspect.

Once you identify a suspect, normal policing techniques for DNA are followed. A surveillance team will monitor the suspect looking for castoff DNA. Something with potential DNA that is discarded in a public place. That sample is gathered. We compare it with our crime scene DNA. If we have a match, that will give you grounds to write a DNA warrant to order the suspect's DNA taken for comparison testing. That comparison DNA is your evidence. The castoff DNA matching will also give you reasonable and probable grounds to arrest the suspect so you can execute the DNA warrant on arrest."

There was silence for a moment then Enoch asked, "Do we need some kind of warrant for the genealogical databases?"

"No. There is case law in the U.S. on this. You can consult your local Crown attorney but it has already been used in court in the States. If you were to write a warrant you would have to write a s. 487.01 Criminal Code warrant for explaining the use of a policing technique similar how you would write a warrant for a wiretap. You are not able to really get that warrant because you can't put a name to it or an offence until you have the results. If you end up with the jackpot that the suspect has their DNA on the databank, then you get your DNA warrant based on that. It is considered castoff in that the suspect has placed it out in the public realm for people to find.

Legal Framework for DNA Evidence

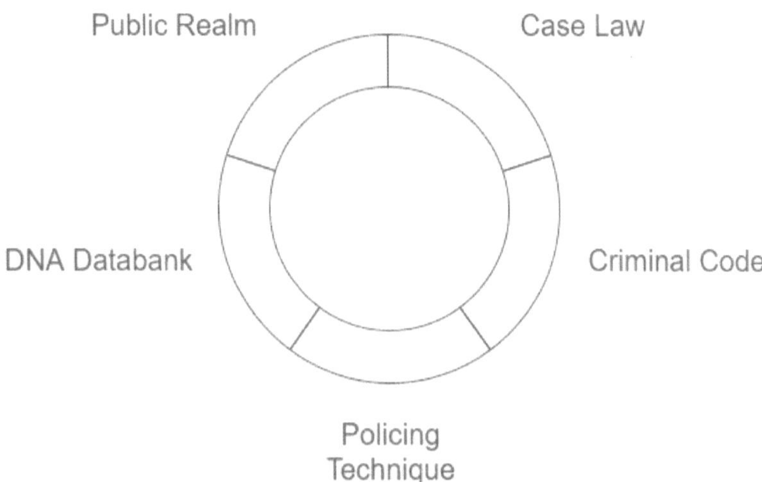

We can prepare the DNA for the genealogical databases and submit it. There is a fee for this as well. Are there any other questions?"

"Have you used sketches made by the DNA?" asked Andy Travis.

"Yes, we have been told it has helped in a few cases. We can also age progress the image but I would caution you there. The further we age it, the less accurate it may become. This DNA is a snapshot of the person at the time the sample was left. That is your best result. It will aid your investigators. Putting it out to the public is a decision you have to make but if it is not accurate because we do have to guess at some things like hair length, it may cause you to have tips and information come in not relevant to your investigation. The age progression would produce that same result but with even less accuracy and even more non relevant tips.

Discuss what you would like us to do. We can give you the person's traits of hair colour, eye colour, and those things I discussed. We can give you an approximated sketch of the suspect at the time the DNA was deposited. We can give you an age progressed sketch of the suspect as he may look today. We can place the DNA on genealogical databases. We have a genealogist we use at the CFS or you can have your investigators do it."

"Let me guess, there's a fee if we use the genealogist," quipped Greg Bouchard.

"That's right."

There was laughter in the room at that.

Enoch then stood and spoke, "Thanks, you have given us a lot to think about. We'll discuss it and get back to you. Please send us that paper on DNA and thank you for this presentation. I think it will be very helpful."

After the teleconference ended, Enoch spoke again, "I'm not sure about this voodoo so I suggest we all take tonight to think about it. There will be a meeting at 1 pm in the Major Crime room to discuss our plans going forward."

The night time brought bad dreams. Depression. Dark thoughts. Enoch felt like a weighted blanket was laid on him whenever he went to bed. He found his hands were trembling without reason. He was angry a lot these days. It was all getting too much. Work was his only safe haven. He cancelled his sessions with Nancy to concentrate on work for these homicides.

Mornings were a struggle after sleeplessness and bouncing all night in bed. He picked up a Starbucks coffee after someone at work had shown him how to use the app to order it. He was no longer getting anything for breakfast. He had no appetite. His day began with a nod to Franklin as he picked up his mail. Instead of walking the floor, he had officers email him what they were up to for the day to brief the Inspector. He only had to worry about the Major Crime Unit and Cold Case Squad officers. He didn't feel like talking to anyone.

Enoch sat with the file of Project B on his desk. His thoughts turned to images he couldn't shake off telling a daughter that her mother was dead and the horrific way she died. He saw in his mind's eye the three scenes. He could smell the coppery tinge of blood in the air and the unearthly colour of the blood on the floor. No one should have to die like this.

He checked his schedule for meetings. He then began reviewing overnight triggers to other cases on Powerccase and checking officer reports. He was ready for his meeting with everyone from yesterday by 1 pm. Skipping lunch, he went to the Major Crime room. Everyone was already seated and waiting.

"Well, we have some decisions to make or at least I do. But I want consensus from all of us before going forward. You have all had time to think about the options. Are we good with this new science that has been presented to us?"

Muttering and muted yes, okay, I like it, came from around the room. Several people mentioned they had read over the paper that CFS had sent by email. The Bear had forwarded it to everyone late afternoon. Enoch had skimmed it but clearly others had read it.

"I guess we move forward. CFS has already been told to search for DNA and if found, process it and compare it to our current databanks. Now what do we think about a description and a sketch."

There was discussion on this point. Everyone agreed with the description of the suspect based on his DNA. It was split in half regarding whether to get a sketch or not. The biggest argument against was it skewing the public away from a suspect who did not look like their interpretation of the sketch. There was also concern about the investigators being biased by the sketch. In the end it was debated and decided they would get the sketch and not put it out in the media. Get it to have it for now and discuss later whether to put it out to the public. They did not believe there would be many potential witnesses who could ID the suspect from the sketch of the suspect in 1963 still alive anyway. It was decided not to get the age progressed sketch at this time.

Next was the conversation about the genealogical databanks. Not everyone was convinced that it would stand up in court. It was outside all of their experience. Enoch picked up the phone and called the senior Crown Attorney, explained the process and rationale as it had been explained to him and the Crown advised she would get back to him.

The meeting continued discussing if there was anyway to move forward if the DNA did not get a trigger on one of the databases. So far, Powercase and ViCLAS had not had significant triggers. There were lots of them but none of the cases were similar enough. They still weren't sure if it was a series of 2 cases or 3 cases. Enoch had asked Travis to start helping to vet the cases on Powercase. The ViCLAS analyst was calling the officers with questions. Still analyzing the case off and on for almost a week. Nothing really strong as a comparison case yet.

The senior Crown called back before the meeting ended to say she had 5 Crowns that she met with who were in the office. She put it to them. Some were already aware of cases in the U.S. where the evidence had been tested and stood up as valid in court. All of them agreed that this was a case where a warrant was not needed for the genealogical database or later getting castoff of a suspect. At that point, a match would require a warrant for another match and that would be the evidence for court. All the lawyers agreed on something. That was a true miracle.

The final decision of the group was made to go forward with the genealogical testing for putting it to the databases to see what we got. It was decided if there was any information to come back that it would be followed up by Greg Bouchard as Sharon Lavric was already overwhelmed as File Coordinator of 3 homicides that were 60 years old.

Chapter 61

Things began to pick up like a train speeding down a hill. Within 48 hours the DNA results were back. They had a good sample. Checked against the databanks there was no hit. They would check with other countries they had agreements with to check their databases. The sample was submitted to the genealogical databases.

A week after the sample was submitted, a description of the suspect based on the DNA arrived along with a sketch. The consensus was there must be a mistake. It was a teenager. Not what they had been expecting. It was decided not to put the sketch or this information out to the public at this time.

The Criminal Profiler was consulted as his report was now ready. His description of the offender was male. He was younger possibly a teenager, white. It was not sexually motivated but motivated by money. Robbery or theft. He noted that the wounds appeared to match and he was linking all three cases as a series. He based this on their location, closeness in time, motive, weapons used and method of death.

They were all stabbings. In Walker's case, he was killed by a single blow with a hunting knife driven in with great force. In the second case, Scheffers, the wounds consisted of hesitation wounds and shallow wounds, none of which were life threatening. They appear all over the body because the victim fought back. The final wounds that killed the victim and bled her out were to the chest. In the Tremblay case, the offender went right for the chest. An area he had learned was fatal. They were savage stabs and deep. Determined to kill the victim. This was consistent with the offender learning.

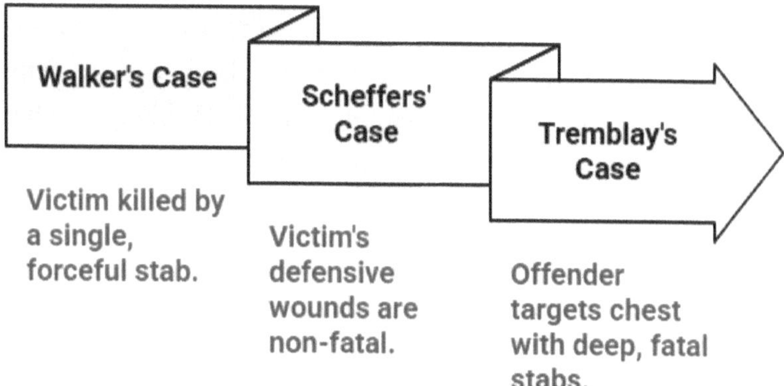

ViCLAS sent a report that the analyst was linking these three cases for similar reasons. Two of the cases were confirmed links due to fingerprints, they had not been updated on the DNA. Neither had the profiler. Enoch called both and they revised their reports to confirmed links due to DNA and fingerprints. Tremblay and Walker had matching offender DNA. Scheffers and Tremblay had matching offender fingerprints.

Travis and Enoch met with the Intelligence analyst. Although there were too few anchor points to be confident, she felt strongly that the offender lived within a block of all the killings. Offenders move and offend in safe zones. These safe zones are around anchor points in the offender's life like home, work, school, someplace they are anchored with.

With few computerized records, they did not have a lot to go on to search further. They talked about conducting a canvass of the neighbourhood. It was decided this was not an effective use of resources because most people or all people from 60 years ago would have moved or died. This was left as a hail mary assignment to discuss again after other avenues had been exhausted.

The results of the genealogical database came back with matches to the paternal lineage and the maternal lineage. Both sides had amateur family genealogists who were creating intricate family trees. One was in Toronto. The other was in Timmins. Greg Bouchard went and met with both to learn more about these family trees. He had been studying genealogy as much as he could to learn about it. He had spent time at the City of Greater Sudbury Archives, the Historical Records at the Greater Sudbury Library and the Sudbury Police Museum. He also haunted on-line archive databases.

After his interviews and armed with their research, he continued following their lines of research into the family tree. After two weeks, he asked to see Enoch one night after everyone had left and they were both working late.

"I have a powerpoint presentation I want to show you," said Greg.

"Just tell me," responded Enoch.

"No, I put this Powerpoint together. I want to show it to you. It won't take long," he stated in earnest.

"All right give me 5 minutes."

"I have it set up on the 5th floor."

"What? In the boardroom?"

"Yes," and off he ran to get ready.

Great, thought Enoch. I'm rubbing off on him and everyone with these Powerpoint briefings. They're going to all become as annoying as I am. He finished reading the report he was reviewing then grabbed a pad of paper and headed upstairs. He found the board room door open, brightly lit. Greg was at the podium. Enoch took a seat near the head of the table close to the screen.

"Okay, Greg. Hit me."

Greg began a very professional Powerpoint. He showed the family tree chart as he had received it from the two family members. He then gave an explanation of everywhere he checked records until it finally came down to family members in their 70's and 80's. He found one family member in Sudbury who had married but never had kids. He also had no siblings. A check of driver's license addresses showed his first driver's license was on Mable Street which was between Melvin Street and Eva Street making it at 90 degrees off Kathleen Street. If you drew straight lines from all of the addresses, they intersected on this house number.

Enoch was ecstatic. This was the killer. This was him. He was sure of it. He told Greg to gear up, they had his current address and they were going to arrest him tonight.

"Wait Staff. We're not ready yet. We have to get cast off first."

"Fuck castoff. This is the guy. We arrest him, interview him. If he doesn't confess then we get him with the DNA."

"Staff there's no rush. It's been 60 years."

"I can articulate reasonable and probable grounds for an arrest tonight."

"But it isn't enough for the Crown's office. We should call the Inspector."

"I'll call him but I want to make the arrest tonight."

Inspector Townsend was huffing and puffing while he spoke on the phone to Enoch telling him not to do anything. Finally Enoch told him to get off his wife and listen to what he had to say. The Inspector snorted and said he was on the treadmill and not on his wife. He then went on to order Enoch to wait and go home. They would have Greg give his presentation in the morning. He reminded Enoch that they had a plan and there was no rush. Enoch calmed down and agree. He sent Greg home and went home himself.

Enoch did not sleep at all. He closed his eyes and he could see all of those crime scenes. This was personal even though he had not even been born when these murders happened. Enoch was beginning to worry he was losing it. He had been ducking phone calls from Nancy and the hospital. He did not want to go through another session or any more testing. He had too much baggage from the other sessions. Plus he now had a mission, to solve these murders. That was priority now.

The following morning, there was an air of excitement on the CID floor as everyone had heard Cold Case had a suspect in 3 old homicides. Greg gave his presentation adding that the suspect had been 15 years old at the time of the murders. When he turned 16, he got his driver's license to an address on Mable Street.

At this point, a meeting with Enoch, Greg and Travis was arranged with Intelligence Branch to get a SPIN (mobile surveillance) team on the suspect. Sharon Lavric would put a package of the suspect together for the team.

The suspect was Alberto Genovese. He was a white male born in Italy and immigrated with his parents to Canada when he was 5 years old. He had been a mining engineer at Inco. He retired when they were taken over by Vale. He lived in New Sudbury on Lillian Street. His wife had died a few years ago. He had no children. No traffic tickets, no arrests or criminal record, only one call on Lillian Street for a noise complaint he put in against a neighbour. Not much else was known about him. They did not have a photo of him.

A team of two Intelligence Officers went out to sit and photograph him at his residence or when he left. It only took a few hours and they got him coming out of the house. They noted he was not heat conscious with no looking around for surveillance. They followed him to the grocery store and got better photos of him. Reporting back to their Sergeant, the photos were added to the project and a SPIN Team was formed with 5 officers from B.E.A.R., Drugs and Intel in the Integrated Crime Unit. They were briefed, given packages and sent out after lunch to get castoff DNA in a public place.

The SPIN team followed their target. For a 76 year old man, he did get around. He still drove his car. He did not smoke or appear to litter. It was a problem compounded by it being winter, January and very cold. After 3 days they had nothing. Finally on the third day they had some luck.

Enoch was listening to the radio of the SPIN Team.

"He's out and into his skate. Going… looks like Lewis. Up toward Wally World I think. Anybody can take the eye now?"

"Yepper, I got it. Onto the big L. Going Davis on big L. Making a switch. Blood flashing for Lewis. And into Wally World. I am passing by."

"I am plugged in front of Wally World. I see his skate. He's alone. Leaving his skate. Do we have a dancer? No? Okay then I'll do it. Radio silent now."

Several minutes went by. SPIN lingo was shorthand for the team and in case anyone was listening, only the team knew what they were saying.

Excited chatter on the radio, "I got it. He blew his nose and discarded the tissue in the mall. That should work?"

"Take that in to the shop right away to the Bear or Ewok. Don't drop it. We'll stay on target," said the SPIN Captain.

"Rog."

The rest of the team chattered on and followed the suspect. Enoch told Franklin he was going to Forensics on the 6th floor. Then he walked up two flights with his heart pounding and excitement building. He went to Bear's office blurting, "They have a cast off."

"I heard. They called me. It will be good. I thought they should stay on him in case we get another cast off. Can't hurt but I'll have Janice package this one and take it to CFS in Sault Ste Marie. We have top priority now. They are closest. They can process it and send the results to Toronto for comparison.

Chapter 62

After 36 hours, CFS responded that the DNA was a match to the Walker and Tremblay Crime scenes. That with fingerprints at Scheffers and Tremblay crime scenes, all three cases were linked together. It was decided they would conduct a planned arrest for all three murders as reasonable and probable grounds now existed for all three. Once his fingerprints were taken it would confirm the prints they had. They would have the DNA warrant on hand when he was arrested and execute it on video at the station when he was being processed after arrest.

Enoch was happy for the first time in a long time. Giddy even. He had not been to any sessions with Doctor O'Brien in several weeks. He had stopped taking the two anti-depressants and anti-anxiety pills awhile ago. He still couldn't sleep through the night without waking every few hours with a nightmare. He was drinking again, telling himself it was to celebrate. He knew all of this was not good but he was sure it would turn around once they had Genovese under arrest.

They had their briefing for the arrest by Enoch. They had a uniform officer standing by for prisoner transport with Sergeant Tamara Phillips who had nothing to do with any of the cases or investigation. Tamara would make the "poster boy" arrest as it was known. A detective completely unbiased by the investigation. Who only knew enough about the crimes for reasonable and probable grounds to make the arrest. She would give an explanation of what she was arresting him for, give him his right to counsel, caution him in any statement he may give. She would ride back to the station with Genovese all the time from contact with him recording everything on an audio recorder.

She would meet Detective Nick Torlone and the Uniform Staff Sergeant to process the prisoner and search him again more thoroughly before placing him in cells. The uniform officer would have also searched him at the scene. Nick would facilitate a call to his lawyer for him to have a private conversation. Should he not have a lawyer, Nick would call the 1-800 number for a legal aid duty counsel who could give legal advise in private to Genovese. Then he after he spoke to a lawyer he would be placed in a cell.

There was to be a cell shot. An officer posing as a prisoner would be in the cell next to him but would not ask him any questions, just record what he said. There was a one party consent wire tap warrant approved for this. The officer would be there until the accused was brought up to his interview he would then be brought out and debriefed by someone to see if the cell shot should continue.

Forensics would take Genovese out of cells first to their Identification room for fingerprints and to execute the DNA warrant. He would be given another opportunity to speak to a lawyer about the DNA warrant. Torlone would be with them while this was being done. These were two pieces of critical evidence as fingerprints and DNA would prove his identity at all three murder scenes. He would be returned to cell in order to sit for a while before being brought up for an interview.

During this time, a search team would be searching his residence looking for anything connected to the murders like old coins and bills, a diary or anything. Once done with all of this, Tamara and the search team would be relieved. Greg Bouchard would take over escort duty. Due to the construction of the police headquarters on 7 floors with cells in the basement floor and the interview rooms for CID on the 4th floor, the prisoner had to be escorted up in an elevator. The transporting officer and Greg would handcuff him and escort him up to the room.

It was important that he be put on the phone to a lawyer as this would mean they would need only a secondary caution with regard to any threats, inducements or promises anyone made since his arrest. They could then interview him without taking him back downstairs to call a lawyer. He would be told if he needed further advice he could stop the interview and speak to a lawyer. This sometimes happened if there was a new crime discovered or if the persons jeopardy changed from suspect to accused where he would now be charged. He was already being charged for three murders and he had been informed of that before speaking to his lawyer.

Detective Greg Bouchard and Detective Sergeant Andy Travis of the Major Crime Unit were prepared for the interview. Detective Nick Torlone was to scribe the interview meaning he would take notes from the monitor room of what was said by everyone so he could create a summary. The interview would be transcribed in detail later. No one else was allowed in the monitor room except these three officers and Enoch should he need to pop in to discuss anything with them.

The rest of the Cold Case Squad and Major Crime Unit, the escorting uniform officer, Enoch and Inspector Townsend would be monitoring the interview from the screen in the Major Crime room. Bouchard and Travis had advice from a Polygraph Examiner, Sergeant Jean Guy Degagne, and the same Criminal Profiler they had used for this profile. Travis was a very experienced police interviewer with several accused murderers interviewed under his belts. Bouchard had been showing a real talent for interviewing on these cases.

Everything went smoothly just as they had planned except for the crying by Genovese when he was arrested. Also he made an admission when being booked, "Why speak to a lawyer when I did it?" It was handled well and he was advised it was his right and he should really exercise it due to the severity of the charges. He spoke to Legal Aid Duty Counsel. He sobbed through his fingerprinting and the taking of his DNA. That was done on video by a pinprick to his index finger onto a card with enough blood to make the size of a quarter on the card.

He said nothing in his cell except, "No, no, no." and "After all this time." The officer in the cell shot had been instructed not to say anything so he did not but he was able to record these two comments. Genovese had himself pulled together when they brought him upstairs for the interview. It was not a tough interview. He was placed in an empty interview room. Travis entered the room.

"Hi, I am Detective Sergeant Andy Travis but you can all me Andy. Mr. Genovese, what do people normally call you?"

"Tony."

"Tony I understand that you are here having been arrested for the murders of Jason Walker, Davida Scheffers and Louise Tremblay all in 1963. Is that what you understand?

"Yes."

"I also understand that you were given your rights and you exercised those rights by speaking to a lawyer about this arrest. Did you speak to a lawyer about these charges and this arrest?

"Yes sir."

"Tony, I want you to know that if anyone has said or done anything to you or want you to say anything, I don't want you to do that. Today I only want you to tell me the truth and say only what you want to say without any threats or promises. Can we agree to that?"

"Yes, sure."

"Tony, I am going to now ask you the most important questions I will ask you today?"

Travis paused, leaned forward a little as he said this looking directly into Genovese's eyes.

"Did you murder Jason Walker?"

"Yes I did."

"Did you murder Davida Scheffers?"

"Yes."

"Did you murder Louise Tremblay?"

"God help me I did."

"All right, thank you for sharing that with me Tony. I want you to know I believe you. Do you want to tell me about it?"

"Yes sir, I do."

Genovese's head looked down and his shoulders slightly slumped as though defeated. What followed was his account of the murders. He described his childhood a little being picked on in the neighbourhood because of his size and being Italian. He still had an accent and trouble with English back then. He spoke about not doing well in grade school but a little better in high school. He did well in college.

He needed money and knew about the booze can known as Walker's. He went over there and broke a window into the basement storeroom. Jason Walker caught him. Genovese had a hunting knife on his belt for protection in the neighbourhood. He used it on Walker jamming it as hard as he could into his chest. He talked about being afraid Walker would kill him or worse, tell his father who he was very afraid of.

He still needed money because he didn't get any from Walker's so he went to the boarding house. His mother knew Mrs. Scheffers and he had been to the boarding house before. He thought no one would be home during the day. He found the cash box and was leaving when Mrs. Scheffer came in the front door. He threw the cash box in the closet and backed up. She was very mad and yelling at him for being in her house. He backed up beside a small table in the hallway where there was a pair of scissor. He grabbed the scissors and threatened her. She reached to take them away and he cut her arm. She grabbed for him and the fight was on. He used the scissors but they were thicker than the knife and more difficult to use. He finally got the scissors open and started stabbing her chest to make her die. And she did.

He had some money but needed more. He eventually decided to go to Madam Desire's brothel. He had heard about that as well. He broke a window to get inside. He was leaving through the back door when she came in with her grocery bag. This time he didn't wait for a fight or for her to yell for help. He was not sure if the house was empty or not so he ran back into the kitchen. She ran after him dropping her groceries on the floor. She started screaming. He grabbed a knife off of the counter and began stabbing her hard in the chest. Then he ran off out the back door.

In all three cases, he left the weapon behind. In all three cases, he needed money and then was motivated by fear his father would learn what he had done. He used the money to buy his mother and father an anniversary present. His father had told him he better get a job and buy something nice or else. His father had taken the belt to him many times. He showed remorse for what he had done. The interview to confession was only a few minutes. His full confession took over an hour with Travis asking clarifying questions.

The result of the confession was clear for murder and that was the three counts for which he had been arrested. DNA, fingerprints and confession. The Crown attorney would later state to the investigators, "Very strong case. And only solved 60 years later."

<u>Chapter 63</u>

With the case closed, his notes submitted, Enoch asked Inspector Townsend for some time off. It was granted. Enoch was very quiet and did not attend the takedown party for the project after the arrest. He went home hoping for his best night sleep but that was not to be. He struggled for two days. Things did not get better for him. The dreams, the memory flashes, no appetite, little sleep, drinking, hands trembling, angry all the time. He made a decision.

The next day was Saturday. He took Jake over to the Travis house telling Andy's wife he was going to go winter camping for a few days. Would they look after Jake? She said no problem of course. Enoch told her he forgot his food but when Andy got home he could pick it up at his house. He knew where the key was hidden. Andy came home late and they fed Jake scraps. The next morning Andy went to pick up the dog food.

Opening the back door to Enoch's house, he saw the dog food bag with a note attached. It read,

"I don't know what has happened to me. I can't stop all these memories, feeling and emotions. I thought it would get better with the arrest but it is getting worse. I have headaches all the time. I think I am going mad. I don't want this for myself. I have realized I have no one and no where to turn. It is time to put an end to things. I miss my wife so much. Travis, please keep Jake as he is a good dog and your wife and kids love him. He deserves a better home. I just can't go on.

Signed Enoch Brown"

Travis read the note and knew what had happened. He ran through the house even though Enoch's truck was gone. He called the on-duty Staff Sergeant to tell him and request the snow mobiles be made ready for the Rural Squad as he had said he was going winter camping. He next called Inspector Townsend who said he was coming out and would initiate Search and Rescue. Travis knew that the Search Manager's first thoughts would be where do we start. So he told Townsend it could be anywhere in the world except maybe it was where this had all started at the native rock paintings.

Travis knew roughly where they were. He raced home to gear up and get his snow mobile. He knew he could go by trail from where he lived in Garson up to Skead, cross Lake Wahnapitae to Lake Matagamasi and follow the lake up. He had been to that spot once in high school when they took a student canoe trip there. He would beat the police machines because they were coming from Azilda where they were stored at District 2.

As he rode out there, Travis kept thinking how bad this was but maybe Enoch talked himself out of it. He had the equipment and had gone winter camping before. Maybe he would be sitting there having his morning coffee or ice fishing. Travis got a text message telling him that Enoch's truck had been found at the boat launch on Lake Matagamasi. Tracks showed he had unloaded a snow mobile and a sleigh. Now Travis knew where he had gone. He moved faster.

As he approached the spot, he could see Enoch snow mobile with sleigh behind it parked on the ice. The sleigh was still packed with all the equipment on it. Foot prints led up and then across the top of the hill to where the rock paintings were. Travis followed the trail. He saw Enoch, kneeling beside a tree. Then he realized he had a rope around his neck and he was hanging forward. He was frozen solid. Travis fell to his knees and roared in frustration.

Before too long, the police snow machines caught up. They had a radio and called for Forensics to attend. A side by side and an argo were arranged to bring a CID officer and Forensics to the scene with the Coroner. Everyone involved in this body recovery was shaken to the core.

It took two days to thaw the body for a post mortem. It was conducted by a pathologist from Toronto as no one local wanted to do it. It was death by hanging. Suicide. Everyone saw it for the sad end that it was. No one understood how he could do it.

The medical PBL team that had worked with him wondered what testing and scans would have shown in the last few weeks since he stopped attending the hospital. There were several theories discussed at the final PBL session. It was agreed by everyone that epigenetic genes could not be proven in this case to have caused the echo memories. The DNA results were back and there was no gene they could identify that would do this. There was still a strong belief that the part epigenetic hereditary traits may have played was a combination of the patient's genome and his environment. This was only a theory. Carrying hereditary memories has never been proven. It has also never been disproven.

"I see the strongest theory with evidence as belonging to a combination of confabulation of memories from details the patient had heard in stories as a child and through his life from his friends, relatives and parents that he had forgotten but were recalled during Cognitive Interviewing and hypnosis. The recall under hypnosis cemented the memories and created more detail to fill in any blanks," offered Doctor Nancy O'Brien.

"What about the "Clever Hans Effect?" queried Doctor Heather Martin.

Doctor Sam Patton spoke, "I think we can safely conclude it absolutely had something to do with these echo memories. Clearly, the patient was an expert at criminal investigations. He was able to extrapolate his childhood stories into a cohesive confabulation then pick up on details that he applied to today's investigative techniques with great success."

Dr Vince Dhwala added, "We have nothing in his genome or brain scans to support past memories and that would fit with the popular belief of past memories or past lives as some of these people whose echo memories he had were still alive when others from other echo memories were alive. What we would be looking for is whether he had these echo memories passed on to him from his parents and grandfathers through epigenetics. Nothing proves this. Lack of proof does not make it true. Doctor Hakkala and I are in agreement there is not enough data for support of these hereditary memory theories. We concur with the conclusions of Doctor O'Brien."

Janet Mack the nurse supervisor asked, "What about any other factors that may have led to his death?"

Doctor Hussain spoke up, "I spoke to the coroner and police. A search of Enoch's home found his medications. He was not taking his prescribed medications for anxiety, depression or PTSD. Sadly, this becomes common in these cases as we all know."

Doctor Hakkala added, "The patient had also not been attending for blood work, brain scans or any of the other testing we had been doing for over a month. That would have been interesting to see what those tests would have shown. Now we shall never know. The brain pathology of the patient on death during the post mortem did not locate anything unusual."

Doctor O'Brien ended the meeting, "We have all the answers I suspect science and psychology can offer us in this case. I will write up our conclusions and close this file. I will also be writing a paper on this case with Doctor Dhwala, Doctor Hakkala, Doctor Martin and Doctor Hussain. I hope this case may help some future patient haunted by these things we now call echo memories and that they are explored further with a better outcome for the patient."

After the paper was submitted, Doctor Nancy O'Brien retired completely from her practise and teaching.

Weeks later, when they caught the abandon building arsonist, he was linked to 3 building fires, 2 homeless encampment fires and all of the deceased people with anti-mortem burn marks. He was caught after the arson team Enoch had created gathered evidence. Finally they're surveillance where the geographic profile predicted the arsonist would strike again paid off as Enoch had told them it would.

He was a man in his 30's who had lost his brother to an opioid overdose. His anger at his brother who died this way led him to punish those he found dead with a small burn mark. He had been preaching to the homeless to stop taking drugs. He was not having much effect. His frustration at not reaching the homeless addicts led to him light fires in abandon buildings where the homeless squatted and encampments where they gathered. Sadly, no one could tell Enoch of the success of his plan and the resolution of this case.

Jake was adopted by the Travis family but he was sad and listless without Enoch.

This ending is not a happy one but everyone recognized it was one that happened all too often with military and first responders with PTSD and other mental health issues. All of the people involved in Enoch's life took a vow with the minister at his funeral service to check on each other and never accept the answer "fine" when asking someone if they were okay again.

<u>Afterward</u>

374

The ending to this book was not what I expected when I began writing it. I think it speaks volumes of the sadness, PTSD and depression in policing today. I hope this brings attention to the idea of suicide. It is real, tragic and misunderstood.

If you are having trouble coping please reach out to mental health professionals, friends, family, work, school, anywhere.

Don't accept "fine" as an answer when asking, "How are you?" It is almost always untrue. Speak up and help people you can see are struggling.